THE CHRONICLES OF SHERLOCK HOLMES

The Further Adventures of Sherlock Holmes

Craig Janacek

The New World Books

Copyright © 2021 Craig Janacek

The Chronicles of Sherlock Holmes Copyright 2021 by Craig Janacek.

All Rights Reserved.

This book is a work of fiction. Names, characters, places, and incidents either are the product of the author's imagination or are used fictitiously and are not to be construed as real. Any resemblance to actual events, locales, or persons, living or dead, is entirely coincidental and not intended by the author.

No part of this book may be reproduced, or stored in a retrieval system, or transmitted in any form or by any means, electronic, mechanical, photocopying, recording, or otherwise, without express written permission of the publisher. The only exception is by a reviewer, who may quote short excerpts in a review.

Grateful acknowledgment to Sir Arthur Conan Doyle (1859-1930) for the use of the Sherlock Holmes characters.

Some excerpts of 'The Adventure of the Tragic Act' are derived from 'The Tragedians' (1884) by Sir Arthur Conan Doyle.
Some excerpts of 'The Adventure of the Most Dangerous Man' are derived from 'The Winning Shot' (1883) by Sir Arthur Conan Doyle.
Some excerpts of 'The Adventure of the Haunted Grange' are derived from 'Selecting a Ghost' (1883) and 'The Haunted Grange of Goresthorpe' (c.1877) by Sir Arthur Conan Doyle.
Some excerpts of 'The Adventure of the Fabricated Vision' are derived from 'The Silver Mirror' (1908) by Sir Arthur Conan Doyle.
Some excerpts of 'The Adventure of the Black Eye' are derived from 'The Story of the Black Doctor' (1898) by Sir Arthur Conan Doyle.
Some excerpts of 'The Adventure of the Wrong Hand' are derived from 'The Story of the Brown Hand' (1899) by Sir Arthur Conan Doyle.
Some excerpts of 'The Mannering Towers Mystery' are derived from 'The Story of B 24' (1899) by Sir Arthur Conan Doyle.
Some excerpts of 'The Adventure of the Twelfth Hour' are derived from 'The Pot of Caviare' (1908) by Sir Arthur Conan Doyle.
'The Adventure of the Fabricated Vision' first published in 'The MX Book of New Sherlock Holmes Stories, Part XXV: 2021 Annual'; David Marcum, Editor; MX Publishing (2021).

ISBN-13: pending

Cover painting 'The Bookworm' (c.1850) by Carl Spitzweg, in public domain.
Printed in the United States of America
The New World Books

First Printing: May 2021

To Owen

"Why should you think that beauty,
Which is the most precious thing in the world,
Lies like a stone on the beach
For the careless passer-by to pick up idly?
Beauty is something wonderful and strange
That the artist fashions out of the chaos of the world
In the torment of his soul.
And when he has made it,
It is not given to all to know it.
To recognize it you must repeat
The adventure of the artist.
It is a melody that he sings to you,
And to hear it again in your own heart
You want knowledge and sensitiveness
And imagination."

'THE MOON AND SIXPENCE' (1919)

WILLIAM SOMERSET MAUGHAM

CONTENTS

Title Page
Copyright
Dedication
Epigraph
LITERARY AGENT'S FOREWORD TO SEEN & OBSERVED   1
LITERARY AGENT'S FOREWORD TO THEIR DARK CRISIS   5
THE ADVENTURE OF THE TRAGIC ACT   9
THE ADVENTURE OF THE MOST DANGEROUS MAN   56
THE ADVENTURE OF THE HAUNTED GRANGE   113
THE ADVENTURE OF THE FABRICATED VISION   155
THE PROBLEM OF THE BLACK EYE   185
THE ADVENTURE OF THE WRONG HAND   230
THE MANNERING TOWERS MYSTERY   270
THE ADVENTURE OF THE TWELFTH HOUR   311
APPENDIX: ON DATES   356
ALSO BY CRAIG JANACEK   366
FOOTNOTES   370
Acknowledgement   401
About The Author   403
About The Author   405

Praise For Author 407
THE FURTHER ADVENTURES OF SHERLOCK HOLMES 409

LITERARY AGENT'S FOREWORD TO SEEN & OBSERVED

"Quite so! You have not observed. And yet you have seen. That is just my point. Now, I know that there are seventeen steps, because I have both seen and observed. By-the-way, since you are interested in these little problems, and since you are good enough to chronicle one or two of my trifling experiences, you may be interested in this."

– A Scandal in Bohemia

We have previously revealed that we were fortunate enough to have come into a large trove of writings by Dr John H Watson chronicling the vast adventures of Mr. Sherlock Holmes. The task of setting them forth before the public has been a slow one, in large part because many of the pages were damaged and required additional work to bring into publishable shape, as well as to add the required historical contexts in a series of careful annotations.

Perhaps not surprisingly, given his complex personality, Sherlock Holmes vacillated in his opinion towards the writings of his friend and biographer. On the one hand, in *The*

Man with the Twisted Lip, Holmes noted that a chronicler 'is always of use.' Furthermore, on at least two occasions – those of the Cornish Horror and of Professor Presbury – he actively encouraged Watson to publish the facts connected with those remarkable cases. However, far more commonly do we find evidence of Holmes actively prohibiting Watson from revealing the details of cases, typically until a great deal of time had passed. Watson reports in *The Adventure of the Six Napoleons* that Holmes said: "If I ever permit you to chronicle any more of my little problems, Watson…" while in *The Adventure of the Norwood Builder,* Watson notes that: "[Holmes] bound me in the most stringent terms to say no further word of himself, his methods, or his successes."

It is these lost tales, which Holmes refused to provide specific approval for Watson to publish, of which we now wish to speak. For, as we will show, Dr Watson managed to find a clever loophole in Holmes's strict injunction.

One interesting discovery in Watson's mass of despatch boxes is that quite a few adventures of Sherlock Holmes have – in fact – been published before, but only after stripping out all mention of Holmes' role in the matter. The world is well aware that Watson utilized Sir Arthur Conan Doyle as his literary agent for the fifty-seven memoirs he wrote that make up the Canon of Sherlock Holmes.[1] Holmes' fame is so immense that the world often forgets that Conan Doyle was an accomplished writer in his own stead. For example, the five tales that make up the Professor Challenger series are so remarkable that the first one, *The Lost World* (1912), gives its name to an entire genre of fictional literature. Conan Doyle's personal favourites were his historical novels,[2] but he also wrote numerous works for the stage, over a hundred poems, several fine works of non-fiction – including the work responsible for King Edward VII granting his knighthood in 1902[3] – and a simply staggering number of essays for various literary journals and newspapers.

Furthermore, and importantly for the matter at hand, Sir Arthur was the reported author of a plethora of short stories, which were published over a fifty-one year time-span between 1879 and 1930 in *The Strand Magazine* and many others.[4] Yet, we have already seen evidence that some of these were actually the disguised chronicles of Sherlock Holmes. In the collection *Treasure Trove Indeed!* (2016) – we reported the lost Holmes work entitled *The Adventure of the Queen's Pendant*, which upon further inspection was previously published by Conan Doyle in modified form as *The Story of the Jew's Breastplate* (1899). Several other discoveries followed, including *The Adventure of the Dawn Discovery* (2018) – originally published as *Our Midnight Visitor* (1891); *The Fatal Fire* (2018) – originally published as *The Tragedy of the Korosko* (1897); *The Adventure of the Defenceless Prisoner* (2019) – originally published as *The Prisoner's Defence* (1916); and *The Adventure of Secret Tomb* (2019) – originally published as *The New Catacomb* (1898).

At the time that these tales were re-released in their original state, with Holmes' role in them restored, we decided to include them in various collections that were roughly organized by theme, interspersed with other lost tales never before seen in any form. However, in the present collection, we now reveal for Dr Watson's loyal reading public four new adventures of Sherlock Holmes – all first released over a century ago by his first literary editor, Sir Arthur Conan Doyle. These include:

1. *The Adventure of the Tragic Act* – originally published as *The Tragedians* (1884; also known as *An Actor's Duel*) in *Bow's Bells* magazine.
2. *The Problem of the Black Eye* – originally published as *The Story of the Black Doctor* (1898) in *The Strand Magazine*.
3. *The Mannering Towers Mystery* – originally published as *The Story of B 24* (1899) in *The Strand Magazine*.
4. *The Adventure of the Twelfth Hour* – originally published as *The Pot of Caviare* (1908) in *The Strand Magazine*. This story was also adapted in 1908 as a

play – called *A Pot of Caviare* (1923) – with slightly different details, and eventually published by *Samuel French Ltd.* (1923).

We hope that via the release of these new adventures, the reader may now appreciate how cleverly Sir Arthur Conan Doyle utilized Dr Watson's words in order to craft his own take on the adventures. He did so without ever mentioning or even hinting at Holmes' direct involvement, thereby permitting them to be enjoyed by the general public despite Holmes' specific prohibition to not release the details. Fortunately, all of the published tales set in print before 1925, have entered the public domain in the United States as of 1 January 2020, and therefore there is no danger in reporting their original forms herein.

§

LITERARY AGENT'S FOREWORD TO THEIR DARK CRISIS

"Would that I had some brighter ending to communicate to my readers, but these are the chronicles of fact, and I must follow to their dark crisis the strange chain of events..."

– The Adventure of the Dancing Men

Sherlock Holmes was no stranger to the supposedly supernatural, though he universally refused to admit it as a possible explanation for any case that he was investigating. He was not interested in 'fairy tales,' as he dismissed all such things. Moreover, as recorded by Dr Watson, Holmes was repeatedly proven correct in such matters.

In the end, Mrs. Ferguson was not a vampire, but instead a devoted mother and wife.[5] Stapleton's painted demon-dog – while admittedly most clever – was no hellhound. Yet – despite the massive popularity of ghost stories during the Victorian age, and the great success of *The Hound of the Baskervilles* upon its publication in 1901-02 – the Canonical tales in which Holmes takes on the supernatural are strangely few and far between.

In fact, much like the curious incident of the dog in the nighttime, we wonder if Holmes purposefully suppressed the publication of many like-themed stories. As noted in the Foreword for the collection *Seen & Observed* (2020), Holmes was in the habit of making such edicts regarding certain cases he did not wish to see set before the public. Fortunately, we have some rare examples of other lost tales that have trickled out over the years, including Holmes' confrontation with a ghost in London – as reported in *The Adventure of the Awakened Spirit* (2017) – and his investigation into the fairy world – as set down in *The Adventure of the Fair Lad* (2019). However, for the most part, such tales are lacking.

While we know little of Dr Watson's personal beliefs regarding such matters – other than his valiant attempt to rationalize the legends of the vampire – such a prohibition on the part of Holmes must have been to the great chagrin of Watson's first literary editor, Sir Arthur Conan Doyle. Sir Arthur was – especially during his later life, after witnessing the horrors of the Great War and the deaths of his son Kingsley and his brother Innes – greatly committed to the cause of Spiritualism. He was also much taken by the works of the American short-story writer Edgar Allen Poe, the master of a macabre. As Conan Doyle explained in his paean to the great writers *Through the Magic Door* (1906-07):

> "Poe is, to my mind, the supreme original short story writer of all time. And all this didactic talk comes from looking at that old green cover of Poe. I am sure that if I had to name the few books which have really influenced my own life I should have to put this one second only to Macaulay's Essays. I read it young when my mind was plastic. It stimulated my imagination and set before me a supreme example of dignity and force in the methods of telling a story. It is not altogether a healthy influence, perhaps. It turns the thoughts too forcibly to the morbid and the strange.... He was a saturnine creature, devoid

of humour and geniality, with a love for the grotesque and the terrible. The reader must himself furnish the counteracting qualities or Poe may become a dangerous comrade. We know along what perilous tracks and into what deadly quagmires his strange mind led him...."

Therefore, it will come as little surprise to the informed reader that when Conan Doyle was surreptitiously provided by Watson with a series of adventures to publish, but with apparently explicit instructions to strip out of them all mention of Holmes, that in so doing, Sir Arthur turned many of them into supernatural escapades. Some of these disguised chronicles of Sherlock Holmes have already been included in other collections, including *The Adventure of the Double-Edged Hoard* (2016), which upon further inspection was previously published by Conan Doyle as *The Silver Hatchet* (1883), and the early Holmes tale entitled *The Lost Legion* (2016), which was originally published as *The Terror of Blue John Gap* (1910).

In the present collection, we now reveal for Dr Watson's loyal reading public four new adventures of Sherlock Holmes – all first released over a century ago by his first literary editor, Sir Arthur Conan Doyle. These include:

1. *The Adventure of the Most Dangerous Man* – originally published as *The Winning Shot* (1883) in *Bow's Bells* magazine.
2. *The Adventure of the Haunted Grange* – originally published as *Selecting a Ghost* (1883) in *London Society* magazine.
3. *The Adventure of the Fabricated Vision* – originally published as *The Silver Mirror* (1908) in *The Strand Magazine*.
4. *The Adventure of the Wrong Hand* – originally published as *The Story of the Brown Hand* (1899) in *The Strand Magazine*.

We hope that via the release of these new adventures, the reader may now appreciate how cleverly Sir Arthur Conan Doyle utilized Dr Watson's words in order to construct his own take on the adventures. He did so without ever mentioning or even hinting at Holmes' direct involvement, thereby permitting them to be enjoyed by the general public despite Holmes' specific proscription to not release the details. Fortunately, all of the published tales, set in print before 1925, have now entered the public domain in the United States as of 1 January 2020, and there is therefore no danger in finally reporting herein their original appearances, as written by Dr John H. Watson.

§

THE ADVENTURE OF THE TRAGIC ACT

Several months after my new suite-mate, Mr. Sherlock Holmes, had invited me to join him in a hansom cab bound for the Brixton Road, I found myself hoping to be included in another one of his extraordinary cases. A brutal August heat wave had made the pursuit of my typical endeavours rather less agreeable, and I was possessing of insufficient funds with which to remove myself from London in favour of some cooler countryside abode. Therefore, I hoped to enjoy some diversion from participating in another of his peculiar adventures. By this time, I already understood that while many of these were undertaken upon private inquiry, others were carried out upon request from a member of the official police force. It was upon one of the later episodes that I interjected my services, humble as they may be.

On the morning in question, I was sitting at my writing desk, engaged in sending a note to my brother Henry. Inspector Lestrade, whose sallow face marked him as one of my suite-mate's most regular callers during the initial months of our acquaintance, had dropped by in order to elicit Holmes' thoughts regarding a series of forgeries emanating from a source in Belgravia. I offered to retire to my bedroom so that the two men could utilize the sitting room in order converse in private, but Holmes dismissed this suggestion with a wave of his long, thin fingers.

Over the course of the next twenty minutes, Lestrade laid out the evidence and facts to date regarding the counterfeits. As I had now witnessed upon multiple occasions, Holmes soon succeeded in unravelling the knot in the case without ever leaving his armchair. He quietly advised that the detective turn his attention towards a young man whose grandfather was a royal duke.

Lestrade's eyes lit up in response to this recommendation, and he bounded from his chair, plainly eager to visit the man in question. However, Holmes forestalled his departure with a question.

"What of the actor's death, Lestrade? It says here," said Holmes, waving to the morning edition of *The Times*, "that he fell to his death during a rehearsal."

"What of it?" replied Lestrade, tersely.

"You were called in to investigate?"

"That's right. However, it was a colossal waste of my time, Mr. Holmes. It was nothing more than a sad accident. In fact, if I had not been so preoccupied with the tragic end of Mr. Latour, I am certain I would have found the connection of the forgeries to the Duke of Oxford by now."[6]

"Quite so," said Holmes, mildly. "So, Scotland Yard has no further interest in Mr. Latour's passing?"

"None."

"Then you won't mind if Watson and I drop by the Lyceum and take a look for ourselves?"

The inspector's brows furrowed and his eyes flickered in my direction. "You and Dr Watson? Why ever would you do such a thing?"

Holmes shrugged. "The doctor here has taken an interest in my trade, which is surely natural, since there are no other consulting detectives currently operating in the Empire, to the best of my knowledge. You may recall how attentive he was when I inspected the site of Mr. Drebber's death? It would, perhaps, prove informative for Dr Watson to inspect another death scene – this one mediated solely by natural causes – so that he can begin to appreciate the difference between the two."

"If Dr Watson cannot tell the difference between a man who was poisoned and one who was fell to his death, he must have slept through his classes at University," said Lestrade, with a knowing chuckle. "Be my guest, Mr. Holmes. And have fun, Doctor." He clapped his hat upon his head and made his way down the steps back out to the Baker Street pavement.

After the sounds of his boots faded, Holmes turned to me with a peculiar gleam in his grey eyes. "What do you say, Watson? Are you up for an outing? Despite the heat, surely a trip to the Strand is preferable to being cooped up in here?"

"Well, I can hardly see the point, Holmes. As Inspector Lestrade said, I believe I am sufficiently well-versed in the various methods by which a man can shuffle off this mortal coil."

Holmes smiled. "Humour me, Watson. I have a suspicion that there is more to the matter than observed by Lestrade. And if I am incorrect, I will make it up to you with a lunch at Simpson's and a concert at St. James's Hall."

"Very well," said I, rising to gather my hat and walking stick. "Lead on, Macduff."[7]

Once we were settled into the seats of a passing cab, I waited to learn in what sort of mood Holmes might be. When travelling about London, I had seen him range from the silent and morose, to the garrulous and prattling. However, on this occasion, he was direct and professional.

"Your quotation was an apt one, Watson. For my dead man in question is Mr. Henry Latour, a French actor who was scheduled for the role of Macbeth in a production opening next week."

"Ah, the Scottish Play!" I cried.

"You say that name as if it was significant. How so?"

"Come now, Holmes. Surely you are familiar with the works of Shakespeare?"

"Of course. I have read each of his thirty-eight plays, even those barely considered Canonical.[8] I am particularly partial to *Twelfth Night*. However, I fail to see how the fact that Latour was rehearsing the part of the Scottish Thane is in any way relevant to his death?"[9]

"Why, the Scottish Play is cursed!"

Holmes frowned. "I am not generally inclined to lend credence to the possibility of curses, Watson."

"I assure you that this one has sufficient examples to make even the most sceptical believe. I am told that it is absolutely forbidden to utter the name of the play within a theatre, or disaster will be henceforth brought down upon the speaker. The number of productions of the Scottish Play which have failed due to deaths or fires is prodigious."

"And why would such an anathema exist in the first place?"

"Well, I have heard it whispered that when Shakespeare set down the lines spoken by the witches, that he copied their incantation from a book that contained a genuine spell. This is what powers the curse."

Holmes shook his head. "Coincidences and imagination, Watson. Nothing more."

"Tell that to Mr. Latour."

Holmes chuckled at my small witticism. "Yes, quite. As you are unfamiliar with the story, permit me to…."

"How could you know that?" said I, interrupting his narrative.

"Simple, Watson. You rose late, and perused the latest copy of *Blackwood's Magazine* while partaking in Mrs. Hudson's excellent rashers and eggs. After that, you went straight to your writing desk. At no time did you pick up any of the morning editions."

I was momentarily taken aback by a comprehension that I lived under such scrutiny. "I did not realize that you paid such close attention to my movements, Holmes."

He waved his long, thin fingers. "Not intentionally, Watson. It is merely a by-product of the careful training that I have undertaken in order to hone my natural abilities. Observation of my surroundings is now second nature to me. I can no more turn it off than I can stop my nose from smelling."

"I see," said I, somewhat mollified that my suite-mate was not actively spying upon me. "Pray continue."

"Well, there is little more to the matter at present. We will need to interrogate some of the witnesses in order to acquire the full story. However, from the paragraph in *The Times*, it appears that this was to be Mr. Latour's first performance in London."

"You said he was French?"

"Indeed. He made his name on the boards of the Theatre National in Paris, where he recently played the role of Laertes."

My eyebrows rose with interest. "It must have been quite the performance to allow him to make the jump from a supporting actor to the lead. And in the Scottish Play, no less. It is a most challenging part."

"Indeed, Watson. Moreover, I hope to learn what precisely induced the Lyceum to hire a relatively unknown Parisian actor over the many quality English thespians who must have been available for the rôle. This is one of the peculiarities that caught my eye when I read about the supposed accident."

By this time, our hansom had rattled up in front of the pillars of the theatre, so we handed our fare to the driver and stepped out. As it was still early in the day, the thick crowds of shirt-fronted men and be-diamonded women normally to be found outside the front and side entrances were conspicuously absent. A few minutes later, a stolid man with a harried expression on his bearded face eventually answered Holmes' loud knocks. He had piercing eyes and a powerful brow, with a thick head of carefully parted reddish-brown hair.

"I am sorry, gentlemen," said the man, "but the theatre is closed."

"Of course, sir," replied Holmes, "We are not here for the show. We have come to ask you some questions about Mr. Henry Latour."

The man shook his head vigorously. "No, no!" he cried. "I have no time for you reporters. You scribblers are going to ensure that no one ever dares set foot in my theatre to see this cursed show."

"We are not Fleet Street men, sir. I am Sherlock Holmes, a consulting detective, and this is my friend, Dr Watson. We are here at the request of Inspector Lestrade from Scotland Yard."

I thought this statement to be a stretching of the truth, but held my tongue.

"Oh, why didn't you say so?" exclaimed the man. "I am Jake Brandin.[10] I run the theatre. Come inside and we will talk."

The manager led us through the lobby and into the auditorium, where we could view the stage. The scenery was currently set as the banquet room of Macbeth's castle.

"Mr. Brandin," asked Holmes. "I wonder if you can tell me what made you hire a Frenchman like Latour for the role of Mac… the Scottish King?"

"Well, Henry was only half-French, on his father's side. His mother is as Scottish as they come. She is a Morton from Dumfries, and Henry spoke English as well as you or me, Mr. Holmes."

"I understand that he lived in Paris?"

"That is correct?"

"And did he seek out a role in your production?"

"Oh no, I offered it to him after I saw him in *Hamlet*. His performance was unforgettable."

"How so? Leave nothing out," commanded Holmes.

"Very well. You see, Mr. Holmes, it is my devout wish that the Lyceum retains its reputation as the premier stage for Shakespeare in the world. Therefore, whenever another theatre decides to put on one of the Bard's works, I always make an effort to attend, in the hope that I might pick up something new that is worth incorporating into our productions. When I heard about the plans of the Theatre National to perform a new translation of *Hamlet*, I determined that this was something that I could not miss.

"However, one thing I dislike about the Parisian performances is their insistence on holding the audience in the foyer until the last possible moment. At times, it seemed as if the door would never open. There is an end to all things, happily, and the hour struck at last. We filed into the theatre one after another, in the orderly French fashion. I was fortunate enough to secure what I wanted – namely, a centre seat in the front row.

"Nothing but the orchestra intervened between me and the footlights. My immediate neighbours were a fellow Englishman named Barker, and an enthusiastic young lady with her elderly mother. The overture was nothing out of the ordinary, so I took that time to expand upon my views of the French stage to my countryman, who seemed somewhat preoccupied.

" 'We cannot approach the French on 'touch-and-go' comedy,' said I. 'For it is their strong point. However, when it comes to Shakespeare, they are lost, sir – utterly lost. If you had seen the Hamlets I have seen – Macready, sir, and the older Kean...'[11]

"Unfortunately, my reminiscences were cut short by the rise of the curtain. The first few scenes were tame enough. The translation lacked the rugged strength and force of our own glorious language. I noticed, however, that some of the veteran theatregoers have become restless in their seats, and began whispering that there was something amiss with their favourite actor."

"What do you mean?" asked Holmes.

Brandin pursed his lips and considered the question. "A man named Gaspard Lablas, the foremost tragedian of the Theatre National – but rather too French for my taste – was the lead, even if his temperament was all wrong for the indecisive prince of Denmark. Worse still, on that night he seemed quite distracted. Still, one cannot easily forget the sinewy, upright form, and the dark, cynical smile of Lablas. A follower of Spurzheim would have prophesied great things, of good or of evil, from that broad, low forehead and massive jaw; and another glance at the cold grey eye and the sensual lip would have warned the physiognomist that, off the boards of the National, this was a man to be shunned – a selfish friend and a vindictive foe.[12]

"Well, you will understand, Mr. Holmes, that given this reputation, I had no interest in ever inviting Mr. Lablas to grace the boards of the Lyceum. While his black, tight-fitting costume may have showed off his splendid figure to advantage, I was much dismayed by his eyes, which seemed to rest upon members of the audience with a dark and threatening scowl. Such a thing would never be tolerated in London, I tell you that!

"Fortunately, my spirits revived somewhat when Mr. Latour entered the stage in the role of Ophelia's brother, Laertes. He looked cool and at his ease, though I thought I could perhaps see a dangerous light in his eye whenever he glanced towards his fellow actor.

"The spirit and fire of Latour's elocution seemed to captivate his hearers. From pit to gallery, there was not one who did not sympathise with the plight of the gallant young Danish nobleman, his sister tragically dead. Latour was applauded to the echo. Poor Mr. Lablas' Hamlet was completely forgotten in the performance of Laertes. I shall never forget the torrent of indignation that rang out when Latour spoke the words in Act Four, Scene Seven:

> *'A sister driven into desperate terms.*
> *Whose worth, if praises may go back again,*
> *Stood challenger on mount of all the age*
> *For her perfections. But my revenge will come.'*

" 'By Jove, sir!" said I, *sotto voce* to my neighbour. 'Those last words were nature itself.' I tell you, Mr. Holmes, it was one of the most powerful things that I have ever witnessed on the boards. Mr. Latour was called before the curtain at the end of the fourth act; however, it was during the scene at Ophelia's grave that he surpassed himself. His howl of 'The devil take thy soul!' as he sprang at Hamlet's throat, fairly brought down the house, and caused me involuntarily to spring to my feet. However, Latour seemed to recollect himself in time, and shook himself clear of his rival. I tell you, Mr. Holmes, that I have rarely seen an actor so inhabit the spirit of a role as Mr. Latour on that evening. Hamlet's invective was also the strongest point in his character. The vast audience seemed to hang on every bitter word that passed between Lablas and Latour.

" 'You will get an English actor to make more stage points,' I noted to the increasingly agitated Mr. Barker; 'but there is a confounded naturalness about all this which is wonderful!'

"You see, Mr. Holmes, my dramatic instinct told me that, in spite of my many years' experience, there was something here which I had never met before. Then there was a great hush in the house as the curtain rose upon the final scene. It was magnificently set upon the stage. The rude, barbaric pomp of the Danish Court sprang to life, like a painted picture. The king and queen were seated in the background, under a canopy of purple velvet, lined with ermine. The walls of the royal banquet-hall were gorgeous with strange trophies, supposedly brought from afar by Viking hands. There was a clear space in the centre; and at either side, a swarm of men-at-arms, courtiers, and all the hangers-on of the royal household. The verisimilitude was astonishing.

"Laertes was leaning carelessly against a pillar, while Hamlet stood with a smile of confidence upon his face, conversing with a courtier. Besides Latour, I could see a man near enough in appearance to have been his brother, got up in a suit of tiny armour that was ridiculously out of proportion to his brawny limbs. There was a look upon his face, however, that would have forbidden a laugh at his expense.

"I tell you, Mr. Holmes, that the excitement was palpable, and all over the house a strange interest began to manifest itself in the proceedings. Not a sound could be heard over the great theatre as the actor playing Osric came tripping forward with the bundle of foils. In fact, while Osric is a minor role, that actor – Jules Grossière by name – did such a fine job that he is even now playing Banquo in our current production. But I digress. Lablas took some little time to satisfy himself, though Latour seemed to choose his weapon without a moment's hesitation.

" 'Gad!' said I to my neighbour. 'Look at the man's eyes! I tell you it is unique!'

"The salute was given, and the courtier with whom Lablas had been speaking drew up to his principal, while behind Latour the brawny soldier took up his position. This man's honest face was pale with anxiety, and I wondered if it was his first time on the stage. Sadly, the costume manager had done a poor job, for I could see that instead of the double-edged Danish sword, Latour had a delicate rapier slung to his side. It was the one small thing that marred an otherwise tremendous performance.

"I was unable to turn away my eyes as the two men approached each other, their feet rapping out quick stamps, and their blades coming together with the sharp ring of steel. The silence was so profound that you might have heard the breathing of the combatants at the extreme end of the pit. As they twisted and turned, I caught glimpses of the dark, savage face of Lablas, and righteous anger upon the face of his antagonist Latour.

"Then there came a momentary cessation in the clash of the swords, and I was forced to admit to my countryman that this was a masterstroke of stage-craft. 'The deception is admirable,' I cried. 'You would swear there was blood running down the leg of Laertes. Capital! Capital! The business is perfect!'

"For some reason, Barker appeared to shudder at my words, but I was too engrossed in the action. I stared as they sprang at each other for the second time, and my eyes were riveted upon the stage for the remainder of the conflict. The combatants were very evenly matched; first one, and then the other, seemed to gain a temporary advantage. The profound science of Lablas was neutralised by the fire and fury of his antagonist's attack. Latour rushed at his opponent so furiously that he drove him back among the crowd of courtiers. I saw Lablas give a deadly lunge under the guard, which Latour appeared to take through his left arm. Then Latour sprang in, and there was a groan and a spurt of blood as Hamlet, Prince of Denmark, tottered forwards to the footlights and fell heavily upon his face.

"The effect upon me and the entire audience was electrical. There was a hush for a moment, and then, from pit to boxes, and from boxes to gallery, there went up a cheer so spontaneous and so universal, that it was like the mighty voice of one man. The whole house sprang to its feet with round after round of applause.

"The French ladies to my side were excitedly saying that it was the finest illusion of the year – it was the best *coup de theatre*, and most realistic stage duel that had ever been fought. However, I shuddered and caught Barker convulsively by the wrist, and said, in an awe-struck whisper, 'I saw it come out of his back!'

"Barker shook his head. 'Yes, as they said, it was the finest illusion of the year,' he replied. I wondered if I alone had seen something that the rest of the audience had missed, for still they applauded and applauded.

" 'Surely he will rise and bow his acknowledgments?' I asked.

" 'One more cheer may do it,' said Barker, stiffly.

"But it did not. For you see, Mr. Holmes, Monsieur Lablas lay there stiff and stark, with a scowl upon his white face, and his life-blood trickling down the boards. Then there was a hot, heavy smell in the orchestra, which was surely never caused by a stage illusion. The second viola began gesticulating wildly, for a little crimson pool had trickled upon his music book, and he saw that it was still dripping down, liquid and warm.

"Then a hush came over the pit, while the boxes were still applauding; and then the boxes grew quiet, and strange whispers went about. Finally, the audience above become silent, too, a great stillness fell upon the theatre, and the heavy brown curtain was rolled down."

The stage manager finished his vivid recitation, and I shook myself free of the spell that he had woven.

"Most illuminating, Mr. Brandin," said Holmes. "You are quite the narrator. You should consider authoring something yourself. So Gaspard Lablas was, in fact, dead?"

"Oh, most definitely."

"And what happened to Mr. Latour?"

The manager shrugged. "Well, his name as an actor was made, that's for certain."

"But he killed a man!" I interjected.

"Was it his fault that a button slipped or a foil snapped? Of course not. Last I heard, the inquiry by Inspector Dubuque of the Paris Police was unable to determine who precisely was to blame for this mix-up.[13] However, Gaspard Lablas was unlikely to be much mourned. He was a fair actor, I admit, but reputedly a most foul man. For his part, Henry Latour had a slight wound in his leg and had been run through the biceps with Lablas' sword. Fortunately, Latour's brother – who is a medical student at Edinburgh – patched him up right as rain. As soon as I could get a word with him, I offered Latour the main part in our upcoming production of the Scottish Play, and he immediately accepted. All was going so well until last night's terrible accident."

"What can you tell me of that?"

"Well, it occurred while we were rehearsing Act Three, Scene Four. When Banquo's ghost interrupts Mr. M's banquet for the second time, although he does not speak, Banquo presents such a grim visage, that it induces a terrible fear into Mr. M. The former thane responds with:

> 'Avaunt! and quit my sight! let the earth hide thee!
> Thy bones are marrowless, thy blood is cold;
> Thou hast no speculation in those eyes
> Which thou dost glare with!'

"In our staging, Mr. Homes, the ghost of Banquo advances upon Mr. M., and chases him up the steps to the battlement, as you can see there." Brandin waved to the stage. "I have replayed the events a hundred times in my mind, but still cannot fathom what went wrong. Mr. Latour raced up the steps, but instead of pausing, he went right over the edge. He fell onto the rocks below and cracked his skull open. I am told he was dead before they even got him to Bart's."

"Do you mind if I look over the set?" asked Holmes.

"Be my guest," said Brandin with a wave.

Holmes spent the next twenty minutes or so engaged in the precise sort of researches that I once witnessed in an empty house off the Brixton Road. No spot of the stage floor went unmeasured by his tape or unmagnified by his glass. Mr. Brandin watched this with some interest, even exclaiming once or twice whenever Holmes went down upon his hands and knees in order to inspect a particular area.

"A veritable foxhound, he is," said the manager, approvingly.

Eventually Holmes returned and thanked Brandin for his time.

The manager smiled and nodded. "I must say, Mr. Holmes, that the man from Scotland Yard did not do half as thorough a job of looking things over."

"No," said Holmes with an explosion of laughter. "I daresay not. Do you have any other pertinent information, Mr. Brandin?"

"Well, I have received word, Mr. Holmes, that Latour's family is rushing here from Paris. His sister, Rose, wired to say that they would arrive this evening."

"Did they mention where they would be staying?"

"The Midland Grand, I believe."[14]

Holmes bade the manager farewell and we made our way back out to the pavement on Wellington Street. Holmes flagged down another hansom, and we were soon rattling up Charing Cross to Euston Road. The cab deposited us in front of the neo-gothic spires and turreted roofline of the St. Pancras Hotel, and we made our way into the luxurious lobby, with its gold-leaf walls and grand staircase.

I soon learned that the hotel manager was an old familiar of Holmes. My friend was informed that a Madame Cora Latour, as well as a Lieutenant Etienne and Madame Rose Malpas, had taken Suite 302. Holmes requested a sheet of paper and scribbled a few lines upon it. Handing this to one of the army of bellmen standing about, the lad soon returned with an invitation to call upon Madame Latour and family.

We rode the hydraulic lift up to the third floor, and knocked upon the door in question. A male voice bade us enter the room, where a large fireplace sat cold and bare, a fit counterpoint to the stolid lamp upon the table and the sombre demeanour in the room. There were three people seated in front of the hearth, two of the gentler sex, and it would take no very profound student of humanity to pronounce at a glance that they were mother and daughter. The third was a young man, his face beardless, dressed in the uniform of an officer of cavalry.

This man jumped to his feet when Holmes and I entered. "Monsieurs, I am Lieutenant Malpas, Third Hussars," he said with only a trace of accent.[15] "Your note said you had information regarding Henry's death? My wife, Rose, and mother-in-law are most desirous to hear your news. We understood it was an accident, but you say that you believe otherwise?"

Holmes nodded and turned to the women. In both there was the same sweet expression and the same graceful figure, though the delicate outlines of the younger woman were exaggerated in her plump little mother, and the hair which spilled from under the latter's matronly cap was streaked with traces of grey, rather than the daughter's golden tresses. It is true that the lieutenant's wife was no regal beauty, and her features had not even the merit of regularity. Yet the graceful girl, with her laughing eyes and winning smiles, would be a dangerous rival to the stateliest of her sex. Unconsciousness of beauty is the strongest adjunct which beauty can have, and Rose Malpas, née Latour, possessed it in an eminent degree. You could see it in every natural movement of her lithe form, and in the steady gaze of her hazel eyes. I thought Lieutenant Malpas was a most fortunate man! As for her mother, well, she struck me as a bustling, kind-hearted little woman, whose cheery laugh was heard less frequently than of old, for great cares had plainly descended upon her.

"Madame Latour, my name is Sherlock Holmes, and this is my friend, Dr John Watson. I am a consulting detective and I have been looking into the events surrounding your son's death."

"On whose behest?" asked Rose.

Holmes looked at her. "My own," said he, mildly. "Although I often am called in by Scotland Yard when they are out of their depths, in this case, I decided to investigate your brother's passing on my own accord."

"Why would you do such a thing?" asked the Frenchman, suspiciously. "Are you seeking payment?"

Holmes shook his head. "I do not intend to send you any professional charges, Lieutenant. When I undertake a case for my own edification, I typically remit them altogether. No, this is one of those times when I investigate something for the sheer motivation of the possibility of learning something new."

"And what have you learned in this case?"

"It is far too early to make any conjectures, Lieutenant. But I wonder where you learned your English?"

"Before I studied at Saint-Cyr, I was fortunate to have obtained a Beaumaris Scholarship. I spent a year at Trinity College, Cambridge."[16]

"Very good." Holmes turned to the dead man's mother. "What can you tell me of your son, Madame Latour?"

The old lady shook her head sadly. "I will not hide it from you, Mr. Holmes. We have all had an anxious time since my husband, the Colonel, died. Nevertheless, I have tried to battle through it all with the uncomplaining patience my mother taught me when I was growing up in Dumfries. The sum that the Colonel had left behind him is not a large one. Were it not for the supervision exercised by my Rose, it would hardly have met our necessary expenses. It was most generous of Lieutenant Malpas to accept such a meagre dowry for her hand."

"I would do it all again, Madame," said the lieutenant passionately. "For Rose is the most beautiful flower of French womanhood to grace the streets of Paris in a hundred years."

His wife blushed attractively at this complement, but Madame Latour shook her head.

"Remember this, Etienne. Rose is a Morton, and nothing but a Morton," said she, emphasizing every second or third word with an energetic little nod of the head, which gave her a strong resemblance to a plump and benevolent sparrow. "She hasn't one drop of French blood in her veins."

"But papa was a Frenchman, wasn't he?" objected Rose. "He served in the Voltigeurs of the Guard."

"Yes, my dear. However, you are a pure Morton. Your father Georges was a dear and good man, though he was a Frenchman, and only stood five feet four. But my children are all Scotch. My father was six feet two, and so would my brother have been, only that the nurse used to read as she rolled him in the perambulator, and rested her book upon his head, so that he was compressed until he looked almost square, poor boy. Nevertheless, he had the makings of a fine man. You see, both Henry and Jack are tall men, so it is ridiculous to call them anything but Morton, and you are their sister. No, no, Rose, you haven't one drop of your father's blood in you!"

I opened my mouth and was about to protest against her erroneous comprehension of physiology; however, I was forestalled by Holmes laying his hand on my arm.

"Go on, Madame Latour," said he. "You were telling me about your son Henry."

"Ah, poor Henry," she wailed. "I never thought that Henry would come to ill. If it was going to be anyone, I thought it might be my second son, Jack. He is at university in Edinburgh, and has long been a grief to me."

"How so?"

"Jack is sowing his wild oats, Mr. Holmes," interjected Rose. "From time to time, vague reports of his escapades are wafted across the Channel, where they startle our quiet household in the Rue Bertrand."

"That is so, dear," her mother continued. "Even his own letters are somewhat of a mystery, for the very language seems to me to be altering in a marvellous manner. I doubt if I could make myself understood if I went back. Jack uses refinements of speech of which poor Rose and I have no idea as to their meaning. I suppose that we cannot expect to keep up to the day when we are living in a foreign country."

"Jack does use some queer words," confirmed Rose. "But it is all harmless fun."

Madame Latour shook her head sadly. "I never thought that one of my own children would come to a violent end. Even with Rose wishing to be a man."

Her daughter brightened at this remark. "Ah, what wouldn't I do," said she, pursing her lips to express her idea of masculine inflexibility. "I would write books, and lecture, and fight, and all sorts of things."

Madame Latour brightened at this memory. "Ah, my dear, my dear, there is no such thing as fighting now-a-days. Not like when your father was a soldier. Why, I remember, when I was a girl, how twenty and thirty thousand people used to be killed in a day. That was when the old Lords Raglan and Lyons went out to Crimea.[17] There was Mrs. McWhirter, next door to us – her son was wounded, poor fellow! It was a harrowing story. He was creeping through a hole in a wall, when a nasty man came up, and ran something into him."

"How very sad!" said I, trying to regain control over the conversation, which seemed to be dangerously veering away from any discussion pertinent to the case of Henry Latour.

"Yes, sir," continued Mrs. Latour. "And I heard young McWhirter say, with his own lips, that he had never seen the man before in his life, and he added that he never wished to see him again. It was at Ink-man."

"Inkerman, mama," said Rose, gently.[18]

"I said so, dear. The occurrence dispirited young McWhirter very much, and, indeed, threw a gloom over the whole family for the time."

She paused and took a moment to reflect upon this thirty-year-old event. Holmes appeared as if he was about to say something, when eventually her mind came round to the present tragedy.

"But Henry, too, was a worry for me," she continued. "Even with his great talent for tragedy, he had no engagement for more than six months before he convinced Monsieur Lambertin to give him the role of Laertes."

"How did that come about?" asked Holmes.

"Well, now, let me think. He was later than usual one night, but when we did hear the turn of his key in the latch, Henry had Mr. Barker in tow. He then simply announced that he had gotten a part in a play at the National."

"Ah, yes, Mr. Barker," said Holmes. "I have also heard his name from the stage manager, Mr. Brandin. What can you tell me of him?"

"A good deal," answered Rose. "He was really a friend of Jack's. However, Henry had come across him at the Café de Provence, and the two fell into talking, so he brought Mr. Barker back here with him. He is a junior solicitor in Edinburgh, but was visiting Paris for a holiday."

"Very good. Pray continue about your brother's new role at the Theatre National."

"Well, Henry and Mr. Barker went around together on a lark. Henry always said that he had not the ghost of a chance at a part, for Lablas, the great tragedian – do you know of him? – had much influence there, and Lablas always did his best to harm and thwart Henry's career."

"Why?"

Rose shook her head. "That was a mystery. Henry never

game him cause of offence that he knew of. I think Lablas was simply a nasty brute."

"My dear," said Madame Latour, "you really must not speak ill of the dead."

"Well, you know he was, mama!"

"Do go on, Madame Malpas," said Holmes.

"Yes, well, Lablas was not at the theatre, and Henry managed to get hold of the manager, old Monsieur Lambertin, and asked him if he needed an actor. According to Henry, Lambertin jumped at the proposal. He even had the goodness to say that he had seen Henry act at Rouen once – it was in a regional revival of Dumas' *Henri III*, I believe – and had been much struck by his talent."

"I should think so!" said the old lady, vehemently.

"Lambertin then told Henry that they were just looking out for a man to play an important role – that of Laertes, in a new translation of Shakespeare's *Hamlet*. It was to come out soon, and Henry had only two days in which to learn it."

"That seems rather sudden."

"Well, it seemed that another man – Monnier by name – was to have played it, but he had broken his leg in a carriage accident."

"How unfortunate," murmured Holmes.

"Henry said that old Lambertin was most cordial about the whole matter."

"Dear old man!" cried Madame Latour. "I am sure I cannot conceive why they should have ever refused such a handsome young fellow as my Henry in the first place," said the fond mother. "I think, even if he could not act at all, they would fill the house with people who wanted to look at him. But he was also a natural on the stage."

"In any case," interjected Rose, "after Henry announced his good news, we all sat down for a fine little supper and we passed away the rest of the time with jests and laughter. I remember the evening like a happy dream, for it was the last we saw of Henry before the dreadful accident with Monsieur

Lablas."

"Yes, I heard of this episode from Mr. Brandin. However, I understand that there were no repercussions for your brother."

"That is true, Mr. Holmes," said Rose. "We were all terribly cut up about it, though. I mean, it is not every day that your brother kills a man, especially one as famous as Monsieur Lablas. Henry decided that he should let things cool down in Paris a bit, so when Mr. Brandin offered the part in London, he took it straightaway."

"If only he had never done such a thing, my poor Henry would still be alive," his mother cried.

"You can't say that, mother," said Rose, with a shake of her head. "Such an accident might have happened anywhere."

"If it is any consolation, Madame Latour, I am in broad agreement with your daughter," said Holmes. I am afraid that, after the events at the Theatre National, nothing Henry did or did not do could have prevented his untimely death."

On that note, Holmes and I took our leave of the bereaved family and made our way back down the grand staircase to the hotel lobby. We were half way across it, when we heard a youthful voice call after us.

"Mr. Holmes!" it said. We turned and saw Lieutenant Malpas chasing after us.

"What can we do for you, Lieutenant?" asked Holmes, a hint of excitement in his voice, as if he sensed that we were about to learn more of the story behind Mr. Latour's death.

"I would tell you the truth, Mr. Holmes," said the young officer, with a rueful smile. "I could not say it in front of Rose, for I am not proud of my actions. You see, there was a time not so long ago when I had fallen in with a poor choice of companions. One night, or rather the following morning, for the cathedral clock had already struck three, changed my life. The streets of Paris were deserted, save for an occasional gendarme or a solitary reveller hurrying home from some scene of pleasure. Even in the Rue d'Anjou – the most dissipated of fashionable streets – there were but few houses that showed a light.

"However, in one of them there was a large room, luxuriously fitted up, where half a dozen men in evening dress gathered to lounge and smoke and gamble. I was one of them. I still recall how the great chandelier reflected its lustre cheerily in the mirrors around, and cast a warm glow on the red velvet of the furniture. The carpet was so thick that hardly a footfall was heard, as one of the men rose from his seat and walked over to lean against the great marble mantelpiece. His name, Mr. Holmes? Well, you may guess that it was Gaspard Lablas."

"It was his home in which we gathered, and by his fame amongst the habitués of the French theatres, he was the unofficial leader of this band. Lablas was a cruel man, but some of the other men were slightly more agreeable."

"Such as?" asked Holmes.

"Well, there was Jules Grossière, from the Variétés, who rarely stirred far from the little glittering spirit cabinet, from which he constantly refilled his brandy glass.[19] Grossière was the cleverest and most unscrupulous of actors, whose duels and intrigues were only less notorious than those of his host, Lablas. Victor Turville was another well-known actor and tight friend of Lablas. Louis Cachet, from the Gaieté, could be found reposing on the couch, puffing at a meerschaum pipe.[20] I believe that one or two less known actors completed the group."

"You seem to have been an odd addition to such a thespian group," noted Holmes.

Malpas grimaced. "Yes, well, you are a more observant man than I, Mr. Holmes. Only later did I realize why they had invited me to join them, which was to take me for all that I was worth. You see, Lablas eventually looked wearily at the table, which was heaped high with cards, dice, and odd pieces of coin and spoke: 'Well, gentlemen,' said the actor, 'you must please yourselves. Shall we have another turn or not?'

" 'We have plenty of time yet,' said Grossière. 'But I fear there is such a run of luck against the unfortunate Lieutenant that he will hardly dare to try again. Positively it is cruel to ask him.'

"I see now, Mr. Holmes, that I was a very young bird, endeavouring to hold my own at Écarté amongst these seasoned old vampires. It should have been evident from the way in which they glanced round at him when Grossière made the remark, that I had been elected as the butt of the company. Nevertheless, I persisted. 'What if I have bad luck?' said I. 'It's all fair play and the fortune of war. I'll try again.'

"So I drank down a tumbler of champagne to try and drown the vision of my sainted mother down at Montpellier, in the sunny south, who was scraping and saving in order to keep me in the manner of a gentleman in Paris.

" 'That is right! Pluckily said!' went up the chorus of voices from around the table, urging me to my doom.

" 'Don't drink your wine like that, though,' said Cachet. 'You will make yourself unsteady.'

" 'I am afraid our military friend is unsteady already,' remarked Lablas.

" 'Not at all, monsieur,' I replied. 'My hand is as steady as your own.'

" 'There is no hand in Paris as steady as my own, young man,' returned Lablas. 'Lieutenant Lallacourt, of your own regiment, could tell you as much. You were with me, Cachet, when I shot away his trigger finger at Vincennes. I stopped his pistol shooting for ever and a day. Do you perceive a little dark spot that is fixed in the centre of the white sheet at the other side of the room? It is the head of a fusee, a mark which I generally use for the purpose of practice, as there can be no doubt as to whether you have struck it or not.[21] You will excuse the smell of gunpowder, messieurs?' he continued, taking a small and highly finished pistol from a rack upon the wall.

"Lablas seemed hardly to glance along the sights. However, as he pulled the trigger, there was a crack and spurt of flame from the other side of the room, and the fusee, struck by the bullet, was scattered in burning splinters upon the floor.

" 'I hardly think you will venture to state that your hand is as steady as mine for the future,' Lablas added, glancing towards me, as he replaced the dainty weapon in its stand upon the wall.

" 'It was a good shot,' I admitted.

" 'Hang the shooting!' said Grossière, rattling up the dice. 'If you want your revenge, Lieutenant, now is your time!'

"And once again money began to change hands, while a hush in the talk showed how all interest was concentrated upon the table. Lablas did not play, but he hovered round the green baize like some evil spirit, with his hard smile upon his lips, and his cold eye bent upon me. Sadly, even when I was the elder hand, I found myself bereft of trump cards, making it almost impossible to score sufficient points to win a game. Eventually, I pushed my chair back in despair.

" 'It is useless!' I cried. 'The luck is against me! But, gentlemen,' I added, beseechingly, 'if I can raise a little money tomorrow, even though it be only a little, you will not refuse to play the same stakes – you will give me a chance?'

" 'We will play just exactly as long as your little sum lasts!' said Turville, with a brutal laugh."

"This is all well and good, Lieutenant Malpas; however, I fail to see the point of your tale," interjected Holmes. "Yes, Lablas was a scoundrel. You were at once his guest and his dupe. It is little wonder that you lost when all were combining to play against you. But what has this to do with Henry Latour?"

"I am coming to that, Mr. Holmes, if you will give me time. You see, I was flushed and excited. I moved to sit apart from the others, and seemed to hear the talk that ensued as in a dream. I had an uneasy feeling that all had not been fair, and yet, do what I would, I could not give one proof to the contrary. Meanwhile, the actors continued to converse amongst themselves.

" 'Pass over the wine,' said Grossière. 'Where were you till one o'clock, Lablas?' he asked his friend.

"Lablas only showed his white teeth in a smile, but was otherwise silent.

" 'The old story, I suppose?' said Turville.

" 'Bah! It is becoming too old a story,' resumed Grossière. 'A story without change or variety is apt to become monotonous. One intrigue is as like another as a pair of small swords, and success is always the end of them.'

" 'They are too easily won,' assented Cachet.

" 'I promise you this will not be too easily won,' said Lablas. 'Though she is a quarry worth flying for, as she is as beautiful as an angel, she is strictly preserved too; and there is a six-foot brother acting as gamekeeper, so there is a prospect of a little excitement.'

" 'Have you made any advance yet?' asked Cachet.

" 'No; I have taken a few preliminary observations, however,' returned the roué.[22] 'I fear it must be done by force, and it will need both courage and tact.'

" 'Who is the girl, Lablas?' said Turville.

" 'That I won't answer.'

" 'Come, do tell us her name,' Turville pleaded.

" 'Curiosity sometimes verges on impertinence,' said Lablas, looking from under his eyebrows at his brother actor. 'Take care that you do not cross the border, for I never tolerate a liberty.'

"Turville was a brave enough man, but he sank his eyes before the fiery glance of the practised duellist. There was a moment's silence, and then Lablas stretched out his hand and said, 'Come, Turville, forgive and forget. I did not mean to speak hastily, but you know my cursed temper. There, I can say no more. After all, there is no reason why I should not give you the name. I may need your assistance; and, in any case, you are men of honour, and you would not thwart me in my plans. I do not suppose any of you know her. Her name is Rose Latour, and she lives in the Rue Bertrand.'"

Holmes' eyebrows rose with interest. "Ah, this is indeed pertinent! Pray continue, Lieutenant."

"You will understand, Mr. Holmes, that at the time, I was as of yet unacquainted with my future wife, so this name meant little to me. But not so to Lablas' fellow actors.

" 'What? The sister of Henry Latour?' cried Grossière.

" 'Yes, the same. Do you know him?'

" 'Know him? Why he plays Laertes to your Hamlet on Monday night!' said Grossière.

" 'The deuce he does!'

" 'Yes, old Lambertin closed with him last night. This will be a pretty complication! As good a fellow as ever breathed.'

" 'I do not see how that affects the question of my carrying off his sister.'

" 'I know the girl, too,' said Grossière. "She is as chaste as she is beautiful. You will never succeed there, Lablas. She is an angel upon earth, and her brother is not the man to be trifled with.'

" 'My dear fellow,' said Lablas. "Don't you see that every word you say is strengthening my resolution? As you said just now, intrigues become monotonous. There is some variety about an abduction.'

" 'You will fail,' said Grossière.

" 'On the contrary, I shall succeed.'

" 'I would stake my head that you will fail.'

" 'If you are willing to stake ten thousand francs, it will be more to the purpose. Shall it be a bet, and I claim twenty-four hours only in which to carry the little Puritan off?'[23]

" 'Done!" responded the comedian.

" 'You are my witnesses, messieurs," said Lablas, turning to the company, and entering the figures in an ivory writing-tablet.

"There was a hush as he wrote, and then my wayward voice broke the silence. 'I will be no partner to this!' I cried.

"You see, Mr. Holmes, I had risen from my chair, and was standing opposite Lablas. There was a murmur of surprise among the actors as their former butt and plaything rose up and dared the arch-spirit of them all. I believe that they would have saved me if they could. Cachet even grasped me by the sleeve, and half pulled me down.

" 'Sit down!' he whispered. 'Sit down! Lablas is the deadliest shot in France!'

"'I will not sit down!" said I. 'I protest against this! If the young lady's helplessness and virtue are powerless to screen her, surely the fact that her brother is your fellow-actor should suffice to save her from your insulting wager.'

"Lablas never raised his eyes from the book in which he was writing. 'How long,' he said, in the cold, measured voice which those who had heard it knew to be more dangerous than the bully's shout, 'how long since have you turned moralist, Monsieur Malpas?'

"'I have not turned moralist,' said I. 'I simply remain a gentleman, a title which I regret to say that you have forfeited.'

"'Indeed! You become personal.'

"'I do not pretend to be immaculate; far from it. But, so help me Heaven! Nothing in the whole world would induce me to be an accomplice in such a cold-blooded, villainous seduction!'

"I like to believe that there was a brave ring in my voice as I spoke, and I imagine that all the fire of the chivalrous South sparkled in my eyes. 'I only regret,' I continued, 'that in confiding your plans to my honour before revealing them will prevent my helping to frustrate them.'

"'Dear, innocent youth!' sneered Lablas. 'I think I see the cause of your conversion to morality. You have some intentions in that quarter yourself, *mon cher*. Is it not so?'

"'You lie, and you know that you lie!' I cried and lunged for the villain.

"Grossière moved to restrain me. 'Here, hold him. Hold his arms, Cachet! Pull him back! Don't let them brawl like roughs!'

"Meanwhile, Turville did the same to my enemy. 'Let me go, I say!' yelled Lablas. 'He called me a liar! I will have his life!'

"'Tomorrow, my dear fellow. Tomorrow,' said Grossière. 'We will see that you have every satisfaction.'

"'There is my card,' I cried, as I threw it down upon the table. 'You shall find me ready whenever it is convenient to you. Capitaine Haut shares my rooms; he will act as my second. Adieu, gentlemen! *Au revoir,* monsieur!'

"And with that retort, I turned on my heel, doing my best to swagger gallantly out of the room. It was only later that I realized that I left all of my remaining money behind. Nevertheless, Mr. Holmes, you must understand that it was at that moment when I threw off my old faults, and felt that my old mother in Montpellier would not have been ashamed of her son if she could have seen me then."

"What was your next course of action, Lieutenant?" asked Holmes.

"Well, I moped in my room for the span of a day, all the while awaiting the knock upon the door which signalled the arrival of the note which spelled out the time and place of my rendezvous with Monsieur Lablas, the meeting from which only one man may return. Eventually, Cachet called upon my friend, Capitaine Haut. It was to be pistols. I was to meet Lablas upon the Bois de Boulogne at dawn.[24]

"You can imagine the rest, Mr. Holmes. My shot missed its mark. But Lablas' did not. I still bear the scar of his bullet upon my left breast," said the Lieutenant, touching the spot. "I count myself most fortunate that it went a few inches too far to the side and spared my heart. For when I awoke, I knew that I owed nothing further to the villain Lablas. My honour had, at first, caused me to hold my tongue regarding his plans for the girl I thought of at the time as Miss Latour. Now, a higher honour required me to speak and warn the household.

"I rose from my sick-bed, to the great consternation of the nurses, and proceeded to don my uniform as quickly as the pain would permit. Fortunately, they had managed to scrub out most of the blood and sewed up the hole with such care that one might never know it was there. It was evening by the time I made my way round to Rue Bertrand, which I recalled Lablas noting was the address in question.

"Night had fallen on the busy world of Paris, and its gay population had poured out on to the Boulevards. Soldier and civilian, aristocrat and workman, all struggled for a footing upon the pavement, while in the roadway the Communistic donkey of the costermonger jostled up against the Conservative thoroughbreds of the Countess de Sang-pur.[25] Here and there, a café, with its numerous little tables, each with its progeny of chairs, cast a yellow glare in front of it, through which the great multitude seemed to ebb and flow. Eventually, I left the noise and bustle of the Boulevard des Italiens behind us, and turn to the right, along the Rue D'Egypte. At the bottom of this there lies a labyrinth of dingy little quiet streets, and the dingiest and quietest of them all is the Rue Bertrand.

"In England, you should call it shabby-genteel. The houses are two-storied semi-detached villas. There is a mournful and broken-down look about them, as if they had seen better days, and were still endeavouring to screen their venerable tiles and crumbling mortar behind a coquettish railing and jaunty Venetian blinds. I have since learned that the street is always quiet, but it was even quieter than usual that night; indeed, it would be entirely deserted but for me, pacing backwards and forwards over the ill-laid pavement. You see, Mr. Holmes, I had come all that way only to realize that I knew not how precisely to speak of Lablas' plan. Surely, they would take me for a villain too, since I had not informed them earlier?"

"So, what did you do?" asked Holmes.

"Well, my decision was made by the appearance of a gendarme, who came clanking noisily round the corner. 'What is your purpose here, Monsieur?' he asked, plainly not observing my uniform in the darkness.

"I was unsure of how to respond. 'I, ah...' I stammered.

"'Out with it! You must be waiting or watching for someone, as the Rue Bertrand is the last place that the romantic dreamer would select for his solitary reverie.'

"'My purpose is my own, and no business of yours.'

"'Oh, is that so?' said the gendarme, his eyebrows rising alarmingly. 'Well, we will see how you feel like talking to the magistrate then!'

"'Very well,' I cried. 'If you must know, I am Lieutenant Malpas, and I have come to call upon Mr. Henry Latour. I believe that he lives there,' said I, motioning to a house just opposite the spot where I had stationed myself, which exhibited not only signs of vitality, but even some appearance of mirth.

"This declaration of purpose, perhaps, caused the gendarme to stop and gaze at me. 'Ah, very good, sir. Sorry to bother you.' He tipped his hat and strode off down the street.

"I realized that I could hardly stand there much longer, or risk attracting even more attention to myself. I turned and looked at the Latour residence. It was neater and more modern looking than its companions. The garden was well laid out, and between the bars of the green persiennes, the warm light glowed out into the street.[26] It had a cheery, English look about it, which marked it out among the fossils that surrounded it. Eventually, as I stood there, the door to number twenty-two opened, and a dainty little figure came out and went tripping down the street. As I watched, even in the venerable Rue Bertrand, which should have been above such follies, there was a parting of window blinds when Rose passed by – for who else could it be?

"As for myself, at that moment, Mr. Holmes, the blasé Parisian lounger vanished once and for all. For, glancing at her face, I was riveted to my place with the sudden conviction that there was something higher in womanhood than I had ever met, even with my varied experiences of the 'Jardin Mabille' and the Cafés Chantants.[27]

"When Rose returned, holding several bags that signified a trip to the local green-grocer, I finally managed to stir from my place. I crossed the street and knocked upon the door. To my surprise and eternal gratitude, I was welcomed inside, where I was introduced to the entire family. This included her brother Henry, who was recuperating from the wounds he had sustained earlier that night.

"I was astonished to learn that Gaspard Lablas – who just the day prior had almost killed me – was himself dead. Over the span of the next several hours, we compared our versions of the mad scheme that eventually led to Lablas' death. During that exchange, I became a fast friend of the family. From there, Mr. Holmes, the conclusion should be self-evident. Within a month, Rose and I were kneeling at the foot of an altar, while a clergyman pronounced the words that refute the commonly received doctrine that one and one are two, and which made me the happiest man upon this earth.

"My only wish now is to ease my wife's pain. If there is something else at work in the matter of Henry's death besides the callous workings of an indifferent universe, then I will do anything to help you find it."

Holmes nodded. "At the moment, Lieutenant, I am optimistic that a conversation with Mr. Barker may shine some additional light upon your brother-in-law's death. Do you have his address in Edinburgh?"

The soldier shook his head. "I can do you one better, Mr. Holmes. I can give you his address in London. You see, both he and Jack came down as soon as they heard about Henry. They are both staying at the Charing Cross Hotel."

§

My friend's brow was furrowed as our cab raced down Southampton Row. Holmes had ordered the driver to make haste, but I knew that – with the typical traffic clogging the streets – we had at least twenty minutes before our arrival.

"What are you thinking, Holmes?"

He shook his head slightly. "It is still premature to form any conclusions, Watson. However, the most apparent possibility is that Mr. Latour's death was a retribution for his own slaying of Monsieur Lablas. It is apparent that there was some sort of bad blood between them, and this may have been exacerbated by the ill intentions Lablas entertained towards Latour's sister, Rose. It is possible that one of Lablas' companions believed that Latour murdered him. I find it suspicious that Jules Grossière was formerly one of Lablas' fellow conspirators and now he is acting in the same play as Mr. Latour. He has both motive and means."

"But Grossière is playing the part of Banquo, Holmes. He was on the stage with Latour when the man fell to his death. Surely, Mr. Brandin or one of the other actors would have noticed if Grossière pushed him?"

"I concur, Watson, that Grossière did not have opportunity. This is why I require more data."

When we reached at Charing Cross Hotel, Holmes slipped a guinea into the hand of one of the lower-attendants, and we were soon escorted to the room belonging to Mr. Stephan Barker. Barker proved to be a tall, dark, young man, with a serious face. He stepped forward and made a small bow.

"Mr. Barker," said Holmes. "We have reason to believe that Mr. Latour's death is somehow related to the accident at the Theatre National where Monsieur Lablas was killed."

The man's eyebrows rose in surprise. "You don't say!"

"Come now, Mr. Barker. I have spoken with Mr. Brandin and heard about how Lablas died with Henry Latour's sword through his chest. Moreover, Lieutenant Malpas has told me that Lablas intended to abduct Rose Latour. I am only missing how these two events connect."

Barker pursed his lips and considered this for a moment. He pulled out a cigar from his breast pocket and slowly lit it. Finally he spoke. "It is strange, Mr. Holmes, how naturally Englishmen adapt themselves to the customs of the country in which they happen to be placed – more especially when those customs happen to accord with their own inclinations. At home, I am a rigid Churchman enough; but on that Parisian Sunday, the still small voice of conscience was even stiller and smaller than usual, as I sauntered round to the Rue Bertrand. I wished to see if my new friend, Henry Latour, would have pity on my loneliness, and venture out for a stroll. Possibly the fair Rose had more to do with my visit than her brother; but, if so, I was disappointed, as that young lady had just tripped off to church, and I was compelled to put up with the male element of the household.

"Henry, for his part, was glad to see me. 'You could not possibly have done better than come,' said my friend, as he stretched his tall frame in a stupendous yawn. 'I have been sitting in this confounded chair, making sure of my part, ever since breakfast and I think I am right at last. I have been doing the *quarte* and *tierce* business too with the poker, in preparation for the last scene.[28] You know I used to be an excellent fencer, and it always brings down the house.'

" 'I suppose your Hamlet can fence?' I remarked.

" 'He is notorious for it,' Henry answered, as a dark shade passed over his handsome face. 'But come, Barker; it is my last free day for some time to come, so we must make the most of it.'

"We certainly did make the most of it, and the young actor proved himself to be an admirable cicerone, doing the honours of picture galleries and museums with an amusing air of proprietorship.[29] He was in excellent spirits about his engagement at the National, to which he often referred as being a splendid opening for his career.

" 'There is only one drawback,' Henry remarked, 'and that is having to play second fiddle to that unmitigated scoundrel, Lablas. He is a profligate fellow, Barker. This very morning they say that he fought a duel in the Bois de Boulogne; shot a young officer of cavalry through the lungs. I shall have a quarrel with him, I fear; for, as Hamlet says, "There is something in me sensitive," and the man's manner jars upon me more than I can tell.'[30]

"It was dark by this time, and we were both somewhat fatigued and hungry after our long peregrination. 'There is a café here,' said Henry, 'on the right-hand side, close to the railway station, where we can have a quiet little meal. That is it, where the lights are. Shall we try it?'

" 'All right,' I said. As we turned to enter, just at that moment, a tall young fellow, with a carpetbag in his hand, who was coming out, ran against us.

" 'Pardon, messieurs,' he said, turning half round and bowing, and was about to pass on, when Henry sprang forward, and caught him by the arm.

" 'Jack, my boy, where in the world did you come from?'

" 'Henry, and Barker, by all that is astonishing!' said the voice of my old college friend, Jack Latour, as he seized us alternately by the hand. 'Why, what an extraordinary thing!'

" 'Extraordinary, indeed,' cried his brother. 'Why, we thought you were in Edinburgh, hundreds of miles away!'

" 'So I ought to be; but it struck me yesterday that a change of air would do me good. The insolent familiarity of the British tradesman was beginning to prey upon my mind. My tailor was exhibiting an increased hankering after his filthy lucre, so I thought I would deprive him for a few weeks of the refining influence of my society.'

" 'The old game, Jack,' said I, shaking my head.

" 'Yes, the old game; and I conclude you fellows are up to the old game, since I find you mooning about the first pub I pass – I beg your pardon, café. Café sounds better than pub, I suppose.'

" 'How do you account for your own presence here?' laughed Henry.

" 'My dear fellow, you don't seriously suppose that I came in search of bibulous refreshment? No; it was a harmless eccentricity that led me within these walls. What do you fellows intend to do with yourselves? There is no use my knocking up Rose and the mother to-night, so I shall stay with you.'

" 'We have nothing particular to do,' I said.

" 'Then come up to the 'Anglais' with me," said Jack.[31] "Two Edinburgh men are up there – Grant and Buckley. Will you come?'

" 'I am willing,' said I.

" 'And I,' said Henry.

"So the bargain was concluded, and we all three repaired to the hotel, where we were introduced to Jack's friends, a couple of reckless, light-hearted medical students of his own kidney.

"There is no reason why I should dwell upon the convivial evening which ensued. I have only alluded to these things as influencing the dark events that were impending. It was close upon one o'clock in the morning before Henry Latour glanced at his watch, and announced that it was high time to break up.

" 'I must run over my part again to-morrow. You come along with me, Jack,' said he, to his brother, 'and we can sleep together without disturbing anyone. I have a key.'

" 'I will walk round with you,' said I; 'I want to finish my pipe.' I am afraid that the sight of a certain window was becoming dearer to me than all the tobacco Virginia ever grew. The brothers Latour were delighted that I should come, so we bade our fellow countrymen adieu, and set off together. We were a hilarious party as long as we kept to the well-lit Boulevards, but when we got into the quiet streets that branch off from them, a curious feeling of depression stole over us, which affected even the irrepressible Jack. We strode on together, each buried in his own thoughts. Everything was very still – so still that we all looked up in surprise when a closed carriage rattled past us, going in our own direction.

" 'That fellow is driving at a deuce of a rate,' remarked Jack. 'Without lights either,' I said.

" 'I wonder where he can be bound for? This is not much of a carriage neighbourhood, especially at such an hour.'

" 'Well, anyway, he isn't going to visit us,' laughed Henry; 'so it is no business of ours.' And so saying, he quickened his pace, and we all three rounded the corner, and passed into the Rue Bertrand.

We were hardly round, before Jack stopped in amazement. 'Why, Henry!' he said; 'what on earth is this? They just exactly are visiting us!'

"There was no doubt about it. The moon had just come from behind a cloud, and was pouring a flood of cold light upon the dingy little street. And there, away down opposite number twenty-two, was a dark blur, which could be nothing but the carriage. It had pulled up.

"You must understand the scene, Mr. Holmes," said Barker. "The house on Rue Bertrand is a simple two-storey one, and

Rose slept alone in one of the upper rooms. So much I gathered, partly from observation, and partly from the servant. They retired to bed early, and when Henry is away, there is only the old lady in the house. They have no shutters to the bedrooms – only blinds."

Holmes nodded. "I can see the scene, just as you describe, Mr. Barker. Pray continue."

"Well, Mr. Holmes, it was Henry who spoke first. 'What is it?'

" 'There are a couple of men on the pavement!' cried Jack.

" 'One of them has a lantern!'

" 'What a lark!' cried Jack. 'It is my Edinburgh tailor, for a dollar!'

" 'They cannot be burglars!' I whispered. 'Let us watch them for a bit.'

" 'By Heaven, there is ladder against a window – against Rose's window!' hissed a voice, which we could hardly recognise as Henry's, it was so altered. The light fell upon his face, and I could see that it was dark with wrath, and that his jaw was fixed and hard, while his features worked spasmodically. 'The villains!' he said. 'Come after me, but quietly!' Swiftly and silently, he started down the street.

"Jack's rage was as great as his brother's, but he was of a less fiery disposition. He ground his teeth, and followed Henry with giant strides. Had I been alone, I should have shouted my indignation, and hurried forward to the rescue. Henry Latour's was the leading mind among us, however, and it is on such occasions that the mind asserts itself. There was something terrible in his very stillness.

"We followed him implicitly down the road. Rain had fallen during the evening, and the ground was very soft. We made little noise as we approached the carriage. We might have made more without fear of detection, for the horses had been left to themselves, and the men we had seen were in the front garden, too much occupied with their own movements and those of their leader to be easily disturbed. The Rue de Bertrand was a cul-de-sac, and the possibility of being disturbed at their work was so slight as to be disregarded.

"Henry slipped behind the carriage, and we followed him. We were effectually concealed, and commanded a view of all that was going on in front of us. Two of the men were standing at the foot of a ladder that was reared against one of the upper windows. They were watching the movements of a third who appeared at that moment at the open casement bearing something on his arms.

"My blood seemed to run in a fiery torrent through my veins as I saw the man place his foot upon the upper step and begin to descend. I glanced at Henry, but he held up his hand as if to ask for one more moment's forbearance. I could see that he knew as well as I did what the poor little white burden was which the man was clasping to his breast. I had lost sight of Jack, but a smothered curse from between the wheels showed me where he was crouching.

"The leader came slowly and gingerly down the ladder. He must have been a powerful fellow, for the additional weight did not seem to inconvenience him. We could see that his face was covered with a mask. His friends below kept encouraging him in whispers. He reached the bottom without an accident.

"'Hurry her into the carriage!' he said.

"Henry rose silently to his feet, with every muscle braced. The time for action had arrived. And at this very moment the prisoner's gag must have slipped, for a sweet, piteous voice rang out on the still night – 'Henry! Brother! Help!'

"Never, surely, was an appeal so promptly answered. The spring was so swift, so sudden, that I never saw him leave my side. I heard a snarl like a wild beast's and a dull thud, and my friend with the man in the mask were rolling on the ground together. It all happened in less time than I take to tell it. Jack and I ran forward to assist Rose into the house; but the two confederates confronted us. I would have passed my antagonist in order to help the lady, but he flew at me with a savage oath, hitting wildly with both hands.

"A Frenchman can never realise the fact that a segment is

shorter than an arc; but I gave my opponent a practical illustration of the fact by stopping him with a facer before he could bring his hands round, and then toppling him over with what is known to the initiated as a Cribb's hit behind the ear.[32]

"He sat down upon a rose-bush with a very sickly smile, and manifested a strong disinclination to rise up; so I turned my attention to Jack. I was just in time to see his adversary make a desperate attempt to practice the barbarous French *savate* upon him; but the student was a man of expedients, and springing aside, he seized the uplifted foot, and gave it a wrench, which brought the discomfited owner howling to the ground with a dislocated leg.[33]

"We led poor trembling Rose into the house, and after handing her over to her frightened mother, hurried back into the garden.

"Neither of our acquaintances were in a condition to come up to time; but the struggle between their leader and Henry Latour was going on with unabated vigour. It was useless to attempt to help our friend. They were so entwined, and revolving so rapidly upon the gravel walk, that it was impossible to distinguish the one from the other. They were fighting in silence, and each was breathing hard.

"But the clean living of the younger man began to tell. He had the better stamina of the two. I saw the glint of the moonlight upon his sleeve-links as he freed his arm, and then I heard the sound of a heavy blow. It seemed to stun his antagonist for a moment; but before it could be repeated he had shaken himself free, and both men staggered to their feet.

"The villain's mask had been torn off, and exposed the pale face of the Frenchman Lablas, with a thin stream of blood coursing down it from a wound on the forehead.

" 'You infernal scoundrel! I know you now!' yelled Henry, who would have sprung at him again had we not restrained him.

" '*Ma foi*! You will know me better before you die!' hissed the man, with a sinister smile.

" 'You accursed villain! Do you think I fear your threats? I will fight you now if you wish; I have weapons! Run in for the pistols, Jack!'

" 'Quietly, old man – quietly,' said I. 'Don't do anything rash.'

" 'Rash!' raved Henry. 'Why, man, it was my sister! Give me a pistol!'

" 'It is for me to name the time and place,' said Lablas. 'It is I who have been struck.'

" 'When, then?'

" 'You shall hear from me in the morning. Suffice it that you shall be chastised before all Paris. I shall make a public warning of you, my young friend.' And with the same hard smile upon his face, he mounted upon the box, and seized the reins.

" 'If this gentleman whose joint I have had the pleasure of damaging considers himself aggrieved,' said Jack, 'he shall always find me ready to make any amends in my power.'

" 'The same applies to my friend on the right,' said I. 'I refer to the gentleman with the curious swelling under his ear.'

"Our 'friends' only answered our kind attentions by a volley of curses. The patron of the *savate* was hoisted into the carriage, and the other followed him; while Lablas, still white with passion, drove furiously off, amid laughter from Jack and myself and curses from Henry, whose fiery blood was too thoroughly roused to allow him to view the matter in its ridiculous aspect.

" 'Nothing like evaporating lotions for bruises,' was the practical piece of advice which our medical student Jack shouted after them as the carriage rumbled away like a dark nightmare, and the sound of its wheels died gradually in the distance.[34]

"At this moment a gendarme – true to the traditions of his order – hurried on to the scene of action. However, after jotting down the number of the house in a portentous notebook, he gave up the attempt of extracting any information from us, and departed with many shrugs.

"My heart was heavy as I trudged back to my hotel that night. There is always a reaction after such excitement, and I was uneasy at the thought of what the morrow might bring forth. I had not forgotten the allusion that Henry had made in the early part of the evening to the duelling proclivities of Lablas, and in particular to the sinister result of his encounter with the young French officer. I knew the wild blood which ran in my friend's veins, and that it would be hopeless to attempt to dissuade him from a meeting. I was powerless, and must let events take their own course.

"When I came down to breakfast in the morning I found the two brothers waiting for me. Henry looked bright and almost exultant as he greeted me, but Jack was unusually serious.

" 'It's all right, old fellow,' said the young actor.

" 'We have worked out what they were thinking," said Jack. 'You see, Barker, they must have known that the street is a very quiet one and that Rose and mother go to bed at eleven o'clock. They took Lablas' closed carriage, and one of them served as the driver, so as to not involve a witness to their perfidy. Lablas must have a ladder in three pieces for just such an affair. They planned to leave the carriage, put up the ladder, open Rose's window, gag her in her sleep, carry her down, and it is done. Lablas would have his way with her.

"I shuddered at the thought of what would have happened if we had not come upon them in time. 'It was a great risk,' said I. 'What if she had been awake and screamed? And Henry might have been at home.'

" 'They must have decided that the three of them could overcome me with a knock upon my head,' said Henry. 'They didn't count on having two more to contend with.'

" 'It's a good thing we were,' said Jack. 'Otherwise, we would have had no clue as to who they were, or where they had taken her. Rose would have been permanently ruined.'

" 'Well, it was a diabolical deed,' said I. 'I am amazed that the profligate actor could call upon so many heartless associates for assistance.'

" 'Yes; look here, Barker,' explained Jack, evidently in considerable perturbation. 'It is a most extraordinary business. The queerest challenge I ever heard of, though I confess that my experience of these things is very limited. I suppose we cannot get out of it?'

" 'Not for the world!' cried his brother.

" 'See here,' said Jack; 'this is the note I got this morning. Read it for yourself.'

"The note, Mr. Holmes, was addressed to Jack, and ran something to the effect of:

> "Sir, –
> On the understanding that you act as second to Mr. Henry Latour, allow me to state that in the exercise of his right M. Lablas selects rapiers as his weapon. He begs you to accompany your principal to the theatre to-night, where you will be admitted to the stage as a supernumerary. You can thus satisfy yourself that the final scene is fought according to the strict rules of the duello. The rapiers will be substituted for stage foils without difficulty. I shall be present on behalf of M. Lablas. I have the honour to remain very sincerely yours,
> PIERRE GROSSIERE."

" 'What do you think of that?' said Jack.

" 'Why, I think that it is a preposterous idea, and that you should refuse,' said I.

" 'It would not do,' said Henry. 'They would try to construe it into cowardice. Besides, what does it matter where I meet the fellow so long as I do meet him? I tell you, Barker,' he continued, laying his hand upon my arm, 'that when I do, I intend to kill him!'

"There was something resolute in the ring of my friend's voice. I felt that, in spite of his advantages, Lablas would meet with a dangerous opponent.

" 'If you should fall, Henry,' said Jack, 'I will take your place, and either lick the blackguard or never leave the stage. It would make a sensation to have Hamlet run through by a supernumerary, wouldn't it?' he concluded, with the ghost of a smile.

" 'Well, write an acceptance at once, Jack,' said Henry. 'My only fear is that our sister's name should get mixed up in the matter.'

" 'No fear of that,' said I. 'It would not be their interest to talk about the ridiculous fiasco they have made.'

" 'You will come to the National tonight, Barker?' asked Henry. 'You can get a place in the front row of the stalls.'

" 'I will,' said I; 'and if you should both fail to avenge your sister, Lablas will have to reckon with me before the curtain falls.'

" 'You are a good fellow, Barker,' said Henry. 'Well,' he added, after a pause, 'my private quarrel must not interfere with my duty to the public, so I will go back and read my part over. Good-bye, old man! We shall see you to-night.'

"And the brothers left me alone to my coffee. How they got through the day, I do not know. I should think even imperturbable Jack found the hours hung rather heavily upon his hands. As for myself, I was in a fever of suspense. I could only pace up and down the crowded streets, and wait for the evening to come. The doors did not open until seven o'clock, but the half-hour found me waiting at the entrance to the National.

"A knot of enthusiasts, eager to secure places, were already clustering round it. I spent the time in perusing a poster, which was suspended to one of the pillars. 'LABLAS' was written across it in great capitals, while in smaller print below there were a few other names, that of Henry Latour being one of them."

"I believe we know the rest of the story, Mr. Barker," interrupted Holmes. "We heard it all from the stage-manager, Mr. Brandin. I would suggest that you steer clear of Paris for the time being, sir, given your complicity in an illegal duel. Henry Latour may be past justice, but the French legal system may decide that you and his brother Jack were accomplices. I have only one question remaining for you. Mr. Brandin described a large man on the stage dressed in ill-fitting armour. Was that

Jack Latour?"

"Of course. Jack cannot act a stitch, but he switched places with a man so that he could be in his place as Henry's second."

"And where is Mr. Jack Latour at the moment?"

Barker shrugged. "He said that he was going round to visit his mother and sister."

"We have just come from the Hotel St. Pancras."

"Then you must have missed him in passing."

§

In the hansom, Holmes appeared tense and preoccupied. I refrained from questioning him, hoping that he would talk when ready. After a few minutes, he sighed and turned to me.

"I fear, Watson, that another crime is about to occur."

"What do you mean, Holmes?"

"I believe we have a rough outline of what has transpired. Duelling has been officially banned in France for several centuries, Watson, but it was such an honoured tradition that it continued behind the scenes until recently. However, the July Monarchy of Louis Philippe finally put a nail in the coffin of the duelling culture, for in 1837, an order went out to the judges that a duel was classified as an attempt at murder and the victor should be punished as a criminal."[35]

"Why then did Lablas' friends not report what had transpired?"

"For two reasons. First, they could hardly do so without exposing their own complicity in an attempting kidnapping and assault. The scandal would have ended their acting careers. Second, their target had fled the country. So, Jules Grossière followed Henry Latour to London, determined to seek a sort of warped revenge."

When we arrived back at the Hotel St. Pancras, Lieutenant Malpas, who was pacing back and forth in an agitated manner, met us in the lobby. The boyish smile was gone from his face.

"What has happened?" asked Holmes, tersely.

"It is Jack."

"What about him?"

"He came here about twenty minutes ago, and seemed his usual charming, blasé self. He was most solicitous of his mother and sister. However, at one point his entire manner changed. He excused himself and went into the room that I share with Rose. When he came out, his face was like thunder. Jack did not speak another word, but instead stormed out of the room. I retraced his steps to try to figure out what his intentions were and when I entered our room, I noticed that my Purdey pistol case had been pulled down from its spot on top of the wardrobe, the lid was open, and one of them was missing.[36] What could he possibly want with a pistol, Mr. Holmes?"

Holmes had listened intently to this narration. "What was Jack doing right before his manner changed?"

"Nothing remarkable," said the soldier, with a shake of his head. "I think he was looking over some souvenirs of Henry's acting career, which my mother-in-law treasures more highly than gold."

"What sort of souvenirs?"

"You know. Ticket stubs, clippings of reviews from the papers, playbills."

Holmes stared at him. "Lieutenant Malpas, you must go upstairs at once and bring me the souvenirs at which that Jack was looking."

The solider nodded and retreated up the stairs to follow Holmes' order. Holmes refused to speak a word while he was gone, but Malpas promptly returned with a soldierly efficiency.

"This is what was on top," said he, holding forth what looked like a playbill.

Holmes snatched it from his hand and ran his eyes down the paper. "I have been painfully slow, Watson," said Holmes bitterly. He held forth the playbill, which read:

THE TRAGEDY OF MACBETH

By William Shakespeare

Macbeth, Thane of Glamis.......................
Henry Latour
Duncan, King of Scotland.........................
Louis Cachet
Malcolm, Duncan's elder son....................
Harry O'Callaghan
Donalbain, Duncan's younger son.............
Laurence Brodribb
Lady Macbeth, Macbeth's wife...................
Florence Baird
Banquo, Macbeth's friend.........................
Jules Grossière
Fleance, Banquo's son..............................
Herbert Pine
Macduff, Thane of Fife.............................
Victor Turville

"I don't understand, Holmes."

"Come now, Watson. Surely, it is quite the coincidence that the three great friends of the dead man Lablas are all actors in this production of Mac…"

"The Scottish Play," I interjected.

"Whatever you call it!' he cried. "It is no happenstance, I tell you, Watson. This is how Grossière brought about the death of Henry Latour. He had assistance from Louis Cachet and Victor Turville, who would have both been offstage during the fatal act. While Grossière, playing the part of Banquo's ghost, distracted Latour, his accomplices added a coating of castor oil to the top of the faux castle rampart. Although they cleaned it up after, I detected a trace of the oil when I was inspecting the stage. Henry raced up the steps and was then unable to stop himself from tumbling off the edge. They hoped that his death would be termed an accident by the police and a manifestation of the Scottish curse by the more credulous."

"So what has happened now?"

Holmes shook his head. "Unfortunately, Jack Latour has recently come to the same conclusion. I suspect that he believes Scotland Yard failed in its duty, and he is now planning to take matters into his own hands."

"What do you mean, Mr. Holmes?" asked Lieutenant Malpas, worriedly.

Holmes turned to the man. "Lieutenant, unless I am mistaken, you are now Madame Latour's only son. Pray treat her well."

The man's face was a picture of bewilderment. "Nothing else would bring me greater pleasure than to care for Rose's mother, but what of Jack? You do not think he is dead?"

Holmes shook his head sadly. "As good as. I am afraid that it will be many years before Jack Latour will be able to set foot in France, and he will be forever barred from England. For no statute of limitations exists in the magnificent fair-play of the British criminal law when the crime is murder."

"Murder!" exclaimed the soldier. "By Jack? Of whom?"

"Unless I miss my guess, Lieutenant, the murders of Monsieurs Grossière, Cachet, and Turville. In retribution for their killing of his brother Henry. I fear that there is nothing I can do to stop him now."

"Surely you are joking, Mr. Holmes," stammered Malpas, uncertainly.

But Holmes was not the sort of man to make such a cruel joke. He was, however, accurate in all accounts.

The following morning's edition of *The Times* carried all of the lurid details of how three French actors were shot to death in their private carriage aboard the Dover train minutes before it was due to pull into its destination station. A tall man with a burly frame and carrying a fancy pistol was seen jumping from the train shortly thereafter. The assailant was still at large, and Scotland Yard requested that anyone possessing information regarding his name or whereabouts come forward immediately.

When I suggested we do so, Holmes merely shrugged. "As you recall, Watson, I was not retained in this case by the police to supply their deficiencies. In fact, Lestrade had washed his hands of the matter. Still, I expect that even he will eventually conclude that it was the medical student Jack Latour who turned avenger. The great tragedy in this case is that even prompter action by Lestrade to bring me into the case at the beginning would have likely been powerless to avert this cycle of retribution. Men sometimes are not masters of their fates, and their faults are written in their stars."[37]

§

About six weeks later, we received a note from Mr. Stephan Barker, who informed us that Jack Latour had successfully taken passage at Dover for France, and there had joined up with the *Légion étrangère*. He was promptly shipped off to Cochin-China before a demand for extradition arrived from Scotland Yard.[38] Barker concluded that he suspected that the British request would vanish into the morass of bureaucracy in the Garrison at Sidi Bel Abbès, and that Jack would remain free so long as he never attempted to return to the shores of England.[39]

"What a startling adventure, Holmes," said I. "I am sorely tempted to commemorate this for one of the popular literary magazines."

"No, Watson," said Holmes, with a shake of his head. "We can hardly claim this as a victory. I am well aware that you intend to embody the experience of my methods of work in the Jefferson Hope case with a small brochure.[40] I cannot say that I am in favour of such a thing; however, I must expressly request that you make no attempt to ever make known the details of Mr. Henry Latour's passing."

"But Holmes," I protested, "the public deserves to hear how these things came about...."

"No, my decision on the matter is final, Watson. We must let the bodies lie where they fell. Despite the carnal, bloody, and unnatural acts, of accidental judgements, casual slaughters, and deaths put on by cunning and forced cause, this is no play to entertain the masses.[41] Let it sink into obscurity."

I must have looked dejected by this decree, as Holmes suddenly smiled. "Come now, my friend. We may hope that there are more adventures to come with happier results. Put those to your pen instead."[42]

§

THE ADVENTURE OF THE MOST DANGEROUS MAN

I. THE PESTILENCE THAT WALKETH AT NOONDAY

When I review my journals for the year 1882, I am often amazed to find that one of the most terrifying cases ever handled by my friend, Mr. Sherlock Holmes, occurred so early in his career. I have previously refrained from setting down the complete details of this problem in hopes of sparing any additional pain to the poor individual who was at the centre of it. Though some particulars did leak out at the time, they were given little attention, and I hope that they caused no permanent mischief. Now that this person has passed on to that place where the horrors of the past can no longer harm her, I feel that I can finally set the matter straight.[43]

Holmes had a peculiar fondness for ranking individuals whom he encountered in the course of his inquiries into both the outré and the criminal. Once, as we strolled along the chalk cliffs near his villa, he told me that he thought the five most challenging cases of his career were – in order – those brought to his attention by the King of Bohemia, Professor James Moriarty, Mr. Hilton Cubitt, Mr. Jabez Wilson, and finally, Miss Helen Stoner.[44] He also ranked the smartest men in London, with John Clay coming in just behind the professor, Holmes' brother Mycroft, and Holmes himself. Then there were the most dangerous men in Europe, which was an ever-changing list as old enemies fell and new ones rose to take their place. Jack Stapleton held the crown briefly. Once Holmes had followed the threads back to the centre of the web of London's criminal world and found Professor Moriarty sitting there like a spider, the former Mathematical Chair became number one, followed closely by his chief of staff, Colonel Sebastian Moran. As these villains were disposed of, Baron Adelbert Gruner and then Henry Peters replaced them on the list. What all of these men had in common was a horrifying ability to bend others to their will. Of all of them, the one with the greatest talent in that foul area was the man of whom I am about to speak. To be completely honest, even to this day, his name summons a shiver of terror down my spine.

On the morning in question, I little thought that we were about to receive a caller whose story would excite considerable curiosity in certain quarters. She would tell of an extraordinary individual, and many guesses would be hazarded as to the identity of the man in question, and the nature of the charges brought against him. However, as the matter unfolded, I realized that Miss Underwood had shown admirable restraint in her judgement. I am not certain that I could have such comportment under similar circumstances.

Holmes was engaged in the task of rummaging through some of his scrapbooks for an item that he thought might assist him in one of his current cases. When our landlady brought in the post, he slit the letters open in turn with the jack-knife. After skimming over each with a distracted air, he crumpled them one by one into balls and tossed them into the cold grate.

"Nothing of interest, Holmes?" I asked.

"Hardly, Watson. Just the usual parade of matters of small consequence, each more absurd than the last. I sometimes think that Scotland Yard and the private firms all conspire to send over to me only the most mundane cases, hoping to keep to themselves the credit of the more peculiar ones."

I inferred from this diatribe that Holmes was in a foul mood, for he well knew that Lestrade and the others came to him with only the most challenging of cases, especially because he usually refrained from taking any personal credit for his role in deducing the solution. I thought perhaps that his recent cases were not going well.

"What is it this time?" I asked.

"See for yourself," said he, with a wave towards the fireplace.

I fished out one of the crumpled letters and smoothed it before me. It was dated from a place called Toynby Hall the preceding evening and ran thus:

> DEAR MR. HOLMES:
> I am very eager to consult you as to how we might keep ourselves safe from the unwanted attentions of a most unpleasant man. I plan to call at quarter-past eleven tomorrow, and I hope this shall be a convenient time for you.
> – Yours sincerely,
> CHARLOTTE UNDERWOOD

"Do you know this Miss Underwood?"

"Not at all," said Holmes.

"Well, perhaps it will be of interest. You never know when the problems of a private client may be just as singular as those that have perplexed the official force."

Holmes was about to respond, when a knock upon the door cut off his words. This was soon followed by the appearance of an extraordinarily beautiful young lady. She was tall and graceful, with a face of perfect symmetry, and a marble complexion. She had a wealth of deep golden hair and large green eyes, though there was a suggestion of strain around the latter.

"Did you receive my note?" she asked. When Holmes nodded, she continued. "I wish to engage your services, Mr. Holmes. We have been plagued by a terrible individual, and yet the police seem powerless to help us."

"Pray take a seat, Miss Underwood. This is my friend, Dr Watson, before whom you may speak freely. You will understand that I am quite busy at the moment, but seeing how you have come a long ways this morning, I will attempt to determine whether I can be of some assistance."

She frowned. "How do you know that?"

He waved his hands. "You dressed several hours ago, for the folds in your dress are no longer crisp, and your travelling boots show signs of scuffing. There is a trace of coal soot upon the hem of your dress, which is commonly seen after stepping off from a long train ride. Finally, you are plainly quite preoccupied by this matter, and yet you come round at a rather late hour. If you were closer to London, you would have arrived at our humble rooms much earlier in the morning, so I conclude that your journey was a long one. Likely at least three hours."[45]

"Three and a quarter," said Miss Underwood, with a satisfied nod. "From Plymouth to Paddington. I see that I have come to the right place."

"Well," said Holmes, "that remains to be seen. It will help me understand the situation if you start from the beginning."

"Of course. It is at Colonel Pillar's place at Roborough, in the pleasant county of Devon, that we have spent our autumn holidays. For some months now, I have been engaged to his eldest son Charley, and we plan for the marriage to take place before the termination of the Long Vacation.[46] Charley is 'safe' for his degree, and in any case, he is rich enough to be practically independent, while I am by no means penniless. The old Colonel is delighted at the prospect of the match, and so is my mother; so that look what way we might, there seems to be no cloud above our horizon. It is no wonder, then, that our last week of July was a most happy one. Even the most miserable of mankind would have laid his woes aside under the genial influence of the merry household at Toynby Hall. Until, that is, the arrival of the foreigner."

"Is it just the three of you at Toynby Hall?" asked Holmes.

"Oh no, there is a whole merry gathering. Beyond the gallant old warrior who is our host; with his time-honoured jokes, and his gout, and his harmless affectation of ferocity, there is Lieutenant Daseby – 'Jack,' as he is invariably called – fresh home from Japan aboard Her Majesty's ship *Shark*.[47] He is on the same interesting footing with Fanny Pillar, Charley's sister, as Charley is with me, so that Fanny and I are able to lend each other a certain moral support. Then there is Harry, Charley's younger brother, and Trevor Hall, his bosom friend at Cambridge. Finally, there is my mother, dearest of old ladies, who the Colonel invited down to join us in Devon.

"We were a most happy bunch, until the day dawned that was the commencement of all our miseries. I shall therefore relate, without exaggeration or prejudice, all that occurred from the day upon which this man, Doctor Octavius Gaster, entered Toynby Hall up to the day that he fled."

"Fled, you say?" interrupted Holmes. He looked as if he was about to ask her a question, then changed his mind and indicated that she should continue her narrative.

"It was the second of August. After dinner was over, we retired to the drawing room, where Fanny and Jack were nestled upon the sofa, while Charley paced restlessly about the room. I was sitting at the window, and when Charley joined me there, he noted that it was a positive shame to waste such a fine evening. Jack and Fan refused to move from their nest amongst the cushions of the sofa, but Charley had gotten the notion stuck in his head. After manoeuvring my mother to permit the two of us to take an unchaperoned walk, I put on my hat and shawl, Charley grabbed his fishing basket, and we stepped out across the lawn. Charley paused for a moment after we had emerged from the gate and seemed irresolute about which way to turn – towards the river or the moor."[48]

Miss Underwood paused for a moment, as if to gather herself. When she looked up, her face was grim. "Had we but known it, Mr. Holmes, our fate depended upon that trivial question."

"What did you choose?" asked Holmes.

She shook her head. "I did not care, so long as I was with Charley, so he voted for the moor, as we would have a longer walk back that way, and therefore more time together. We walked for some ways until we came to a pool, but by the time we got there, Charley had lost his whim for fishing. He suggested that we have a short rest and then walk back by the pathway. The place was extremely gloomy, and I shivered a bit, not from cold but due to some inexplicable fright.

"Charley tried to reassure me and cure my blues, which his easy laugh can usually accomplish. However, on that night, nothing could shake the feeling of dread that had stolen over me. Then we saw the figure on the rocks."

"This would be the man of whom you speak – Dr Gaster?" asked Holmes.

"That is correct, Mr. Holmes," said Miss Underwood, with a shudder. "Charley saw him first, and even he – a braver man I have never met – turned pale at the sight and staggered back a bit. For myself, I could scarcely suppress a scream. I clung to my lover in speechless terror, and glared up at the dark figure above us. Charley quickly passed from fear into anger – as men generally do – and hulloed the stranger, asking him who he was and what the devil he was doing.

"For his part, the man seemed glad to see us and soon disappeared from the top of the hill. In another moment, he emerged upon the banks of the brook and stood facing us. Weird as his appearance had been when we first caught sight of him; the impression was intensified rather than removed by a closer acquaintance. The moon shining full upon him revealed a long, thin face of ghastly pallor, the effect being increased by its contrast with the flaring green necktie which he wore. A scar upon his cheek had healed badly and caused a nasty pucker at the side of his mouth, which gave his whole countenance a most distorted expression, more particularly when he smiled.

"The knapsack on his back and stout staff in his hand announced him to be a tourist, while the easy grace with which he raised his hat upon perceiving the presence of a lady showed that he could lay claim to the *savoir faire* of a man of the world.[49] There was something in his angular proportions and the bloodless face, which – taken in conjunction with the black cloak which fluttered from his shoulders – irresistibly reminded me of a bloodsucking species of bat which Jack Daseby had brought back with him from Japan upon his previous voyage, and which was the bugbear of the servants' hall at Toynby.[50]

" 'Excuse my intrusion,' he said, with a slightly foreign lisp, which imparted a peculiar ring to his voice. 'I should have had to sleep on the moor had I not had the good fortune to fall in with you.'

" 'Confound it, man!' said Charley; 'why couldn't you shout out, or give some warning? You quite frightened Miss Underwood when you suddenly appeared up there.'

"The stranger once more raised his hat as he apologised to me for having given me such a start. He introduced himself and then said in that peculiar intonation of his, 'I am a gentleman from Stockholm, Sweden, and am viewing this beautiful land of yours. Perhaps you could tell me where I may sleep, and how I can get from this place, which is truly of great size?'

" 'You're very lucky in falling in with us,' said Charley. 'It is no easy matter to find your way upon the moor.'

" 'That can I well believe,' remarked our new acquaintance.

" 'Strangers have been found dead on it before now,' continued Charley. 'They lose themselves, and then wander in a circle until they fall from fatigue.'

" 'Ha, ha!' laughed the Swede; 'it is not I – who have drifted in an open boat from Cape Blanco to Canary – that will starve upon an English moor.[51] But how may I turn to seek an inn?'

" 'Look here!' said Charley, whose interest was excited by the stranger's allusion, and who is at all times the most open-hearted of men. 'There is not an inn for many a mile round; and I daresay you have had a long day's walk already. Come home with us, and my father, the Colonel, will be delighted to see you and find you a spare bed.'

" 'For this great kindness, how can I thank you?' returned the traveller. 'Truly, when I return to Sweden, I shall have strange stories to tell of the English and the hospitality!' "

"I fail to see what the problem is, Miss Underwood," said Holmes, appearing to grow tired of her tale. "Certainly, Dr Gaster has a misfortunate countenance, but he seems pleasant enough."

She shook her head. "You should hear his stories, Mr. Holmes. They are of the most gruesome nature. In fact, as we walked back to Toynby Hall, Charley asked him about his open boat comment.

" 'Ah, yes,' answered the stranger; 'many strange sights have I seen, and many perils undergone, but none worse than that. It is, however, too sad a subject for a lady's ears. She has been frightened once to-night.'

"I reassured him that I was no longer frightened, and that he may continue. 'Indeed there is but little to tell,' said Gaster 'and yet is it sorrowful. A friend of mine, Karl Osgood of Uppsala, and myself started on a trading venture. Few white men had been among the wandering Moors at Cape Blanco, but nevertheless we went, and for some months lived well, selling this and that, and gathering much ivory and gold. It is a strange country, where there is neither wood nor stone, so that the huts are made from the weeds of the sea. At last, just as we had collected what we thought was a sufficiency, the Moors conspired to kill us, and came down against us in the night. Short was our warning, but we fled to the beach, launched a canoe and put out to sea, leaving everything behind. The Moors chased us, but lost us in the darkness. When day dawned, the land was out of sight. There was no country where we could hope for food nearer than Canary, and for that we made. I reached it alive, though very weak and mad; but poor Karl died the day before we sighted the islands.'

"'That is terrible!' cried Charley, 'to come so close, and perish at the end.'

"'I gave him warning!' said the Swede. 'I cannot blame myself in the matter. I told him that the strength that he might gain by eating them would hardly be made up for by the blood that he would lose. Karl laughed at my words, caught the knife from my belt, cut them off, and ate them; and he died.'

"'Ate what?' asked Charley.

"'His ears!' said the stranger."

I gazed at Holmes' client in horror at these words, but there was no suspicion of a smile or joke upon Miss Underwood's face.

"Dr Gaster said his friend Karl was what we would call headstrong," she continued, "but that Karl should have known better than to do a thing like that. He then said something quite peculiar. Gaster said that had Karl but used his will he would have lived, as he himself did."

"His 'will,' eh?" said Holmes, his posture shifting, which I knew indicated that he was growing interested in the story. "Pray continue. What was your response to this suggestion?"

"Well, Charley asked him if he thought that a man's will could prevent him from feeling hungry."

"And what did Dr Gaster answer?" asked Holmes.

"He said 'What can it not do?' He then relapsed into a silence that was not broken until our arrival in Toynby Hall. The stranger seemed buried in thought, but once or twice, I had the impression that he was looking hard at me through the darkness as we strode along together.

"Well, as you can imagine, Mr. Holmes, considerable alarm had been caused by our delayed return to the Hall, and Jack

Daseby was just setting off with Charley's friend Trevor in search of us. They were delighted, therefore, when we marched in upon them, and considerably astonished at the appearance of our companion. Jack made a comment to the effect that Dr Gaster's face would never be his fortune. This was meant only for the ears of Charley and me, but to Jack's discomfiture our guest overheard him. Fortunately, Dr Gaster took it quite well and laughed off the whole embarrassing situation. Charley tried to hurry him out of the room, but as he went, the Swede gazed at me with a disturbing intensity. Looking back, I think that it was from that moment that I began to have a strange indefinable fear and dislike of the man."

"I fail to see the basis for your concern, Miss Underwood," said Holmes. "Certainly, Dr Gaster seems to have a somewhat ghoulish appearance and perhaps even personality, but that hardly makes him a danger."

"There is more, Mr. Holmes. Weeks passed and Octavius Gaster was still a guest at Toynby Hall, and, indeed, had so ingratiated himself with the proprietor that any hint at departure was laughed to scorn by that worthy soldier. I remember that the Colonel would cry, 'Here you've come, sir, and here you'll stay; you shall, by Jove!' Whereat, the Swede would smile and shrug his shoulders and mutter something about the attractions of Devon, which would put the Colonel in a good humour for the whole day afterwards.

"Of course, my darling Charley and I were too much engrossed with each other to pay very much attention to the traveller's occupations. We used to come upon him sometimes in our rambles through the woods, sitting and reading in the loneliest situations. He always placed the book in his pocket when he saw us approaching. I remember on one occasion, however, that we stumbled upon him so suddenly that the volume was still lying open before him.

" 'Ah, Gaster,' said Charley, 'studying, as usual! What an old bookworm you are! What is the book? Ah, a foreign language. Swedish, I suppose?'

" 'No, it is not Swedish,' said Gaster; 'it is Arabic.'

" 'You don't mean to say you know Arabic?' asked Charley.

" 'Oh, very well – very well indeed!' Gaster replied.

" 'And what is it about?' I asked, turning over the leaves of the musty old volume.

" 'Nothing that would interest one so young and fair as yourself, Miss Underwood,' he answered, looking at me in a way that had become habitual to him of late. 'It treats of the days when mind was stronger than what you call matter; when great spirits lived that were able to exist without these coarse bodies of ours, and could mould all things to their so-powerful wills.'[52]

" 'Oh, I see; a kind of ghost story,' said Charley. 'Well, *adieu;* we won't keep you from your studies.'

"We left him sitting in the little glen still absorbed in his mystical treatise. It must have been imagination that induced me, upon turning suddenly round half an hour later, to think that I saw his familiar figure glide rapidly behind a tree. I mentioned it to Charley at the time, but he laughed my idea to scorn. I alluded just now to a peculiar manner that this man Gaster had of looking at me. His eyes seemed to lose their usual steely expression when he did so, and soften into something that might be almost called caressing. They seemed to influence me strangely, for I could always tell, without looking at him, when his gaze was fixed upon me.

"One night, I was awakened from my slumbers by some sort of thrill which ran through me even as I dreamed. I stole softly to the window, and peered out through the bars of the Venetian blinds, and there was the gaunt, vampire-like figure of our Swedish visitor standing upon the gravel-walk, and apparently gazing up at my window.[53] It may have been that he detected the movement of the blind, for, lighting a cigarette, he began pacing up and down the avenue. I noticed that at breakfast next morning he went out of his way to explain the fact that he had been restless during the night, and had steadied his nerves by a short stroll and a smoke."

"Well, Miss Underwood, when you consider it calmly," said Holmes, "the aversion which you have against the man and your distrust of him appear to be founded on very scanty grounds. A man might have a strange face, and be fond of curious literature, and even look approvingly at an engaged young lady, without being a very dangerous member of society."

"I agree with you, Mr. Holmes, and had come to the same conclusion. I say this to show that even up to that point. I was perfectly unbiased and free from prejudice in my opinion of Octavius Gaster. Yet, his behaviour continued to repulse me. When he was preoccupied with his books and journals, I would occasionally come upon him in the throes of considerable amusement. These spasms of merriment episodes would invariably petrify me with astonishment, for his expression in those moments was unlike anything I have seen on the face of other men."

"What was it like?" asked Holmes.

"I can only describe it as one of savage exultation."

"Well, he is certainly a curious enigma," said Holmes. I could tell that he was becoming interested in her story, despite his initial protestations. "Was there anything else?"

"Well, it soon became apparent to me that Dr Gaster felt some strong emotion regarding my person. Wherever we went, I could feel his eyes upon me. They hardly ever wandered away, unless others were speaking to him. Moreover, he attempted to do minor favours for me. What he could possibly hope to gain from such actions is beyond me, for the day fixed for my marriage to Charley grows nearer every day – and this fact was not concealed from our guest. In fact, I began to fear that Gaster would reveal his feelings to the others, and Charley would therefore be forced to evict him from Toynby Hall. I suppose I pitied the unfortunate foreigner, for his hopes can never be fulfilled."

"But you do not pity him any longer?" asked Holmes.

"No," said she, shaking her head. "I gave him no encouragement, of course. In fact, I did my best to be as cool to him as possible without drawing notice to my actions. I thought by doing so, I might dissuade him, and induce him to turn the direction of his love onto more attainable subjects – not that there were any such individuals at the Hall, but some lady he might meet in the future, perhaps. Alas! I had not counted upon the utter recklessness and want of principle of the man; but it was not long before I was undeceived.

"It was three nights ago when everything unravelled. You see, there is a little arbour at the bottom of the garden, overgrown with honeysuckle and ivy, which has long been a favourite haunt of Charley and myself. It was doubly dear to us from the fact that it was here, upon the occasion of my former visit to Toynby Hall, that words of love had first passed between us.

"After dinner, I sauntered down to this little summer-house, as was my custom. Here I used to wait until Charley, having finished his cigar with the other gentlemen, would come down and join me. On that particular evening, he seemed to be longer away than usual. I waited impatiently for his coming, going to the door every now and then to see if there were any signs of his approach. I had just sat down again after one of those fruitless excursions, when I heard the tread of a male foot upon the gravel, and a figure emerged from among the bushes. I sprang up with a glad smile, which changed to an expression of bewilderment, and even fear, when I saw the gaunt, pallid face of Octavius Gaster peering in at me.

"There was certainly something about his actions which would have inspired distrust in the mind of anyone in my position. Instead of greeting me, he looked up and down the garden, as if to make sure that we were entirely alone. He then stealthily entered the arbour, and seated himself upon a chair, in such a position that he was between the doorway and me.

" 'Do not be afraid,' said he, undoubtedly noticing my scared expression. 'There is nothing to fear. I do but come so that I may have talk with you.'

"I asked him if he had seen Mr. Pillar, trying hard to seem at my ease.

" 'Ha! Have I seen your Charley?" he answered, with a sneer upon the last words. 'Are you then so anxious that he come? Can no one speak to thee but Charley, little one?'

"I told him in no uncertain words that he was forgetting himself. He could not talk like that to me. But he went on.

" 'It is Charley, Charley, ever Charley!' continued the Swede, disregarding my interruption. 'Yes, I have seen Charley. I have told him that you wait upon the bank of the river, and he has gone thither upon the wings of love.'

"I was shocked, but attempted to not to lose my self-control. I asked him why he had told Charley such a lie.

" 'That I might see you; that I might speak to you' he answered. 'Do you, then, love him so? Cannot the thought of glory, and riches, and power, above all that the mind can conceive, win you from this first maiden fancy of yours? Fly with me, Charlotte, and all this, and more, shall be yours! Come!' And he stretched his long arms out in passionate entreaty.

"Even at that moment the thought flashed through my mind of how like they were to the tentacles of some poisonous insect. I rose to my feet and cried out that he insulted me, and told him that he would pay heavily for such treatment of an unprotected girl.

" 'Ah, you say it,' he cried, 'but you mean it not. In your heart so tender there is pity left for the most miserable of men. Nay, you shall not pass me – you shall hear me first!'

"I asked him to let me go, but he refused to do so until I told him that there was nothing that he could do to win my love. I almost screamed at him, losing all my fear in my indignation. I remember my specific words: 'How dare you speak so?' I cried. 'You, who are the guest of my future husband! Let me tell you, once and for all, that I had no feeling towards you before save one of repugnance and contempt, which you have now converted into positive hatred!'

" 'And is it so?' he gasped, tottering backwards towards the doorway, and putting his hand up to his throat as if he found a difficulty in uttering the words. 'And has my love won hatred in return? Ha!' he continued, advancing his face within a foot of mine as I cowered away from his glassy eyes. 'I know it now. It is this – it is this!' Then he began to strike at the horrible cicatrix upon his face with his clenched hand. 'Maids love not such faces as this! I am not smooth, and brown, and curly like this Charley – this brainless schoolboy; this human brute who cares but for his sport and his….'

" 'Let me pass!' I cried, rushing at the door.

" 'No; you shall not go – you shall not!' he hissed, pushing me backwards.

"I struggled furiously to escape from his grasp. His long arms seemed to clasp me like bars of steel. I felt my strength going, and was making one last despairing effort to shake myself loose, when some irresistible power from behind tore my persecutor away from me and hurled him backwards onto the gravel walk. Looking up, I saw Charley's towering figure and square shoulders in the doorway.

" 'My poor darling!' he said, catching me in his arms. 'Sit here – here in the angle. There is no danger now. I shall be with you in a minute.'

" 'Don't, Charley, don't!' I murmured, as he turned to leave me. But he was deaf to my entreaties, and strode out of the arbour. I could not see either him or his opponent from the position in which he had placed me, but I heard every word that was spoken. 'You villain!' said a voice that I could hardly recognise as my lover's, so angry was the tone. 'So this is why you put me on a wrong scent?'

" 'That is why,' answered the foreigner, in a tone of easy indifference.

" 'And this is how you repay our hospitality, you infernal scoundrel!'

" 'Yes; we amuse ourselves in your so beautiful summer-house.'

" 'We! You are still on my ground and my guest, and I would wish to keep my hands from you; but, by heavens….' Charley was speaking very low and in gasps now.

" 'Why do you swear? What is it, then?' asked the languid voice of Octavius Gaster.

" 'If you dare to couple Miss Underwood's name with this business, and insinuate that....'

" 'Insinuate? I insinuate nothing. What I say I say plain for all the world to hear. I say that this so-called chaste maiden did herself ask....' I heard the sound of a heavy blow, and a great rattling of the gravel.

"I was too weak to rise from where I lay, and could only clasp my hands together and utter a faint scream.

" 'You cur!' cried Charley. 'Say as much again, and I will stop your mouth for all eternity!'

"There was a silence, and then I heard Gaster speaking in a husky, strange voice. 'You have struck me!' he said; 'you have drawn my blood!'

" 'Yes, and I will strike you again if you show your cursed face within these grounds. Don't look at me so! You don't suppose your hankey-pankey tricks can frighten me?'

"An indefinable dread came over me as my lover spoke. I staggered to my feet and looked out at them, leaning against the doorway for support. Charley was standing erect and defiant, with his young head in the air, like one who glories in the cause for which he battles. Octavius Gaster was opposite him, surveying him with pinched lips and a baleful look in his cruel eyes. The blood was running freely from a deep gash on his lip, and spotting the front of his green necktie and white waistcoat. He perceived me the instant I emerged from the arbour.

" 'Ha, ha!' he cried, with a demoniacal burst of laughter. 'She comes! The bride! She comes! Room for the bride! Oh, happy pair, happy pair!'

"And with another fiendish burst of merriment he turned and disappeared over the crumbling wall of the garden with such rapidity that he was gone before we had realised what it was that he was about to do. I admonished Charley for having hurt Gaster, but he shrugged this off, saying that he certainly hoped he had wounded the scoundrel. I felt rather faint and sick, but was otherwise uninjured. Charley explained that the rascal had cunningly and deliberately planned to get me alone. Gaster had told Charley that he had seen me down by the river, a ruse that would have taken Charley away from the house for a prolonged period. Fortunately, as Charley was going down to the Tavy, he met young Stokes, the keeper's son, coming back from fishing, and Stokes told Charley that there was nobody there. Somehow, when Stokes said that, a thousand little things flashed into Charley's mind at once, and he became in a moment so convinced of Gaster's villainy that he ran as hard as he could to the arbour."

Her tale complete, our visitor sat back and clasped her hands in front of her.

Holmes nodded his head. "A wise intuition on the part of Mr. Pillar, for it seems that he arrived in the nick of time. Yet, I am unclear what you wish of me, Miss Underwood? Gaster – while plainly a villain of the first water – is unlikely to be found guilty of a crime. And, as you have noted, he has fled from the house. Who knows where he might have gone?"

She shook her head. "Nevertheless, I fear, Mr. Holmes, that he intends to take his revenge upon Charley. You should have seen the look in Gaster's eyes before he leapt over the wall."

"And did you share your concerns with your fiancée?"

"Of course," said she, mournfully, "but he laughed them away in the manner that I knew he would. He said that all these foreigners have a way of scowling and glaring when they are angry, but it never comes to much. Still, I am very afraid of Gaster. I wish Charley had not struck him. Gaster may have left us in peace otherwise, but I doubt that he will forgive such an insult."

"Nevertheless, he has not reappeared?" asked Holmes.

"No. In fact, the next few days for me, at least, were a period of absolute happiness. With Gaster's departure a cloud seemed to be lifted off my soul, and a depression that had weighed upon the whole household completely disappeared. Once more

I was the light-hearted girl that I had been before the foreigner's arrival."

"And what has now changed that you seek my assistance?"

"I cannot say for certain. However, I have begun to have dreams that something terrible is coming. Some looming cloud upon the horizon that I try to hold back, and yet it washes over me, and consumes me."

"Unfortunately, Miss Underwood," said Holmes, shaking his head, "my other responsibilities are such that I cannot possibly leave London at the moment. I have a royal duke who is in mortal fear of his life, a major who has been wrongfully accused of cheating at cards, and scandal regarding the substitution of a rather valuable painting.[54]

"I will pay you whatever you require," she pleaded.

"It is not a matter of money. You see, Miss Underwood, I am a detective, not a sentry. I can hardly watch over your fiancée at all times. I would urge that Mr. Pillar take all reasonable precautions; however, beyond that advice I cannot see any other avenue that requires my services at present. However, should some new definitive threat appear, a telegram would bring me down to your aid."

On that note, Miss Underwood bade us good-bye and bustled off to catch her return train.

"Do you think she is hysterical?" I asked, as we listened to her steps descending the stairs back to Baker Street. "Her xenophobia is quite profound."

"It is difficult to say, Watson. Her fear of this one specific foreigner does not necessarily imply a more general attitude to those born beyond our dominion. We might dismiss her fancies as the by-product of a disordered nervous system or a morbid imagination, but I wonder if these are not delusions after all. In fact, her womanly intuition that the rascal Gaster is a danger may be accurate. Yet, even if the man is planning something, it is the yet-to-be committed crime that is so exceedingly difficult to counter. For his wrath is as likely to fall tomorrow, as it is several years in the future."

"Then they must live with a sword of Damocles hanging over their heads," said I.

"Well, I can make some inquires. And in the meantime, we must hope that nothing untoward happens to that lady or her fiancée."

§

Sadly, it was not very long before we heard once more of this dangerous Swede. Almost a month had passed, and Holmes was reading the agony column in the *Daily Telegraph*, when he suddenly sat up with a rare curse.

"What is it?" I exclaimed.

"Word of Gaster," said he, grimly. He handed the paper to me, and I read:

> CAUTION – The public are hereby cautioned against a man calling himself Octavius Gaster. He is to be recognised by his great height, his flaxen hair, and deep scar upon his left cheek, extending from the eye to the angle of the mouth. His predilection for bright colours – green neckties, and the like – may help to identify him. A slightly foreign accent is to be detected in his speech. This man is beyond the reach of the law, but is more dangerous than a mad dog. Shun him as you would shun the pestilence that walketh at noonday. Any communications as to his whereabouts will be thankfully acknowledged by A.C.U., Lincoln's Inn, London.[55]

"I do not understand, Holmes. What about this has you so concerned?"

"The author only left his initials, but the 'U' suggests that this barrister-at-law may be a relative of Miss Underwood. Why would he post this missive unless something has happened either to her or to Mr. Pillar?"

"Should we go round to see him?"

"At once, I think."

A quick hansom ride over to Holborn deposited us in front of the chambers belonging to the man who proved to be Miss Underwood's brother. The stately buildings, constructed over the span of several centuries, and framed by its private gardens and famous public square conveyed a solid sense of English respectability, which contrasted greatly with the uncanny tale that had brought us here.

A secretary showed us into the barrister's office. Arthur Cooper Underwood was a handsome man in his early thirties, with dark features, and a morose expression.

"We have come in response to your advertisement, Mr. Underwood," said Holmes. "Miss Charlotte Underwood – your sister, I presume – came to see me a month ago. Has something happened at Toynby Hall to induce you to place such a notice in the papers?"

The barrister shook his head sadly. "Her fiancée, Mr. Charles Pillar, is dead."

Holmes looked shaken at this news. "How did it happen?" he asked, a strain in his voice.

"It was during the annual shooting competition. As I understand it, shooting had always been a hobby of Charley's, and he was the captain of the Roborough Company of Devon volunteers, which boasted some of the crack shots of the county. The match was to be against a picked team of regulars from Plymouth."

"Ah, I see it now," said Holmes. "He was felled by a stray bullet."

"Not at all. In fact, Charley simply dropped dead after firing the winning shot. The physician who saw to him said that it appears that his heart had failed."

"What!" I cried. "He was so young!"

The barrister shrugged. "Some congenital weakness, I suppose," said he. "However, my sister collapsed with grief, and fell into a terrible case of brain-fever. Lottie was restless and delirious for three weeks. They recovered her in the sickroom at Toynby Hall, and when she finally rose, she wrote to me at once, begging me to insert this warning to the general populace. She reported to me all of the facts, no matter how small and unnoticed at the time, which form a chain of evidence that – though worthless in a court of law – may yet have some effect upon the mind of the public. She thought that if Octavius Gaster cannot be found guilty, at least we can warn all honest households to avoid him."

"So you agree that Gaster was involved in Mr. Pillar's death?" asked Holmes.

"I can see how it looks, Mr. Holmes – a hysterical woman hunts down a harmless savant in the advertisement columns of the newspapers! On but the shallowest of evidence she hints at crimes of the most monstrous description! And yet, after hearing her explanation – which seems so authentic that it can hardly be doubted – I cannot help but think her fears are correct and that great caution must be taken with this man. In fact, I was most eager to represent her in this matter."

"But you have no word of Gaster's whereabouts?"

"None."

"And your sister is still in Devon?"

"Yes, Colonel Pillar will not hear of her departing until she is fully recovered. And our mother is with her."

"Would you wire to them to expect me?" asked Holmes. "I plan to go down on the next train."

"For what purpose?"

"I dismissed your sister's fears when she came to me four weeks ago. I would see this matter to the end. If Gaster is still in the area, she too may be at danger."

Mr. Underwood looked shaken at this news. "Well, Lieutenant Daseby and Mr. Hall are still at Toynby. Surely they can protect her."

"I certainly hope so," said Holmes, his tone grim, as if he doubted the prospect of the words coming from his mouth.

§

Holmes was never one for the rolling green hills and quaint roofs of the little farm-steadings that dot the countryside, but his mood on that day was even graver than usual. He spent the entire ride from Paddington alternatively restlessly drumming his fingers upon the arm of his seat and pacing back and forth in our cramped carriage, all the while emitting a dense haze of the strongest shag from his travelling pipe.

Needless to say, his anxiety made it difficult for me to concentrate upon my yellow-backed novel, and I was mighty glad to see the inside of Plymouth Station. About half an hour later, the hired trap pulled into the drive of Toynby Hall. As we rode up to the house, we noted that the rear of it abutted the great wilderness of Dartmoor, which stretched away to the horizon, ruddy and glowing in the light of the sinking sun, save where some rugged tor stood out in bold relief against the scarlet background.[56]

Upon our arrival, Holmes gave our names and asked to be taken to see Miss Underwood. The butler looked at him with a strange expression but beckoned us to follow him. We were shown along a passage lined with rick thick matting into the drawing room, where an older lady seemed unconscious of our approach. She was sitting in a basket chair in the corner, engaged on a piece of fancywork. After Holmes cleared his throat, she looked up at us through gold-rimmed spectacles.

"May I help you, gentlemen?" she asked.

After he introduced ourselves, Holmes explained the purpose of our visit. "We have come from London, Mrs. Underwood," – for resemblance of the old lady to Arthur and Lottie was unmistakable – "after speaking to your son, in order to see your daughter."

"I see. I hardly know what to say, Mr. Holmes," she replied, vacantly. "In fact, I wonder if we were right to come over to Devon in the first place. I always thought Charley an excellent match, and I did everything in my power to smooth every little difficulty in the way of the couple. Surely Lottie herself had none of the doubts and fears and perplexities that I had when I was her age and that gay young blood, Mr. Nicholas Underwood, came a-wooing into the provinces, and forswore Crockford's and Tattersall's for the sake of a poor country parson's daughter."[57]

"It must have been quite the blow when Mr. Pillar died so suddenly," said Holmes, attempting to steer her recollections back to more recent events.

"Well, I have found in my own experience that life is hardly fair, sir," said Mrs. Underwood, in a tone which suggested that the dear old soul believed this truism to be an entirely original remark, and founded exclusively upon her own individual experiences.

"Has there been any further inquiry into the cause of Mr. Pillar's death?" asked Holmes.

"No. Some imbalance of the humours I suppose," said she, shaking her head sadly. "Still, my experience has always shown me that moderation is an excellent thing for young people. Poor dear Nicholas used to think so too. He would never go to bed of a night until he had jumped the length of the hearthrug. I often told him it was dangerous; but he would do it, until one night, he fell on the fender and snapped the muscle of his leg. This injury made him limp until the day of his death, for Dr Pearson mistook it for a fracture of the bone, and put him in splints, which had the effect of stiffening his knee. They did say that the doctor was almost out of his mind at the time from anxiety, brought on by his younger daughter swallowing a halfpenny, and that that was what caused him to make the mistake."

Holmes' brow furrowed in puzzlement at this rambling and seemingly unrelated story; however, I had served as the physician for a sufficient number of older ladies who shared this a curious way of drifting along in their conversations, and occasionally rushing off at a tangent. It made it rather difficult to remember their original propositions, but I was well used to just pressing forward.

"May we speak with Lottie, Mrs. Underwood?" I asked, gently.

She shook her head. "I am afraid not."

"Has she had a relapse of the brain fever?"

"Oh no, doctor. My daughter has vanished."

"What?" cried Holmes. "She was abducted?"

"We hardly know, sir. Lottie woke up yesterday morning and seemed a bit remote. But that is hardly a surprise, given that her fiancée has only been in the ground for three weeks. She said she was going out for a walk, and she never returned. We called up the constable, and he has led search parties over the moors. But so far he has failed to turn up any trace of her."

"There are no clues whatsoever?"

"Well, a porter at the railway station has deposed to having seen a young lady resembling her description get into a first-class carriage with a tall, thin gentleman. It is, however, too ridiculous to suppose that she can have eloped after her recent grief, and without my having had any suspicions as to her inclinations."

"Could the man have been Dr Gaster?" asked Holmes.

"Of course not!" she exclaimed. "My daughter told me that that if she was upon a bridge with Octavius Gaster standing at one end, and the most merciless tiger that ever prowled in an Indian jungle at the other, she should fly to the wild beast for protection."

"And what was your opinion of Dr Gaster?"

"He was a very well informed young man, sir," she remarked. "However, I wish that he would have winked his eyes more. I do not like to see people who never wink their eyes. Still, my life has taught me one great lesson, and that is that a man's looks are of very little importance compared with his actions."

"And what were his actions?"

"Well, I think the fool fell madly in love with Lottie."

"Oh yes?"

"I really think so, sir," continued her mother. "He had a way of looking at my daughter which was very like that of my poor dear husband, Nicholas, before we were married."

"Did you share your opinion with your daughter?"

"Of course. I told her it was utterly preposterous, as Dr Gaster knew as well as the next man that she was engaged. But I thought that time would show."

It was apparent that we would get no further pertinent details from Miss Underwood's mother, so Holmes promised her that he would not rest until her daughter had been located, and we made our way back into the smoking-room, where a balmy southern breeze was blowing through the open windows.

"Do you really think that Miss Underwood went somewhere with Dr Gaster?" I asked. "That seems preposterous."

Holmes shook his head. "I am afraid so, Watson. His influence is stronger than I imagined."[58]

"But why would she go with the man she hated so violently? She thought him responsible for her fiancée's death."

"I am developing a theory, Watson. However, there is still much to learn about Dr Gaster's actions and movements. Let us see who else may help us reconstruct the scene."

Holmes asked one of the servants to inquire about whether any of the guests would be willing to speak to him. A few minutes later, two men entered the room.

The first was a tall young chap, golden-moustached, blue-eyed, with a stiff bearing and expression of authority. The second man was a hearty, full-blooded fellow, full of spirits and energy, though his natural ebullience was rather dashed by the recent loss of his friend. They introduced themselves as Lieutenant Jack Daseby and Mr. Trevor Hall, respectively.

"How did you know Mr. Pillar?" asked Holmes.

The navy officer shrugged. "I hardly can think of a time when I didn't know him. My father's house is in Bickleigh, the next village over from here. Charley and I are of the same age, and we have been mates since the day we could first walk, more or less."

"And we met at Cambridge," said Mr. Hall. "I am reading

maths, while Charley was in for history. But we are in the same college and became fast friends on the bowling green."

"Have you not been recalled to term?"

"Of course," said Mr. Hall. "After the rifle match, I was due to return to the mill, and Jack to his ship, which has been re-commissioned. Charley and Lottie were going to settle down into the life of a staid respectable couple. However, our planned dissolution was thrown all akimbo by Charley's death. We both obtained a bereavement leave until Lottie recovers, though in truth, Fanny does most of the work."

"And what of Dr Gaster?" asked Holmes. "Have you seen him about?"

"I hope that monster doesn't try to turn up around here," cried Lieutenant Daseby.

"So you did not care for the man?"

"From the very beginning, I thought him a second-hand corpse," said the sailor. "That face of his was something to behold. Of course, he was quite knowledgeable about all sorts of things. He could discourse about things upon the coast of Japan that I did not know myself."

"Indeed," added the Cantab.[59] "He even knew more about rowing than Charley. He went on and on about levers of the first order, and fixed points and fulcra, until Charley was fain to drop the subject."

"At first, he seemed rather modest, even deferential," said Trevor. "Such that no one could possibly feel offended at being beaten upon their own ground. There was a quiet power about everything he said and did which was very striking."

"That's true," said Mr. Hall. "You should have seen him with Towzer."

"Who is Towzer?" asked Holmes.

"He's my pure-bred bulldog – a living, breathing example of the national animal of England. Of course, I will admit that Towzer is a bit savage."

"A bit!" cried Daseby. "He might be fond of you, Trevor, but he fiercely resents any liberties from the rest of us.[60] Let us just say that Towzer is rather unpopular."

"He is not all that bad," said Mr. Hall, sullenly.

"Nevertheless, seeing as Towzer is the pride of Trevor's heart," continued Daseby, "it was agreed not to banish the beast entirely, but instead to lock it up in the stable and give it a wide berth. From the first, it seemed to have taken a decided aversion to our visitor, and showed every fang in its head whenever he approached it."

"You see, Towzer has good sense!" said the student, proudly.

"On the second day of his visit, however," said Daseby, "we were passing the stable in a body, when the growls of the creature inside arrested Gaster's attention. 'They are ugly animals – very ugly!' said the Swede. 'Would you come into the stable and unchain him, that I may see him to advantage. It is a pity to keep an animal so powerful and full of life in captivity.'"

"I warned Gaster that Towzer is rather a nipper," said Trevor, "but the man claimed to not be afraid. He was so pompous, that I could not resist the idea of paying him a little lesson. I opened the stable door. I heard Charley mutter something about it being past a joke, but any answer I had to that would have been drowned out by the hollow growling from inside."

"The rest of us retreated to a respectable distance," said Daseby, taking up the tale, "while Gaster stood in the open doorway with a look of mild curiosity upon his pallid face. 'And those,' he said, 'that I see so bright and red in the darkness – are those his eyes?'"

"I agreed with him, as I stooped down and unbuckled the strap," said Mr. Hall. "But what happened next is rather inexplicable. Gaster commanded Towzer to come. Then the growling of the dog suddenly subsided into a long whimper, and instead of making the furious rush that I expected, he rustled among the straw as if trying to huddle into a corner. I wondered what the deuce was the matter with him."

"The Swede repeated his order to come in that sharp metallic accent of his," said Daseby. "There was an indescribable air of command in his words. To my astonishment, the dog trotted out and stood at his side, but looking as unlike the usually pugnacious Towzer as is possible to conceive. His ears were drooping, his tail limp, and he altogether presented the very picture of canine humiliation. The Swede then stroked him, and called him a fine dog, but singularly quiet. He then ordered Towzer back, and can you believe it, the brute turned and slunk back into its corner. We heard the rattling of its chain as it was being fastened, and the next moment Trevor came out of the stable-door with blood dripping from his finger."

"I don't know what could have come over the confounded beast," said Mr. Hall. "I've had him three years, and he never bit me before."

Holmes nodded as if he expected just such a conclusion to that peculiar tale. "Were there any other episodes that made you mistrust him?" asked Holmes.

"Well, if you spoke to Lottie, she must have told you about the incident in the arbour. When Gaster waylaid her and she was saved by Charley in the nick of time. That is when Charley boxed his ear. Charley was a bit sorrowful for having done so, for – unlike the rascal Gaster – Charley was a gentleman through and through. He hated the thought that he had struck a guest. But who can blame him? It was really more than flesh and blood could stand."

"That's right," said Daseby. "Charley eventually shrugged it off and quoted the cook in 'Pickwick' – saying that it was done now, and couldn't be helped.[61] Of course, before that episode, there was the picnic. That was a strange one."

"What happened then?" asked Holmes.

"It was my idea," continued the officer, "for I wanted to compress as much fun as we could in the time we had remaining to us, and the motion was carried without a division. Of course, Gaster – with his usual obsequious nature - claimed to not even know what the word meant. Charley told him that it was another of our English institutions for him to study – that the picnic is our version of a *fête champêtre*.[62] Charley then decided that there were nothing like ruins for a picnic, so he chose Bere Ferris Abbey as the spot."[63]

"It is about six miles from here," said Mr. Hall.

"Seven by the road," said the Lieutenant, with military exactness. "We each took charge of making a dish or collecting the necessary items of china and silverware into a hamper. By the time we were done, we had salmon, salad, hard-boiled eggs, vegetables, and a selection of liquor. Gaster volunteered to wait upon the ladies and made the salad, and I recall that Lottie offended him by saying that he should focus on the latter task. She meant to go apologize, but I told her to leave him alone. A man with a mug like that has no right to be so touchy. I thought he would come round right enough.

"We took the wagonette round to the ruins, and Gaster made himself as agreeable as usual," continued Daseby, "and his salad was pronounced a *chef-d'oeuvre*, while his quaint little Swedish songs and his tales of all climes and countries alternately thrilled and amused us.[64] It was after luncheon, however, that the conversation turned upon a subject that seemed to have special charms for his twisted mind. I forget who it was that broached the question of the supernatural. Was it you, Trevor?"

"That's right," said the Cantab. "I had perpetrated a little hoax down at Cambridge, and related the story to the group for their amusement. However, my narration seemed to have a strange effect upon Gaster, who tossed his long arms about in impassioned invective as he ridiculed those who dared to doubt about the existence of the unseen. I recall his exact words. 'Tell me,' he said, standing up in his excitement, 'which among you has ever known what you call an instinct to fail? The wild bird has an instinct that tells it of the solitary rock upon the so boundless sea on which it may lay its egg, and is it disappointed? The swallow turns to the south when the winter is coming, and has its instinct ever led it astray? Moreover, shall this instinct, which tells us of the unknown spirits around us, and which pervades every untaught child and every race so savage, be wrong? I say, never!' "

"And then Charley and I egged him on to tell us more," said the sailor. "So the Swede repeated his words, disregarding our amusement, and then continued. 'We can see that matter exists apart from mind; then why should not mind exist apart from matter?' I told him to give it up, for it was getting ridiculous."

"But he insisted that we have proofs of it," continued Mr. Hall. "I recall that his grey eyes gleamed with excitement as he spoke. He asked, 'who that has read Steinberg's book upon spirits, or that by the eminent American, Madame Crowe, can doubt it? Did not Gustav von Spee meet his brother Leopold in the streets of Strasbourg, the same brother having been drowned three months before in the Pacific? Did not Home, the spiritualist, in open daylight, float above the housetops of Paris?[65] Who has not heard the voices of the dead around him? I myself....'

" 'Well, what of yourself?' asked Lottie, in a breath.

" 'Bah! it matters nothing,' said Gaster, passing his hand over his forehead, and evidently controlling himself with difficulty. 'Truly, our talk is too sad for such an occasion.' "

"In spite of all our efforts," concluded Daseby, "we were unable to extract from Gaster any further relation of his own experiences of the supernatural."

"Ah, that is a pity," said Holmes, shaking his head. "It would have been useful to peer deeper into the man's twisted brain. Well, it cannot be helped. For now, I wish to examine the place where Mr. Pillar died."

Mr. Hall looked troubled. "I am not sure what good that will do you, sir, but the range is only a mile from Toynby Hall. We can drive you over there in the trap and you can see it for yourself. Though, personally, I have little wish to ever again lay eyes upon that accursed place."

§

II. THE LOSING SHOT

Although now hated by the eyes of all who once loved Charley Pillar, I know of few more attractive spots than the shooting-range at Roborough. I could well imagine it when set up for a match. The glen in which it is situated is about half a mile long and perfectly level, so that the targets are able to range from two to seven hundred yards, with the further ones simply showing as square white dots against the green of the rising hills behind. The glen itself is part of the great moor and its sides, sloping gradually up, lose themselves in the vast rugged expanse.

Its symmetrical character suggests to the imaginative mind that some giant of old had made an excavation in the moor with a titanic cheese-scoop, but that a single trial had convinced him of the utter worthlessness of the soil. One might even think that said giant had dropped the despised sample at the mouth of the cutting that he had made, for there was a considerable elevation there, from which I judged the riflemen would fire, and thither we bent our steps.

"For their part, after Gaster fled, in public neither Charley nor Lottie mentioned his name or alluded in any way to what had passed in the arbour," said Mr. Hall, as we went along in the trap. "Of course, everyone wondered where the Swede had vanished to so suddenly. Charley told me the details in confidence, and Lottie told Fanny, who in turn told Jack. Harry wrested the information of out someone. Therefore, really the only people who were in the dark were Mrs Underwood and the Colonel. In any case, we were all absorbed in the coming shooting competition that we almost forgot about the outrageous conduct of the former guest. The competition was our main subject of conversation and bets were freely offered by all of us gentlemen on the success of the Roborough team, though no one was unprincipled enough to seem to support their antagonists by taking them."

"I even ran down to Plymouth, and 'made a book on the event' with some officers of the Marines," said Lieutenant Daseby.

"Which you did in such an extraordinary way that we reckoned that in case of Roborough winning, you would lose seventeen shillings; while, should the other contingency occur, you would be involved in hopeless liabilities," said the Cantab, wryly. His attempt to interject some cheer into the general gloom was rewarded with a small smile from his friend.

"On the day of the match," continued Mr. Hall, "the regulars from Plymouth had already arrived here before us. They brought with them a considerable number of naval and military officers, while a long line of nondescript vehicles showed that many of the good citizens of Plymouth had seized the opportunity of giving their wives and families an outing on the moor."

"An enclosure for ladies and distinguished guests had been erected on the top of the hill," continued Jack Daseby, motioning with his finger, "which, with the marquee and refreshment tents, made the scene a lively one. The country people had also turned out in force, and were excitedly staking their half-crowns upon Charley's team, whom they considered their local champions. These bets were enthusiastically taken up by the admirers of the Plymouth regulars."

"And where were you during the match?" asked Holmes.

"Over here," said Mr. Hall, leading us to a spot off to the side. "They had erected a sort of rudimentary grandstand, from which we could look round at our ease upon all that was going on."

Holmes and I both regarded the place I was soon absorbed in the glorious view. Away to the south, I could see the blue smoke of Plymouth curling up into the calm summer air. Beyond that was the great sea, stretching away to the horizon, dark and vast, save where some petulant wave dashed it with a streak of foam, as if rebelling against the great peacefulness of nature. From the Eddystone to the Start, the long rugged line of the Devonshire coast lay like a map before me.[66]

I was still lost in admiration when Holmes' voice broke half-reproachfully on my ear. "Mr. Pillar did not die at sea, Watson," said he.

"No," said Lieutenant Daseby, gloomily. "It was right there," said he, pointing to a spot on the slope from where I had judged the shooters might lie.

"Was there anything special about this competition?" asked Holmes. "Any strange circumstances?"

The sailor shook his head. "Not until near the end. It was standard rules. Ten men on each side. The teams shot alternately; first, one of our fellows from Roborough, then one of them, and so on – you understand. First, they fired at the two hundred yards range – those were the targets nearest of all. They fired five shots each at those. Then they fired five shots at the ones at five hundred yards – the middle targets; and then they finished up by firing at the seven hundred yards range – you can see by the scuffs in the grass where the target stood far over there on the side of the hill. Whoever made the most points won. The bull's-eye in the centre of the target counted for five points if they hit that. The centre ring counted for four and the outer ring and only gave three points. To help the spectators tell where a shot has hit, a marker puts out a coloured disc, and covers the place."

"Charley explained all of this to Lottie," continued Mr. Hall, "as she was quite ignorant of such things. However, once she got it, she became enthusiastic and even went so far as to keep her own score upon a pad of paper. Then the warning bell sounded, and Charley pushed his way through the chaff of the crowd – all trying to get their last bets in – in order to join his team."

"The competition began like so many others before it," said Lieutenant Daseby. "There was a great waving of flags and shouting before the ground could be got clear, and then all of the shooters took off their coats – red for the regulars and grey for the volunteers – and laid them upon the greensward. When the first rifle fired, throwing up a little curl of blue smoke, Fanny shrieked and Lottie gave a cry of delight. The two teams were evenly matched, and at the end of the competition at the short range each side had scored forty-nine out of a possible fifty."

"Charley joined us during the intermission," continued Mr. Hall, "and Lottie praised his marksmanship, for he had made a 'bull' each time. Charley was modest about the whole thing, and mentioned that the regulars had some terribly good long-range men among them. He also noted that the five hundred yards targets would not be so easy, especially when the sights were up."[67]

"So Mr. Pillar was at his ease?" asked Holmes.

"Well, now that you mention it, Mr. Holmes," said the sailor, "by the look in his face, something was troubling him. I thought it a little strange for him to have nerves, as he was a crack-shot. Perhaps he was feeling the pressure of not letting down his teammates, who were counting on him as their best man? It was not until later that I found out what was the matter, for Lottie had confided to Fannie during the match, who then told me."

"What was it?" asked Holmes.

"It was that infernal Swedish fellow, Gaster," said Daseby." It was only the week before that he had vanished from Toynby Hall, but he must have stuck around the area."

I could see that Holmes was interested in this news. "Dr Gaster was at the competition?"

"That's right. I did not spot him, but Charley did, and pointed him out to Lottie."

Mr. Hall looked thoughtful. "You know, I too saw Gaster here that day. However, I was so engrossed in the outcome of the match and then, of course, the whole thing with poor Charley, that it slipped my mind. It is a weird coincidence to be sure, but I suppose the man had some interest in the competition, as it had been one of our principal topics of conversation for days beforehand."

"And where was Dr Gaster during the shooting?" asked Holmes.

"He was standing on that little knoll," said Mr. Hall, pointing, "close to the place where the riflemen were lying. I only remember because the foreigner's tall, angular figure was so distinctive. In fact, now that I think about it, his singular appearance and hideous countenance excited some sensation among the burly farmers around him; though Gaster seemed utterly unconscious of this attention. I suppose the man was used to it."

"And what was he doing?" asked Holmes.

"Well, he was craning his long neck about, this way and that, as if in search of somebody. Eventually, he looked over in the direction of our group and it seemed to me that, even at that distance, I could see a spasm of hatred and triumph pass over his livid features."

"And you did not do anything about this?"

Mr. Hall shrugged. "He could be upset about his forced departure from Toynby, but what was it to us? He was out of our circle."

Holmes shook his head. "He may have intended one of you harm."

"Well, I can hardly see how that would have been possible," protested the Cantab. "We were all together, save Charley, who was himself surrounded by a score of armed men."

"Very well," said Holmes. "What happened next?"

"The contest at the five hundred yards range was a close and exciting one," said Lieutenant Daseby, taking up the story. "Roborough led by a couple of points for some time, until a series of 'bulls' by one of the crack marksmen of the regulars turned the tables upon them. At the end of it was found that the volunteers were three points to the bad – a result which was hailed by cheers from the Plymouth contingent, and by long faces and black looks among the dwellers on the moor."

"And what of Dr Gaster?" asked Holmes of Mr. Hall. "Did you observe him again?"

"Yes, I glanced over at him once or twice. In fact, during the whole of this competition, Octavius Gaster had remained perfectly still and motionless upon the top of the knoll on which he had originally taken up his position. It seemed to me that he knew little of what was going on, for his face was turned away from the marksmen, and he appeared to be gazing into the distance. Once I caught sight of his profile, and thought that his lips were moving rapidly as if in prayer, or it may have been the shimmer of the hot air of the almost Indian summer which deceived me. It was, however, my impression at the time."

"That is very interesting," said Holmes. "You say he did not move from his spot?"

"Well, I could hardly swear to it. My attention was primarily upon the competition. But it would have been difficult for him to move far and return to the exact same spot."

"Quite so. And then what?"

"And then came the competition at the longest range of all, which was to decide the match," explained the sailor. "The Roborough men had settled down steadily to their task of making up the lost ground; while the regulars seemed determined not to throw away a chance by over-confidence. As shot after shot was fired, the excitement of the spectators became so great that they crowded round the marksmen, cheering enthusiastically at every 'bull.' We ourselves were so far affected by the general contagion that we left our harbour of refuge, and submitted meekly to the pushing and rough ways of the mob, in order to obtain a nearer view of the champions and their doings.

"The military stood at seventeen when the volunteers were at sixteen, and great was the despondency of the rustics. Things looked brighter, however, when the two sides tied at twenty-four, and brighter still when the steady shooting of the local team raised their score to thirty-two against thirty of their opponents. There were still, however, the three points which had been lost at the last range to be made up for. Slowly the score rose and desperate were the efforts of both parties to pull off the victory. Finally, a thrill ran through the crowd when it was known that the last red-coat had fired, while one volunteer was still left, and that the soldiers were leading by just four points."

I had a great fondness for English sport, and I will admit that Lieutenant Daseby's story had worked me into a state of all-absorbing excitement by the nature of the match. "If the last representative of Roborough could but hit the bull's eye, the match would be won!" I cried.

"That's right, Dr Watson," said the lieutenant. "The silver cup, the glory, the money of our adherents, all depended upon that single shot. You can imagine how excited we all became when, by dint of some shoving and craning of ours neck, we caught sight of Charley coolly shoving a cartridge into his rifle, and realised that it was upon his skill that the honour of Roborough depended."

"We were so animated by this," continued Trevor Hall, "that Jack and I managed to vigorously push our way through the crowd, followed by Lottie, Fanny, Mrs. Underwood, and the Colonel. We eventually all found ourselves almost in the first row and commanding an excellent view of the proceedings. As for myself, there were two gigantic farmers standing on the side of me – I think Lottie was wedged between them – and while we were waiting for the decisive shot to be fired, I could not help listening to the conversation, which they carried on in broad Devon.

" 'Mun's a rare ugly 'un,' said one.

" 'He is that,' cordially assented the other.

" 'See to mun's een?'

" 'Eh, Jock; see to mun's moo', rayther! – Blessed if he bean't foamin' like Farmer Watson's dog – t' bull pup whot died mad o' the hydropathics.'[68]

Mr. Hall looked over at me when his finished this story. "Say, you don't have a relative round these parts, do you, doctor?"

I assured him that I had neither kith nor kin in Devon, and he nodded. "Well, you can imagine that I turned round to see the favoured object of these unflattering comments, and my eyes fell upon Dr Gaster, whose presence I had entirely forgotten in my excitement. His face was turned in our direction; but he evidently did not see me, for his eyes were bent with unswerving persistence upon a point midway apparently between the distant targets and himself.

"I have never seen anything to compare with the extraordinary concentration of that stare, which had the effect of making his eyeballs appear gorged and prominent, while the pupils were contracted to the finest possible point. Perspiration was running freely down his long, cadaverous face, and, as the farmer had remarked, there were some traces of foam at the corners of his mouth. The jaw was locked, as if with some fierce effort of the will which demanded all the energy of his soul."

"Well, I did not see him at the match," said Lieutenant Daseby, shaking his head. "However, to my dying day that hideous countenance shall never fade from my remembrance, nor cease to haunt me in my dreams. They say that you should not judge a book by its cover, but in Gaster's case, it seems that his soul is as rotten as his face."

"Do you think the farmer might be right, Mr. Holmes?" asked Mr. Hall. "Could mental disease be the cause of all the vagaries of this extraordinary man?"

"From what I have heard thus far, there is little doubt that Dr Gaster is quite mad," said Holmes. "Pray continue."

"Well," said the sailor, "a great stillness fell upon the whole crowd as Charley – having loaded his rifle – snapped up the breech cheerily, and proceeded to lie down in his appointed place. Old McIntosh, the volunteer sergeant, murmured encouragements to him. 'A cool head and a steady hand, that's what does the trick, sir!' the grey-headed soldier said. Charley smiled at this as he lay down upon the grass, and then proceeded to look along the sight of his rifle amid a silence in which the faint rustling of the breeze among the blades of grass was distinctly audible.

"For more than a minute he hung upon his aim. His finger seemed to press the trigger, and every eye was fixed upon the distant target, when suddenly, instead of firing, the rifleman staggered up to his knees, leaving his weapon upon the ground. To the surprise of everyone, his face was deadly pale, and perspiration was standing on his brow."

Holmes appeared much interested in this part of the account. "You are certain about this? He was sweating?"

"Of course," said Lieutenant Daseby. "But what man wouldn't in Charley's shoes? He needed to hit a bull at seven hundred yards, or be the source of disappointment to not only his fellow volunteers but all the local rustics who had wagered on them."

"What did Mr. Pillar do next?"

"Well, he asked McIntosh, in a strange, gasping voice, if there was anybody standing between the target and him."

"Oh?" said Holmes, his eyebrows rising. "And was there?"

"Of course not. Not a soul. The sergeant was astonished at the question, and answered in the negative. However, this did not seem to appease Charley. With a fierce energy, he seized McIntosh by the arm, and pointed in the direction of the target, 'There!' he cried. 'Don't you see him there, standing right in the line of fire?' A half a dozen voices shouted at him that there was no one there, so Charley mopped his forehead and settled himself back into position, raising his weapon slowly to his eye. However, he had hardly looked along the barrel before he sprang up again with a loud cry."

"He was not himself," said Mr. Hall, shaking his head sadly. "His tone was fierce, and his words strange and wild. Charley swore that he could see a man dressed in volunteer uniform, and very like himself. He even accused the crowd of a conspiracy, asking all of us if we could not see a man resembling himself walking from that target, and not two hundred yards from him."

"Then the officer from the Plymouth team came forward to protest," said Daseby. "He said that Charley must either take his shot or he would remove his men off the field and claim the victory. Charley protested that he would shoot the man whom he saw on the range, but they growled at him for spouting rubbish. One of the Plymouth boys even went so far as to suggest that Charley's nerves were not equal to the occasion and this was some ploy to back out. I almost gave that imbecile a sound boxing of his ears, but was more concerned about what was wrong with Charley."

"One of them supposed it was Martell's three-star brandy," said Mr. Hall, "and that Charley had 'the 'devils,' claiming that he had them himself and knew a case when he saw it."[69]

"And was this a possibility?" asked Holmes.

"Hardly!" cried Mr. Hall. "Charley would have a round with the rest of us, but he took no more liquor than Jack or I. It is impossible!"

"The crowd kept pestering Charley to shoot," continued the sailor, "so Charley eventually agreed, though he groaned and muttered that it was sheer murder. I shall never forget the haggard look that he cast round at the crowd. As he lay down on the grass and raised the gun for the third time to his shoulder, he even murmured to McIntosh that he was aiming right through the invisible figure." Daseby paused, his face contorted with pain.

"And then what happened?" I asked.

"What happened?" he said, looking at me and shaking his head. "Why he took the winning shot. There was one moment of suspense, a spurt of flame, the crack of a rifle, and a cheer that echoed across the moor, and might have been heard in the distant village. As the little white disc came out from behind the marker's shield and obliterated the dark 'bull,' proclaiming that the match was won, a hundred honest Devonshire voices cried 'well done, lad!'

"But when Sergeant McIntosh and the other lads on the team went to hoist him on their shoulders – intending, I think, to carry him in honour all the way back to Roborough – they realized that something terrible had happened. You see, Mr.

Holmes, Charley never rose from that spot on the grass. He was cold and dead upon the ground, with the rifle still clenched in his stiffening fingers."

"I think Lottie was the first to really understand that Charley was dead," said Mr. Hall. "Some intuition told her, when the rest of us were still stunned in incredulous silence that such a thing could happen to a man in the prime of health. Lottie flew to his side and sank down, moaning short, quick cries of despair. For their part, the crowd was deadly still, with only murmurs of pity and whispers to leave the poor lass alone."

"I begged her to control her sorrow," said Lieutenant Daseby, his voice broken with grief, "though how I could expect her to do such a thing I hardly know. Still, I managed to gently raise her from poor Charley's body for a moment. And then she collapsed into a merciful oblivion."

"Mr. Underwood said that the doctor considered it a case of heart failure," noted Holmes.

"Indeed," said Daseby, shaking his head. "I still can hardly believe it."

"You had no reason to consider foul play?"

"Foul play!" cried the Cantab. "But everyone loved Charley!"

"Not everyone," said Holmes. "You yourself noted that Dr Gaster was present on the fatal day. Surely he held a grudge against Mr. Pillar?"

"Well, of course," admitted Mr. Hall, "but the man never went near him."

"Are you certain?"

"As the sky is blue. One of us would have noticed – Lottie especially. She never took her eyes from Charley."

"I agree," said the sailor. "There were a hundred people here, Mr. Holmes, and each of them knew that Charley was the best shot for Roborough. At any given time, I wager a dozen people had Charley in their sights. Surely one of them would have noticed a man as remarkable-looking as Gaster approaching him and mentioned it after Charley's passing?"

"Perhaps," said Holmes. "Well, I fear that there is little more to learn here. I now wish a word with Mr. Pillar's father."

The two men looked at each other for a moment, and then Mr. Hall spoke. "We are happy to take you back round to Toynby Hall, Mr. Holmes, but the Colonel doesn't speak to many people these days. He perked up a bit when Lottie came out of her fever, but when she vanished yesterday, it was another blow to the old man. What Inkerman could not manage, the loss of Charley and Lottie has done.[70] Still, we can give it a try."

At Toynby, the two men passed the care of Holmes and me over to Fanny Pillar, Lieutenant Daseby's fiancée. She was a striking-looking woman, slender and tall, with a smooth complexion, dark, Italian eyes, and a wealth of deep red hair. If she took after her brother, I thought he must have been a handsome fellow. Miss Pillar led us up the stairs and along a passageway to a semi-private apartment within the greater building, to where that ill-used veteran may retreat at the end of the day.

"He rarely stirs from his rooms now," said she, sadly.

Indeed, Colonel Pillar looked to be a broken man. From all that we had heard, Charley had been a fine young man, and evidently a great source of pride to the old warrior. Although his daughter and younger son still breathed, there is nothing like the death of one's first child to crush a father's soul. If Charley had perished bravely upon some field of valour, the colonel might have been able to take some solace in his son's honoured passing, but this senseless death during a shooting competition was too much for the old man's spirit.

He was dozing in his chair when we entered, but stirred when touched by Miss Pillar. "I cannot help you, Mr. Holmes," said he, after Holmes asked about his views on his son's passing. "I cannot understand why Charley was taken from me. It is a cruel world."

"Then I will not disturb you any longer. I only wish to know what you did with your son's rifle."

The man frowned. "His rifle? That cursed thing! I locked it

up – in the attic. I would have burned it, but I knew how much Charley loved it, and I suppose that Harry should have it someday. It was with me from Eupatoria to Sebastopol."[71]

With that, the man began to sob, and Miss Pillar patted his hand until he drifted off to the land of dreams, which I hoped treated him better than this world had done.

We stepped out of the room, and Miss Pillar joined us a moment later. "I fear we may lose Father over this," said she. "Just a few weeks ago were some of the happiest of his life. It was hard for a while after Mother died, but Lottie was like a ray of sunshine in the house. Once she came, he never even once cursed the Liberal Administration over the Irish question.[72] After he had a post-dinner glass of port, he used to whisper to her – in a tone loud enough for each of us to hear – that Charley was a lucky dog to have found her, and that it was proof that Charley was not a fool. I wish I understood why she would leave us so suddenly. She did not even say a word to her mother! Now such a deep sadness has gotten into Father's system, and it may finish him."

"What was your father's opinion of Dr Gaster?"

"Well, like most of us, after we had gotten over our initial revulsion of his face, Father welcomed him as if he had been an old friend of the family. In fact, he was the soul of hospitality. He told Gaster that he should look upon Toynby Hall as his own place, and as long as he cared to stop he was very welcome."

"Was your father always so convivial?"

She considered this. "Generally, yes. We are pretty quiet down here, and I think he feels that any visitor is an acquisition. However, I suppose that his attachment to Gaster was greater than to most guests. In fact, by the day after his arrival, Father would not even hear of his potential departure. The two of them would talk for hours about Crimea, and I think that Gaster knew more about it than Father himself, if you can believe such a thing."

"Yes, I had heard that Dr Gaster was well-read."

"He was certainly a social success. He essentially installed himself as a member of the household."

"I would like to see your brother's rifle."

"Of course." She led us to the stairs that gave access to the attic, and we all climbed up into that dusty space. The item Holmes sought was quickly located, and he opened the case with what I considered an excessive amount of care. To my surprise, he went so far as to don a pair of gloves before he handled Charley's Enfield rifle.[73] After a few minutes, he laid this aside and uncapped the bottle of gun oil. Sniffing this, he nodded briefly, and then replaced everything in the case.

"Miss Pillar," said he, "it is imperative that you lock away this case for the time being. I will explain more when I can, but for now, the most pressing matter is to locate Miss Underwood."

Charley's sister frowned in puzzlement but nodded her understanding of Holmes' instructions and we left her in the attic. As we made our way down to the main floor, Holmes laid his hand upon my arm.

"We are dealing with a most dangerous man, Watson. I fear that Charley Pillar is not the first man that Dr Gaster has killed. I wired to Stockholm and learned that he fled that city in a cloud of suspicion regarding the unexpected death of Professor Retzius of the Karolinska Institute."[74]

"That is hardly conclusive."

"Then there is this. I came across it a week ago while making enquires after Miss Underwood's visit to Baker Street." He handed me an old cutting from the *Western Morning News*, dated several months prior, which read:[75]

> SUDDEN DEATH IN THE DOCKS
> The master of the bark-rigged steamer *Olga*, from Tromsberg, was found lying dead in his cabin on Wednesday afternoon.[76] The deceased was, it seems, of a violent disposition, and had had frequent altercations with the surgeon of the vessel. On this particular day, he had been more than usually offen-

sive, declaring that the surgeon was a necromancer and worshipper of the devil. The latter retired on deck to avoid further persecution. Shortly afterwards the steward had occasion to enter the cabin, and found Captain König lying across the table quite dead. Death is attributed to heart disease, accelerated by excessive passion. An inquest will be held to-day.

"Do you think the surgeon was Gaster?"

"I am sure of it."

"Holmes, are you certain that we should even attempt to capture him?"

"What do you mean?"

"Well, if he is able to kill men – first the master of the Olga, then Charley Pillar – with nothing more than the power of his mind, how are we to face him? I do not mind knives or even a gun, but this seems beyond our ability to fight."

"No, no, Watson," said he, shaking his head. "I refuse to admit that the man possesses such supernatural powers. I give you that a charismatic mesmerist may exert some control over someone who is weak-minded...."

"Miss Underwood hardly struck me as someone who was excessively impressionable," I interjected.

"No, but she was extremely vulnerable after the death of her fiancée. Such a thing cannot happen to us, for no man, no matter how compelling, can hold sway over a prepared mind."

"So you deny the powers of animal magnetism?"

"To the man of a precisely scientific mind, the work of Dr Mesmer must be discredited, for the evidence is impossible to verify."

"And yet there are so many accounts of it working."

"Of course. The credulous are eager, Watson, to believe absolutely anything put before them – no matter how ridiculous – if delivered in a convincing enough fashion. Do not forget that Poe deceived half the world with his Valdemar hoax."[77]

"So you think that Gaster may have killed these men in some

other manner?"

"I do not think it, Watson," said Holmes, shaking his head. "I know it. For Charley Pillar was poisoned."

"Poisoned!" I cried. "Are you certain?"

"Of course. In fact, Dr Gaster made it rather easy, for there are only a handful of many poisons that produce such distinct symptoms as manifested in Mr. Pillar, and even fewer than may be absorbed through the skin. As you know, I dabble with them a good deal, and I will someday draw up a monograph containing the accumulated knowledge drawn from these practical experiences. In this case, unless I am far off base, Mr. Pillar's gun-oil has been replaced with a solution of mercuric nitrate."

"Hatter's disease!" I exclaimed.[78] "Of course. His pale face, the perspiration, the gasping voice, even the supposed vision of the man in his way."

"Indeed," said Holmes. "Poor Mr. Pillar never stood a chance against a villain as cunning as Dr Gaster. I suspect that the Swede substituted the mercury as soon as he learned about Charley's passion for the shooting match. Gaster knew that Charley would be practicing regularly, and after each use of his rifle, he would re-oil it. Unfortunately, for Charley, the mercury worked as a lubricant as well as his usual gun-oil, so he never noticed the switch. However, each time, he touched the rifle he absorbed a bit more of the toxin into his system. In his own way, Gaster is quite brilliant. It would take a minor genius to time it just so that Charley's heart would give out during the competition."

"Holmes!" I exclaimed. "You sound as if you admire the man."

"Well, I admit that the most rewarding game to hunt is the beast that offers the greatest possibility of danger. And there is little doubt that Dr Octavius Gaster is a beast wearing the skin of man."

"But how are we to track him? He could have taken Miss Underwood anywhere by now."

"Plainly, Dr Gaster did not quit the area after Mr. Pillar's death. Surely, someone would have remarked upon a man of such remarkable appearance. So, where did he stay? Not in an inn. No, I fancy he had a rather rougher accommodation. And I know just the person to lead us there."

Holmes descended the steps back to the ground floor, and made his way to the billiard-room, where we found a youth of some fifteen years engaged in the task of aimlessly bouncing the ball off the cushions of the table. He was pace-faced and fair-haired, with light blue eyes dulled by a deep pain.

"Harry" – for the youth could only be Charley's younger brother – "did your brother indicate where he and Miss Underwood met Octavius Gaster?" asked Holmes, after he introduced us and the reason for our presence at Toynby Hall.

"Course!" said the lad. "He was trying for trout, so they went to one of the brooks upon the moor."

"Can you show us?"

"Now?" he said, with a glance out of the window. "We have hardly an hour of daylight left. We will have to walk back in the gloaming."

"Is that a problem?" said Holmes.

"Well, not many like to cross the moor at night, but I don't mind.[79] Let me grab some lanterns and my hat."

Our guide so attired, we passed down the winding lane together, and through the little wooden gate, which opened on to the Tavistock road. Harry took the turn towards the moor and we followed the brook in question, which ran through a most desolate part of the country. Harry noted that by the path, it was several miles from Toynby Hall; however, he suggested – with the aplomb of the young and active – that we strike out across the moor, regardless of rocks and furze bushes. Holmes agreed, and not a living creature did we meet upon our solitary walk, save a few scraggy Devonshire sheep, who looked at us wistfully, and followed us for some distance, as if curious as to what could possibly have induced us to trespass upon their domains.

It was almost dark before we reached a little stream, which came gurgling down through a precipitous glen, and meandered away to help to form the Plymouth 'leat.'[80] Above us towered two great columns of rock, between which the water trickled to form a deep, still pool at the bottom.

"This pool had always been a favourite spot of Charley's," said Harry.

I looked around. I thought it might be a pretty cheerful place by day; but now, with the rising moon reflected upon its glassy waters, and throwing dark shadows from the overhanging rocks, it seemed rather distant from than the typical haunt of a pleasure-seeker. I sat down upon a mossy bank to rest.

"It is a dismal sort of place to fish, isn't it?" I asked.

Harry shrugged. "I suppose if you are in a queer sort of mind, it might seem a bit depressing."

I thought that an understatement. The noise that the water made was like the gurgling in the throat of a dying man.

If the charnel-house atmosphere of the place affected Holmes, he gave little notice of it. "And this is where your brother and Miss Underwood met Gaster?"

"That's right," said Harry. "He told me that it was up there."

He pointed, and I followed the direction of his finger. I have already mentioned that the pool by which we were standing lay at the foot of a rough mound of rocks. This mound towered about sixty feet above our heads.

"Wait here a minute," said Holmes. He reversed our steps and scrambled up the loose stones. A few minutes later, I spotted his tall dark figure standing atop the mound, peering down into the rugged hollow in which Harry and I sat. The moon was just topping the ridge behind, and the gaunt, angular outlines of Holmes' cape stood out hard and clear against its silvery radiance. There was something ghastly in his sudden and silent appearance, especially when coupled with the weird nature of the scene. I could only imagine how Miss Underwood would have felt if it had been a complete stranger standing above them, rather than the familiar form of my friend.

Holmes hailed us to come up, and I lost no time in quitting that eerie place. We joined him at the top, where he continued to question Harry Pillar.

"If we came along the path from Toynby, then Gaster must have come from deeper in the moor."

"That's right," said the lad.

"Where might he have come from?"

Harry considered this. "Well, there are half a dozen places I can think of. There's the Roman graves, the Eylesbarrow mine, a cave at Lover's Leap, and the huts on Black Tor."[81]

"And are any of them habitable?"

"I suppose so. Especially the longhouse at Lower Uppacott, though there are better ones over near Hound Tor."[82]

"Can you show us?"

"Sure. Follow me."

As we went along, Harry told us that Dartmoor was pocked with ancient sites, which most of the locals considered to be sacred. However, some thought to disturb the possible crocks of gold, seeking lost treasures. "They still tell of the legend of a parson," said our guide, "who began to place a black dot upon map showing the location all of the money pits upon the moor. Soon, his map had more black dots than a ladybird has upon its back. He began to open the sites, and was seen counting his money into the wee hours, until one night, a huge storm rolled over the moor. Furious lightning and booming thunder made it impossible for anyone to sleep that night. However, the next morning, people were surprised to find that there was no damage to anyone's home or farms – save for one. The parson's house was blasted to ruins, and fires still burned in the remnants of its thatch and furniture. They say that the smell of brimstone made it clear who made the parson pay for his greed."

"That is a remarkable legend," said I. "Are there more like it?"

"Oh yes!" said Harry. "Everywhere you go, someone will tell you of some haunt or another. I think that Dartmoor is a great place, really," said Harry, rather philosophically. "It is very sad and wild, dotted as it is with the dwellings of prehistoric man, strange monoliths, and graves. In those old days, my schoolmaster tells me that there was evidently a population of very many thousands here, but now you may walk all day and never see one human being."

After this monologue, we stumbled along in silence, keeping as far as we could to the rugged pathway, sometimes losing it as a cloud drifted over the face of the moon, and then regaining it further on with the return of the light. Finally, we came to the place Harry had in mind, which was a rough home built of granite, with the remnants of a thatched roof. It was slanted down the slope of a hill, and I deduced that the higher ground was once the dwelling of the human inhabitants, while the animal quarters occupied the lower shippon. Gazing into the ruin, I could make out an old pitch-black hall, with only a few small windows, their panes of glass long broken. There were doorways at both ends, and a cool breeze whistled through the space.

Lighting a lantern, Holmes led us inside, where the pitted floor was slimy with the excrements of centuries past. The house lacked a fireplace; instead, there was an open furze hearth, the smokes of which had long ago darkened the barren rafters above us.

"Note the embers," said Holmes, pointing to the hearth. "Not more than two days old."

"That could have been anyone," said Harry. "The shepherds sometimes use this during a storm."

Holmes bent down and picked up something from near the fire pit. He sniffed this and then held it forth for Harry and me to see. It was a brown substance. "Not unless they happen to utilize the smokeless tobacco of the Ettan Company," said Holmes. "Which is only manufactured in Stockholm."[83]

"So Gaster was here!" I exclaimed.

"I think we can consider that proven, Watson. The question is where he would go next. Surely, if the other habitations on the moor are of an equal quality to this, he would hardly fain to bring Miss Underwood back to one of them. However, where can he have gone without his possessions?"

Harry looked troubled by this. "Well, sir, now that you mention it, his possessions have vanished."

"What!" cried Holmes. "I was told that Gaster has not been back to Toynby Hall since he fled over the garden wall."

"That's true, sir. Yet, they are gone. The morning after Gaster left, Charley sent a servant up to the Swede's room with instructions to pack up any things he might find there, and leave them at the nearest inn. It was discovered, however, that all Gaster's effects had been already removed."

"How?" asked Holmes. "When?"

The lad shrugged. "That is a perfect mystery."

"Even to the servants?"

"Yes, sir. None of them admit to speaking to Gaster either that night or the following morn."

"And you trust them? They might have been bribed."

The lad shook his head. "I doubt that. Most of them have been with the family for ages. They are devoted to Father. They might have agreed to help Gaster in ignorance that the man had left in disgrace, but they wouldn't lie about it when questioned."

"Well, I would like to have a word with them anyhow," said Holmes.

"Suit yourself," said Harry.

When we got back to Roborough, despite the lateness of the hour, the enterprising lad led us around the building, introducing us to each of the servants. Unfortunately, despite Holmes' close questioning, none of them seemed to know anything regarding the matter, until we came to the gamekeeper's son, a boy called Stokes. Holmes found his answers rather more enlightening than the others.

"Stokes," said Holmes, "do you recall the night that Dr Gaster departed the Hall?"

The lad furrowed his brow. "I remember the following morning that he was gone, but not much about the night before." He shrugged. "Mayhaps it was a quiet evening?"

"Was it?" asked Holmes. "Surely you and the other boys were talking about the upcoming shooting match and placing bets about the victors?"

"Well, now that you mention it, sir, I got in a fight with Morris."

"Who is Morris?"

"He is the stable boy," continued Stokes. "Morris said that I bet him four quid that the Roborough team would beat Plymouth by at least three points. Of course, I did no such thing. After the competition – which we won by a sole point – he tried to make me pay up, but I refused on general principle. Imagine him making up such a story. As if I would not remember making such a bet!"

I saw by the sudden gleam of excitement in his eyes that Holmes was onto something, but it was not until we departed Toynby Hall that he informed me of his flash of intuition.

"I have him now, Watson!" he exclaimed.

"How?" I asked, mystified.

"By the lacunas in the memories of those he mesmerizes. If we trace individuals who possess such lapses, we can plot a chart of his path."

I shook my head. "That's impossible."

"Not at all, Watson. Merely very difficult. However, with the invaluable assistance of our friend, the provincial press, we can do it. But not from here. Baker Street shall be our command centre."

§

In the end, locating Miss Underwood required both Holmes' myriad advertisements in the provincial press for people who had holes in their memories during the last two days – which led to a vast correspondence that required much winnowing of the wheat from the chaff – and coordination with Mr. Arthur Underwood – whose own warning had garnered multiple communications regarding men matching the description of Octavius Gaster. Baker Street was positively buzzing with activity, as innumerable district messengers, commissionaires, and post office clerks all scrambled to deliver messages to and from Holmes, sitting like a spider in the middle of his web.

The sitting room wall opposite our armchairs was quickly transformed by a giant map transfixed with a series of coloured pins – white for tips of doubtful authenticity, yellow for those that were more promising, and red for those of the highest certainty. From this, a trail began to emerge. The next day, Holmes verified that a couple by the name of Mr. and Mrs. Francis Overhill had sailed aboard the S.S. *Mount Batten* on September 24 from Plymouth to Saint-Malo.

"The city of pirates," said Holmes, rubbing his hands together in glee at this news.[84] "A fitting stop for a man who has abducted his companion against her will."

"And you are certain that the Overhills are Gaster and Miss Underwood?"

"As certain as the fact that the sun will rise tomorrow. First, there is no record of such a couple in the GRO.[85] Second, the supposed Mr. Underwood was described as being over six feet tall, with a scar upon his left cheek that was partially hidden by a three week-old beard. He had changed his hair colour – but he could hardly disguise his accent, which was remarked upon by the steward. And this observant fellow noted the fact that Mrs. Underwood had a curiously vacant expression upon her face, as well as a distracted way of responding to questions."

"Then we will find them in Brittany?"

He shook his head. "I doubt that he will stay there long. It is too small for his purposes. People will eventually begin to talk about the peculiar attitude of his supposed wife. No, Gaster will wish to blend into the surroundings of a much larger city."

"Paris!" I cried.

"Most probably, Watson," said Holmes, nodding. "There are few places better to lose oneself than the City of Lights. In the dark alleys of Pigalle, who will remark upon yet another woman who appears to be under the influence of some narcotic? I trust that the foreign press will be as accommodating as our own in terms of its advertisement rates."

Two days later, Holmes' tactic paid off, when a man wrote to say that he had rented his small villa off the Rue Tardieu for a preposterously small price to a tall man with a left cheek scar, though he could not for all the world now say why he gave the man such a steep discount.

The following morning we were on the boat train to Dover and soon sailing over the Channel. While Holmes could have simply turned the evidence against Dr Octavius Gaster over to Scotland Yard and asked them to coordinate with the Paris Police, Holmes thought that Miss Underwood would do better if we were physically present for her liberation. Holmes had also kept her brother up to date regarding the progress of his investigation, and while he could not get away from Lincoln's Inn, Lieutenant Jack Daseby, Mr. Trevor Hall, and even young Harry Pillar all insisted upon meeting us at the Gare du Nord.

Holmes had coordinated with a member of the French detective service named François Le Villard about our plans to obtain the emancipation – by force if necessary – of Miss Underwood from the clutches of Dr Gaster. This plan was met with some scepticism, and required Holmes to obtain the backing of our Ambassador to France, before it could be carried off.

Fortunately, all of this was accomplished before Gaster got wind of our impending arrival, and on the night in question, the man was surprised to see such a regiment suddenly arranged against him at his rented villa. Upon our sudden entrance, he turned sharp round upon us and flushed up to his flaxen hair. There was no possibility of armed resistance on the part of Gaster, for at least three of us were armed with revolvers, and Harry Pillar looked as if he could by himself rip the Swede's head off with his bare hands.

"Ha, ha!" laughed the man, mirthlessly. "You have found me. Very good! Very good!" There was something horrible in this mirth of his, for though he writhed his body about as if with laughter, no sound was emitted from his lips. "Well, what would you do now, gentlemen? Will you shoot me, as I stand here?"

"It would be more than you deserve, you cur," snarled Jack Daseby.

"Cur!" cried Gaster. "You insult me, sir."

"No, I insult mongrels everywhere, for even the most rabid of them is worth more than you."

The man grinned until the hideous gash across the angle of his mouth made him look more like the reflection in a broken mirror than anything else. "Ha, ha! Well, we shall see who has the last laugh, Mr. Daseby."

"You can laugh your way to prison, Doctor," said Holmes.

"Prison! I think not, Mister Busybody. This is a private matter between myself and these gentlemen, who think that they can carry away my fiancée."

"Your fiancée!" cried Mr. Hall.

"That is right," said Gaster, his hideous grin mocking us. "If you think to lay a hand upon her and take her from my side, I am certain that she will make the most strenuous complaint to the Paris Police."

"I am afraid that where you are going, she cannot follow you," said Holmes.

The man narrowed his eyes. "Your name, sir?"

"My name is Sherlock Holmes."

"Well, then, Mr. Sherlock Holmes, you will rue having ever crossed my path. Those who oppose my will soon learn to regret it."

"Do not attempt to scare me with your necromancer act, Dr Gaster. It will not serve. You see, I am well aware of your predilection for mercuric nitrate. As Captain König and Charley Pillar learned far too late."

"I do not know of what you speak," said Gaster, coolly.

"While the initial inquest missed it, after I wired to Tromsberg, Dr Zorn of the Swedish Pathological Society discovered traces of that toxin in Captain König's body, which had been returned home after you murdered him aboard his skip. Moreover, once I told him what to look for, the Medical Officer for Tavistock found evidence of mercury in Mr. Pillar. This shall be more than sufficient to charge you with murder."

A ghastly look settled upon the face of Octavius Gaster when Holmes revealed the charlatan for what he was. His cicatrix began twitching spasmodically, which heralded the beginning of a hideous laugh. This horrible sound continued until the Paris Police arrived to haul him away, and I swore I could hear it even as the Black Maria drove away.[86]

I thought that Holmes had earned a bitter enemy that night, but he seemed little concerned, even when we later learned that Dr Gaster had escaped from the custody of the detectives tasked with escorting him back to England in order to stand trial for multiple homicides. The two men could not explain what had happened, only that their memories of the train ride to Calais were curiously blank.

I asked Holmes if he was worried that Gaster would attempt to carry out his promise of revenge, but he merely shook his head.

"Octavius Gaster is a most dangerous man," said he, "but only to those weak enough to fall under his spell. For at heart, he is the perfect compound of coward, bully, and petty tyrant. As such, he instinctively avoids confrontation with anyone who is capable of resisting his methods. No, I think we have little to fear in the future from that individual."

Our rescued lady was initially in a rather grim mental condition, having been thoroughly dominated by the will of Dr Gaster. Initially, Miss Underwood even defended him, though with slow and patient care, she eventually came to understand that the emotional bond she had to him was entirely artificial.[87]

Finally, when she became more lucid, Miss Underwood recalled to us one night prior to his disappearance, when Fanny Pillar momentarily stepped out of her sick room at Toynby

Hall. During Miss Pillar's absence, Miss Underwood saw a gaunt, bloodless face peering in through the half-open window. She remembered hearing a voice that said, 'I have dealt with thy so beautiful lover, and I have yet to deal with thee.' The words were repeated over and over, until they developed a familiar ring. Eventually, the lady could hear them sounding in her ears the entire day. Yet she could not tell it from a dream, and when she awoke, she was amazed to hear that she had been in Paris at all. She could remember nothing of her time there, which I supposed was a blessing of a sort.

Charley's bosom friend, Mr. Trevor Hall, tenderly nursed her back to health and in time, the pair came to an understanding. Although not announced in the paper – in hopes of keeping the news from the inquisitive eyes of Dr Gaster – a quiet ceremony transformed the unhappy Miss Lottie Underwood to the – if not precisely happy, at least – content Mrs. Charlotte Hall. And perhaps that is all that most of us can hope for in life – for I have found that the happiest fairy tale endings rarely transpire in the real world, while the darkest stories are sadly all too common.

As for Lieutenant Jack Daseby, he was true to his word. Whenever his ship docked at some distant port, he would make inquiries for a person matching the description of Dr Octavius Gaster. These were universally unsuccessful – as he dutifully reported to Holmes in a series of despatches – until one tragic day in 1890, when the HMS *Shark* was lost with all hands off the coast of Pernambuco. I shall always wonder if the sinking of that ship was a natural accident, or if Gaster somehow managed to engineer its demise. If so, I expect that he has long since moved on from the Brazils, and any attempt of Holmes to track him there would be futile. Yet, the world shall not rest easy until the malign pestilence that is Octavius Gaster no longer walks free under its sun.

§

THE ADVENTURE OF THE HAUNTED GRANGE

It was a blustery morning in early November of '83 when the services of Mr. Sherlock Holmes were engaged by one of the most eccentric individuals to ever cross the threshold of 221B Baker Street. I had gone out for a constitutional walk along the Serpentine in Hyde Park – Holmes had waved off my suggestion that he join me with a murmured indication that he planned to spend some time organizing his commonplace books. When I returned, however, I found a curious pair occupying the settee across from my friend.

They were plainly a man and wife, each of about sixty years. The man was short and portly, with mutton chop whiskers covering his jowls, and eyes that twinkled with a sort of inner mirth behind his thick glasses. He was dressed in a sombre style that I thought had last been seen in fashionable circles around the days of the Regent.[88] His wife was a match for him in stature and girth, and her animated face suggesting an engaging personality. Her lace-frilled dress was also of a rather ancient style and a pair of pince-nez was perched upon her thin nose.

"Ah, Watson!" exclaimed Holmes. "Just in time. Mr. Silas

D'Odd and his wife, Mrs. Matilda D'Odd – of Goresthorpe Grange in Norfolk – were just about to describe their problem.[89] From what I have heard thus far, you might be interested."

I took a seat in my usual armchair and waited for Mr. D'Odd to resume his tale.

"Pray continue, sir," said Holmes. "I assure you that, other than the fact that you are a retired grocer from the East End, I know nothing about your circumstances."

The man started at this statement. "I say, sir, what do you mean?"

"Come now, Mr. D'Odd. Your accent can hardly belong to someone who hails from more than a stone's throw from Stepney, and yet your gait does not possess any of the distinctive features of the riverside and seafaring people who are the primary inhabitants of that locale. Combine that with the slight stoop in your back, and your habit of rubbing your hands down your legs, and it suggests a man who spent a score of years behind the counter of a grocer's shop."

"Very well," said the visitor, his tone suggesting that he was somewhat mollified. "Yes, what you say is true. My business was quite successful, but the trade can be rather dangerous. One of my colleagues, Mr. Stephen Maple, had three smashed ribs and a broken leg after being assaulted by an irate customer. Therefore, when the time came to consider alternate avenues for my future, I sold the shop for a tidy sum and thereby reached a financial independence sufficient to take possession of Goresthorpe Grange.

"My habits are conservative, you understand, Mr. Holmes, and my tastes refined and aristocratic. I have a soul that spurns the vulgar herd. Our family, the D'Odds, date back to a prehistoric era, as is to be inferred from the fact that their advent into British history is not commented on by any trustworthy historian.[90] Some instinct tells me that the blood of a Crusader runs in my veins. Even now, after the lapse of so many years, such exclamations as 'By'r Lady!' rise naturally to my lips, and

I feel that, should circumstances require it, I am capable of rising in my stirrups and dealing an infidel such a blow – say with a mace or broadsword – that would considerably astonish him."

"Yes, I see," said Holmes, his face unusually straight, though I thought I detected a hint of a twinkle of amusement in his grey eyes. "I presume your present difficulty has something to do with your new abode?"

"Indeed. Goresthorpe Grange is a feudal mansion – or so it was termed in the advertisement that originally brought it under my notice. The Grange's right to this evocative adjective had a most remarkable effect upon its price, and the advantages gained may possibly be more sentimental than real. Still, it is soothing to me to know that I have slits in my staircase through which I can discharge arrows; and there is a sense of power in the fact of possessing a complicated apparatus by means of which I am enabled to pour molten lead upon the head of the casual visitor, should I so require. These things chime in with my peculiar humour, and I do not grudge to pay for them. I am proud of my battlements and of the circular uncovered moat that girds me round. I am proud of my portcullis and my donjon and my keep. There is but one thing wanting to round off the mediaevalism of my abode, and to render it symmetrically and completely antique. Goresthorpe Grange was not provided with a ghost."

Holmes' eyebrows rose with interest. "A ghost! Do I hear you right, Mr. D'Odd? Your problem is your lack of a ghost? I am afraid that I cannot help you with such things. This agency stands firmly rooted to the earth. I have little to say about such spirits."

Mr. D'Odd shook his head. "You misunderstand me, sir. I said that the lack of a ghost at Goresthorpe Grange was my original problem. That issue has already been solved. However, in so doing, we have stumbled upon a small complication."

"Small complication!" cried Mrs. D'Odd, speaking for the first time. "We were robbed! I made Argentine," – this appeared to be a pet name for her husband – "come speak to you."

"Oh," said Holmes, "well, robbery is rather more in line with my area of expertise. Pray continue."

"As to the ghost, any man with old-fashioned tastes and ideas as to how such establishments should be conducted," said Mr. D'Odd, his equanimity undisturbed by his wife's protestations, "would have been disappointed at the omission. In my case, it was particularly unfortunate. From my childhood, I had been an earnest student of the supernatural, and a firm believer in it. I have revelled in ghostly literature until there is hardly a tale bearing upon the subject that I have not perused. I even learned the German language for the sole purpose of mastering a book upon demonology. When I was a young lad, I had secreted myself in dark rooms in the hope of seeing some of those bogles with which my nurse used to threaten me; and the same feeling is as strong in me now as then.[91] It was a proud moment when I felt that a ghost was one of the luxuries which money might command."

"Was there a mention of an apparition in the advertisement for the castle?" asked Holmes, a hint of wry amusement in his voice.

"Well," said Mr. D'Odd, spluttering a bit, "no, I suppose not. However, on reviewing the mildewed walls, and the shadowy corridors, I had taken it for granted that there was such a thing on the premises. As the presence of a kennel presupposes that of a dog, so I imagined that it was impossible that such desirable quarters should be untenanted by one or more restless shades. Good heavens, what can the noble family from whom I purchased it have been doing during these hundreds of years! Was there no member of it spirited enough to make away with his sweetheart, or take some other steps calculated to establish a hereditary spectre? Even now, I can hardly speak rationally upon the subject."

"Well, you did show great patience, my dear," said Mrs. D'Odd, patting his arm.

"That is true. You see, Mr. Holmes, for a long time I hoped

against hope. Never did a rat squeak behind the wainscot, or rain drip upon the attic floor, without a wild thrill shooting through me as I thought that at last I had come upon traces of some unquiet soul. I felt no touch of fear upon these occasions. If it occurred in the nighttime, I would send Mrs. D'Odd – who is a most strong-minded woman – to investigate the matter, while I covered up my head with the bedclothes and indulged in an ecstasy of expectation. Alas, the result was always the same! The suspicious sound would be traced to some cause so absurdly natural and commonplace that even the most fervid imagination could not clothe it with any of the glamour of romance.

"I might have reconciled myself to this state of things," continued Mr. D'Odd, "had it not been for Jorrocks of Havistock Farm. Jorrocks is a coarse, burly, matter-of-fact fellow, whom I only happened to know through the accidental circumstance of his fields adjoining my demesne. Yet this man, though utterly devoid of all appreciation of archaeological entities, is in possession of a well-authenticated and undeniable spectre."

"Oh, yes?" said Holmes, somewhat doubtfully.

"Indeed!" cried Mr. D'Odd. "Can you possibly believe it, sir? Jorrocks is densely unconscious of his good fortune and the air of respectability that the ghost gives his house. He little dreams how I covet every one of those moans and nocturnal wails that he describes with unnecessary objurgation. Things are indeed coming to a pretty pass when democratic spectres are allowed to desert the landed proprietors and annul every social distinction by taking refuge in the houses of the great unrecognised."

"So you sought to rectify the situation somehow?" asked Holmes.

"Precisely, sir. I have a large amount of perseverance. Nothing else could have raised me into my rightful sphere, considering the uncongenial atmosphere in which I spent the earlier part of my life. I felt now that a ghost must be secured, but how to set about securing one was more than either Mrs. D'Odd or myself was able to determine."

"Until I thought to have one sent down from London," said Mrs. D'Odd, no hint of irony apparent in her voice.

"Sent down?" said Holmes, sceptically. "Like furniture?"

"You see, my dear?" said Mr. D'Odd to his wife. "At first blush, Mr. Holmes thinks the idea unlikely too."

"If I recall correctly, you said it was idiotic," she replied, crossly.

"Yes, well, I may have spoken in haste. Clearly, it was not so challenging to get such a thing after all."

"What?" exclaimed Holmes, his eyebrows rising. "How did you manage it?"

"Well, I engaged the services of Matilda's cousin, Mr. Jack Brocket. Do you know him?"

"No," said Holmes, shaking his head. "The name is unfamiliar."

"He's a clever fellow, and has tried his hand at many things, though he wants of some perseverance to succeed at any. Jack is what you might term a general agent, and handles most of our remaining business in London. Though I have found that Jack's commission is generally considerably larger than all of the other items of the bill put together."

"It was he who managed the business about the crest," insisted Mrs. D'Odd.

"It was only a resuscitation of the old family coat-of-arms, my dear," her husband protested. "Still, when I thought about it some more, I reckoned that it was a good idea. It is one of my maxims, Mr. Holmes, to act promptly when once my mind is made up. Therefore, the very next day, I called upon Mr. Brocket and put the question to him. After a considerable discussion, he concluded that he would be happy to look into the matter, and I returned home rather excited by his confident manner."

"So excited that he hung his boots and spectacles upon a peg with his other garments before retiring to rest," said Mrs. D'Odd, dryly.

"Yes, well," continued Mr. D'Odd, weakly, "Jack and I might have toasted once or twice to his future success in this matter."

"More like five or six times," sniffed Mrs. D'Odd.

"What happened next?" asked Holmes.

"I picked out the room of the house most suitable for the reception of a new ghost, supposing my wife's cousin to succeed in his negotiation with the spirit-mongers. After that, there was nothing to do but wait patiently until I heard some news of the result of his inquiries. A few days later, this letter arrived." He removed a note from his waistcoat pocket and handed it to Holmes.

After glancing at this, Holmes passed it to me. The note was scribbled in pencil upon the back of a playbill, and was sealed with what appeared to be a tobacco-stopper. It read:

> My dear Argentine,
> Am on the track. Nothing of the sort to be had from any professional spiritualist, but picked up a fellow in a pub yesterday who says he can manage it for you. Will send him down unless you wire to the contrary. Abrahams is his name, and he has done one or two of these jobs before. You shall find his fee to be quite reasonable, and I can always receive a cheque for my small role in the matter.
> Your affectionate cousin,
> John Brocket

"While somewhat on the short side," Mr. D'Odd continued, "this note was at least encouraging. My respect for Jack Brocket's business capacities began to go up very considerably. He certainly seemed to have managed the matter wonderfully well. I need hardly say that I did not wire a cancelation, but awaited the arrival of Mr. Abrahams with all impatience. In spite of my belief in the supernatural, I could scarcely credit the fact that any mortal could have such a command over the spirit-world as to deal in them and barter them against mere earthly gold. Still, I had Jack's word for it that such a trade existed; and here was a gentleman with a Judaical name ready to demonstrate it by proof positive. How vulgar and commonplace Jorrocks' eighteenth-century ghost would appear should I succeed in securing a real mediaeval apparition!" he concluded, gleefully rubbing his hands together.

"And Mr. Abrahams soon appeared?" asked Holmes.

"Indeed. Jack Brocket was as good as his word. The shades of another evening were beginning to darken round Goresthorpe Grange, when the man in question arrived. I hurried down to meet him, half expecting to see a choice assortment of ghosts crowding in at his rear. Instead of the sallow-faced, melancholy-eyed man that I had pictured to myself, the ghost-dealer was just a plain little fellow. His sole stock-in-trade seemed to consist of a small leather bag jealously locked and strapped, which emitted a metallic chink upon being placed on the stone flags in the hall."

"And what did Mr. Abrahams have to say for himself?"

"Well, he claimed to have some tricks in his bag. In fact, Mr. Abrahams smiled a smile of superior knowledge. 'You wait,' he said; 'give me the right place and the right hour, with a little of the essence of *Lucoptolycus*' – here he produced a small bottle from his waistcoat pocket – 'and you won't find no ghost that I ain't up to.[92] You'll see them yourself, and pick your own, and I can't say fairer than that.' I asked him when he planned to summon the ghosts. He said ten minutes to one in the morning. He thought that hour preferential to midnight, a time when other spirit-seekers are crowding for attention. He then asked to be shown about the premises in order to locate the ideal place where he would attract the ghost – for they can be quite particular as to the place in which they manifest themselves. After he saw the banqueting room, Mr. Abrahams declared that was the ideal spot, and asked to be left alone in order to commune with the spirits. He said that he needed to make sure they were calm enough for me to converse with them, and asked me to return at half-past twelve."

"You left him alone with your valuables?" asked Holmes.

Mr. D'Odd shrugged. "We were just downstairs. And, in any case, Mr. Abrahams' request struck me as a reasonable one, so I left him with his feet upon the mantelpiece, and his chair in front of the fire, fortifying himself with some stimulants against his potentially refractory visitors. From the room beneath, in which I sat with Mrs. D'Odd, we could hear that – after sitting for some time – he rose up and paced about the hall with quick impatient steps. We then heard him try the lock of the door, and afterward drag some heavy article of furniture – upon which he apparently mounted – in the direction of the window. I heard the creaking of their rusty hinges, and I knew it to be situated several feet above the little man's reach. Mrs. D'Odd thought that she could distinguish his voice speaking in low and rapid whispers after this, but that may have been her imagination. I confess that I began to feel more impressed than I had deemed it possible to be. There was something awesome in the thought of the solitary mortal standing by the open window and summoning in from the gloom outside the spirits of the nether world. It was with a trepidation, which I could hardly disguise from Matilda, that I observed that the clock was pointing to half-past twelve and that the time had come for me to share the vigil of my visitor.

"He was sitting in his old position when I entered, and there were no signs of the mysterious movements which I had overheard, though his chubby face was flushed as if due to recent exertion.

" 'Are you succeeding all right?' I asked as I came in, putting on as careless an air as possible, but glancing involuntarily round the room to see if we were alone.

" 'Only your help is needed to complete the matter,' said Mr. Abrahams, in a solemn voice. 'You shall sit by me and partake of the essence of *Lucoptolycus*, which removes the scales from our earthly eyes. Whatever you may chance to see, speak not and make no movement, lest you break the spell." His manner was subdued, and his usual vulgarity had entirely disappeared.

I took the chair which he indicated, and awaited the result.

"My companion cleared the rushes from the floor in our neighbourhood, and, going down upon his hands and knees, described a half-circle with chalk, which enclosed the fireplace and ourselves. Round the edge of this half-circle, he drew several hieroglyphics, not unlike the signs of the zodiac. He then stood up and uttered a long invocation, delivered so rapidly that it sounded like a single gigantic word in some uncouth guttural language. Having finished this prayer, if prayer it was, he pulled out the small bottle which he had produced before, and poured a couple of teaspoonfuls of clear transparent fluid into a phial, which he handed to me with an intimation that I should drink it.

"The liquid had a faintly sweet odour, not unlike the aroma of certain sorts of apples. I hesitated a moment before applying it to my lips, but an impatient gesture from my companion overcame my scruples, and I tossed it off. The taste was not unpleasant; and, as it gave rise to no immediate effects, I leaned back in my chair and composed myself for what was to come. Mr. Abrahams seated himself beside me, and I felt that he was watching my face from time to time, while repeating some more of the invocations in which he had indulged before.

"A sense of delicious warmth and languor began gradually to steal over me, partly, perhaps, from the heat of the fire, and partly from some unexplained cause. An uncontrollable impulse to sleep weighed down my eyelids, while at the same time, my brain worked actively, and a hundred beautiful and pleasing ideas flitted through it. So utterly lethargic did I feel that, though I was aware that my companion put his hand over the region of my heart – as if to feel how it were beating – I did not attempt to prevent him, nor did I even ask him for the reason of his action. Everything in the room appeared to be reeling slowly round in a drowsy dance, of which I was the centre. The great elk's head at the far end wagged solemnly backward and forward, while the massive salvers on the tables performed cotillions with the claret-cooler and the epergne.[93] My head fell upon my breast from sheer heaviness, and I should have become unconscious had I not been recalled to myself by the opening of the door at the other end of the hall.

"This door led on to the raised dais, which, as I have mentioned, the heads of the house used to reserve for their own use. As it swung slowly back upon its hinges, I sat up in my chair, clutching at the arms, and staring with a horrified glare at the dark passage outside. Something was coming down it – something unformed and intangible, but still a something. Dim and shadowy, I saw it flit across the threshold, while a blast of ice-cold air swept down the room, which seemed to blow through me, chilling my very heart. I was aware of the mysterious presence, and then I heard it speak in a voice like the sighing of an east wind among pine-trees on the banks of a desolate sea. I will not repeat its verses – for they were far too horrible – and I could not speak in turn. The words seemed to be choked in my throat; and, before I could get them out, the shadow flitted across the hall and vanished in the darkness at the other side, while a long-drawn melancholy sigh quivered through the apartment.

"I turned my eyes toward the door once more, and beheld, to my astonishment, a very small old woman – her wizened hands like the talons of an unclean bird – who hobbled along the corridor and into the hall. She passed backward and forward several times, and then, crouching down at the very edge of the circle upon the floor, she disclosed a face – the horrible malignity of which shall never be banished from my recollection. Every foul passion appeared to have left its mark upon that hideous countenance.

"I endeavoured to shake my head in horror; upon which she aimed a blow at me with her crutch, and vanished with an eldritch scream. By this time, my eyes turned naturally toward the open door, and I was hardly surprised to see a man of tall and noble stature walk in. His face was deadly pale, but was surmounted by a fringe of dark hair that fell in ringlets down his back. A short pointed beard covered his chin. He was dressed in loose-fitting clothes, made apparently of yellow satin, and a large white ruff surrounded his neck. He paced across the room with slow and majestic strides. Then turning, he addressed me in a sweet, exquisitely modulated voice. When he was done, he bent his head courteously, as though awaiting my reply, but the same choking sensation prevented me from speaking; and, with a deep bow, he disappeared.

"He had hardly gone before a feeling of intense horror stole over me, and I was aware of the presence of a ghastly creature in the room, of dim outlines and uncertain proportions. One moment it seemed to pervade the entire apartment, while at another it would become invisible, but always leaving behind it a distinct consciousness of its presence. Its voice, when it spoke, was quavering and gusty. I raised my hand in a deprecating way, but too late to prevent one discordant outbreak of hideous laughter that echoed through the room. Before I could lower my hand, the apparition was gone.

"I turned my head toward the door in time to see a man come hastily and stealthily into the chamber. He was a powerfully built fellow; his face once sunburnt, with earrings in his ears and a Barcelona handkerchief tied loosely round his neck. His head was bent upon his chest, and his whole aspect was that of one afflicted by intolerable remorse. He paced rapidly backward and forward like a caged tiger, and I observed that a drawn knife glittered in one of his hands, while he grasped what appeared to be a piece of parchment in the other. His voice, when he spoke, was deep and sonorous. He looked toward me beseechingly; however, before I could make a sign, I was paralysed by the horrible sight that appeared at the door.

"It was a very tall man, if, indeed, it might be called a man, for the gaunt bones were protruding through the corroding flesh, and the features were of a leaden hue. A winding-sheet was wrapped round the figure, and formed a hood over the head, from under the shadow of which two fiendish eyes, deep set in their grisly sockets, blazed and sparkled like red-hot coals. The lower jaw had fallen upon the breast, disclosing a withered, shrivelled tongue and two lines of black and jagged fangs. I shuddered and drew back as this fearful apparition advanced to the edge of the circle. The creature stretched out its fleshless arms to me as if in entreaty, but I shook my head; and it vanished, leaving a low, sickening, repulsive odour behind it. I sank back in my chair, so overcome by terror and disgust that I would have very willingly resigned myself to dispensing with a ghost altogether, could I have been sure that this was the last of the hideous procession.

"A faint sound of trailing garments warned me that it was not so. I looked up, and beheld a white figure emerging from the corridor into the light. As it stepped across the threshold, I saw that it was that of a young and beautiful woman dressed in the fashion of a bygone day. Her hands were clasped in front of her, and her pale proud face bore traces of passion and of suffering. She crossed the hall with a gentle sound, like the rustling of autumn leaves, and then, she turned her lovely and unutterably sad eyes upon me. Her voice died away in a beautiful cadence as she concluded, and she held out her hands as if in supplication. I have always been sensitive to female influences. Besides, what would Jorrocks's ghost be to this? Could anything be in better taste? Would I not be exposing myself to the chance of injuring my nervous system by interviews with such creatures as my last visitor, unless I decided at once? She gave me a seraphic smile, as if she knew what was passing in my mind.

"That smile settled the matter. 'She will do!' I cried; 'I choose this one;' and as I took a step towards this apparition, in my enthusiasm I passed over the magic circle that had girdled me round. However, at that moment, another voice pierced my consciousness. My dear Matilda was screaming in my ear, over and over again. I could hardly grasp the meaning of her words. A violent throbbing in my head seemed to adapt itself to their rhythm, and I closed my eyes to the lullaby of 'robbed, robbed, robbed!' A vigorous shake caused me to open them again, however, and the sight of Mrs. D'Odd in the most furious of tempers was sufficiently impressive to recall all my scattered thoughts. I realized that I was lying on my back on the floor, with my head among the ashes which had fallen from last night's fire, and a small phial in my hand."

"Do you still have it?" asked Holmes, leaning forward eagerly.

"Oh, yes," said Mr. D'Odd. "I thought you might ask after it." He reached into his pocket and handed over a plain glass tube, stopped with a cork. "Here you go."

Holmes accepted this item and set it aside. "What happened next?"

"Well, I staggered to my feet, but felt so weak and giddy that I was compelled to fall back into a chair. As my brain became clearer, and stimulated by the exclamations of Matilda – who stood in the grey light of dawn, wringing her hands and repeating her monotonous refrain – I gradually began to recollect the events of the night. I found that the seer had vanished, along with the pride of Goresthorpe Grange, the glorious plate that was to have been the delectation of generations of D'Odds.[94] It was only very slowly that my misty brain took these things in, and grasped the connection between them."

"The rope hanging from the window," said Mrs. D'Odd, "may have assisted with this insight."

"That is quite the tale, Mr. D'Odd," said Holmes, with a shake of his head. "Did you notice anything out of the ordinary prior to the appearance of Mr. Abrahams at your manor?"

Mr. D'Odd considered this question for a moment. "Now that you mention it, sir, the night prior to his arrival, I almost thought that a ghost had been sent down in advance. As I walked round the moat that night before retiring to rest – using a rather fine medieval bill as my walking stick – I came upon a dark figure engaged in surveying the machinery of my portcullis and drawbridge.[95] His start of surprise, however, and the manner in which he hurried off into the darkness, speedily convinced me of his earthly origin. I put him down as some admirer of one of my former female retainers, who was mourning over the muddy Hellespont that divided him from his love.[96] Whomever he may have been, he disappeared and did not return, though I loitered about for some time in the hope of catching a glimpse of him and exercising my feudal rights upon his person with the point of my bill."

"And have you gone to Scotland Yard?"

"Indeed, but the man I talked to – Lestrade, I think he gave his name – was rather unhelpful. He was chuckling the entire time, so much that I wonder if he had not partook a pint or three over his luncheon. At the end, he suggested that it was unlikely we would ever see our plate again. The inspector said that our time would be better spent conversing with our insurance agent, but that if we persisted in attempting to locate Mr. Abrahams, he thought you would be the man for the job."

"Yes, I wager he did," said Holmes, dryly. "So you wish to know where Mr. Abrahams and your plate have gone?"

"Yes!" cried Mrs. D'Odd.

"Partly," said the husband, speaking simultaneously. He looked at his wife apologetically, before continuing. "You see, Mr. Holmes, I am not altogether dissatisfied with the service that Mr. Abrahams has provided – though the amount of his fee, and the manner in which he took it, remains a matter that I would very much like to further discuss with him. However, the more serious question in my mind is the role of Mr. Brocket in identifying Mr. Abrahams. Did he know that Mr. Abrahams meant to defraud us? Worse, could he have actively conspired against us?"

Mrs. D'Odd was shaking her head vigorously as her husband put forth this question. "Jack would not do such a thing."

Mr. D'Odd grimaced. "As you can see, Mr. Holmes, this is something of a sore subject between us. However, the fact of the matter remains that neither Mrs. D'Odd nor I are getting any younger. Moreover, we were never blessed with children to whom we might leave the remainder of our estate – for despite his best efforts, Mr. Abrahams has put only a small dent in that sum. Mr. Brocket, as Matilda's cousin, would naturally stand to inherit a sum – which might be either small or quite large, depending on how we leave things in our final will and testament – upon our passing on to the realm that sits on the other side of the veil. So, my question for you, in sum, Mr. Holmes, is whether or not he is so deserving?"

Holmes nodded. "Very good, sir. This particular enquiry is well within the realm of operations for this agency. I shall look into the matter. Your account was quite clear. I have only one remaining question for you. Where was your staff – for surely a manor the size of Goresthorpe must have them – during the whole operation of Mr. Abrahams and his accomplice?"

The pair looked at each other meaningfully before Mrs. D'Odd answered. "We were somewhat between servants at the time, Mr. Holmes."

"I see," said Holmes, in such a way to suggest rather the opposite.

"You may find Mr. Brocket at 16A, Victoria Street," said Mr. D'Odd, pressing on. "He has professional chambers there."

"Oh, I think that Mr. Brocket can wait. I will start with an inspection of the scene of the crime. No, no, do not delay for us, Mr. D'Odd," said Holmes, with a wave of his hand. "I have a brief inquiry or two to make before we go up to Norfolk. We will be on the next train."

After the D'Odds had departed, Holmes turned to me with a smile. "I presume, Watson, that you are sufficiently interested to join me in this investigation?"

"Of course. Though I confess that I did not think you one for ghosts."

"On that, you are indubitably correct. However, Mr. D'Odd strikes me as a great eccentric, and – as I have, from time to time, been accused of the same – I appreciate his unique spirit."

"What inquiries do you plan to make?"

"If we wish to catch the next train to Norwich, we do not have time to go out to Stepney, nor interview Mr. Brocket. Yet, I wish to know more of the antecedents of both Mr. D'Odd and his agent. I shall wire to my agent in the East End, as well as to

Mr. Pike.[97] We shall see what they can dig up during our time in Norfolk. Come, Watson, grab your hat and coat. No need for an overnight bag, we will catch the late return."

Before departing Baker Street, Holmes inspected the phial containing the final drops of the liquid consumed by Mr. D'Odd prior to the onset of his visions. "Excellent, there is still a drop left." He carefully packed it in a wool-padded box, adding a scribbled note. "I could test this myself, of course, but in the interest of time, I shall send it over to a colleague. Dr Stube is a well-known analyst of such substances, and should have an answer for us by the time we return from Goresthorpe."

On our way to Liverpool Street Station, Holmes had the cabman stop twice, the first at a district messenger office to convey the box to Dr Stube, and the second so that he could dash into a telegraph office. These tasks complete, Holmes and I rattled along the remainder of the trip talking of inconsequential matters.

It was not until we were settled into a private second-class carriage that Holmes allowed me to turn the discussion to Mr D'Odd's case. Holmes had produced a large briarroot pipe and, after a matter of a few minutes, a dense wreath of smoke surrounded him. His slender figure loomed through the haze, from the midst of which his voice issued like the oracle of Delphi.

"What do you make of these spirits seen by Mr. D'Odd, Holmes?" I asked. "It is strange that a common thief could bring about the appearance of such apparitions."

He shook his head. "Watson, I am shocked. You have been trained as a medical student, have you not? You should look at things from an eminently practical point of view. Your strange speculative way of thinking is almost German in nature. It is a great fault."

"Oh?" said I, somewhat rankled by this dismissive attitude. "So you do not believe in the possibility of ghosts? I find that those who profess not to believe in such things are often those who are mortally afraid of them, while the men who admit at least the possibility of their existence would go out of their way to see one."

He chuckled. "Do not be cross with me, Watson. You must consider me a third type. A 'credo-quod-tango.'[98] I walk on the narrow path of certain fact. I cannot fathom the possibility of the orthodox spectre with his curse, and his chain warranted to rattle, and his shady retreat down some back stairs or into the cellar. No, it is impossible."

"I cannot agree."

"Well, then, let's hear your idea of a credible ghost, Watson."

"It's not such an easy matter, you see, to explain it to another, even though I can define it in my own mind well enough. You admit, Holmes, that it is widely believed that when a man dies he is done with all the cares and troubles of this world, and is for the future – be it one of joy or sorrow – a pure and ethereal spirit."

"A theory yet to be proven," he interjected.

"A theory held for all of human history, back to the Egyptians in their pyramids," I retorted. "Well now, what I think is that it is possible – just possible, mind you – for a man to be hurried out of this world with a soul so impregnated with one all-absorbing passion such that it clings to him even after he has passed the portals of the grave."

"I suppose you mean," said Holmes, waving his pipe from side to side through the cloud that surrounded him, "love, or patriotism, or some other pure and elevating passion?"

"Such thoughts might well be entertained by one who is but a spirit, but it is different, I fancy, with such grosser feelings as hatred or revenge. These one could imagine, even after death, clogging the poor soul so that it must still inhabit the coarse clay that is most fitted to the coarse passions that absorb it. Thus I would account for the unexplained and unexplainable things that have happened even in our own time, and for the deeply rooted belief in ghosts which exists – smother it as we may – in every breast, and which has existed in every age."

Holmes snorted in amusement. "Your argument is persuasive, Watson, save for one thing."

"What is that?"

"As I have never seen any of your 'impregnated spirits' with mine own eyes, I must beg leave to continue to doubt their existence."

"It's very easy to laugh at the matter," I answered, "but there are few facts in this world that have not been laughed at, sometime or another. Perhaps you have simply not been in the right place."

"What do you mean?"

"Well, suppose there was said to be white crows or some other natural curiosity in Yorkshire, and someone assured you that there was not, because he had been all through Wales without seeing one. You would naturally consider the man an idiot, would you not, Holmes? Therefore, perhaps you simply need to spend some time in a verifiably haunted house. You may change your tune."

He smiled. "Well then, Watson, perhaps we shall see one tonight, if Mr. Abrahams was good enough to actually perform his promised summoning."

When we arrived at Thorpe Station, there were two telegrams waiting for Holmes, who read them through with interest.

"What have you learned?" I inquired.

"Well, it seems that Mr. D'Odd is an open book. According to my agent, he was once just plain Mr. Dodd, but the general consensus is that his general store on the Mile End Road was completely above board. He came to his fortune honestly – a rare feat in this day and age! – and has long been obsessed with how he might go about being raised to the peerage. He hoped – rather implausibly – to join the Rothschilds in that honour."[99]

"And Mr. Brocket?"

"Ah, that is another story. Jack Brocket appears to be something of a rake. As Mr. D'Odd noted, he professes to be a general agent, though it seems that he is really living – to a great extent – upon his wits. It will be most interesting to hear precisely how he met the villainous Mr. Abrahams."

Holmes hired a trap to convey us out to Goresthorpe Grange, which proved to be a tumbledown old pile at the meeting of the Morsely and Alton roads where the new turnpike stands now.[100] It stood cold, bleak, and desolate with the wind howling past it. Great curtains of ivy climbed the walls, and a flag – emblazoned with what I presumed was the D'Odd family crest – flew from the highest tower. The drawbridge was down and Holmes strode across it to lift the heavy brass knocker.

The door was soon opened by our host, who showed us excitedly along a long stone-flagged corridor running the whole length of one wing of the house, one wall of which was entirely solid, while the other had openings for windows at every three or four paces. I imagined that when the moon was full, it would shine in the dark passage such that it would be flecked with patches of white light. We went along about the rambling corridors and old-fashioned rooms until he finally led us to the banqueting hall. It was a long low room, hung round with red curtains, and a large fireplace opposite the entrance blazed with light. Scattered about were valuable tapestries, a virginal, and other interesting relics of the old family to whom it had belonged.[101] Long line of faces adorned the walls, from the burly Norman robber, through every gradation of casque, plume, and ruff, to the sombre Chesterfieldian individual who appears to have staggered against a pillar in his agony at the return of a maiden MS that he gripped convulsively in his right hand.[102]

"Mr. Brocket resuscitated these family portraits," said Mr. D'Odd.

"You must allow that Jack selected them very judiciously," noted his wife, smiling gleefully.

The man nodded. "I confess that in this instance Jack did his work well, and it was the thing that made me think that it was only fair to give him an order – with the usual commission – for a family spectre, should such a thing be attainable. Would you care for a cup of sack, gentlemen? I do love the good old names!"[103]

Holmes declined this offer for the both of us and took in these additional details without comment, as he continued to inspect the room. Coats of mail and implements of war glimmered fitfully as the light of the fire played over them, and the wind crept under the door, moving the hangings to and fro with a ghastly rustling. At one end there was the raised dais, upon which in ancient times the host and his guests used to spread their table, while a descent of a couple of steps led to the lower part of the hall, where the vassals and retainers held wassail. The floor was uncovered by any sort of carpet, but a layer of rushes had been scattered over it. In the whole room, there was nothing to remind one of the nineteenth century – it could have easily been the fifteenth. Near the fireplace, there was a circle of chalk with hieroglyphics round the edge, while on a side table was a cigar-box and brandy bottle.

Holmes pointed to a bare area on the oak table in the centre. "This is where the silver plate was stolen?"

"That is correct," said Mr. D'Odd.

Holmes then strode over to one of the diamond-paned casement windows, below which an ancient steel-banded chest had been dragged. "And this was the open window with a rope running out of it?"

"Yes," answered out host.

"Very good, Mr. D'Odd. I now propose that Watson and I have a look about the outside of the house. I do not anticipate any resolution to your matter today, but shall be in touch shortly."

Having made our parting with the D'Odds, Holmes led me back outside the house and around the moat until he came to a place roughly opposite from what I took to be the window of the great hall. His gaze was focused on the ground, and he suddenly stopped.

"Here we are, Watson. Note the footmarks imprinted in the mud – two sets, one more frequent than the other. I can see some on the other side of the moat as well. Plainly, Mr. Abrahams had an accomplice below, who received the sacks of precious metal which had been let down through the open window. Mr. Abrahams then lowered himself down the rope, waded across the moat, and the two made off with their ill-gotten loot. Shall we see where their tracks lead us?"

He followed these – though I could hardly see what he was looking at – through Mr. D'Odd's estate until we passed into a neighbouring field.

Eventually, the owner noted our trespass. "Hey there!" cried a stout, sandy-haired, middle-aged man coming along a path through the thickets. "Where do you think you are going?"

"My apologies, sir," said Holmes, "I am Mr. Sherlock Holmes, and this is my friend, Dr John Watson. I am a private inquiry agent and am investigating a recent disturbance at Goresthorpe Grange."

"Ah, you might be interested in something then. Follow me. The name's Jorrocks, by the way."

Holmes looked at me and shrugged before setting off to follow the man. Jorrocks led us to an outbuilding, where he picked up a small bag.

"Two nights ago," said Jorrocks, "about four o'clock, I noticed two men making their way across my fields. I sent a blast of my fowling piece over their heads and they ran off faster than a pair of scampering rabbits. But they dropped this." He handed over the bag.

"A choice assortment of jemmies and centre-bits," said Holmes, looking inside.[104] "Mr. Jorrocks," said Holmes, "Might I have a word with you about your neighbour, Mr. D'Odd?"

The man considered this for a moment, and then spit out a wad of tobacco that had been occupying a corner of his mouth. "What would you know about daft old D'Odd?"

"So you think Mr. D'Odd is somewhat disturbed in his head?"

"The man is mad as a hatter." The farmer shook his head. "I told D'Odd when he first came round to see the Grange that he was barmy to want to purchase such an old ruin. The garden round it had long been choked up by a rank growth of weeds, while pools of stagnant water – filled with the accumulated garbage of the whole village – poisoned the air for miles around."

"But Mr. D'Odd was not dissuaded by this?" asked Holmes.

"Oh, no! To the man's credit, he spared no expense to fix the place up. A small army of labourers cleared the garden, while the moat was dredged and the garbage hauled away. I suppose the place even looks somewhat presentable these days."

"How does he maintain it without any servants?"

"Ha! He had servants, until they all got fed up."

"Over what?"

"As I understand it, Mr. D'Odd suggested to the house-steward Watkins that he should set himself – or possibly someone else – on fire in the interests of the establishment. Well, as you can imagine, Watkins did not take kindly to such a proposal. The other servants sympathized with Watkins' opinion to the degree that they left the house in a body the same afternoon."

"Immolate himself! " I cried. "To what end?"

"Why, to create a ghost, of course. You need a terrible crime of some sort to leave such an imprint behind, as I well know."

"Indeed," said Holmes. "Mr. D'Odd had noted that your own farm is haunted."

"That's right," spat Jorrocks. "The damn ghost's existence dates back, I believe, to the reign of the Second George, when a young lady cut her throat upon hearing of the death of her lover at the battle of Dettingen. I wish she had kept her knife in her pocket, as I am sick to death of her gibbering and her caterwauling, not to mention the bloodstains that keep appearing upon the floor.[105] Of course, the ironic thing is that Goresthorpe Grange is already haunted."

"Oh, yes?" cried Holmes.

"Well, before D'Odd bought the place and cleaned it up, it was a dreary place by day and an eerie one by night. Strange stories were told of the Grange, sounds were said to have come from those weather-beaten walls, such as mortal lips never uttered. The elders of the village still speak of one foolhardy soul – Job Garston by name – who, forty-some years ago, had

had the temerity to sleep inside. It is said that when Garston was led out in the morning, he had become a whitehaired and broken man. In fact, he was raving mad until the day of his death."

"So this ghost is common knowledge in the area?"

"Of course. Legend holds that the spirit of Godfrey Marsden, a villain of the first water, still walks those halls. After Job Garston's experience, no one would set foot in the place until a pair of lads – names of Jack and Tom, if I recall correctly – who were down in these parts round '76 got it in their heads to spend the night in the Grange. The two of them never spoke of what they saw, but you could tell from the look in their eyes the following morn that it was something terrible. When someone suggested that they repeat the experience, the two of them just shuddered. They went away and never returned."[106]

"You said one of them was named Jack?" asked Holmes. "Do you recall his surname?"

"Let me think," said Jorrocks. "Ah yes. His mother was a Marsden – there are still some families in the area by that name – but she married a Brocket. Her son was Jack Brocket."

§

On the return train to London, Holmes appeared pleased with what we had learned in Norwich. "Well, Watson, a pretty picture, don't you think? Mr. Brocket seems to be rather deeply involved in the whole matter. By the time we get back, it will be far too late to call upon him, but first thing in the morning we should have ourselves a chat with this gentleman."

As the sun rose on the following day, Holmes generously did not insist upon an early start, but instead joined me in savouring Mrs. Hudson's breakfast. Before we had finished, the following note arrived for Holmes:

Dear Mr. Holmes,
Your very singular case has interested me extremely.

The bottle that you sent, labelled 'essence of Lucoptolycus,' contained a strong solution of chloral, and the quantity which you describe your client as having swallowed must have amounted to at least eighty grains of the pure hydrate.[107] This would of course have reduced him to a partial state of insensibility, gradually going on to complete coma. In this semi-unconscious state of chloralism, it is not unusual for circumstantial and bizarre visions to present themselves – more especially to individuals unaccustomed to the use of the drug.
– I remain, dear sir, sincerely yours,
T. E. STUBE, M.D.
ARUNDEL STREET

"There we have it, Watson," said Holmes. "A definitive explanation for Mr. D'Odd's visions."

I shook my head, unconvinced. "The ghosts he saw were so clear. Can chloral hydrate alone account for such a thing?"

"Mr. D'Odd's mind was saturated with ghostly literature, and he told us himself that he had long taken a morbid interest in classifying and recalling the various forms in which apparitions have been said to appear. You must also remember that he was expecting to see something of this very nature, and that his nervous system was worked up to an unnatural state of tension. Under the circumstances, I think that – far from the sequel being an astonishing one – it would have been very surprising indeed to any one versed in narcotics had he not experienced some such effects. Now let us see the London agent of the D'Odd's."

Mr. Brocket's professional chambers were situated in a four-storey building of offices opposite Victoria Station. A spiral stone staircase was adorned with a series of arrows and fingers painted upon the whitewashed wall that indicated the direction of that gentleman's sanctum at the very top floor.

The door was opened by a youth who was evidently astounded at the appearance of a client, and we were promptly ushered into the presence of a young man, not more than five-and-twenty years of age. He had a strong, masculine face, with a well-groomed brown moustache and bright green eyes, and was dressed in a flashy suit. Mr. Brocket – for it could only be him – was sitting behind an enormous desk that must have dated back several centuries, where was engaged in writing furiously in a large ledger.

After Holmes introduced ourselves, he set aside the ledger and plunged into business at once. "What can I do for you, Mr. Holmes?"

"We have come, Mr. Brocket, because we understand that you might be able to procure us a spirit," said Holmes.

"Spirits you mean!" shouted the man, plunging his hand into the waste-paper basket and producing a bottle of whisky with the celerity of a conjuring trick. "Let's have a drink! Dr Watson here looks like a man who appreciates a bit of a morning pick-me-up."

I had held up my hand as a mute appeal against such a proceeding so early in the day. However, on lowering it again, I found that I had almost involuntarily closed my fingers round the tumbler that Mr. Brocket had pressed upon me. I set this down hastily, lest anyone should come in upon us and set me down as a toper.[108]

"Not spirits," Holmes explained, smilingly, as if there was something very amusing about the young fellow's eccentricities. "An actual apparition – a ghost. If such a thing is to be had, I should be very willing to negotiate."

"Ah, I see. Have you been up to Goresthorpe Grange?" inquired Mr. Brocket, with as much coolness as if Holmes had asked for a drawing-room suite. He tipped his head back and the gin vanished from his glass.

"Quite so," answered Holmes.

"And how did things work out for Silas?"

"You have not heard?"

"No," said he, shaking his head and waving his hand about

his office. "As you can see, I have been swamped with work."

"Well, your efforts were quite the success. I would very much like it if you could re-create for us how you precisely went about procuring Mr. D'Odd's ghost?"

The man shrugged. "Ah, you want one of your own, sir? Sure enough. Easiest thing in the world," said Mr. Brocket, filling up his glass again. "Let us see!" Here he took down a large red notebook, with all the letters of the alphabet in a fringe down the edge. "The first thing I did was consult my index. Silas wanted a good old-fashioned ghost – I presume you feel the same – not a spectre or wraith or bogle, correct? So that's to be found in 'G.' " He quickly read from the list. "G – gems – gimlets – gas-pipes – gauntlets – guns – galleys. Ah, here we are. Ghosts. Volume nine, section six, page forty-one. Excuse me!" Then Mr. Brocket ran up a ladder and began rummaging among the pile of ledgers on a high shelf.

"Here it is!" cried the agent, jumping off the ladder with a crash, and depositing an enormous volume upon the table. "I have all these things tabulated, so that I may lay my hands upon them in a moment." He paused to fill up his glass again. "What were we looking up, again?"

"Ghosts," said Holmes, dryly.

"Of course; page 41. Here we are. Therefore, the first person I suggested was: 'T.H. Fowler & Son, Dunkel Street, suppliers of mediums to the nobility and gentry; charms sold – love philtres – mummies – horoscopes cast.' Nevertheless, Silas thought that there was nothing in his line there. Next, I proposed this one: 'Frederick Tabb,' sole channel of communication between the living and the dead. Proprietor of the spirits of Byron, Kirke White, Grimaldi, Tom Cribb, and Inigo Jones.'[109] That was about the figure, I thought!"

"But Mr. D'Odd did not agree?"

Mr. Brocket shook his head in disbelief. "No, Silas objected that there was not anything romantic enough in those sorts. Good heavens! Can you believe how particular the man is? He could not fancy a ghost with a black eye and a handkerchief tied round its waist, or turning summersaults, and saying, 'How are you tomorrow?' So I reasonably proposed another: 'Christopher McCarthy; bi-weekly séances – attended by all the eminent spirits of ancient and modern times. Nativities – charms – abracadabras, messages from the dead.' I thought that he might be able to help us, though Silas was not so certain. Nevertheless, I agreed to have a hunt round myself the next day, and see some of these fellows. I know their haunts – if you will excuse the pun – and I thought it would be odd if I could not pick up something cheap. But none of them quite seemed right."

"And then you found Mr. Abrahams?"

"Indeed. Or perhaps I should better say that he found me."

"How so? Did you place an advertisement?"

"No, no," said Mr. Brocket, shaking his head. "I was in the bar of the 'Lame Dog' – do you know it?"

"On Wilton Road," said Holmes.

"That's the one!" agreed Mr. Brocket. "Anyhow, I was talking about Silas' problem with a pal of mine, and Mr. Abrahams must have overheard me. He came over said that I would not find a better man for the job. When I asked him if he could really do it, he simply said, 'try me. Me and my bag. Just try me.'"

"So you send him round to see Mr. D'Odd?"

"Oh yes. Mr. Abrahams was so confident of his abilities – and truth be told, I was not having much luck in other quarters. It seems that, after all, it is not the simplest of matters to persuade a ghost to switch the location of its haunting."

"I can imagine," said Holmes, dryly. "One final question, if you please. I wonder, Mr. Brocket, if you know how Mr. D'Odd first came to learn about Goresthorpe Grange being for sale?"

The man pursed his lips. "I believe it was an advertisement in the paper."

"Indeed," said Holmes. "That is just what Mr. D'Odd said. I wonder, though, if you know the identity of the prior owners of the estate?"

Brocket pursed his lips and shook his head. "That is an excellent question. I could look it up for you. It should only take a few hours of work – two sovereigns worth, I think."

"Thank you, Mr. Brocket, for your kind offer of assistance. However, as it so happens, I have already inquired. Mr. Jorrocks of Havistock Farm was most helpful. It seems that the estate once belonged to the Marsden family. Do you know them?"

The man stared at Holmes for a long moment, a spasm of indecision rippling across his face. "Why, yes, in fact, that is my mother's name." He laughed. "You have me there, Mr. Holmes. I admit that I found the Grange for Silas because it has long been in my family. But only a very small portion of the sale devolved upon me, I promise you."

"And the ghost? I believe that Mr. Jorrocks indicated that the Grange was already in possession of a ghost."

The man paled at this question. "Ah, yes, the ghost. Or, should I say, ghosts. Well, it seems that they have moved on to the next plane of existence, since Silas and Matilda have never seen them."

"But you have?"

"Yes," the man paused to fill up his glass and drain it again. "It was about five or six years ago. My college chum, Tom Hulton, and I were down at holiday visiting relatives, and had gotten into an argument about the existence of ghosts. I was – at the time – rather incredulous about the possibility. To settle the matter once and for all, we decided to spend the following night in the old family manor.

"I knew that the Grange had certainly – as far as foul crimes were concerned – as orthodox a title to be haunted as any building on record. You see, Mr. Holmes, I discovered from my family papers that the last tenant was a certain Godfrey Marsden. He lived there about the middle of last century and was a byword of ferocity and brutality throughout the whole countryside. Eventually, he consummated his many crimes by horribly hacking his two young children to death and strangling their mother. In the confusion of the Pretender's march into England, justice was laxly administered, and Marsden succeeded in escaping to the Continent where all trace of him was lost.[110] There was a rumour indeed among his creditors, the only ones who regretted him, that remorse had led him to commit suicide, and that his body had been washed up on the French Coast. However, those who knew him best laughed at the idea of anything so intangible having an effect upon so hardened a ruffian. Since his day, the Grange had been untenanted – the extended family moving to less gloomy dwellings nearby – and had been suffered to fall into the state of disrepair in which it then was.

"I confess that the morning after our debate about ghosts I began to feel that I had been slightly imprudent in aiding and abetting Tom in his ridiculous expedition. It was that confounded Irish whisky. I always put my foot into it after the third glass. Nevertheless, Tom was even more excited about the plan we had made, and swore he had been awake all night planning and preparing everything for the evening. He planned to take pistols – though what good those would do against the spirit of Godfrey Marsden I can hardly say – as well as our pipes and a couple of ounces of bird's-eye tobacco, plus our rugs, and a bottle of whisky for fortification.

"That evening, as the sun began to set, we walked over to the old Grange. Turning the key in the rusty lock and, having lit a candle, we began to walk down the dusty hall. Tom proposed waiting in a large, dingy room, but I wanted to find a smaller place where we could light a fire and be sure at a glance that we were the only people in it.

"Tom laughed at this request, but agreed and we went back along the hall, until we came to a door which led into a small room, cleaner and more modern looking than the rest of the house, and with a large fireplace opposite the entrance. It was hung with dark red curtains, and when we had our fire ablaze, it certainly looked more comfortable than I had ever dared to expect. Tom, for his part, seemed unutterably disgusted and discontented by the result. He thought it looked more like a hotel than a haunted house, and I eventually came round to his line of thinking. Perhaps our curious surroundings flavoured the bird's-eye and mellowed the whisky, and our own suppressed excitement that gave zest to the conversation. Certainly a pleasanter evening neither of us ever spent."

"I thought you said that you had seen a ghost in the Grange?" asked Holmes.

"Oh, I am coming to that part, Mr. Holmes, don't you worry. You see, around midnight, I began to change my mind. Outside, the wind was screaming, and the moon shone out fitfully from between the dark clouds that drifted across the sky. And then I heard a noise in the corridor – the sound of a heavy door slamming."

Holmes' lip curled up. "It is amazing what the wind may accomplish, Mr. Brocket."

"Scoff if you wish, Mr. Holmes, but the next thing really set my nerves a tingle. A gentle pit pat, pit pat started in the room close to Tom's elbow. We both sprang to our feet, for what else could this be but the blood of those poor youngsters who were cut up by that model father of theirs, dripping down from their bedroom above?"

"It sounds like a leaky roof, and the rain had gotten in," said Holmes, mildly.

Jack Brocket shook his head. "So thought Tom at first, but when he looked at the liquid, it was the colour of blood."

I admit that I was spellbound by the agent's tale, but Holmes was less impressed. "So is water when tinged with rust."

"True enough, Mr. Holmes," said Brocket, "though I admit that I did not think of that at the time. Instead, all I could think about was how the Grange was cursed, and that I had seen enough. I begged Tom to come away with me, but he shook off my grasp, and cried that a drop or two of blood should not cow me. He pushed past me and dashed into the corridor. What a moment that was! If I should live to be a hundred, I could never shake off my vivid remembrance of it. Outside, the wind was still howling past the windows, while an occasional flash of lightning illuminated the old Grange. Within, there was no sound save the creaking of the door as it was thrown back and the gentle pit-pat of that ghastly shower from above. Then Tom tottered back into the room and grasped me by the arm. When he spoke, it was in an awestruck whisper. He said that there was something coming up the corridor.

"A horrible fascination led us to the door, and we peered together down the long and dark passage. One side was pierced by numerous openings through which the moonlight streamed throwing little patches of light upon the dark floor. Far down the passage, we could see that something was obscuring first one of these bright spots, then the next, then another. It vanished in the gloom, and then it reappeared where the next window cast its light, and then it vanished again. It was coming rapidly towards us. Now it was only four windows from us, now three, now two, one, and then the figure of a man emerged into the glare of light that burst from our open door. He was running rapidly and vanished into the gloom on the other side of us. His dress was old fashioned and dishevelled, what seemed to be long dark ribbons hung down among his hair, on each side of his swarthy face. But that face itself – when shall I ever forget it? As he ran, he kept it half turned back, as if expecting some pursuer, and his countenance expressed such a degree of hopeless despair, and of dreadful fear, that – frightened as I was – my heart bled for him.

"As we followed the direction of his horror stricken gaze, we saw that he had indeed a pursuer. As before we could trace the dark shadow flitting over the white flecks of moonlight, as before it emerged into the circle of light thrown by our candles and fire. It was a beautiful and stately lady, a woman perhaps eight and twenty years of age, with the low dress and gorgeous train of last century's fashion. We both remarked that beneath her lovely chin, upon one side of the neck were four small dark spots, and on the other side, one larger one. She swept by us, looking neither to the right nor left, but with her stony gaze bent upon the spot where the fugitive had vanished. Then she too was lost in the darkness. A minute later, as we stood there still gazing, a horrible shriek, a scream of awful agony, rang out high above the wind and the thunder, and then all was still inside the house.

"I don't know how long we both stood there, spellbound, holding on to each other's arms. It must have been some time, for the fresh candle was flickering in the socket when Tom, with a shudder, walked rapidly down the passage, still grasping my hand. Without a word, we passed out through the mouldering hall door, out into the storm and the rain, over the garden wall, through the silent village and up the avenue. It was not until we were in my comfortable little smoking room, and Tom – from sheer force of habit – had lit a cigar, that he seemed to recover his equanimity at all.

" 'Well, Jack,' were the first words he said, 'what do you think of ghosts now?'

" 'We have seen a horrible sight,' said I. 'What a face he had, Tom! And those ghastly ribbons hanging from his hair, what were those, Tom?'

" 'Ribbons! Why, Jack, do you not know seaweed when you see it? And I've seen those dark marks that were on the woman's neck before now, and so have you I have little doubt.'

" 'Yes,' said I, 'those were the marks of four fingers and a thumb. It was the strangled woman, Tom. God preserve us from ever seeing such a sight again!' And I never have, Mr. Holmes. Of course, I have never set foot in the Grange again either. I assisted Silas with the purchase and provisioning of the place all from a respectable distance."

"And your friend Mr. Hulton," asked Holmes. "I presume he will corroborate your story?"

"Yes, if you can find him. The following morning, he went down to London, and soon afterwards set sail for the coffee estates of his father in Ceylon. Since then, I have lost sight of him. I do not know whether he is alive or dead. But of one thing I am very sure – that if he is alive, he never thinks without a shudder of our terrible night in the haunted Grange of

Goresthorpe."

§

"What did you make of Mr. Brocket, Watson?" asked Holmes, as we departed the man's chambers. "Did you note that the ledger in which he was so furiously scribbling when we entered was upside down?"

I shook my head. "I can hardly say, Holmes. I must admit that his story was quite vivid."

"Indeed. The question is whether he truly believes it, or is he merely a confidence artist of unusual skill?"

"So what is our next course of action?"

"It may be a little early in the morning for most of us to indulge, but I think we should go round to the 'Lame Dog' for a quick pint. It is just a few blocks away."

He led me to the public house in question, which plainly catered to a class of clientele who little minded the rougher side of life. There, I spent an agreeable hour playing billiards with a former Army sergeant, while Holmes became friendly with the regular patrons. Eventually he signalled to me that he had concluded his interviews and he settled our tab.

When we stepped back out to the pavement, I asked whether he had any success.

"Oh, yes. I had, at first, considered the possibility that the house steward Watkins – who certainly had a bone of contention with his former employer – was somehow involved. However, I think we now have a much clearer suspect. For it seems that the so-called Mr. Abrahams is none other than Jemmy Wilson, also known as the Nottingham crackster."[111]

"Excellent!" I cried. "We can have Lestrade pick him up."

Holmes shook his head. "I am afraid that it will not be that easy, Watson."

"Why not?"

"First, there is no proof. We would be relying upon Mr. and Mrs. D'Odd picking Wilson out of a line-up. Even if we trusted that their poor vision was capable of such a task – you saw the thickness of their glasses – if you were the prosecution, Watson, would you want to put Mr. D'Odd on the witness stand? The man – while engagingly eccentric – plainly has a few screws loose.[112] A clever barrister for the defence will turn him into a laughingstock. And even if we managed to put away Wilson for a year or two, that action will not suffice to get back the D'Odd's plate, as Wilson will never give up the location where he has stashed it."

"So do you have a better plan?"

He smiled. "In fact, I do. How would you like to be raised to the peerage, Watson?"

§

As I was to learn the following afternoon, it seemed that my peerage was to be a temporary one. Holmes had bundled me into a carriage, which stopped at Leicester Square long enough for a young woman to climb aboard with us. She was fashionably dressed, beautiful, and possessed of a queenly presence. I thought she was an aristocrat of some sort, though Holmes introduced her as simply Miss Minnie Cavill.

"Where are we going, Holmes?" I asked, as the carriage turned south and passed over Westminster Bridge.

"Near Horsham."

"Whatever for?"

"Do you recall the Arnsworth Castle business?"

"Of course."[113]

"Well, then you know that Lord Arnsworth was quite appreciative of my efforts on his behalf. I wired to him yesterday asking for a brief loan of his great hall, as well as his esteemed name, and he readily agreed."

"I do not understand."

Holmes smiled. "I have put about a certain type of public house that Lord Arnsworth was forced to relinquish his medieval plate several years ago as the security for an advancement of money that had gone awry via a series of poor investments. His fortunes now reversed, Arnsworth has been unable to re-purchase the original plate, but is hopeful of locating a suitably old replacement – for which he is willing to pay handsomely."

"And you believe that Jemmy Wilson will offer him the plate pilfered from the D'Odd's?"

"Indeed. Plate is far harder to move than coin or bullion, Watson. Most pawnbroker's will not touch it unless it comes direct from a noble house – as they well know that Scotland Yard is constantly on the look-out for stolen items that have entered their stores, especially soon after a major robbery has occurred."

"Wilson could melt it down," I noted.

"True enough. Though he would get far less for the melted silver than he would for the originally- crafted items. I believe it is likely that he will plan to hold onto the plate for a while, until the coast is clear. However, I also think it probable that – should a sufficiently lucrative possibility arise – he will be hard put to resist it. And why should he? The robbery of the D'Odd's occurred in Norfolk. How that could possibly be linked to a request to purchase medieval plate in Sussex will be beyond the imagination of even someone as clever as Jemmy Wilson. Indeed, Lord Arnsworth has had a note this afternoon that a gentleman by the name of Mr. Isaacs plans to call upon him this evening with a potential collection of plate for his consideration. I can only conclude that Isaacs and Abrahams are one and the same."

"And my role in this charade?"

"Why, you will be Lord Arnsworth, and Miss Cavill here shall be your lovely wife," said he, indicating our lovely companion. "She is – as you may have guessed – one of the rising stars of the stage. You should have seen her as Lady Anne at Drury Lane.[114] She brought down the house. I once did a small favour for her when she was rather short of funds, and she has graciously agreed to repay me now by playing this small part. I hardly anticipate any danger from Jemmy Wilson, but is always better to be safe than sorry. I thought you were rather more ready to handle a scuffle than the real Lord Arnsworth – who is just shy of sixty."

"What about you?"

As I watched, Holmes' face transformed to that of another man. "Your servant, sir," said he, with a formal bow. Miss Cavill laughed and clapped her hands at his performance. His face returned to its normal appearance. "I shall be your butler, Stevens."

I shook my head in rueful admiration of Holmes' penchant for the dramatic, but could conceive of no better strategy by which we might catch Jemmy Wilson red-handed.

When we arrived at Arnsworth Castle, we found that the owners were most excited to be a part of Holmes' planned subterfuge. They even went so far as to insist that I stuff myself into one of Lord Arnsworth's suits, while Miss Cavill was permitted to wear some of Lady Arnsworth's jewels – all to provide an extra verisimilitude to Holmes' stage production. My friend had brought with him his own change of clothes, and a quarter of an hour later, he had fully transmogrified himself into the butler Stevens.

We had not long to wait in our costumes before there was a peal at the outer bell, and the sound of a fly pulling up.[115] Mr. Isaacs proven to be a sturdy little podgy fellow, with a pair of wonderfully keen sparkling eyes and a mouth that was constantly stretched in a good-humoured, if somewhat artificial, grin. He carried a large and obviously heavy leather bag.

"And 'ow are you, sir?" he asked, wringing my hand with the utmost effusion. "And the missus, 'ow is she? And all the others — 'ow's all their 'ealth?"

I intimated that we were all as well as could reasonably be expected. Mr. Isaacs glimpsed Miss Cavill out of the corner of his eye, and at once plunged at her with another string of inquiries as to her health, delivered so volubly and with such an intense earnestness, that I half expected to see him terminate his cross-examination by feeling her pulse and demanding a sight of her tongue. All this time his little eyes rolled round and round, shifting perpetually from the floor to the ceiling, and from the ceiling to the walls, taking in apparently every article of furniture in a single comprehensive glance.

Having satisfied himself that neither of us was in a pathological condition, Mr. Isaacs suffered me to lead him upstairs, all the while he was inspecting the castles' corridors and chambers with a most critical and observant eye, fingering the old tapestry with the air of a connoisseur, and remarking in an undertone that it would 'match uncommon nice.' It was not until he reached the banqueting-hall, however, that his admiration reached the pitch of enthusiasm. A repast had been laid out for him, to which he did ample justice. He had carried the heavy bag along with him, and deposited it under his chair during the meal. It was not until the table had been cleared and Isaacs and I were left together, with just the supposed butler attending us, that he broached the matter on which he had come down.

"I hunderstand," he remarked, puffing at a trichinopoly, "that you want my 'elp in fitting up this 'ere 'ouse with some plate."

I acknowledged the correctness of his surmise, while mentally chuckling at those restless eyes of his, which still danced about the room as if he were making an inventory of the contents.

"And you won't find a better man for the job, though I says it as shouldn't," continued our visitor.

"You don't mean to say that you carry an entire set of plate about in your bag?" I remarked, with the diffidence I thought expected by a lord.

"Not at all, sir. This is just the prime example," said he. He reached into his bag and removed a large platter. "Now this is a noble, solid piece – none of your electro-plate trash![116] That's the way as things ought to be done, sir. Plenty more where that came from, all down in the fly with my associate. I can't say fairer than that."

As all Mr. Isaacs' protestations of fairness were accompanied by a cunning leer and a wink from one or other of his wicked little eyes, the impression of candour was somewhat weakened.

He turned to Holmes in his guise as the butler. "Send up some brandy and the box of weeds, my good man. The master and I can sit here by the fire and do the preliminaries." He looked back at me. "I can see that you like it, sir, so now it is just a matter of how much it will take to transfer this fine plate from my hands to your sideboard. I must tell you that the individual whom I represent is most loathe to relinquish the plate, it having been in their family for generations. But when times are tough, as they say, sir, we must resort to tough choices."

"Would you like your brandy first, sir," asked Holmes, "or a cigar? We have genuine Havanas."

"What's that?" asked Isaacs. "Both of them together, of course."

"Very good, sir. Here you are," said Holmes, proffering a cigar.

Mr. Isaacs held out his hand. At that instant, the cigar vanished and I heard a sharp click and the jangling of metal. Isaacs turned and stared at the glittering handcuffs that had appeared as if by magic on his wrist.

"What's all this then?" he cried.

"It's five years, I think, Jemmy Wilson, unless you have a lenient magistrate," said Holmes. "I have no doubt that Mr. and Mrs. D'Odd will testify that this plate is identical to the one stolen from Goresthorpe Grange three nights ago. However, it is not just robbery this time. You compounded your crime with the poisoning of Mr. D'Odd."

The man stared around, but eventually decided that his chances of making a break for it were slim to none and the game was up. "Well, now, it's all just a bit o' fun, that's all. I didn't mean no harm. I made sure the old blighter didn't take too much of the chloral – just enou' to give him some pleasant dreams. Which is what he asked for, ain't it?"

§

Before we departed London, Holmes had wired in advance to Scotland Yard informing them that he intended to bring the Nottingham cracker to justice that evening, and if Inspector Lestrade was interested, he should avail himself of meeting us at Arnsworth Castle – ideally in the company of a pair of burly constables. Lestrade had seen Holmes be correct too many times before to discount such advice. In the end, the inspector gladly took the handcuffed Jemmy Wilson into custody, even if he little comprehended the entire tale of Goresthorpe Grange, which Holmes had attempted to relate in a somewhat abbreviated fashion.

Upon further questioning of Jemmy Wilson – and his accomplice Archie Tully, who had been waiting in the fly below – the pair of them admitted that they had simply overheard Jack Brocket's indiscreet inquiries, and promptly availed themselves of the tempting opening. It appeared that Mr. Brocket was innocent of any malicious intent when he sent the supposed ghost-procurer to the home of Mr. and Mrs. D'Odd.

Both their plate and their faith in their cousin restored, the D'Odd's were exceptionally pleased with the outcome of the case. A few weeks later, an additional note arrived from Mr. D'Odd. Holmes glanced at the words and then tossed it aside, turning his attention back to the black-letter edition he had picked up at a stall the prior evening. Out of curiosity, I read the note over, which ran:

> Mr. Sherlock Holmes, Esq. 221B Baker Street, London, NW1
> My dear Mr. Holmes,
> I am writing to let you know that I remain most grateful for your assistance with the successful return of the family plate. It would have been a severe inconvenience to replace it, especially at Mr. Brocket's

rates. Your commission was exceptionally fair, and I will recommend your services to all of my friends and acquaintances, should they ever find themselves in a troubling spot. If you, in turn, should ever wish to call upon us, you will find yourself most welcome. However, please note that we have recently made a change in our residence.

It seems that Mr. Abrahams – for by such name will I long remember him – was quite efficacious in his side-business of spirit mongering. Wouldn't you know it, but the night after our plate was returned, we began to be visited by a rather unhappy apparition. I had thought to select only one such spectre, and the lady was just as I imagined. However, I had not bargained for the other one. He is certainly old-fashioned, though possessed of some rather ghastly ribbons that hang from his hair. Nevertheless, I am displeased by how it seems as if she is always be chasing after him. And Jorrocks was right about the nocturnal wails. One night was plenty enough for me. A lifetime of such shrieking would be enough to turn my remaining hairs white.

In fact, my night's experiences have cured me of my mania for the supernatural, and have quite reconciled me to inhabiting the humdrum nineteenth-century edifice on the outskirts of London upon which Mrs. D. has long had in her mind's eye.

Your affectionate friend,
SILAS D'ODD, ESQ.
THE ELMS, BRIXTON

I set this down and went about my day. It was not until a few days later that an unexpected thought popped into my brain. If Jack Brocket had never told Silas D'Odd about the legend of the ghosts of Godfrey Marsden and the poor lady that he had strangled, then how did the description match so precisely?

Mr. Sherlock Holmes may be unwilling to admit to the possibility of the supernatural, but I am not so certain.

§

THE ADVENTURE OF THE FABRICATED VISION

It was a late January morning in 1887, when one of the most curious cases of his career to date confronted my friend, Mr. Sherlock Holmes. I had found that while Holmes possessed a rather abstract interest in certain metaphysical aspects of society and history – such as miracle plays, the Buddhism of Ceylon, or the razor of Ockham – he was always sceptical that there was a transcendent reality beyond what is readily observable to the senses. Yet, as I look back over the course of our adventures together, the case of Mr. Henry Darnley has – for me, at least – always suggested that something nebulous remained hidden behind the veil of our limited perception.[117]

I had stopped by the well-remembered suite of rooms at Baker Street that I had shared with Holmes prior to my marriage.[118] I made a point of calling regularly, as I did not wish for us to drift apart, and I was always keen to hear details of how Holmes was employing his extraordinary powers.

He seemed if not demonstrative – for such was not his way – at least pleased enough to see me. We sank into our respective armchairs across from the fireplace and he offered me a cigar from the coalscuttle. So ensconced, we fell into a long conversation regarding both his various adventures in the criminal underbelly of London, as well as some of the more outré medical cases which had recently come through my practice, for he had long had a curiosity regarding the intersection of pathology and crime.

"This reminds me, Watson, that you may be interested in my next client," said he.

"Oh, how so?"

Holmes glanced at his pocket watch. "I am expecting him any minute now. Lestrade, who felt that there was no criminal element at play, has sent round him. However, the man seemed desperate enough, and wrote that he wished to consult with me regarding an episode of madness in one of his employees."

"Well, I am hardly a psychologist, Holmes. I would much rather stitch up a man's skin and sinew than attempt to repair his broken mind."

"I too am unclear how I may be of assistance, and yet, the state of my finances is not such that I can afford to turn away a potential client – especially if the case is too peculiar for the imagination of Scotland Yard. Ah, I think I hear him now."

At that moment, there was a loud ring at the bell, followed by the familiar steps of my former landlady. She gave a crisp knock before entering, holding before her a card upon the brass salver. Holmes motioned for me to pick it up. I did so, and I read it aloud:

> TIMOTHY JOHNSON, ACA[119]
> JOHNSON, ROBERTS & COMPANY
> CHARTERED ACCOUNTANTS
> 2 FINCH LANE

Holmes nodded. "Pray ask him to step up, Mrs. Hudson."

A few minutes later, a tall, thin man of between fifty and sixty years entered the room with a diffident step. His suit was well cut and pressed, and his cheeks were closely shaven. However, his dull grey eyes and pale face suggested a man who saw little of the sun whenever it made one of its rare appearances over the City.

Holmes introduced me as his trusted friend and indicated that the accountant should feel free to speak plainly in front of me.

Mr. Johnson nodded his head in response to these instructions. "Are you familiar, Mr. Holmes, with the affair of Sir Roger Shoemaker?"

"The alderman of Cordwainer?" replied Holmes.[120] "I have been following it in *The Times*."

"Then you are aware that Sir Roger is from an ancient and respected family. His purported misdeeds are the talk of the nation."

"Indeed. But what has this to do with your firm?"

"Sir Roger has been accused of defalcation.[121] He utilized the firm of White and Wotherspoon to keep his accounts, such that – should he be proven guilty – that venerable company is on the verge of being dragged down with him. My firm was engaged by the prosecuting lawyers to review White and Wotherspoon's accounts for evidence of malfeasance. It was a gigantic task, as there were twenty thick ledgers to be examined and checked, and the lawyers gave us less than three weeks to evaluate them all in time for the trial – which was scheduled for the 21st of this month."

"Ah yes, I recall reading that it has been postponed?"

"Indeed. But only for three days, and that was two days ago. We are running out of time to prove our case. Tomorrow afternoon, if I am unable to supply proof of Sir Roger's guilt, the case for the prosecution will collapse."

Holmes shrugged. "I fail to see how I may be of help?"

"You see, Mr. Holmes, I had originally considered utilizing a team of accountants upon this task. However, I worried that the ledgers might be so convoluted that – where a group of individuals might miss a pattern of clues – a single man might be able to see the forest for the trees, if you will excuse the metaphor. I asked myself who was on track to become a junior partner. Who was my most reliable and hard-working man? I could only conclude that Henry Darnley was the man I needed. I left this vital bit of business entirely in his hands, confident that he would justify my choice."

"And did he?"

"That is the precise question, Mr. Holmes. At first, I had no doubts. He was at the office every day from ten to five, and then a second sitting from about eight in the evening to one in the morning. I have often thought that Mr. Darnley has accountancy seeped into his marrow."

"A queer obsession," I noted.

He looked over at me. "Ours is perhaps not the most glamourous occupation, Doctor. We are not the type to go running after villains and throwing them in chains, or sewing up a man who is bleeding to death. Yet there is drama in an accountant's life. When we find ourselves in the still early hours, while the entire world sleeps, hunting through column after column for those missing figures which will turn a respected alderman into a felon, well, you will hopefully understand that it is not such a prosaic profession after all."

Johnson turned back to Holmes and continued his account. "I spoke to Mr. Darnley on the 4th of January. It was a Monday, and I could tell that he had worked upon the case throughout the weekend, without pause. And I could see by the light in his eyes that he was onto something. No heavy game hunter ever got a finer thrill when first he caught sight of the trail of his quarry, even if the jungle through which Darnley had to follow Sir Roger's tracks before he got his kill was made up of twenty thick ledgers, rather than a tangle of trees and vines. Hard work – but rare sport, too, in a way!"

Holmes waved his hand. "The colourful metaphors are strictly unnecessary, Mr. Johnson. Just the facts will do. Pray continue."

"Well," said the man, looking somewhat put out, "I checked in with Darnley regularly, and he appeared to be making good progress upon the stack of twenty ledgers. He told me on the 6th of January that he had completed three of them. While the rascal Shoemaker had covered his tracks well, Darnley was convinced that he could pick them up for all that. By the 17th, the lawyers began to clamour for their material, as the trial was but four days away, and Darnley had finished reviewing only three-quarters of the ledgers. He promised to do the rest in a forced march, but noted that he already had enough evidence to give the lawyers, and anything else would be to spare. Darnley said that he had Shoemaker fast on a hundred counts, and that he expected that he would get a large share of the credit when the judge realized Shoemakers's true nature – a slippery, cunning rascal. Darnley claimed to have proof of false trading accounts, false balance-sheets, dividends drawn from capital, losses written down as profits, suppression of working expenses, manipulation of petty cash – a fine record!"

"And has something happened to Mr. Darnley?"

"You are most perspicacious, Mr. Holmes. In fact, three nights ago, Mr. Darnley collapsed in his home, slumped in his chair over the final ledger. His housekeeper found him and summoned his physician. Mr. Darnley is, at this moment, residing in Dr Andrew Sinclair's private hospital, raving about visions of the past."[122]

"A tragic tale of over-work, Mr. Johnson, but I fail to see your problem," said Holmes. "Darnley is alive. He may not be fit to testify directly, but his notes have not vanished, have they?"

"No," said Johnson shaking his head. "His figures are in the solicitor's possession, even as we speak. However, like Pepys before him, Darnley utilized a form of brachygraphy that we have been largely unable to decipher.[123] Moreover, even if we could, his notes are not in such a form that would be admissible in court. Darnley must himself testify regarding the nature of Shoemaker's crimes, or the case for the prosecution is likely to be thrown out. However, I can ill afford to put a lunatic before the court. We would be the laughingstock of the City. So, I ask you, Mr. Holmes – is Mr. Darnley fit to stand before a judge? Is his evidence against Shoemaker accurate, or yet another a fantasy?"

Holmes furrowed his brow. "This seems like the work for another accountant."

"There is no time for that!" cried Johnson. "We need an answer by tomorrow, and an accountant would take weeks."

"Then a psychologist. What does Dr Sinclair say?"

"That is unclear. When I spoke to the doctor, he seemed uncertain if Mr. Darnley was simply overstrained, or if he experienced an actual vision from the past. If it is the former, then I may feel confident in his work, for that was what broke him. However, if Darnley is seeing visions, I cannot allow the barrister for the defence – Sir Kenneth Bailey of Inner Temple – to examine him. Sir Kenneth is far too sharp – he would ferret out that Darnley has been in the hospital, and would probe and inquire until all comes out. Then we would be ruined. I simply cannot take the risk. I would rather say that we found nothing in the ledgers of White and Wotherspoon that would implicate Sir Roger than destroy the future of the firm."

§

Holmes was eventually persuaded to look into Mr. Johnson's case, which meant a trip to question the invalided Mr. Darnley. Dr Sinclair's hospital was located off Shoreditch, so Holmes engaged a hansom cab to take us along the New Road, veering right at Angel to follow City Road.

The hospital was a small affair, with under twenty beds, but to my professional eye, it looked to be smartly-run and clean. Nurses scurried about busily, and the patients appeared to be cared for well.

We were soon shown into the office of Dr Sinclair, where we found him seated behind his desk. This was littered with a precarious pile of medical notebooks, as well as several musty volumes – which looked to be historical records rather than professional texts. However, a mere glance at the man was sufficient for me to recognize a fellow man of science. He was rather past sixty, with a mane of flowing white hair. His face was rather square, his jaw strong, and piercing blue eyes shone under a thatched brow.

Holmes introduced us and the reason for our visit. At first, Dr Sinclair seemed somewhat reluctant to discuss the particulars of his patient; however, when Holmes explained that Mr Darnley's professional reputation was at stake, the physician relented.

"Very well," said Sinclair, reaching for his notebook and flipping through it. "Ah, yes, here we go. Mr. Darnley first came to see me on the 6th of January. He complained, not of a pain *per se*, but only a sort of fullness of the head with an occasional mist over the eyes. He thought perhaps some bromide, or chloral, or something of the kind might do him good."[124]

"Ah!" said Holmes, with interest. "And did you prescribe such an agent?"

Dr Sinclair shook his head. "I did not. I could tell that he was nervous and highly-strung and told him that drugs would not help him. Instead, I prescribed rest."

"And what was Mr. Darnley's response to your prescription?" asked Holmes.

"I am afraid that he did not take it well."

"How so?"

"If I recall correctly, I believe that he called me an 'ass,' and a 'foolish spouter of perfect nonsense.' He said that rest was out of the question, and that I might as well shout to a man who has a pack of wolves at his heels that what he wants is absolute quiet."

"A vivid image," said Holmes.

"Yes, well, that is hardly the most vivid image that Mr. Darnley has seen this month."

"What do you mean?"

Instead of answering, Dr Sinclair continued his tale. "Mr. Darnley returned to see me three days later. He was under considerable pressure, and I believe that he originally had little intention of seeing me again. Yet he felt that he had to, for a queer experience drove him to me. All in all, he is a curious psycho-physiological study."

"What was the peculiar experience?" asked Holmes. "You spoke of an image?"

"Yes, or perhaps I should say a vision, to be more precise. You see, Mr. Darnley has developed a mania of sorts regarding an old silver-framed mirror in his room. Now, if you are familiar with accountants, Mr. Holmes, you will know that they are a precise sort, and Darnley is no exception. He kept an exact record of his symptoms and sensations. I have been studying these notes, and they are interesting in themselves, and also because now – when I try to get him to speak of what he saw in the mirror – the visions all seem blurred and unreal, like some queer dream betwixt sleeping and waking."

"And what precisely did he see?"

"Upon the first occasion – which appeared as he was working at his desk – it was the vague outline of a woman's head, her eyes filled with a passionate emotion."

"It sounds as if he had dropped asleep over his figures, and that his experience was nothing more than a dream," said Holmes.

Dr Sinclair smiled. "I see that you are a sceptic, Mr. Holmes. Well, there is no doubt that is one possible explanation, and I suggested as such to Mr. Darnley. However, he responded that – and I quote – 'as a matter of fact, I was never more vividly awake in my life.' Still, I persisted in arguing this hypothesis with him, and told him that it was a subjective impression – a chimera of the nerves – begotten by worry and insomnia. I am not certain that he believed me, and he left my office an unsatisfied man."

"And your diagnosis?"

"It was plain that he was overly straining his nerves, risking a complete breakdown, even endangering his sanity. He was on the verge of a full-blown brain fever."

I concurred with Dr Sinclair's judgment, and said as much.

Holmes nodded. "What happened next?"

"Well, I was most concerned for him, so two days later – on the evening of the 11th of January – I went round to Darnley's house – he lives at Clerkenwell Close across from St. James's – in order to ensure that he was well."

"And was he?"

"Hardly. He gave me a smile at the door, but one that looked as if his nerves would break over it. When I asked how he was doing, Darnley said that he had determined that the mirror was a sort of barometer that marked his brain-pressure. For each night, he would reach out and rub it before going back to work. He then observed that it would cloud up before he reached the end of his task."

"He sounds quite unstable," I interjected.

"Indeed. Darnley was obsessed with that silver mirror, so I agreed to have a look at it. It was a highly polished affair, for all its age. He pointed out that something was scribbled in crabbed old characters upon the metalwork at the back. I examined this with a lens, but could make nothing of it. 'Sanc. X. Pal.' was my final reading of it, but that did not bring us any farther. I advised him to put it away into another room. However, he only laughed, saying something to the effect that after all, whatever he may see in it is – by my own account – only a symptom."

Holmes nodded gravely. "For a madman, he is most perceptive. It is in the cause that the danger lies – not the visions."

Dr Sinclair frowned. "What cause?"

"That remains to be determined," said Holmes. "Pray continue."

"I went round again on the morning of the 14th, and Darnley seemed somewhat improved. He reported that on the 12th, he had made good progress on the ledgers that had so consumed his time and thoughts. Therefore, he could afford to follow my advice to drop work for a day. It was quite evident that the visions depended entirely upon his nervous state, for he reported that he had sat in front of the mirror for an hour the night before, with no result whatever. His soothing day had chased them away. However, he had plainly not fully abandoned his obsession with the mirror. He had examined the mirror the prior evening under a good light, and besides the mysterious inscription *'Sanc. X. Pal.,'* he was able to discern some signs of heraldic marks, very faintly visible upon the silver."

"Ah, additional marks," said Holmes, with interest. "Could you recognise them?"

"They are plainly very ancient, as they are almost obliterated. As far as I could make out, the symbols are three spearheads, two above, and one below. Some sort of armorial bearings. Mr. Darnley agreed with my identification. I admit, Mr. Holmes, that his case deeply interested me. I cross-questioned him closely on the details of his vision. For I was torn in two by conflicting desires – the one that my patient should lose his symptoms, the other that the medium – for so I began to regard him – should solve this mystery of the past. I advised continued rest, but could not oppose him too violently when Darnley declared that he felt perfectly well again. He said that he intended that nothing else should stop him until his task was finished, so such a thing as rest was completely out of the question until the ten remaining ledgers had been checked."

"And how did he end up here?"

"Well, as he was adamant about continuing his excessive work and was refusing my advice, I stopped visiting him. I regret that decision now, of course, for I might have prevented his complete collapse. However, he eventually broke under the intolerable strain. He had worked himself to the limit. I was called in and had him brought here for the rest that he so desperately needed. After his collapse, he was insensible for the first two days, and only began to speak intelligibly last evening."

"Surely it is unusual for a man to suffer an attack of brain-fever solely from an immoderate amount of work?" said Holmes. "In my experience, it is usually a traumatic event that precipitates such a frenzy."

"I concur, Mr. Holmes, and in this case, I believe that there was something beyond work alone which brought low Mr. Darnley."

"Yes? What was it that drove him over the edge?"

Dr Sinclair smiled wryly. "You will not believe me if I told you. You should hear it from Darnley himself. Come, let us see if he is awake."

Sinclair rose, and picked up both his notebook on Darnley's case, as well as two of the old volumes from his desk. He led us out into the main corridor, and we made our way along the passage's whitewashed walls and umber-coloured doors. We climbed a stone staircase, and stopped in front of one of the propped-open doors.

The doctor rapped with his free hand, and a pale face looked up from the bed. "Mr. Darnley, how are you doing this afternoon?"

Darnley was a small man, nearing only thirty years of age, yet with thinning brown hair and thick glasses. He wore the provided white garments – so that everyone would know his place in the hospital – and from beneath these gowns, I noted his skin appeared rather rashy. When he spoke, his voice had a trace of a Scottish inflection. "Ah, Dr Sinclair, it is good to see you, sir!" he cried. "My figures must be out by a certain date; unless they are so, I shall lose the chance of my lifetime, so how on earth am I to rest? I'll take a week or so after the trial."

"You are resting now, Mr. Darnley," said the doctor, gently.

"Nonsense!" the little man cried. "Stop work? It is absurd to ask such a thing. It is like a long-distance race. You feel queer at first and your heart thumps and your lungs pant, but if you have only the pluck to keep on, you get your second wind. I will stick to my work and wait for my second wind. If it never comes – all the same, I will stick to my work. Two ledgers are done, and I am well on in the third."

"According to Mr. Johnson, you have completed rather more than that, Mr. Darnley," said Sinclair.

"Have I?" said Darnley, looking confused. "That is good. Still there is more work to be done. Well, I'll stand the strain and I'll take the risk, and so long as I can sit in my chair and move a pen, I'll follow the old sinner's slot."[125]

"I have brought two visitors who are interested in your case," said the doctor.

"Your employer, Mr. Johnson, sent us," Holmes explained. "I am Sherlock Holmes, and this is my associate, Dr John Watson."

"I assure you, gentlemen, that Dr Sinclair has done all that is possible. If only I had listened to him sooner, I would not even be in this predicament. Please thank Mr. Johnson for his kindness, but I shall not require your services."

"Mr. Darnley," said Holmes, gently, "we are not here to assume Dr Sinclair's duty. Rather, we have come to ask you about Sir Roger Shoemaker."

The man began to chuckle to himself. "Ah, I see. You know, I saw the fat fellow once at a City dinner, his red face glowing above a white napkin. He looked disdainfully at the little pale man sitting at the end of the table, believing that I could be neither a help nor a threat to his schemes. He would have been pale too if he could have seen the task that would be mine. Good Lord! Well, I will have at it, and if human brain and nerve can stand the strain, I'll win out at the other side."

"Your work is already done, Mr. Darnley," said Holmes. "The ledgers are complete and your notes in the hands of the prosecuting lawyers."

"Are they?" Darnley cried, shaking his head. "Yes, I remember now. Well then, the hunt is over. I must say that I am glad to be done with those endless figures."

"I am most interested in your mirror, sir."

"My mirror, you say? Perhaps it would have been wiser after all if I had packed away the mirror. I had an extraordinary experience with it. Yet I find it so interesting, so fascinating, that even now I think that I will keep it in its place. Still, I wonder what on earth the meaning of all that I have seen is?"

"Perhaps if you tell us of what you viewed in the mirror, while it is still fresh in your mind?" suggested Holmes.

The little man nodded. "Of course. The mirror is so situated, you understand, that as I sit at the table I can usually see nothing in it but the reflection of the red window curtains. I will – from time to time – reach out and adjust it. However, a queer thing happened a few nights back. I had been working for some hours, very much against the grain, with continual bouts of that mistiness of which I had complained to Dr Sinclair. Again and again, I had to stop and clear my eyes. Well, on one of these occasions I chanced to look at the mirror. It had the oddest appearance. The red curtains that should have been reflected in it were no longer there, but the glass seemed to be clouded and steamy, not on the surface – which glittered like steel – but deep down in the very grain of it. This opacity, when I stared hard at it, appeared to slowly rotate this way and that, until it was a thick white cloud swirling in heavy wreaths. So real and solid was it, and so reasonable was I, that I remember turning, with the idea that the curtains were on fire. But everything was deadly still in the room – no sound save the ticking of the clock, no movement save the slow gyration of that strange woolly cloud deep in the heart of the old mirror."

"Only clouds?" asked Holmes. "I thought you had perhaps seen people?"

"Not at first. Then, as I looked, the mist, or smoke, or cloud, or whatever one may call it, seemed to coalesce and solidify at two points quite close together, and I was aware, with a thrill of interest rather than of fear, that these were two eyes looking out into the room. A vague outline of a head I could see – a woman's by the hair, but this was very shadowy. Only the eyes were quite distinct; such eyes – dark, luminous – filled with some passionate emotion, fury, or horror, I could not say which. Never have I seen eyes that were so full of intense, vivid life. They were not fixed upon me, but stared out into the room. As I sat erect, I passed my hand over my brow, and made a strong conscious effort to pull myself together. The dim head then faded into the general opacity, the mirror slowly cleared, and there were the red curtains once again."

"Fascinating," said Holmes. "Why do you think you saw this particular shape? And who is the woman?"

"The very questions I asked myself, sir!" cried Darnley. "And I wondered what was the dreadful emotion that I read in those magnificent brown eyes? I can only say that they came between my work and me. For the first time, the following morn I had done less than the daily tally that I had marked out. Perhaps that is why I had no abnormal sensations that second night."

"But they returned again?"

"Oh yes, Mr. Holmes, and each time more vivid and distinct than the last. The next time, I suppose it was about one in the morning, and I was closing my books in preparation for staggering off to bed, when I saw her there in front of me. Nothing had appeared in the mirror all evening. I would even reach out and rub it, as if it were the bottle of a genie in the Arabian Nights – to no avail. Then everything changed. The stage of mistiness and development must have passed unobserved, and there she was in all her beauty and passion and distress, as clear-cut as if she were really in the flesh before me. The figure was small, but very distinct – so much so that every feature, and every detail of dress, are stamped in my memory. She was seated on the extreme left of the mirror. A sort of shadowy figure crouched down beside her – I could dimly discern that it was a man. Behind them, it was cloudy, in which I saw vague figures – figures that moved. It was not a mere picture upon which I looked, I tell you. It was a scene in life, an actual episode. She crouched and quivered. The man beside her cowered down. The vague figures made abrupt movements and gestures. All my fears were swallowed up in my interest. It was maddening to see so much and not to see more."

"Can you describe the woman?" asked Holmes.

"To the smallest point. She was very beautiful and quite young – not more than five-and-twenty, I should judge. Her hair was of a very rich brown, with a warm chestnut shade fining into gold at the edges. A little flat-pointed cap came to an angle in front, and was made of lace edged with pearls. Her forehead was high, too high perhaps for perfect beauty; but one would not have it otherwise, as it gives a touch of power and strength to what would otherwise be a softly feminine face. The brows are most delicately curved over heavy eyelids, and then came those wonderful eyes – so large, so dark, so full of over-mastering emotion, of rage and horror, contending with a pride of self-control that holds her from sheer frenzy! The cheeks were pale, the lips white with agony, the chin and throat most exquisitely rounded. She sat and leaned forward in the chair, straining and rigid, cataleptic with horror. The dress was black velvet, a jewel gleaming like a flame in the breast, and a golden crucifix smouldered in the shadow of a fold. This is the lady whose image still lives in the old silver mirror."

"Amazing!" interjected Dr Sinclair. "What dire deed could it be which has left its impress there, so that now, in another age, if the spirit of a man be but worn down to it, he may be conscious of its presence?"

"Hmmm, perhaps," said Holmes. "Was there anything else?" he asked Darnley.

"Ah, yes," cried Darnley, "there was one other detail. On the left side of the skirt of the black dress was, as I thought at first, a shapeless bunch of white ribbon. Then, as I looked more intently or as the vision defined itself more clearly, I perceived what it actually was. It was the hand of a man, clenched and knotted in agony, which held on with a convulsive grasp to the fold of the dress. The rest of the crouching figure was a mere vague outline, but that strenuous hand shone clear on the dark background, with a sinister suggestion of tragedy in its frantic clutch. The man was frightened – horribly frightened. That I could clearly discern. What had terrified him so? Why did he grip the woman's dress? I believed that the answer lay amongst those moving figures in the background. They had brought danger both to him and to her. The interest of the thing fascinated me. I thought no more of its relation to my own nerves. I stared and stared as if in a theatre. However, I could get no farther. The mist thinned. There were tumultuous movements in which all the figures were vaguely concerned. Then the mirror was clear once more that evening."

"But the vision returned a final time?" asked Holmes.

"Indeed. It was on the 20th of January, I believe. That day, I spent some twenty or thirty minutes carefully positioning the mirror in order to optimize my viewing of it, and then returned to my work. That night, the mirror in its silver frame was like a stage, brilliantly lit, in which a drama was in progress. There was no longer any mist. The oppression of my nerves had wrought this amazing clarity. Every feature, every movement, was as clear-cut as in life. To think that I, a tired accountant, the most prosaic of mankind, with the account-books of a swindling bankrupt before me, should be chosen of all the human race to look upon such a scene!"

"So it was the same scene as before?"

"It was the same scene and the same figures, Mr. Holmes, but the drama had advanced a stage. The tall young man was holding the woman in his arms. She strained away from him and looked up at him with loathing in her face. They had torn the crouching man away from his hold upon the skirt of her dress. A dozen of them were round him – savage men, bearded men. They hacked at him with knives. All seemed to strike him together. Their arms rose and fell. The blood did not flow from him – it squirted. His red dress was dabbled in it. He threw himself this way and that, purple upon crimson, like an overripe plum. Still they hacked, and still the jets shot from him. It was horrible – horrible! They dragged him kicking to the door. The woman looked over her shoulder at him and her mouth gaped. I heard nothing, but I knew that she was screaming. And then, whether it was this nerve-racking vision before me, or whether – my task finished – all the overwork of the past weeks came in one crushing weight upon me, the room danced round me, the floor seemed to sink away beneath my feet, and

I remembered no more."

"And that was the last time you have looked into the mirror?"

"It was. To be honest, I am not certain that I have the strength to do so again. The visions are too much for my nerves. And yet, I wonder whether I shall ever penetrate what they all mean?"

"As you may have heard, Mr. Holmes," said Dr Sinclair, "Mr. Darnley's landlady found him early the following morning stretched senseless before the silver mirror."

"I knew nothing myself until yesterday mid-day, when I awoke in the deep peace of the doctor's nursing home," said Darnley.

"And you have listened to this story before, Dr Sinclair?" asked Holmes.

"Oh yes, Mr. Darnley told it to me last night. At first, I would not allow him to speak of such matters, for I did not wish to bring about a recurrence of his brain fever. But he seems to be making progress, so I attended with an absorbed interest."

"And what do you make of it?"

"You don't identify this with any well-known scene in history?" he asked, with suspicion in his voice.

Holmes assured him that he knew nothing of history, and I confirmed that this was one of his limits, along with his rather narrow knowledge of astronomy and politics.

"Well, you share that trait with Mr. Darnley here," said Dr Sinclair, chuckling. "What of you, Dr Watson?"

I rubbed my moustache. "I admit that there is something familiar about it, but I cannot put my finger on it."

"Well, I suppose that I may forgive you, for we are talking about an episode that transpired over three hundred years ago. Have none of you any idea from whence that mirror came and to whom it once belonged?" Sinclair continued.

"Have you?" I asked, for he spoke with meaning.

"It's incredible," said Sinclair, "and yet how else can one explain it? The scenes, which Mr. Darnley described before, suggested it, but now it has gone beyond all range of coincidence. This morning, I consulted some pertinent tomes, and made various notes about what I have found." He stepped forward and placed the two musty volumes upon Darnley's bed.[126]

"These you may consult at your leisure," he continued. "I also have some notes here which you can confirm. There is not a doubt that what you have seen, Mr. Darnley, is the murder of David Rizzio by the Scottish nobles in the presence of Mary, which occurred in March 1566.[127] Your description of the woman is accurate. The high forehead and heavy eyelids combined with great beauty could hardly apply to another woman. The tall young man was her husband, Henry Stuart, also known as Lord Darnley."[128]

The accountant's brow rose in amazement. "What a coincidence!"

"Ah, but your tongue has a trace of Glaswegian accent," said Holmes. "Surely you have some Scottish blood?"

"Of course. My father hails from a small village outside of Glasgow – and I was born there, before we moved to London when I was a boy of ten."

"There is more," said Dr Sinclair. "Rizzio, says the chronicle, 'was dressed in a loose dressing-gown of furred damask, with hose of russet velvet.' With one hand, he clutched Mary's gown, with the other, he held a dagger. Your fierce, hollow-eyed man must have been Lord Ruthven, who was new-risen from a bed of sickness.[129] Every detail is exact."

"But why to me?" asked Darnley, in bewilderment. "Why of all the human race did they appear to me?"

"Because you were in the fit mental state to receive the impression," said Dr Sinclair. "And because you chanced to own the mirror which gave the impression."

"The mirror! You think, then, that it was Mary's mirror – that it stood in the room where the deed was done?"

"I am convinced that it was Mary's mirror," continued Dr Sinclair. "She had been Queen of France.[130] Her personal property would be stamped with the Royal arms. What we took to be three spear-heads were really the lilies of France."

"And the inscription?"

"Ah yes! 'Sanc. X. Pal.' You may expand it into *Sanctae Crucis Palatium*. Someone has made a note upon the mirror as to whence it came. It was the Palace of the Holy Cross."

"Holyrood!" cried Darnley.[131]

"Exactly. Your mirror came from Holyrood," concluded the doctor. "You have had one very singular experience, and have escaped. I trust that you will never put yourself into the way of having such another."

"Fascinating," said Darnley, drawing the top volume into his lap, and beginning to flip through the pages, each time licking his index finger.

Holmes had been silent during this exchange. "You have indeed had a singular experience, Mr. Darnley, and I echo Dr Sinclair's advice. I have but one final question for you, sir. Where did you acquire the silver mirror?" he asked.

Darnley considered this for a moment. "It was given to me by an old friend from school who had a taste for antiquities, and he – as I happen to know – picked it up at a sale. I believe that he had no notion where it originally came from."

"Your friend's name?"

"Patrick Rootes."

"And his address?"

"12 Devonshire Square."

"Very good," said Holmes, turning to the physician. "Dr Sinclair, I trust that you agree that Mr. Darnley has recovered to the degree necessary to testify in tomorrow's trial of Sir Roger Shoemaker?"

"Yes, I suppose that would be safe enough, as long as he comes back here afterwards to recuperate after the strain of a deposition. We have more work to do to prevent a recurrence of his brain fever. I certainly do not think he is ready to gaze into the mirror again."

"On that, I wholeheartedly agree with you," said Holmes. "In fact, Mr. Darnley, if I may be so bold, may I suggest that you donate it. The British Museum would be glad to have it, and your credit from the doubtlessly successful impending prosecution of the Shoemaker case will be even further compounded."

§

"So you intend to recommend to Mr. Johnson that Darnley be allowed to testify?" I asked as we departed the hospital.

Holmes pursed his lips. "A difficult question, Watson. On the one hand, we can plainly see that the man is not yet fully himself again. However, his ultimate mental collapse did not begin immediately. Therefore, any findings from the initial ledgers are, at least, likely valid."

"And the later ledgers? What if those contain the critical details that implicate Sir Roger?"

"Indeed. This is why we must determine how far we may trust Mr. Darnley's sanity."

"What then is our next course of action?"

"A visit to Mr. Darnley's house. I should very much like to see this silver mirror for myself."

"For what purpose?"

"Are you not curious, Watson, to see if the visions may be recreated?"

I frowned and peered at him. "Are you serious, Holmes?"

The corner of his mouth curled up. "We shall see."

As it was almost two miles between Dr Sinclair's hospital and the abode of Mr. Darnley, Holmes waved down a passing hansom. That conveyance swiftly rattled down Old Street and deposited us at our destination a quarter of an hour later. Darnley's apartment was situated in a plain brick building, its staring façade lit by the harsh glare and tawdry luminosity of the public house across from it.

A thought occurred to me. "I do say, Holmes, unless I missed it, you neglected to borrow Mr. Darnley's key."

He smiled and removed several skeleton keys from his coat pocket. "As you know, Watson, the opening of locks is a particular hobby of mine. Unless Mr. Darnley has equipped his door with a particularly sophisticated lock, it should prove to be only a matter of minutes before I have it open."

Obscured in a convenient archway from the probing eyes of any passing constables, Holmes was true to his word. We were soon inside Mr. Darnley's house, with Holmes leading the way along the dark passage, ducking his head into each door as we went. He soon found the room that he was seeking. "Hallo, Watson! This is a rather impressive thing!"

I followed Holmes into the chamber that – judging by the paper-strewn desk – Darnley utilized as a study. In the corner of the room, turned in such a way as to primarily display the red window curtains across from it, was the silver mirror. It was large – three feet across and two feet high – and leaned against the back of a side-table to the left of the desk. The frame was flat, about three inches across and was plainly very old. The glass part projected with a bevelled edge, and had the magnificent reflecting power that is only – as it seems to me – to be found in very old mirrors. There was a feeling of perspective when you look into it such as no modern glass could ever give.

I said as much to Holmes, and he merely shook his head. "You see what you want to believe, Watson."

"What do you mean?"

"Your brain equates – at a level likely even below your perception – that something this old must be expensive and therefore of high quality."

I bristled slightly at this charge. "So you do not think it is a splendid piece?"

He shrugged. "It is a mirror."

"Not at all. If Dr Sinclair's theory is correct; it is a direct channel to the past."

"Yes, well, let us explore that hypothesis further. If you will do me the favour, Watson, of sitting at Mr. Darnley's desk and gazing into the mirror – no, do not touch it, leave it just as is – I will inspect the marks to confirm Dr Sinclair's impressions."

I did as he requested and stared into the silver mirror for a span of some twenty minutes. However, try as I might, the mirror remained just that. No swirling clouds or beautiful women appeared in it.

Meanwhile, Holmes was engaged in inspecting the back of the mirror with his large magnifying glass. After this task was complete, he used a stray rag to polish the edge of the frame. He finally straightened his back and turned to me. "I perceive that you have had no visions, Watson," said he.

"No," I admitted. "And from this, you conclude that Mr. Darnley is mad."

He shook his head. "Not so. In fact, from what I have seen here, I am quite convinced by Mr. Darnley's story. He has undoubtedly had a vision of the murder of David Rizzio in front of Mary, Queen of Scots."

§

Despite my cry of astonishment at this pronouncement, Holmes would speak no more of it. Instead, he merely smiled diffidently. "There are still a few loose ends, Watson; however, I believe that I may just provide a valuable service to Mr. Johnson tomorrow morning. The remaining tasks are trivial; therefore, may I suggest that you return to your wife, for your dinner will soon be cold. However, should you be interested in learning the final details, pray come round Baker Street in the morning. Say, at quarter to ten."

Knowing that I was more likely to squeeze water from a stone than a secret from Sherlock Holmes when he was in one of his dramatic moods, I followed his advice to the letter. When I arrived at Baker Street at the appointed time the following morn, I was surprised to find both Mr. Johnson and Inspector Lestrade sitting upon the settee. The apartment was much as I left it, though a new odour filled the air, and several of the retorts on Holmes' chemical bench appeared to have been recently utilized.

Holmes waved me to my old armchair. "Do not fear, Watson, I have not shared with our guests anything beyond what we learned at Dr Sinclair's hospital. However, the impending dénouement requires the presence of one more individual. Ah, I think I hear him now."

A knock upon the door was soon followed by the appearance of a dashing young fellow, whose clean-shaven face was marked by a bright, smiling expression. His suit appeared new and somewhat showy, while his black shoes gleamed.

"Mr. Patrick Rootes of 12 Devonshire Square?" asked Holmes, using the name of Mr. Darnley's friend.

"That's right," said Rootes.

"Pray have a seat, sir," said Holmes, guiding the guest to the basket chair.

"I have come as you asked, Mr. Holmes," said Rootes, settling into his seat, "but I am unsure of how I may be of assistance?"

"All in good time, Mr. Rootes. We are gathered here today to help Mr. Henry Darnley recover his lost sanity. This is Mr. Timothy Johnson, Mr. Darnley's employer, and the other gentleman is Inspector Lestrade of Scotland Yard. Now, would you be so kind as to tell us of your relationship with him?"

The man shrugged. "We have been acquaintances since our schooldays."

"Just acquaintances?" asked Holmes. "Mr. Darnley described you as a friend."

"Well, just so. Friends then," Rootes nodded.

"And Mr. Darnley noted that you have a passion for antiquities."

"That is correct."

"Does Mr. Darnley share your interest?"

"No, I would not say that. Henry cares mainly about numbers. All else is rather unimportant to him."

"Why then did you gift him a valuable antique silver mirror?"

The man pursed his lips. "Well, let me think. Ah yes, I recall now. I had gone round to his place before the holidays and noted that it was severely lacking in décor. A few days later, I found the mirror at a broker's in Tottenham Court Road for sixty shillings – you will never believe the sorts of odd treasures that old Rosenberg has in his shop – and immediately thought of Henry. I figured it would brighten up his office, and brought it round with my belated compliments of the season."

"A most generous gift," said Holmes. "I have examined the mirror and believe it to be early seventeenth century."

"Mid-sixteenth, more likely," said Rootes.

"Indeed," said Holmes with a smile. He then turned to me. "I would value your professional opinion, Watson. What do you make of Mr. Darnley and his visions?"

I considered this question. "Well, there are many medical reasons for such misfirings of the temporal lobe.[132] Certain forms of mania – such as Hecker's hebephrenia – are accompanied by distinct hallucinations.[133] Even the aura that proceeds an epileptic's fit is sometimes mistaken for a vision."

"You speak of the permanent organic causes," said Holmes. "But there are more temporary kinds, are there not."

"Such as higher visions?"

"Ah, do you refer to the supernatural, Watson?"

"I suppose you might call them such," said I. "These would include the visions seen by William Blake or Joan of Arc. I believe that Dr Sinclair is of the opinion that Mr. Darnley's images fall into this category."

Holmes shook his head. "Let us set aside the illusions of madness and of ergotism.[134] No, I speak of the ingestion or inhalation of certain substances, such as the fungal spores which once drove poor Professor Sidney to his fatal actions."[135]

"Do you think that Mr. Darnley is addicted to the use of some narcotic?"

"While I note that the visions of Darnley and Mr. Coleridge have much in common," said Holmes, "he does not have the wasted look of a habitual opium user.[136] No, I have an alternate hypothesis in mind." He turned back to Rootes. "You said that you met Henry Darnley at school. Would that perchance be accountancy school?"

"Yes. That is correct."

"Would you be so kind as to inform Inspector Lestrade where it is that you work, Mr. Rootes?"

The man's eyes darted towards the policeman. "In the city. Old Broad Street."

"At Gresham Chambers, if your landlady is to be believed," said Holmes.

"Yes," said Rootes, his voice strained.

Holmes smiled broadly, like a cat with a canary. "And what firm precisely?"

The man licked his lips and hesitated.

However, Mr. Johnson suddenly jumped up from his chair. "White and Wotherspoon have their offices in Gresham Chambers!"

"What is all this?" said Lestrade, a perplexed furrow in his brow.

"Three weeks ago, Lestrade, Mr. Darnley was tasked by Mr. Johnson here," said Holmes, "with an inspection of the ledgers of White and Wotherspoon to determine if that venerable firm was complicit in the embezzlement carried out by Sir Roger Shoemaker. It is a rather odd coincidence – is it not? – that one of White and Wotherspoon's employees should happen to call upon Mr. Darnley at this precarious time?"

"A man cannot call upon his friend at holiday time?" cried Rootes, springing to his feet. "Is the giving of gifts now against the law?"

"No," said Holmes, spinning about and pointing one of his long, thin fingers at Rootes. "But surely the poisoning of one's friend is a matter for Scotland Yard."

"Poison!" exclaimed the inspector. "Who is dead?"

"Not all poisons are lethal, Lestrade," said Holmes. "The one in question is rarely fatal, for such an event would hardly further the cause of White and Wotherspoon. Should Mr. Darnley have suddenly died in mysterious circumstances, it would have been simple enough for the prosecution to request an extension to the date of the trial. However, if Mr. Darnley were found to have gone mad, then all of his work would be cast into question. Only the most lenient of magistrates would permit any additional delay for Mr. Johnson's firm to repeat their investigation of the ledgers due to such an unusual situation. I inquired as to who was presiding over Sir Roger's trial, and I assure you that Sir James Hannen is not the most indulgent of judges."

"That is a grave accusation, Mr. Holmes," said Rootes. "You can be certain that you will hear from my solicitor about such libellous claims. However, I have no need to stand here and listen to any more of this nonsense." He moved to the door, but Holmes slid into his way. The man turned to Lestrade and held out his arms in a pleading manner. "This amateur has no official capacity to detain me, Inspector. If he resists my departure with force, will you permit such an assault upon my person?"

Lestrade appeared troubled and shook his head. "This is all rather circumstantial, Mr. Holmes. What proof do you have?"

"I am getting to that, Lestrade," said Holmes. "If you would each do me the favour of resuming your seats, I shall make all clear."

Lestrade nodded slowly, as if mentally calculating the number of past situations in which Holmes had provided him with the correct solution to a case. "I suggest, Mr. Rootes," said the inspector, finally, "that you do as he says. Let us hear him out. If there is no proof, you have my word that you shall be detained no longer."

"And if I choose not to listen any longer?" asked Rootes.

"Then I am afraid that you will listen in chains," said Lestrade, slowly pulling a pair of steel cuffs from his pocket, and dangling them menacingly.

The man silently glared at the inspector, but took his seat. The others followed in turn, save only Holmes.

"As I was saying," resumed Holmes, pacing about the room. "Mr. Henry Darnley has slowly and gradually been poisoned with bromine, a substance that – when it builds up in the system – leads to irritability, hallucinations, and eventually stupor."

"Bromism!" I exclaimed. "Yes, I noted that Mr. Darnley has a rash, which may be seen in individuals who have consumed an excess of bromine."

"Ha!" cried Rootes. "And how precisely did I poison Henry? I have not even laid eyes upon him this year!"

"That is where you were exceptionally clever, Mr. Rootes. You are a most unfortunate individual. If Mr. Johnson had not asked me to investigate, I daresay that you would have gotten away with it." He turned to me. "Did you notice, Watson, that when Mr. Darnley turned the pages of the history book given to him by Dr Sinclair that he always first licked his index finger?"

I considered this for a moment. "Yes, I believe he did."

"Such a habit is something that is deeply ingrained. Either you are a person does it or you are not. Darnley likely developed such a routine during his schooldays, a fact that did not go unnoticed by his old acquaintance here, Mr. Rootes. Moreover, when Rootes eventually found himself in a situation where he needed to discredit the reputation of his supposed friend, he ingeniously decided to employ this habit of Mr. Darnley's as the means by which the bromine was ingested. Whenever Darnley would touch or manipulate the position of the mirror, some of the bromine was transferred to his fingers and from there to his tongue."

"That is a very fancy theory, Mr. Holmes," said Lestrade, a hint of doubt creeping into his voice. "Can you prove it?"

"Sadly, there is no method by which to prove that Mr. Darnley has bromine in his body; however, we may test the mirror itself.[137] Moreover, I have done so. Yesterday, I inspected the mirror and I took various swabs from its surface." He waved towards his chemical bench. "The results are conclusive. The mirror in Mr. Darnley's home office has been generously coated with potassium bromide. You may have these experiments repeated, should you wish, Lestrade; however, I assure you that the results shall not vary."

"So what?" said Rootes, with a sneer. "If there was bromide on that mirror, it was either there when I purchased it, or Henry put it on himself."

Holmes reached into his pocket and pulled out a stack of receipts. "Why then, Mr. Rootes, did you purchase a quart of potassium bromide from no less than six chemists in the vicinity of your home in the two days after you acquired the mirror?" Holmes turned to Lestrade and handed him the papers. "You may send a man round to Mr. Rosenberg's shop and Mr. Darnley's home, Lestrade; however, I strongly doubt that you will find a supply of potassium bromide at either locale. If you choose to do so, I trust that you will – in the interim – at least detain Mr. Rootes. We do not want him making a run for the coast."

§

Once the steel cuffs clicked onto his wrists, Rootes broke down and confessed. The rival accountant admitted that he had perpetuated the bromine poisoning of Mr. Henry Darnley on behalf of his employers, who threatened him with a loss of employment on the one hand, and proffered a generous bonus on the other. As Lestrade hauled him away, Rootes was wailing about how he never intended to harm Darnley, how his friend was still alive and recovering his wits, so no harm was really done. "How much time could I get?" was the last thing I heard him cry.

As I followed the case of Sir Roger Shoemaker in the papers over the next few weeks, I learned the answer was one year in Exeter Gaol – Rootes' term having been reduced for his statement blaming his actions upon the orders of his former employers at White and Wotherspoon. That venerable firm collapsed under the combined weight of Rootes' testimony and the evidence unearthed in their ledgers by the work of Mr. Henry Darnley. In turn, both Mr. White and Mr. Wotherspoon agreed to testify against Sir Roger in exchange for lower sentences of their own. For his crime of defalcation, Judge Sir James Hannen sentenced Sir Roger to fifteen years, though he hung himself after just five days.

A few weeks later, I called upon Holmes on my way back from my rounds. He was seated in his armchair, droning away upon a new violin, no recognized tune arising from those notes. At my arrival, he set down the violin, and welcomed me to my old chair. Eventually, our talk turned to the case of Mr. Henry Darnley.

"I suppose I shall always wonder, Holmes, whether Mr. Darnley saw a true vision."

He stared at me in concern. "What do you mean, Watson? Patrick Rootes confessed to poisoning the man. It was merely a drug-induced hallucination."

"Surely you will admit, Holmes, that his visions were curiously precise? In my experience, those images that appear during such intoxications are rarely so accurate. Even Dr Sinclair was amazed. Could this not be a remarkable synchronicity between the centuries – Henry Stuart, Lord Darnley, calling forward to plain old Henry Darnley, the accountant, through the medium of the mirror once belonging to his wife Mary, Queen of Scots?"

"I will admit, Watson, only to Patrick Rootes' cunning. You see, there is a major impediment to your theory of psychic connections."

"Which is?"

"That was not the mirror of Mary, Queen of Scots."

"What!" I cried. "But the inscription! Holyrood! The lilies of France!"

Holmes shook his head. "I went round to see Mr. Rosenberg at his shop in Tottenham Court Road. The broker was most friendly, and showed me his ledger where the purchase of the mirror by Mr. Rootes was documented. Rosenberg is a most thorough individual, and the bill of sale plainly states 'One silver-framed mirror, mid-sixteenth century, three feet across and two feet high, bevelled edge, unmarked."

"Unmarked!"

"Yes, Watson. Mr. Rootes added those marks himself. Surely, it is too great a coincidence that the actual mirror of Mary, Queen of Scots, would come into the possession of a man who shared the name of her murderous husband. Rootes took note of his friend's unique surname, and employed the legend of David Rizzio's murder to play upon Darnley's somewhat limited imagination. He knew that Darnley was a rather thorough gentleman, and would carefully inspect his new piece of décor, especially after the effects of the bromine began to take effect. Rootes counted upon Darnley deciphering the marks and making the link to the ancient legend. From there, Darnley's future bromine-induced visions took a predictable route."

"But Darnley denied knowing the legend of Rizzio," I protested.

"He may have forgotten it, but as a Scotsman, he undoubtedly learned it as a child. It was there; stowed deeply in the box-room of his brain, ready to be unearthed when the moment was right."

"So there was nothing spiritual about it?" said I, disappointedly.

"Surely life is fantastic enough, Watson, and does not require the existence of even stranger things," said he, with a laugh, as he placed his violin to his chin.

I nodded my farewell, and as I descended the seventeen steps, I listened to the long-drawn, haunting notes of the Berlioz symphony wash over me.[138] Perhaps Holmes was right, I thought. Perhaps life was fantastic enough. For whom could have predicted that a simple former army surgeon would have such adventures as others could only dream. Yet, I will always wonder about the amazing clarity of Mr. Henry Darnley's visions – undoubtedly induced by bromine as they were – and whether some trace of them came from a place beyond the edge of the unknown.

§

THE PROBLEM OF THE BLACK EYE

"The state of the provincial papers is appalling, Watson," said Mr. Sherlock Holmes, one June morning in the year 1895. To punctuate his disgust, he wadded the offending newssheet into a ball and tossed them into the cold grate.

"Is there a particular matter that has so provoked your ire?"

"The murder of Dr Lana. The London press has only partially covered it, and thus I sought out some of the local accounts in hopes of gleaning more pertinent details."

"In vain, I see."

"Indeed. They add little of interest to what has already been reported."

"And what is it about the case that has so piqued your curiosity?"

"You have not heard anything about the problem?"

I shook my head. "Not a word."[139]

"In summary, it seems rather cut and dry. On the one hand, we have a doctor who has recently broken his engagement with a young lady. On the other, we have an angry brother of said lady. When the former is found slain in his study, the latter is clearly the focus of attention, especially when a witness has reported that he was seen near the doctor's home on the night in question."

"So?" I asked. "As you said, it seems most straightforward."

"And yet, there is one thing out of place, which upsets the whole narrative that the prosecution has built against the brother."

"Which is?"

"A green eye-patch."

"I am afraid that you have lost me, Holmes."

"The local police found a green eye-patch at the scene of the crime. It was plainly not the property of the doctor, nor did anyone ever see it in the possession of the brother, who had little need for such a device. So, what was it doing there?"

I shrugged. "I can hardly say. What do the police think?"

He snorted in derision. "The police have – as far as I can gather – completely ignored it. They even called in Lestrade, and he too seems to have made nothing of it."

"But you think it is meaningful?"

"It is singular. And anything singular must be explained. If not, that hanging thread will unravel the entire tapestry of the crime."

"What do you propose to do about it?"

"I suggest that we catch the next train from Euston to Liverpool. Will you come?"

"It may be nothing more than a wild goose chase."

"So thought Lestrade when I formerly proposed that a hotel bill might solve one of his most pressing cases," said Holmes, merrily, as he reached for his long grey travelling-cloak and close-fitting cloth cap. "And yet, Lady St. Simon was a myth, after all."

§

Half an hour later, we were sitting in our own first-class carriage of the London and North Western Railway line. Holmes' tall, gaunt figure was stretched out to the point where his knees almost touched the seat across from him, while I reclined in the window seat. He was languidly stuffing his old brier-root pipe with some Eastern tobacco.

"You seem rather relaxed," I noted.

"There is little to do at the moment, Watson," said he.

"I may be of more use if I were to have a complete picture of the case," said I.

"Quite so. Here is what I know from my perusal of the *Lancaster Weekly*.[140] Bishop's Crossing is a small village lying ten miles in a southwesterly direction from Liverpool.[141] Here in the early nineties there settled a doctor named Aloysius Lana. Nothing was known locally either of his antecedents or of the reasons that had prompted him to come to this Lancashire hamlet. Two facts only were certain about him: the one that he had gained his medical qualification with some distinction at Glasgow; the other that he came undoubtedly of a tropical race, and was so dark that he might almost have had a strain of the Indian in his composition. His predominant features were, however, European, and he possessed a stately courtesy and carriage, which suggested a Spanish extraction. Dr Lana's swarthy skin, raven-black hair, and dark, sparkling eyes under a pair of heavily tufted brows made a strange contrast to the flaxen or chestnut rustics so common to that corner of England.

"Dr Lana appeared to be a confirmed bachelor, and years passed before his engagement was suddenly announced to Miss Frances Morton, of Leigh Hall. Miss Morton was a young lady who was well known upon the country-side; her father, James Haldane Morton, having been the Squire of Bishop's Crossing. However, both her parents were deceased, and she lived with her only brother, Arthur Morton, who had inherited the family estate. Their engagement was in February, and it was arranged that the marriage should take place in August.

"However, on the 4th of June, Dr Lana called upon Miss Morton, and a long interview followed, from which he was observed to return in a state of great agitation. Miss Morton remained in her room all that day, and her maid found her several times in tears. In the course of a week it was an open secret to the whole village that the engagement was at an end, that Dr Lana had behaved shamefully to the young lady, and that Arthur Morton, her brother, was talking of horse-whipping him."

"What was the cause of their rupture?"

"On this, the papers are silent, Watson. Nevertheless, it must have been a serious one. For there was an advertisement in *The Lancet* as to the sale of a practice which mentioned no names, but which was thought by some to refer to Bishop's Crossing, and to mean that Dr Lana was thinking of abandoning the scene of his success. Such was the position of affairs when, upon the evening of Monday, June 21st, there came a fresh development which changed what had been a mere village scandal into a tragedy which may very well end up arresting the attention of the whole nation. Some detail is necessary to cause the facts of that evening to present their full significance.

"The sole occupants of the doctor's house," continued Holmes, "were his housekeeper, an elderly and most respectable woman, named Martha Woods, and a young servant – Mary Pilling. The coachman and the surgery-boy slept out. It was the custom of the doctor to sit at night in his study. This was situated next to the surgery in the wing of the house that was farthest from the servants' quarters. This side of the house had an exterior door of its own for the convenience of patients, so that it was possible for the doctor to admit and receive a visitor there without the knowledge of any one. As a matter of fact, when patients came late it was quite usual for him to let them in and out by the surgery entrance, for both the maid and the housekeeper were in the habit of retiring early."

"And I suppose on the night in question, the housekeeper heard nothing?" I remarked.

"On the contrary, Watson. On this particular night, Martha Woods went into the doctor's study at half-past nine, and found him writing at his desk. She bade him goodnight, sent the maid to bed, and then occupied herself until a quarter to eleven in household matters. It was striking eleven upon the hall clock when she went to her own room. She had been there about a quarter of an hour or so when she heard a cry or call, which appeared to come from within the house. She waited some time, but it was not repeated. Much alarmed – for the sound was loud and urgent – she put on a dressing gown, and rushed at the top of her speed to the doctor's study.

"She tapped on the door and spoke to Dr Lana for a moment. He reported that everything was alright and that she should return to her room."

I leaned forward with interest. "She is certain that the voice belonged to the doctor?"

Holmes smiled. "Capital, Watson. This is a crucial detail. I intend to ask her the same question myself. For now, however, we can only relate what has been reported in the papers. Mrs. Woods returned to her room, and looked at the clock as she turned out the lamp. It was half-past eleven. Some point between that time, and three o'clock in the morning, when an urgent caller knocked at his surgery door and found him dead, Dr Lana was murdered. The brother of his former fiancée, Mr. Arthur Morton, has been arrested for the crime."

"But he claims to be innocent?"

"Indeed. Instead, Mr. Morton says that he never spoke to the man that evening."

"And you believe him?"

Holmes waved his hand. "It is too soon to form conjectures of innocence or guilt, Watson. However, there are features present that induce me to conceive the possibility that the simple answer may not be the correct one. Sadly, as we have seen time and time again, if we wait for the official force to uncover the truth, it may prove to be too late. No, I can hardly stand idly by and ignore such a potentially interesting case. Now, we have a good three hours until we alight at Lime Street Station and I fully intend to spend it beyond the gates of horn."[142]

Holmes was true to his word, so I took the opportunity to pull my pocket Shakespeare from my coat pocket and brush up on his wonderful Ephesus comedy.[143] With this companion, the hours raced by. When I next looked up, we were gliding under Mr. Baker and Stevenson's massive arched iron shed.[144]

Holmes had wired to Lestrade, such that the lean and ferret-like inspector was waiting for us upon the platform. He had transformed his routine city attire for a brown dustcoat and leather-leggings, but was otherwise looking somewhat put out.

"I do not understand your interest in this incident, Mr. Holmes," said Lestrade, as he shook my hand. "It is a simple matter. Judge Aldrich will hear the case tomorrow, and the verdict is as evident as the back of my hand."

Holmes reached out his hand in a rare act of greeting. The inspector's eyebrows rose in surprise, but he returned the gesture. Holmes suddenly twisted Lestrade's hand slightly such that the back of it was now pointed to the ground.

"Quick, Lestrade," said he. "How many moles do you have on the back of your right hand?"

The man frowned. "Well… two, I think."

"Incorrect," said Holmes, releasing his hand. "There are three, as you can now plainly see."

Lestrade glanced at his hand. "Yes, indeed. What is your point?" he asked, irritably.

"That some things so ordinary that they are easily overlooked. But have no concern, Lestrade. I merely wish to provide a few observations to assist you in your case. I will remain in the background, and you may pocket any credit which derives from my inquiries."

"Very well," said Lestrade, grudgingly. "We will have to take the ferry over to Birkenhead. I have engaged a carriage to take us to Bishop's Crossing. I knew that you would want to look over the scene of the crime as your first course of action."

Holmes shrugged. "I doubt that there is much to see at this late hour. It goes without saying that the doctor's study has already been well trampled, as if from a herd of elephants, by the local constabulary."

"Then what would you do?"

"First, I want to hear some of the details which have been

omitted from the papers. How was the body found?"

Lestrade consulted his pocket notebook. "At the side of the table, away from the window, Dr Lana was discovered stretched upon his back and quite dead. It was evident that he had been subjected to violence, for one of his eyes was blackened, and there were marks of bruises about his face and neck. A slight thickening and swelling of his features appeared to suggest that the cause of his death had been strangulation. He was dressed in his usual professional clothes, but wore cloth slippers, the soles of which were perfectly clean. The carpet was marked all over, especially on the side of the door, with traces of dirty boots, which were presumably left by the murderer, as they were too small to belong to the doctor. There had been a heavy shower that afternoon."

"Did you take impresses?"

"Of course," said Lestrade. "I am the first to admit that your monograph on the uses of plaster of Paris has been much admired in the Yard."

"And what did you conclude from them?"

"They were made from rather rough boots. But the softness of the carpet blurred the marks, and made it impossible to make any additional trustworthy notes."

"Surely you could tell the size?"

"Yes, they were a ten."

"And the shoe of Mr. Arthur Morton?"

"Nine," said Lestrade. "But that means little. A clever man could easily put on a pair of boots bigger than his natural size to disguise his identity."

Holmes's face was rapt at this unusual display of imagination on the part of the inspector. "I concur, Lestrade. Yet, your hypothesis would imply a rather calculated act upon the part of Mr. Morton. Does he strike you as possessing such a cold-blooded temperament?"

Hee shrugged. "Who knows what goes on in the mind of a man?"

"I do. Or at least, often I am able to deduce it," said Holmes, with a wry smile. "A woman, on the other hand, is a book with a tightly locked clasp."

"Do you suspect a woman?" said Lestrade, his brow furrowed.

"It is far too soon to make any conclusions, Lestrade," said Holmes with an airy wave of his hand. "However, if your theory of missized boosts is correct, then such a cool premeditation does suggest that a woman may be involved."

"Miss Morton may have decided to punish her former fiancée for his cruel mistreatment of him," I postulated.

"Or Dr Lana may have broken off the engagement because of the presence of another woman on the scene," said Holmes. "Surely a woman could wear men's boots to throw the police off the scent."

Lestrade shook his head. "We feel certain that the assailant was a man, for – even if you discount the size of the footprints – there is the nature of the injuries. The doctor was no weak man. I hardly think a woman could have inflicted such violence."

"What then is your conclusion?"

"It is evident that someone had entered by the surgery door, killed the doctor, and had then made his escape unseen. However, beyond that point the local police found it very difficult to go. There were no signs of robbery, and the doctor's gold watch was safe in his pocket."

"What of a safe?"

"I asked the same thing myself," said Lestrade, complacently. "He kept a heavy cash-box in the room, and this was discovered to be locked but empty. The housekeeper, Mrs. Woods, had an impression that a large sum was usually kept there, but the doctor had paid a heavy corn bill in cash only that very day, and it was conjectured that it was to this and not to a robber that the emptiness of the box was due."

"That would have been a pretty bill," said Holmes. "Have you traced it?"

"I have a man on it," said Lestrade. "It is only a matter of time before we know the amount."

"Was there anything else missing?"

Lestrade smiled broadly. "Oh yes, one thing, which was most suggestive. The portrait of Miss Morton, which had always stood upon the side-table, had been taken from its frame and carried off. Mrs. Woods had observed it there when she waited upon her employer that evening, and now it is gone."

"Ah, and from this you conclude that Mr. Arthur Morton, the young squire, was involved? That he could not leave his sister's likeness behind?"

"Yes," said Lestrade. "However, there is much more than that, Mr. Holmes. There is the evidence of a late visitor, Mrs. Alice Madding, the wife of the village grocer. The poor man was dangerously ill of typhoid fever, and Dr Lana had asked her to look in the last thing and let him know how her husband was progressing. At some period between eleven and twelve – she could not be positive as to the exact hour – she called upon the doctor and was unable to get any reply from him. She observed that the light was burning in the study, but having knocked several times at the surgery door without response, she concluded that the doctor had been called out, and so returned home.

"There is a short, winding drive with a lamp at the end of it leading down from the house to the road. As Mrs. Madding emerged from the gate, a man was coming along the footpath. Thinking that it might be Dr Lana returning from some professional visit, she waited for him, and was surprised to see that it was Arthur Morton. In the light of the lamp, she observed that his manner was excited, and that he carried in his hand a heavy hunting crop. She spoke to him briefly, and she recalls his tone being harsh. Later, at three o'clock that morning, her husband suffered a worsening of his condition, and she was so alarmed by his symptoms that she determined to call the doctor without delay. As she passed through the gate, she was surprised to see Mr. Arthur Morton lurking among the laurel bushes."

"She is certain that it was Morton?" I asked.

I noted that the corner of Holmes' mouth turned up at this question.

"Well," said Lestrade, "it was certainly a man, and to the best of her belief it was Mr. Arthur Morton. Preoccupied with her own troubles, she gave no particular attention to the incident, but hurried on upon her errand.

"When she reached the house," the inspector continued, "she perceived to her surprise that the light was still burning in the study. She therefore tapped at the surgery door. There was no answer. She repeated the knocking several times without effect. It appeared to her to be unlikely that the doctor would either retire to bed or go out while leaving so brilliant a light behind him, and it struck Mrs. Madding that it was possible that he might have dropped asleep in his chair. She tapped at the study window, therefore, but without result. Then, finding that there was an opening between the curtain and the woodwork, she looked through.

"The small room was brilliantly lighted from a large lamp on the central table, which was littered with the doctor's books and instruments. No one was visible, nor did she see anything unusual at first, except that in the further shadow thrown by the table a dingy white glove was lying upon the carpet. Then suddenly, as her eyes became more accustomed to the light, a boot emerged from the other end of the shadow, and she realized, with a thrill of horror, that what she had taken to be a glove was the hand of a man!

"Dr Lana was prostrate upon the floor. Understanding that something terrible had occurred, she rang at the front door, roused Mrs. Woods, the housekeeper, and the two women made their way into the study, having first dispatched the maidservant to the police station. Once the local constable entered, it was apparent to him that Dr Lana was dead. He looked over the scene, and by the following morn, the news had gone round the entire village. Once the constable heard about the disagreement between Dr Lana and the Morton siblings, a motive became clear. In conjunction with the report of Mrs. Madding, suspicion could only turn in one direction, and Arthur Morton, the young squire, was immediately arrested."

"It seems to me that the evidence against him is circumstantial," observed Holmes.

"But damning," Lestrade persisted. "He was devoted to his sister, and it was shown to the police that ever since the rupture between her and Dr Lana, Arthur Morton had been heard again and again to express himself in the most vindictive terms towards her former lover."

"Hearsay," interjected Holmes.

"Perhaps," admitted Lestrade. "But Mrs. Madding's testimony is not. For Arthur Morton had, as stated, been seen somewhere about eleven o'clock entering the doctor's drive with a hunting crop in his hand."

"What then is your theory?"

Lestrade smiled and rubbed his hands together. "Arthur Morton broke in upon the doctor, whose exclamation of fear or of anger was loud enough to attract the attention of Mrs. Woods. When Mrs. Woods descended, Dr Lana had made up his mind to talk it over with his visitor, and therefore, sent his housekeeper back to her room. This conversation lasted a long time, had become more and more fiery, and finally ended by a personal struggle, in which the doctor lost his life."

"It takes a powerful individual to strangle another man to death when the victim is anticipating the attack," noted Holmes.

"Ah, well, Mr. Holmes, there is also the fact – revealed by a post-mortem performed by Dr Fickert of Liverpool – that Dr Lana's heart was much diseased. This ailment, quite unsuspected during his life, would have made it possible that death might, in his case, ensue from injuries that would not be fatal to a healthy man. After Lana was dead, Arthur Morton then removed his sister's photograph, and made his way homeward, stepping aside into the laurel bushes to avoid meeting Mrs. Madding again at the gate. How is that for a fine theory, Mr.

Holmes? I dare say it fits all of the facts."

The case that Lestrade presented was a formidable one, and I said as much.

"Is it, Watson?" said Holmes. "There seem to be some items which you have overlooked, Lestrade."

"Such as?" asked the inspector, sharply.

"Have you found the missing picture of Frances Morton in her brother's possession?"

"No, but he may have burned it! He had ample time before his arrest."

Holmes shook his head. "Why take it, only to destroy it?"

"How can I say why a man performs this or that action in the mad throes of murdering a man?" protested Lestrade.

"And the boots? Did you find size ten boots at Leigh Hall?"

Lestrade shook his head. "No, but we did find that Mr. Morton's boots were very muddy."

Holmes' lip curled up in a sardonic grin. "As were all boots in the village if there had been a heavy shower."

"Well, their appearance is not inconsistent with the theory that they were made by the accused. Plaster of Paris is not infallible. A size nine boot might have made those marks. Is there anything else?"

"Well, there is the eye-patch for instance."

"The eye-patch!" cried Lestrade. "What of it?"

"If the papers are accurate, Mrs. Wood picked up from the floor a green eye-patch, which the housekeeper could not remember to have seen before."

"It's completely irrelevant, Mr. Holmes! Such a patch might be in the possession of any doctor. There is nothing to indicate that it was in any way connected with the crime."

"You may be correct, Lestrade," said Holmes, mildly. "Still, you will not mind if we call upon Miss Frances Morton, will you?"

§

Despite Lestrade's grumblings that Holmes was wasting his time, once we arrived at Bishop's Crossing, we located a man who was willing to take us around to Leigh Hall in his trap. The inspector strode away with firm instructions to Holmes that he was to report any findings forthwith. Lestrade noted that he could be found at the 'Seven Stars' public house, where he had set up a temporary base of operations, as the local constabulary was several miles away.

Great ridges that ran parallel down the peninsula dominated the rural countryside, while the towns were tucked into the shallow tree-filled valley between them. The Morton family estate was perched upon a great hill, with a long-winding drive leading up to the three-story manor. The irregular plan suggested that it had been added to in fits-and-starts over the centuries, while the narrow mullioned windows of one wing spoke to a time when the structure was used for defence rather than pleasure.

Holmes presented his card to the man who answered the door. After a few moments, we were shown into a well-appointed sitting room, where we were soon joined by the lady of the house. In person, Miss Morton was tall and stately, with brunette hair and a low, but clear, voice. She indicated her willingness to discuss the case with us.

"Where did you meet Dr Lana?" asked Holmes.

"At a garden party last September. A friendship sprang up between us."

"But you knew of him before?"

"Of course. He was quite well known in the village. I simply never had a need to consult with him."

"What did you know about his reasons for coming to Bishop's Crossing?"

"He did not like to talk about his past. He simply said that after he completed his studies at Glasgow that he wished for a quiet life."

"But surely Bishop's Crossing already had a doctor. Did he

buy out a practice?"

"No, he established it."

"It must have been hard for a newcomer to attract clients away from the doctor with whom people were accustomed to consulting?"

She nodded. "Yes, I believe that it was quite difficult at first. However, he soon proved to be a capable surgeon and an accomplished physician. I suppose that it was the case of the Honourable James Lowry, the second son of Lord Belton, which really made Dr Lana's name. Mr. Lowry was riding through the village last summer when his carriage overturned. He sustained a terrible head wound; however, Dr Lana rapidly performed a remarkable surgical intervention, and Lowry fully recovered. Lord Belton was most grateful for his son's cure and ensured that Dr Lana's social success was as rapid as his professional. He was the means of introducing Dr Lana to county society, where I understand that he quickly became a favourite through the charm of his conversation and the elegance of his manners."

"An absence of antecedents and of relatives is sometimes an aid rather than an impediment to social advancement," said Holmes.

"Precisely, Mr. Holmes," Miss Morton agreed. "And, to be honest, the distinguished individuality of the handsome doctor was its own recommendation."

"But you said that you did not meet him until last fall? I understand that Dr Lana has lived here for many years?"

"Indeed. The locals used to make merry over it," said she, with a sad smile. "His female patients used to gossip that they found one fault – and one fault only – with him. Given that his house was a large one, and that – as was well known – his success in practice had enabled him to save considerable sums, it is hardly a surprise that the local matchmakers were continually coupling his name with one or another of the environs' eligible ladies."

"And yet, as the years passed, he resisted such charms and

remained a bachelor," said Holmes. "Did he ever tell you why?"

Her eyes narrowed. "Have you been talking to Mr. Bankley?"

"I assure you, Miss Morton," said Holmes, with a shake of his head, "that I have never even heard of Mr. Bankley. However, your reaction is such that I may have to seek him out."

She glared at him. "There is no need. I will tell you what foul rumour he put about. He claimed that Dr Lana was already married, and that it was in order to escape the consequence of an early misalliance that he had buried himself at Bishop's Crossing."

"But you know that not to be true?"

"Aloysius assured me that there was nothing to it. He was merely waiting for the right woman," said she, quietly. "Our friendship quickly ripened into love, and we were devoted to each other."

"I understand that there was some discrepancy in age, he being thirty-seven, and you, what, three and twenty?"

"Twenty-four, actually. Perhaps that would have been as issue if my father were still alive, for he was a conservative soul. However, my brother was satisfied, and – save in that one respect – there was no possible objection to be found with the match."

"And why did Dr Lana call off your engagement?"

She shook her head. "It is not pertinent."

"I will be the judge of that."

"It is a private matter. I do not wish to speak of it."

Holmes frowned. "I can hardly prove your brother's innocence if you so tie my hands, Miss Morton."

"I assure you, Mr. Holmes, that the matter between us has no possible bearing upon Dr Lana's death. Have you met my brother? No? Well, I urge you to do so. You will soon learn that Arthur has not a wicked bone in his body. He is rather high-spirited and impetuous, yes. I give you that. But he is respected and liked by everyone – just ask about the village. His frank and honest nature is incapable of such a crime."

"If not your brother, then who did kill Dr Lana?" asked

Holmes.

"I hardly know, Mr. Holmes. I had not seen much of him of late," said she, sadly. "But I urge you to find the man responsible, and bring him to justice."

§

"What do you think, Watson?" asked Holmes, after we had departed Leigh Hall.

"She may as well have been describing herself, Holmes. High-spirited and impetuous. However, I think that she might score some strong points for the defence, should they put her in front of a jury."

Holmes shook his head. "Emotion should not enter into the equation, Watson. Mr. Arthur Morton is either guilty or he is not. These are facts, and emotion cannot alter them. Furthermore, I fear that Miss Morton is not being entirely honest with us."

"Do you believe that she is covering for her brother?"

"Possibly. Or even herself."

"I say, Holmes, surely you don't think that she killed the doctor!"

He shrugged. "She has more motive than most, and as Congreve said, 'heaven has no fury like love turned to hatred.'[145] Still, even powered by rage, it is somewhat unlikely from a physical perspective. I will concede that. However, it is not impossible, so we cannot yet eliminate it from our list of potential scenarios."

"What shall we do next?"

"The logical order is to proceed with the testimony of Mr. Arthur Morton."

The accused was confined in a Liverpool gaol, though Lestrade had submitted the formalities required to obtain orders that permitted both Holmes and I to see him. Therefore, we retraced our steps back to the city, and within an hour, we were escorted into Mr. Morton's cell.

He was young, not more than five-and-twenty, with a robust, masculine face. However, he was remarkably pale and gave me the impression of a man who was suffering from some fervent distress. He sprang up in response to our arrival.

"Who are you?" asked Morton. "Have you come with news?"

Holmes introduced us and the purpose for our visit. "Inspector Lestrade and the local constabulary are convinced that you are guilty, Mr. Morton."

"I am not!" he cried. "I swear it."

"Well," said Holmes, "you will be happy to learn that, for myself, I have some doubts about the plausibility of their narrative, for the evidence may be pointing to another party, presently unknown. Will you answer my questions truthfully?"

"Of course! Ask me anything."

"Firstly, who is Mr. Bankley?"

The man looked mystified. "The postmaster? What does he have to do with anything?"

Holmes nodded, as if this confirmed his theory. "It is of no matter," said he with a wave of his hand. "Mrs. Madding testified that she met you turning in at Dr Lana's gate. Do you deny this?"

"Not all at. She told me that the doctor was not in. She had been to the surgery door, and he was out."

"She also reported that you addressed her with harsh words."

"Perhaps," said he, with a shrug. "I was most anxious to have a conversation with Dr Lana. I could see up the drive to his home that the light was on in his study, so was surprised when she said that he was out. Nevertheless, she assured me that such was the case. I figured that if he had left a light on, he must have stepped out briefly and would presently come in again. So I passed through the gate, intending to wait for him, while Mrs. Madding went upon her homeward way."

"And what the purpose of the conversation you wished to have with him?"

"It had to do with some urgent family matters."

"Regarding your sister, Frances?"

He sat silent in response to this question.

"Very well," said Holmes. "Do you deny that this conversation would probably have been of an unpleasant nature?"

"No. I do not deny it."

"And how did Dr Lana respond?"

Morton shook his head. "He did not. I never spoke with the man. Mrs. Madding told me he was out, so I waited until about three in the morning for his return. But, as I had seen nothing of him up to that hour, I gave it up and returned home."

Holmes' eyebrows rose. "So you never spoke to Dr Lana on the evening in question?"

"I had not spoken to Dr Lana for several weeks prior to his death. I know no more about it than the fool constable who arrested me."

"Surely you were once a close friend of the deceased man?"

"Circumstances brought about a change in my sentiments."

"Circumstances which you would prefer not to mention."

"Just so."

Holmes shook his head. "By your silence, both you and your sister, Mr. Morton, are making things more difficult than they need be."

"It is not my secret to share, Mr. Holmes. Besides, I am not guilty. They cannot convict an innocent man."

"I am afraid, Mr. Morton, that is far from certain," said Holmes, gravely. "The British criminal law system is not infallible. Men have been hanged on the basis of far less convincing evidence."[146]

Morton paled in response to these words, yet held firm on his refusal to discuss the matter of his sister.

"I have only one final question for you at this time," said Holmes. "Do you own a green eye-patch?"

The man frowned. "A green eye-patch? Why would I own such a thing?"

"So you deny it?"

"I do."

"You have never had an injury to one of your eyes which required you to wear a patch?"

"Never."

§

"Do you believe him, Holmes?" I asked, once we had emerged from the gaol.

He nodded slowly. "I do."

"What now?"

"We cannot assume that Lestrade and the local police have adequately gathered the pertinent statements from all of the potential witnesses. As you noted on the train, Watson, some questions remain for Mrs. Woods. Let us return to Bishop's Crossing."

Back in the village, Holmes was rapidly pointed in the direction of Dr Lana's former residence, which was marked by a red lamp. An old woman, with a scared look and restless, picking fingers, opened the door. Holmes explained the purpose of our visit to her, and she reluctantly showed us inside.

"I don't think I will be of much help to you, sir," said the housekeeper. "I have already told everything I know to the man from Scotland Yard."

"This is important, Mrs. Woods," said Holmes. "I wish for you to close your eyes."

"My eyes?" said she, plainly taken aback. "Whatever for?"

"I find that the mind is more conductive to recalling important details if it is not preoccupied with extraneous input."

"Well, I hardly think that it would be proper...."

"We could call in the maid," said I. "She can watch over you."

She pursed her lips and nodded. "Very well."

Once I had collected Mary Pilling and explained her role, Holmes resumed his questioning. I could sense from a tightness around his grey eyes that he had grown somewhat impatient at the delay, but his tone was gentle.

"What did Dr Lana say when you tapped at his door at half-past eleven o'clock?"

Her eyes closed, Mrs. Woods considered this. "He asked: 'Who's there?' That's all."

"And what did you say?"

"I replied: 'I am here, sir – Mrs. Woods.'"

"Was this not a strange question for Dr Lana to ask? Who else could it have been at that hour?"

Her eyes opened and she shrugged. "From within the house? Just me or Mary."

"And why would it matter to him which of you had knocked?"

"I can hardly say, sir."

"Very well," said Holmes. "Close your eyes again and concentrate. What did he say after you had identified yourself?"

Following his instructions, Mrs. Woods closed her eyes and thought about this. "He said: 'I beg that you will leave me in peace. Go back to your room this instant!' I told him that I thought I heard his calling, but he did not answer me."

"That seems a rather harsh way to respond," said Holmes. "For, as you explained at the time, you were responding to a cry, were you not? You were not disturbing him out of the blue."

Mrs. Woods nodded. "Just so, sir! Truth be told, I was fairly surprised and hurt at his tone. To think that those were the last words he spoke to me."

"Did he often raise his voice to you?"

"Oh no, sir. He was an exceptional master. His manner was always most proper. Except for that one night, no one could possibly find fault with him."

"I have one final question for you, Mrs. Woods," said Holmes. "Are you certain that the voice you heard in the study was that of Dr Lana?"

"Oh yes, sir. The man from Scotland Yard asked me the same thing, and I told him that there was no doubt. I would swear to it."

"Have you heard of impressionists, Mrs. Woods?"

"Like Mr. Monet?" she asked, frowning in confusion. "I have read about him in the papers. What does he have to do with Dr Lana?"

"No, I refer to someone who possesses a remarkable talent for mimicking the voices of another. They are quite popular in the music halls about Leicester Square. There is one gentleman who sounds so similar to the Grand Old Man that even Gladstone's wife can't tell them apart."[147]

She frowned. "Well, I wouldn't know much about that," said Mrs. Woods. "And who would want to mimic Dr Lana?"

"Who indeed?" said Holmes, with a smile. "Thank you for your assistance, Mrs. Woods. It has been most valuable."

§

"So you believe, Holmes, that Mrs. Woods was talking to someone else?" I asked, once we had stepped outside. "Was it the murderer?"

Holmes shrugged. "I believe nothing as of yet, Watson. I am merely attempting to assemble the various threads, in hopes of eventually assembling them into a cohesive whole."

"Are there more threads still to be gathered?"

"I think it likely. Despite Miss Morton's protestations to the contrary, I would like a word with Mr. Bankley."

Holmes explained that in a small village, the postmaster is also in a position to be the gossip-master, something that Miss Morton has essentially verified. "Many of the secrets of his neighbours, Watson, will be in the possession of Mr. Bankley."

Holmes rapidly identified the local post office, where Bankley proved to be a red-faced, demonstrative man, who plainly relished his role as the centre of the village gossip-mill. He was most eager to talk with Holmes.

"I am glad you are here, Mr. Holmes. Neither the local police force, nor that inspector from Scotland Yard bothered to ask me what I thought of the matter."

Holmes nodded in apparent commiseration. "A grievous

oversight. What was your impression of Dr Lana?"

Bankley shook his head, "Poor man. He was a good sort. Shame what happened to him. He was our 'black' doctor."

"Why do you call him that?" I asked.

"That's what everyone called him, since shortly after his arrival. 'The Black Doctor of Bishop's Crossing.' On account of his pitch-black hair, which was unique in these parts."

"It sounds like a term of ridicule and reproach," I interjected.

"Perhaps at first it was, but as the years went on, it became a title of honour. It was familiar to the whole countryside, and his reputation extended far beyond the narrow confines of the village. It also helped distinguish him from the other practitioner in the district."

"Who was that?" asked Holmes.

"Edward Rowe, the son of Sir William Rowe, the Liverpool consultant. Sadly, the son had not inherited the talents of his father, and Dr Lana, with his advantages of presence and of manner, soon beat him out of the field. His practice closed."

"What happened to Dr Rowe after that?"

"I heard he went back to Liverpool. He was not a bad doctor, just not an extraordinary one. I suppose we now have an empty practice. Perhaps he can be induced to return, given Dr Lana's death." He paused and shook his head. "And to think that the son of James Haldane Morton, J.P. could be capable of such a thing."

"So you believe him to be guilty?"

The man shrugged. "That's what the police are saying, and they are usually right about such matters, aren't they? Still, if you had asked me a few days ago if it was in Arthur Morton's nature, I would have laughed in your face."

"But there was friction between them, was there not?"

"Well, yes. That is true. It is only natural after the way that Dr Lana treated Miss Morton."

"Do you have any idea of the nature of their argument?"

"Well, I have my theories."

"Go on."

"Very well. You see, upon the 3rd of June, Dr Lana received a letter from aboard."

"Oh, yes? From where?" asked Holmes.

"Buenos Aires. I only remarked it, you understand, because of the curious envelope and the exotic stamp of the Argentine Republic."

"Ah, was Dr Lana in the habit of receiving letters from abroad?"

"Not at all. In fact, I believe this was the first. Before this time, no one even knew from which country he hailed."

"Did you happen to notice the handwriting on the envelope?" asked Holmes. "Was it a man or a woman's?"

"A man's."

"You are certain?"

"Oh, yes. If you do this job for as long as I have, you can tell a great deal about a person from their handwriting."

Holmes smiled. "I concur. And what could you tell about the letter sender?"

"It seemed the hand of a once-strong man brought low by either illness or drink."

"Ah!" said Holmes. "An interesting observation, Mr. Bankley. What did you do with the letter?"

"I handed it to the local postman, of course. As far as I know, it would have been delivered that evening."

"Surely you draw a connection between Dr Lana's receipt of that letter and his visit to Leigh Hall the following morning?"

"Obviously," said Bankley. "Something in that letter caused Dr Lana to break off his engagement with Miss Morton. That was plain to the entire village once they heard about the letter. In what particular respect the doctor had behaved badly was unknown – some surmised one thing and some another. However, it was observed, and taken as the obvious sign of a guilty conscience, that afterwards he would go for miles round rather than pass the windows of Leigh Hall, and that he gave up attending morning service upon Sundays where he might have met the young lady. My notion is that Dr Lana was still married back in his native land. The letter was from the father of the jilted bride, who had finally tracked him down. That is why he held out for so many years, causing the local matchmakers to give him up in despair. However, once he met Miss Morton, he could hardly help himself. Now that you mention it, I feel doubly sorry for poor Miss Morton. She has lost two suitors due to Dr Lana."

"How is that?" asked Holmes.

"Well, she was once engaged to Edward Rowe. He broke his engagement with Miss Morton in shame, after losing his practice to Dr Lana and shuffling back to Liverpool. Then Dr Lana himself also broke his engagement with her, right before getting himself killed." He paused, and his eyes widened. "Say, you do not think that Lana's father-in-law could have done this? Is Mr. Morton innocent?"

Holmes smiled. "That is a most interesting theory, Mr Bankley. I shall look into it."

After we took our leave of the man, Holmes strode slowly in the direction of the 'Seven Stars' public house.

"It is time to touch base with Lestrade. I doubt that he has much news for us, and he surely will make little of what additional data we have acquired, but we promised as much. So, how would you summarize the case, Watson?" Holmes asked.

"I think that you might be correct, Holmes, that the police are on the wrong track. There are several facts that support Mr. Morton's innocence. First, it is certain that Dr Lana was alive and in his study at half-past eleven o'clock. Mrs. Woods is convinced of it, unless you persist in your theory of a mimic?"

"I would simply say that it is not one hundred percent definite that Dr Lana was alive. But pray continue."

"Well, given the doctor's agitation, I would contend that it is probable that at that time, he was not alone. The sound that had originally attracted the attention of the housekeeper, and her master's unusual impatience that she should leave him in peace, seem to point to that."

"I concur, Watson."

"If this were so, then it appears to be likely that Dr Lana met his end between the moment when the housekeeper heard his voice, and the time when Mrs. Madding made her first call – which was no later than midnight – and found it impossible to attract his attention. However, if this were the time of his death, then it was certain that Mr. Arthur Morton could not be guilty, as it was after that when Mrs. Madding had met the young squire at the gate."

"If your hypothesis is correct, Watson, and someone was with Dr Lana before Mrs. Madding met Mr. Arthur Morton, then who was this someone, and what motives had he for wishing evil to the doctor?"

"I admit that if we could throw light upon this, it would go a long way towards establishing Arthur Morton's innocence."

"However, in the meanwhile, it is possible to say — as I am certain that Lestrade is arguing — that there was no proof that anyone had been there at all except the young squire. Meanwhile, on the other hand, there was ample proof that his motives in visiting Dr Lana were of a sinister kind. When Mrs. Madding called, the doctor might have retired to his room, or he might – as she thought at the time – have gone out, and returned afterwards to find Mr. Arthur Morton waiting for him."

"But that is pure conjecture, Holmes," I protested. "And what of the fact that the photograph of his sister Frances, which had been removed from the doctor's room, has – as Lestrade admitted – not been found in her brother's possession? Surely he would not have destroyed it."

Holmes shook his head. "This argument, does not count for much, Watson, as he may have stashed it anywhere in that great pile of a building."

By this time, we had arrived outside our destination. Entering the pub, we found Lestrade looking rather smug. His face was flushed with victory.

"Well, Mr. Holmes," said he, in a mocking tone, "have you traced your eye-patch?"

"Not as of yet, though there are one or two avenues still in need of pursuing."

"Well, I would tell you not to bother. This one is sewn up as tight as a bug in a rug."

"Oh?" said Holmes, his right eyebrow cocked upwards. "Have you found something of note?"

"You can say that," the inspector said, with a loud laugh. "Do you recall the serving girl, Mary Pilling? She finally came clean, and admitted that she was awakened about a quarter to ten on the night in question. She peeked out her window, where she saw a fine landau parked outside the front door to the house."

"A landau?" said Holmes. "That is most remarkable."

"Indeed it is," Lestrade continued. "It is proof that Arthur Morton is responsible for Dr Lana's death."

"How so?"

"Remember the time-line, Mr. Holmes," said Lestrade, smugly. "The one flaw in the case for the prosecution was that Mrs. Woods heard a cry at almost precisely eleven o'clock. And yet, Mrs. Madding saw Mr. Morton approaching the house sometime after that."

"Certainly," said Holmes, mildly. "But you have a new theory which explains it?"

"I do! Mr. Morton arrived by landau at a quarter to eleven, now proven by the testimony of Mary Pilling. He beats Dr Lana to death at eleven, arousing Mrs. Woods. Mrs. Woods speaks through the door to someone whom she believes to be Dr Lana, but is in fact Mr. Morton impersonating his voice. Morton then flees the scene in panic, but soon realizes that he must have left behind clues to his guilt. Therefore, he turns around to revisit the scene of the crime, where he encounters Mrs. Madding. He is at first alarmed by her appearance, but then reassured that she did not notice anything amiss. After she leaves, he spends the next few hours removing all traces of his presence there, and therefore, Mr. Morton is just leaving when Mrs. Madding returns at three o'clock."

"How did he get in and out of Dr Lana's study?"

"Why, he took the key with him, of course!"

"And you are certain that the landau belonged to Mr. Morton?"

"Mary Pilling identified it. It seems the girl was rather sweet upon Mr. Morton, and knew his conveyance by heart. There is no doubt."

Holmes nodded appreciatively. "It is quite the story, Lestrade. I congratulate you."

"So you admit that I am correct?" said Lestrade, triumphantly. "You should not feel bad, Mr. Holmes. You cannot always be right."

"Indeed. Well, there are still a few things that I think remain unanswered. However, I hope to satisfy myself about those issues soon. To do so, there are two physicians in Liverpool with whom I wish to consult."

"Regarding what?" said Lestrade, his brows constricted in a frown.

"A little whim of mine," said Holmes airily. "It may be nothing at all. Watson, you should remain here. The trial will commence in the morning, and you will not want to miss that. I will return as soon as I am able to do so."

§

After Holmes departed on his errand, I sat in the common room of the 'Seven Stars' and endeavoured to write up all that I had learned thus far while it was fresh in my brain. When complete, I read it over and found it to be a bald statement of the singular and romantic series of events that centred public attention upon this Lancashire tragedy. The unknown origin of the doctor, his curious and distinguished personality, the position of the man who was accused of the murder, and the love affair that had preceded the crime, all combined to make the matter one of those dramas that promised t0 absorb the whole interest of a nation.

I thought that – by this time – throughout the three kingdoms, the public was now discussing the case of the Black Doctor of Bishop's Crossing.[148] In the village itself, many were the theories put forward to explain the facts, which I overheard from the various passers-by who stopped in for a pint of ale. However, it may safely be said that among all these notions, there was not one that prepared the minds of the public for the extraordinary sequel, which caused so much excitement upon the first day of the trial, and came to a climax upon the second.

The case had been referred to the Northern Circuit Court of the Assizes, so early the following morn – Holmes nowhere to be found – I departed the public house and took a train from Wigan to Lancaster. Outside the Castle's courtroom, I shuddered at the Hanging Corner, where public executions took place.[149] I hoped for poor Mr. Arthur Morton's sake that Holmes would soon unearth evidence that cleared the squire's name before he met his fate in that grim site.

The long files of the *Lancaster Weekly*, with their report of the case lie before me as I write the conclusion to this tale.[150] However, in the interest of space, I must content myself with a synopsis of the case up to the point when, upon the evening of the first day, the evidence of Miss Frances Morton threw a singular light upon the case.

Mr. Robert Carr, the counsel for the prosecution, had marshalled his facts with unusual skill, and as the day wore on, it became more and more evident how difficult was the task that Mr. Peter Humphrey – who had been retained for the defence – had before him. Several witnesses were put up to swear to the intemperate expressions that the young squire had been heard to utter about the doctor, and the fiery manner in which he resented the alleged ill-treatment of his sister. Mrs. Madding repeated her evidence as to the visit that had been paid late at night by the prisoner to the deceased. Furthermore, it was shown by the testimony of Mr. Bankley, the postmaster, that the prisoner was aware that the doctor was in the habit of sitting up alone in this isolated wing of the house. The suggestion was put forth that Mr. Morton had chosen this very late hour to call because he knew that his victim would then be at his mercy. A servant at the squire's house was compelled to admit that he had heard his master return at about three o'clock that morning, which corroborated Mrs. Madding's statement that she had seen him among the laurel bushes near the gate upon the occasion of her second visit. The muddy boots and an alleged similarity in the footprints were duly dwelt upon, and it was felt when the case for the prosecution had been presented that – however circumstantial it might be – it was none the less so complete and so convincing that the fate of the prisoner was sealed, unless something quite unexpected should be disclosed by the defence.

It was four o'clock when the prosecution closed. A few minutes later, I heard a familiar voice behind me.

"How does it look for Mr. Morton, Watson?" asked Holmes.

"Holmes!" I cried, whirling about. "By Jove, man! Where have you been?"

"In Liverpool, as I said I would be. And it was a most productive outing, if I do not say so myself."

"It had better be. The prosecutor, Mr. Carr, looks to have this case sewn up."

Holmes smiled, and his two eyes were shining like stars. It was a clear sign that he was overcome with a deep inward merriment, though about what precisely I could hardly fathom. "I would not count upon that, Watson. In fact, if only such things were legal, I would recommend you wager your wound pension upon Mr. Morton being set free."

"What did you find?"

"All in good time, Watson. Let Mr. Humphrey have his day in the sun."

At half-past four, when the Court rose, as Holmes predicted, a new and unlooked for development occurred. I extract the incident, or part of it, from the journal which I have already mentioned, omitting the preliminary observations of the counsel.

Considerable sensation was caused in the crowded Court when the first witness called for the defence proved to be Miss Frances Morton, the sister of the prisoner. Miss Morton had not, however, been directly implicated in the case in any way, either at the inquest or at the initial police-court proceedings, and her appearance as the leading witness for the defence came as a surprise upon the public. I glanced over at Holmes, who smiled enigmatically, but did not say a word.

As soon as she began to answer the questions put to her by Mr. Humphrey, it was evident throughout the courtroom that Miss Morton was suffering from extreme emotion. She alluded to her engagement to the doctor, and touched briefly upon its termination, which was due – she said – to personal matters connected with his family. Finally, she surprised the Court by asserting that she had always considered her brother's resentment to be unreasonable and intemperate.

"Are you saying, Miss Morton," asked her counsel, that you do not feel that you have any grievance whatsoever against Dr Lana?"

"That is correct. In my opinion, he acted in a perfectly honourable manner."

Mr. Carr jumped up and proceeded to cross-examine the witness. "Did your brother take another view, Miss Morton?" he asked.

"Yes, he did," she admitted.

"Why?"

"He possessed an insufficient knowledge of the facts."

"And did Mr. Morton, or did he not, utter threats of personal violence against Dr Lana?" Carr persisted.

Miss Morton paused, and then nodded slightly.

"The Court requires a verbal answer, Miss Morton," said Judge Aldrich.

"In spite of my entreaties to the contrary, yes," she acknowledged.

"And on the evening of the tragedy," continued Mr. Carr, "did Mr. Morton announce to you his intention regarding the doctor?"

"Objection," cried Mr. Humphrey. "Hearsay."

"I will allow it," said Judge Aldrich. "Answer the question,

Miss Morton."

"He said that he planned to 'have it out with him.'"

"And – for the record – by 'him' you refer to Dr Lana?"

"That is correct," she admitted. "I did my best to bring him to a more reasonable frame of mind."

"But you failed?" asked Mr. Carr.

Her chin rose proudly. "My brother is very headstrong where his emotions and prejudices are concerned. But I knew that he would cool down in time and nothing would come of it. He would never hurt Dr Lana."

Mr. Carr shook his head. "Move to strike that last from the record. Speculation. The witness cannot know such a thing for certain."

"Sustained," agreed Judge Aldrich.

Carr turned to the twelve men in the box.[151] "The jury will remember that the young lady had been engaged to Dr Lana, and that it was the prisoner's anger over the sudden termination of this engagement which drove her brother to the perpetration of this crime."

"Objection!" cried Mr Humphrey. "Premature summation."

"Sustained," agreed the judge. "The counsel for the prosecution will avoid addressing the jury." He turned back to the counsel for the defence. "Mr. Humphrey, do you have anything more for your witness?"

Up to this point, I thought that the young lady's evidence had appeared to make a case against the prisoner rather than in his favour. The additional questions of her counsel, however, soon put a very different light upon the matter, and disclosed an unexpected line of defence.

"Do you believe your brother to be guilty of this crime?" asked Mr. Humphrey.

"I cannot permit that question, Mr. Humphrey," interjected Judge Aldrich. "We are here to decide upon questions of fact – not of belief."

Mr. Humphrey nodded and changed his question. "Do you know that your brother is not guilty of the death of Doctor

Lana?"

"Yes," replied Miss Morton, definitively.

"How do you know it?" asked the counsel.

Miss Morton smiled before her answer. "Because Dr Lana is not dead."

There followed a prolonged sensation in the Court, which interrupted the cross-examination of the witness. Mystified, I turned to Holmes, and found him restraining a convulsive attack of laughter.

"And how do you know, Miss Morton, that Dr Lana is not dead?" asked Mr. Humphrey, once the commotion had been brought to order.

"Because I have received a letter from him since the date of his supposed death."

"Have you this letter?"

"Yes, but I should prefer not to show it."

"Have you the envelope?"

"Yes, it is here."

"What is the post-mark?"

"Liverpool."

"And the date?"

"June the 24th."

"That being today, three full days after his alleged death," said Mr. Humphrey. "Are you prepared to swear to this handwriting, Miss Morton?"

"Certainly."

"I am prepared to call six other witnesses, my lord," continued Mr. Humphrey, "to testify that this letter is in the hand of Doctor Lana. Including the author of the seminal monograph 'Graphology: Deductions from Handwriting,' who is here visiting from London."

"Didn't you write that, Holmes?" I whispered.

Holmes merely nodded slightly in response, his lips sill curled upwards in merriment.

Judge Aldrich appeared dumbfounded by this shocking turn of events. "Then you must call them tomorrow," he finally managed.

The counsel for the prosecution had also been paralyzed by the surprise testimony of Miss Morton, but he rallied. "In the meantime, my lord," said Mr. Carr, "we claim possession of this document, so that we may obtain expert evidence as to how far it is an imitation of the handwriting of the gentleman whom we still confidently assert to be deceased. I need not point out that the theory so unexpectedly sprung upon us may prove to be a very obvious device adopted by the friends of the prisoner in order to divert this inquiry."

"It is no fake, I assure you," said Miss Morton.

"But you will not produce the letter itself?" persisted Mr. Carr. "Can you explain this, Miss Morton?"

"It is not my secret to share."

"Then why have you made this public?" asked Mr. Carr.

"To save my brother."

A murmur of sympathy broke out in the Court, which was instantly suppressed by the Judge.

"Admitting this line of defence," said Judge Aldrich, "it lies with you, Mr. Humphrey, to throw a light upon who this man is whose body has been recognised by so many friends and patients of Dr Lana as being that of the doctor himself."

The foreman of the jury spoke up. "Has any one up to now expressed any doubt about the matter?"

Mr. Carr shook his head strenuously. "Not to my knowledge."

"We hope to make the matter clear tomorrow," said Mr. Humphrey. He permitted himself a slight smile.

"Then the Court adjourns until tomorrow," concluded Judge Aldrich.

This new development of the case excited the utmost interest among the general public. Press comment was prevented by the fact that the trial was still undecided, but the question was everywhere argued as to how far there could be truth in Miss Morton's declaration, and how far it might be a daring ruse for the purpose of saving her brother. The obvious dilemma in which the missing doctor stood was that – if by any extraordinary chance he was not dead – then he must be held responsible for the death of this unknown man, who resembled him so exactly, and who was found in his study. This letter, which Miss Morton refused to produce, was possibly a confession of guilt, and she might find herself in the terrible position of only being able to save her brother from the gallows by the sacrifice of her former lover.

Holmes, for his part, refused to say a word about it. I knew this to be one of those rare examples where Holmes had paused in acting as a purely analytical engine, and instead yielded to his secret craving for appreciation and acclaim. He could never resist the touch of the dramatic, and when more so than in front of a public trial?

The Court next morning was crammed to overflowing, and a murmur of excitement passed over it when Mr. Humphrey was observed to enter in a state of emotion, which even his trained nerves could not conceal, and to confer with the opposing counsel. A few hurried words – words that left a look of amazement upon Mr. Carr's face – passed between them, and then the counsel for the defence – addressing the judge – announced that, with the consent of the prosecution, the young lady who had given evidence upon the sitting the evening before would not be recalled.

Judge Aldrich frowned. "But you appear, Mr. Humphrey, to have left matters in a very unsatisfactory state."

Mr. Humphrey bobbed his head. "Perhaps, my lord, my next witness may help to clear them up."

"Then call your next witness," commanded the judge.

"I call Dr Aloysius Lana."

The learned counsel has made many telling remarks in his day, but he has certainly never produced such a sensation with so short a sentence. The Court was simply stunned with amazement as the very man whose fate had been the subject of so much contention appeared bodily before them in the witness box. Those among the spectators who had known him at Bishop's Crossing saw him now, gaunt and thin, with deep lines of care upon his face. However, in spite of his melancholy bearing and despondent expression, there were few who could say that they had ever seen a man of more distinguished presence.

Dr Lana bowed to the judge. "Might I be allowed to make a statement?" he asked.

"It is my duty to inform you that whatever you say might be used against you," said the judge.

Dr Lana nodded his understanding and he bowed once more. "My wish," said he, "is to hold nothing back, but instead to tell with perfect frankness all that occurred upon the night of the 21st of June. Had I known that the innocent had suffered, and that so much trouble had been brought upon those whom I love best in the world, I should have come forward long ago; but there were reasons that prevented these things from coming to my ears. It was my desire that an unhappy man should vanish from the world that had known him, but I had not foreseen that others would be affected by my actions. Let me to the best of my ability repair the evil that I have done.

"To anyone who is acquainted with the history of the Argentine Republic," he continued, "the name of Lana is well known. My father, who came of the best blood, of old Spain, filled all the highest offices of the State and would have been President but for his death in the riots of San Juan.[152] A brilliant career might have been open to my twin brother Ernesto and myself had it not been for financial losses, which made it necessary that we should earn our own living. I apologize, sir if these details appear to be irrelevant, but they are a necessary introduction to that which is to follow.

"I had, as I have said, a twin brother named Ernesto, whose resemblance to me was so great that even when we were together people could see no difference between us. Down to the smallest detail, we were exactly the same. As we grew older this likeness became less marked because our expression was not the same, but with our features in repose, the points of difference were very slight.

"It does not become me to say too much of one who is dead, the more so as he is my only brother, but I leave his character to those who knew him best. I will only say – for I have to say it – that in my early manhood I conceived a horror of him, and that I had good reason for the aversion that filled me. My own reputation suffered from his misdeeds, for our close resemblance caused me to be credited with many of them. Eventually, in a peculiarly disgraceful business, he contrived to throw the whole odium upon me in such a way that I was forced to leave the Argentine forever, and to seek a career in Europe. The freedom from his hated presence more than compensated me for the loss of my native land. I had enough money to defray my medical studies at Glasgow, and I finally settled in practice at Bishop's Crossing, in the firm conviction that in that remote Lancashire hamlet I should never hear of him again.

"For years my hopes were fulfilled, and then at last he discovered me. Some Liverpool man who visited Buenos Ayres put Ernesto upon my track. He had lost all his money, and he thought that he would come over and share mine. Knowing my horror of him, Ernesto rightly thought that I would be willing to pay him to leave me alone. I received a letter from him saying that he was coming over to England. This visit was at a crisis in my own affairs, and his arrival might conceivably bring trouble, and even disgrace, upon some whom I was especially bound to shield from anything of the kind. I took steps to insure that any evil which might come should fall on me only, and that" – here he turned and looked at the prisoner – "was the cause of conduct upon my part towards Miss Morton which has been too harshly judged. My only motive was to screen those who were dear to me from any possible connection with scandal or disgrace. That scandal and disgrace would accompany my brother was only to say that what had once been true in Argentina, would be again in Lancashire.

"My brother himself arrived one night not very long after my receipt of the letter. I was sitting in my study after the servants had gone to bed, when I heard a footstep upon the gravel outside, and an instant later, I saw his face looking in at me through the window. He was a clean-shaven man like myself, and the resemblance between us was still so great that, for an instant, I thought it was my own reflection in the glass. He had a dark patch over his eye, but our features were absolutely the same. Then he smiled in a sardonic way, which had been a trick of his from his boyhood, and I knew that he was the same brother who had driven me from my native land, and brought disgrace upon what had been an honourable name. I went to the door and I admitted him. That would be about a quarter to eleven o'clock that night.

"When he came into the glare of the lamp, I saw at once that he had fallen upon very evil days. He had come from Liverpool, and he was tired and ill. I was quite shocked by the expression upon his face. My medical knowledge told me that there was some serious internal malady. He had been drinking also, and his face was bruised as the result of a scuffle that he had fought with some sailors. It was to cover his injured eye that he wore this patch, which he removed when he entered the room. He was dressed in a pea jacket and flannel shirt, and his feet were bursting through his boots. His poverty had only made him more savagely vindictive towards me. His hatred rose to the height of a mania. I had been rolling in money in England, according to his account, while he had been starving in South America. I cannot describe to you the threats that he uttered or the insults that he poured upon me. My impression was that hardships and debauchery had unhinged his reason. He paced about the room like a wild beast, demanding drink, demanding money, and all in the foulest language. I am a hot-tempered man, but I thank God that I am able to say that I remained master of myself, and that I never raised a hand against him. My coolness only irritated him the more. Ernesto raved, he cursed, he shook his fists in my face, and then suddenly a horrible spasm passed over his features, he clapped his hand to his side and, with a loud cry, he fell in a heap at my feet.

I raised him up and stretched him upon the sofa, but no answer came to my exclamations, and the hand which I held in mine was cold and clammy. His diseased heart had broken down. His own violence had killed him.

"For a long minute, I sat as if I were in some dreadful dream, staring at the body of my brother. The knocking of Mrs. Woods, who had been disturbed by that dying cry, aroused me. I sent her away to bed. Slowly and gradually, as I sat there, a plan was forming itself in my head in the curious automatic way in which plans do form. When I rose from my chair, my future movements were finally decided upon without my having been conscious of any process of thought. It was an instinct that irresistibly inclined me towards one course.

"Ever since that change in my affairs to which I have alluded, Bishop's Crossing had become hateful to me. My plans of life had been ruined, and I had met with hasty judgments and unkind treatment where I had expected sympathy. It is true that any danger of scandal from my brother had passed away with his life; but still, I was sore about the past, and felt that things could never be as they had been. It may be that I was unduly sensitive, and that I had not made sufficient allowance for others, but my feelings were as I describe. Any chance of getting away from Bishop's Crossing and everyone in it would be most welcome to me. Moreover, here was such a chance as I could never have dared to hope for, a chance that would enable me to make a clean break with the past.

"There was this dead man lying upon the sofa, so similar in appearance to me that, save for some little thickness and coarseness of the features, there was no difference at all. No one had seen him come and no one would miss him. We were both clean-shaven, and his hair was about the same length as my own. If I changed clothes with him, then Dr Aloysius Lana would be found lying dead in his study, and there would be an end of an unfortunate fellow, and of a blighted career. There was plenty of ready money in the room, and this I could carry away with me to help me to start once more in some other land. In my brother's clothes, I could walk by night unobserved as far as Liverpool, and in that great seaport, I would soon find some means of leaving the country. After my lost hopes, the humblest existence where I was unknown was far preferable, in my estimation, to a practice – however successful – in Bishop's Crossing, where at any moment I might come face to face with those whom I should wish, if it were possible, to forget. I determined to effect the change.

"And so I did. I will not go into particulars – for the recollection is as painful as the experience – but in less than twenty minutes my brother lay, dressed down to the smallest detail in my clothes, while I slunk out by the front door dressed in those of my brother. Taking the back path that led across some fields, I started off to make the best of my way to Liverpool, where I arrived the same night. My bag of money and a certain portrait were all I carried out of the house, and I left behind me in my hurry the shade that my brother had been wearing over his eye. Everything else of his I took with me.

"I give you my word, sir, that never for one instant did the idea occur to me that people might think that I had been murdered, nor did I imagine that anyone might be caused serious danger through this stratagem by which I endeavoured to gain a fresh start in the world. On the contrary, it was the thought of relieving others from the burden of my presence that was always uppermost in my mind.

"A sailing vessel was due to leave Liverpool this very day for Corunna, and upon this I booked my passage, thinking that the voyage would give me time to recover my balance, and to consider the future.[153] However, before I left my resolution softened. I thought that there was one person in the world to whom I would not cause an hour of sadness. She would mourn me in her heart, however harsh and unsympathetic her brother might be. She understood and appreciated the motives upon which I had acted, and if the rest of her family condemned me, she, at least, would not forget. Therefore, before I left, I thought to send her a note under the seal of secrecy to save her from a baseless grief. If under the pressure of events she broke that seal, she has my entire sympathy and forgiveness.

"It was only last night that I opened a paper for the first time since I fled Bishop's Crossing, so during all this time I have heard nothing of the sensation which my supposed death had caused, nor of the accusation that Mr. Arthur Morton had been concerned in it. It was in a late evening paper that I read an account of the proceedings of yesterday, and I have come this morning as fast as an express train could bring me from Liverpool to testify to the truth."

Such was the remarkable statement of Dr Aloysius Lana, which brought the trial to a sudden termination. As the crowd pushed its way out of the courtroom, abuzz with excited discussion regarding the astonishing facts that had turned the case upon its head, I turned to Holmes.

"I presume you orchestrated this, Holmes?"

"Indeed, Watson," said he, with a restrained smile. "I facilitated Dr Lana's writing of the letter, as well as his arrival here today."

"But how did you know that he was alive?"

"As I said at the beginning, the solution lay in the peculiar finding of the green eye-patch. I knew that if I were to explain it, all would become clear. What possible role could it play in the death of the man found in Dr Lana's study? Moreover, what else does an eye-patch do, besides cover an eye? Accordingly, I sought out Dr Fickert, the Liverpool physician who performed the post-mortem, and asked him what he recalled of the victim's blackened eye, which you may recall Lestrade offhandedly mentioning. Dr Fickert's answer made me rethink the entire nature of the case, Watson. For he reported that the victim's eyes was no longer black in the conventional sense, or even plum-coloured, but instead a striking shade of yellow."

"How does that help?"

"Come now, Watson! Surely, it is plain? You know of my difficult work in determining how far bruises may be produced after death. However, it is far simpler to determine the dating of a bruise in a living subject. As I am certain you learned at the University of London, the evolution of an ecchymosis almost invariably follows a certain pattern. It begins as a plum-coloured swelling, and then darkens by the second day as more blood escapes into the subcutaneous space. Between the third and fifth days, the degradation of haemoglobin to bilirubin produces a striking yellow colour, which fades over another four or five days until the healing process is complete. From this, we may deduce that the victim upon the floor of Dr Lana's study obtained his so-called 'black eye' some three to five days before his death. As none of the witnesses remarked that Dr Lana had such a contusion in the days leading up to his demise – which certainly would have been something worth mentioning, I think! – I thereby concluded that the corpse did not belong to the doctor. But if not him, it could only be someone who resembled him almost perfectly. And that could only be a sibling – ideally a twin.

"From there, it was simplicity itself to inquire at the Waterloo Dock, where I learned that one Ernesto Lana was a passenger aboard Lamport and Holt's SS *Inventor*, which arrived on the afternoon of June 18th. If Ernesto got in a fight shortly after disembarking, that would give us the three days required for his eye to reach its present state at the time of his death on the 21st. As the *Inventor* was still in port, I managed an interview with the ship's doctor, who confirmed that Ernesto had complained of a weak heart during the voyage. When I described how the man met his end, the ship's doctor agreed that Ernesto's symptoms were consistent with such a death."

"Amazing, Holmes," said I, with sincere admiration. "Who would have thought that it was not Aloysius Lana lying on the floor of his study?"

He shrugged modestly. "It merely required a refusal to ignore the elephant in the room. Lestrade would do well to avoid grasping at the simplest solution which presents itself."

§

As to Dr Aloysius Lana, he returned to the village from which he had made so dramatic a disappearance, and a complete reconciliation was effected between him and the young squire, the latter having acknowledged that he had entirely misunderstood the other's motives in withdrawing from his engagement. That another reconciliation followed several months later may be judged from a notice extracted from a prominent column in *The Morning Post:*

> *A marriage was solemnized upon September 19th, by the Rev. Stephen Johnson, at the parish church of Bishop's Crossing, between Aloysius Xavier Lana, son of Don Alfredo Lana, formerly Foreign Minister of the Argentine Republic, and Frances Morton, only daughter of the late James Morton, J.P., of Leigh Hall, Bishop's Crossing, Lancashire.*

"It is a good thing that Dr Lana glanced at a paper before he got on that boat to Corunna," said I, after reading this announcement.

"What are you talking about, Watson?" asked Holmes, who was engaged at his chemical bench in the task of distilling a particularly noxious-smelling vapour.

"Dr Lana's decision not to leave Liverpool. How he instead sent Miss Morton a letter and then travelled to Lancaster to avert a miscarriage of justice."

Holmes stared at me for a moment. "Really, Watson, you did not believe all of that nonsense that Dr Lana spouted at the trial, did you?"

"Nonsense!" I cried. "What do you mean?"

"Well, there was some truth to it, I suppose. But the good doctor omitted a great deal from his testimony."

"Like what?"

"The landau, for instance."

"The landau?" I replied, weakly. "The one Mary Pilling saw? The one belonging to Mr. Morton?"

He shook his head. "It most certainly did not belong to Arthur Morton. That would make no sense with the revised timeline, Watson. Morton did not appear at the scene until about half-past eleven o'clock, by which time Dr Lana had already fled the house."

"Then to whom did it belong? His brother?"

"Unquestionably this was the method by which Ernesto Lana had arrived at Bishop's Crossing from Liverpool, and there was an outside possibility, I grant you, that he had simply stolen it. However, that explanation would require an extraordinary coincidence that Ernesto happened to steal the one type of carriage precisely matching the one owned by Mr. Morton. No, it was far more plausible that the landaus were alike on purpose."

"You have lost me, Holmes," I admitted.

"Come now, Watson!" he exclaimed. "First, was it merely a coincidence that Ernesto learned the whereabouts of his brother, tucked – as he was – away in a small Lancashire village? Second, how did the bankrupt Ernesto have the funds with which to purchase passage from Buenos Aires to Liverpool? Clearly, Ernesto had an accomplice, who drove him to the destination where he met his pitiful end. Furthermore, why would Dr Lana flee? It was a foolish choice and not one that such an intelligent man would have come to if left to his own devices. Instead, just after Mrs. Woods' retreat to her room, Ernesto's accomplice arrived at the study and persuaded Dr Lana that he would be blamed for his brother's death. Posing as a friend, the accomplice took Dr Lana away with him in his landau to Liverpool. There, he sequestered Dr Lana at his home, convincing him to take a ticket out to Corunna and avoid reading the local papers, so that Lana would never learn the repercussions of his departure."

"But who would do such a thing?" I cried.

"Well, surely it must be a man with a deep grudge against

Dr Lana, Miss Frances Morton, and Mr. Arthur Morton, to wish to see them all suffer so. The man who orchestrated this entire narrowly-averted tragedy, Watson, was none other than Dr Edward Rowe."

"The former doctor of Bishop's Crossing!"

"And former fiancée of Miss Morton," said Holmes. "You see, Watson, Dr Rowe was obsessed with his rival, and spent years trying to ferret out Dr Lana's antecedents. When he finally succeeded, he put his plan in motion. It was rather brilliant. In one possible outcome, Ernesto would kill his brother, at which point Dr Rowe would swoop in and shoot the man, pretending to have arrived a moment too late to save poor Dr Lana. In the aftermath, he would reclaim both his former position and likely the affections of Miss Morton. If Ernesto failed in his mission to kill his brother, then things would transpire as they ultimately almost did. Once Dr Lana was safely shipped off, he was as good as dead, and Dr Rowe could again reclaim what he had lost."

"That is horrific, Holmes. How did you determine it was him?"

He shrugged. "It was quite simple. Once I knew that Dr Lana was alive, my suspicions immediately turned to his former rival. I quickly learned that it was Dr Rowe who had purchased the ticket to Corunna in Dr Lana's name. Moreover, I inquired of the local newspaper boy near Dr Rowe's house, who confirmed that the doctor had stopped his regular delivery of the local papers in favour of only those written by the international press. In so doing, he slyly prevented Dr Lana from learning about the consequences of his supposed death. Until I snuck into the house in the guise of a plumber and spoke to Dr Lana, he was completely in the dark regarding what Dr Rowe had done to him."

"But why did this not come to light at the trial?"

"That was not my idea, Watson," said Holmes, shaking his head. "In fact, I advised strongly against it. Nevertheless, Dr Lana was most adamant that enough damage had been done.

He refused to implicate Dr Rowe, and instead dreamt up a story which was plausible enough to convince the Court that he acted alone."

"So Dr Rowe gets off scot-free?"

"Not quite," said Holmes, with a cold smile. "After I saw Dr Lana into the carriage that transported him to recuperate for a night at the North Western Hotel, I turned back to Dr Rowe, his face pale at the revealing of his perfidy. I told him that I had it on good authority that the South American line was a reliable passage on which to take a berth. I thought the good people of the Argentine Republic might appreciate it if he were to immigrate there forthwith.[154] I have already made inquiries, Watson, and was pleased to learn that Dr Rowe took my advice. I would hate to have to make public the full details of his misdeeds."

§

THE ADVENTURE OF THE WRONG HAND

"Lestrade or Gregson?" asked Mr. Sherlock Holmes of our visitor.

It was a still pleasant early October day in 1895. Holmes had few cases of late, and I could tell by the way he eagerly welcomed in the young lad, that he was hopeful of something sufficiently interesting to stoke the fires of his mental engines. Little did Holmes know at the time that soon he would be engaged in one of the most gruesome investigations in which I have had the opportunity to participate – one where he would be forced to banish a ghostly revenant – despite his frequent derisive declarations about the general absurdity of those consumed by supernatural concerns.[155]

"Excuse me, sir?" said the young lad. He was but a year or two over twenty, with cheeks that had missed a day of shaving, deep shadows under his eyes, and a worried expression furrowing his brow. He had introduced himself as Matthew Travers, a student-dresser at the Shadwell Seaman's Hospital.[156]

"Was it Lestrade or Gregson who referred you to me?"

"It was Inspector Lestrade," said Travers, his blue eyes wide with wonder. "But how did you know that?"

Holmes shrugged. "It was a simple deduction. You have splashes of fresh mud upon your left leg trousers. It has been uncommonly dry of late, so one of the few places to acquire such a stain would be near the water-main break upon Whitehall Street, which I read about in the morning edition of *The Times*. I asked myself where a man who works in Shadwell would be visiting in Whitehall and the obvious answer is Scotland Yard. You also hold in your hand a note with our address printed upon it. I do not recognize the hand; however, the paper is quite similar to that utilized by the clerks at the C.I.D."

"Yes, sir. The inspector's assistant wrote it down for me."

"So you went to see Scotland Yard and they referred you to me," said Holmes, his mouth curling in a smile, which I thought was a sign of his growing interest. "Pray tell what it is that has you so concerned. Did you come on behalf of a patient whom you suspect was the victim of foul play?"

"No, sir. Quite the opposite. We get all sorts of bad injuries coming through there, but they can generally be explained by simple accidents, for the life of a sailor is rough and dangerous. But yesterday, we had a gentleman through who wanted a person's hand."

"A hand?" I exclaimed. "By Jove, Holmes! Do we have another cardboard box case?"

Holmes shook his head. "Let Mr. Travers finish his story, Watson." He turned back to his client. "Start at the beginning, if you will."

The lad nodded his head. "At the Seaman's Hospital, I work under the house-surgeon, Jack Hewett. He keeps a little bell, which he strikes to call me when he needs something. Yesterday, he called me in to ask me what had become of the appendages of the Lascar who had his hands amputated the day prior."

"Who was this Lascar?" asked Holmes.

Travers shrugged. "He was just a simple sailor working the East India Dock who got his hands caught in the steam winch. There was nothing we could do for those mangled hands but take them off and cauterize the stumps."

"So what did you tell Dr Hewett?"

"I said that the hands were in the post-mortem room. He

then ordered me to pack one of them in antiseptics and give it to Dr Hardacre."

"Who is Dr Hardacre?"

"I am not certain, sir. I have never seen him before, though he seemed on quite intimate terms with Dr Hewett. I did what the surgeon asked, Hardacre thanked me, and he then departed. But the more I thought about this, the more I wondered what possible use that a man could have for such an object?"

"Did you ask Dr Hewett?"

"I did sir. He laughed and said that Hardacre always had some peculiar ideas. When his friend requested a brown man's hand, Dr Hewett asked what in the world it was for, but Hardacre wouldn't say."

"But Hewett gave it to him anyway?"

"That's what I asked, sir," said Travers. "But Dr Hewett just replied that Hardacre would get around to telling him some day, and he trusted his friend had a good explanation for such a strange request."

"I take it you have a different opinion?" said Holmes, with a smile.

Travers threw his hands up in the air. "What possible reason could an honest doctor have for such a thing, I ask you?" he cried. "It seems so nefarious. I troubled myself about this all night, and could hardly sleep. I finally resolved to tell the police about Dr Hardacre and let them figure out what he was up to."

"Inspector Lestrade was not interested in your tale?"

"He said that there was no crime, as far as he could see. Then he said that if I really wanted someone to look into it, I should come around here. That you were just the man to investigate something this unusual."

Holmes smiled. "Lestrade has always lacked the imagination necessary to distinguish the simply unusual, from the truly remarkable. I believe your case, Mr. Travers, to fall into the latter category, and would be glad to inquire into the habits of Dr Hardacre."

"Um, thank you, sir," said Travers. "There is only one problem...." His voice trailed off uncertainly.

"Ah, yes. I understand that the state of the typical student-dresser's chequebook is often an alarming one. Do not concern yourself with my professional charges, Mr. Travers. I believe this is one case where I will be most happy to waive them altogether."

The look of relief upon the lad's face was plain. I hoped that he would be able to sleep easier that night.

After Travers had departed, Holmes stood and walked over to my small medical shelf, where he took down the Medical Directory. Turing the pages, he stopped at the 'H' page, and he ran his finger down this. "There are several Hardacres, Watson. However, I fancy that only one could be the man who has so worried poor Travers." He passed me the volume, and I read the record aloud:

> "Hardacre, Philip, M.D., 1879, Bromley, Kent. House-surgeon, from 1879 to 1881, at Royal Free Hospital. Winner of the Bruce Pinkerton prize for Nervous Lesions, with essay entitled 'Phantoms of the Mind.' Member of Psychical Research Society. Author of 'Hallucinations: Pathology or Presence?' (*Lancet 1879*). Medical Officer for the parishes of Bromley, Bickley, Sundridge, and Hayes."

"The very model of a hard-working and impecunious country doctor," concluded Holmes. "What do you say to a trip down to Kent, Watson?"

The Bromley station was a quick fifty-minute journey from Victoria. The railway had transformed this once quiet rural village into a bustling market town. A few questions led us to the red lamp that marked the row home of Dr Hardacre.

A stout, tall, brown-whiskered, and eminently respectable person, who proved to be Hardacre himself, answered Holmes' knock upon the door.

"Ah!" said the man sadly, after Holmes had explained the

purpose of our visit. He invited us into his parlour and waved us to some comfortable armchairs. "Yes, my failed experiment. I did not realize that my request, albeit a peculiar one, would raise so many eyebrows."

"Pray explain, Doctor," said Holmes.

"Very well. Do you know Sir Dominick Holden?"

Holmes shook his head. "I am afraid not."

However, the name was a familiar one to me. "The famous Indian surgeon?"

"That is correct, Dr Watson," said Hardacre. "Sir Dominick is my uncle. And it was upon his behalf that I sought out the Lascar's hand."

"I understand now!" said I. "Sir Dominick is one of the foremost authorities on the study of Comparative Pathology. I once read his textbook at Netley.[157] He must have wanted the hand for a new monograph."

However, Hardacre grimaced and shook his head. "No, Doctor. It is not quite so simple."

"Go on, Dr Hardacre," said Holmes.

"Well, Sir Dominick Holden, C.B., K.C.S.I., and I don't know what besides," said Hardacre, "was – as Dr Watson has noted – the most distinguished Indian surgeon of his day.[158] He was in the Army for a stint, and afterwards he settled down into civil practice in Bombay. He visited – as a consultant – every part of India, though his name is best remembered in connection with the Oriental Hospital, which he founded and supported.[159] The time came, however, when his iron constitution began to show signs of the long strain to which he had subjected it, and his brother practitioners – who were, perhaps, not entirely disinterested upon the point – were unanimous in recommending for him to return to England. As I understand it from Lady Holden, Sir Dominick held on for as long as he could, but at last, he developed nervous symptoms of a very pronounced character. Therefore, he came back, a broken man, to his native county of Wiltshire. He bought an ancient manor house surrounded by a considerable estate upon the edge of

Salisbury Plain, and devoted his old age to the study of his lifelong learned hobby.

"We of the family were, as may be imagined, much excited by the news of the return of this rich uncle to England. At this point, I should note that I am one of five cousins descended from Sir Dominick's three sisters. On his part, although by no means exuberant in his hospitality, he showed some sense of his duty to his relations, and each of us in turn had an invitation to visit him. From the accounts of my cousins, it appeared to be a melancholy business, and it was with mixed feelings that I at last received my own summons to appear at Rodenhurst. My wife was so carefully excluded in the invitation that my first impulse was to refuse it, but the interests of our children had to be considered, and so, with her consent, I set out a few days ago upon my visit to Wiltshire, with little thought of what that visit was to entail."

"So you expected to inherit part of his estate?" interjected Holmes. "Is Sir Dominick childless?"

"Oh, no. His daughter Victoria lives at Rodenhurst with Sir Dominick and Lady Anne. She will inherit the bulk of his fortune. Nevertheless, my wife thought it probable that Sir Dominick would look favourably upon me as a fellow medical man, and leave us some small bequest when he finally passed on. However, all such thoughts were dashed from my mind when I learned of his troubles."

"Which are?"

"Well, he would not tell me at first. We were sitting over our first glass of wine, and the servants had left the room, when the conversation took a turn that produced a remarkable effect upon my host and hostess. I cannot recall what it was that started the topic of the supernatural, but it ended in my relating to them that the abnormal in psychical experiences was a subject to which I had – like many neurologists – devoted a great deal of attention. I concluded by narrating my experiences when – as a member of the Psychical Research Society – I had formed one of a committee of three who spent the night in a haunted house. Our adventures were neither exciting nor convincing, but such as it was, the story appeared to interest my hosts in a remarkable degree. They listened with an eager silence, and I caught a look of intelligence between them that I could not understand. Lady Holden immediately afterwards rose and left the room.

"Sir Dominick pushed the cigar-box over to me, and we smoked for some little time in silence. That huge, bony hand of his was twitching as he raised the cheroot to his lips, and I felt that the man's nerves were vibrating like fiddle-strings. My instincts told me that he was on the verge of some intimate confidence, and I feared to speak lest I should interrupt it. At last, he turned towards me with a spasmodic gesture like a man who throws his last scruple to the winds.

" 'Would you repeat the experience, sir?' he asked me.

" 'Which one?' I replied.

" 'Spending the night in a haunted house.'

"At first I laughed, but then saw that he was completely serious. 'Well, if it will do some good.'

"Sir Dominick replied that it was uncertain that any good would come of it. 'However,' said he, 'I think that your understanding may have a higher evidential value,' said he, 'if you are not told in advance what you may expect to encounter. You are yourself aware of the quibbles of unconscious cerebration and subjective impressions with which a scientific sceptic may throw a doubt upon any subsequent statement as to what you witnessed. It would be as well to guard against them in advance. Nonetheless, the experience is so terror-inducing; I cannot in good conscience allow you to undergo it without strong warning.'

"I admit that I was half intrigued and half frightened by his words," continued Hardacre. " 'What shall I do, then?' I asked him.

"Sir Dominick admitted that he was constantly plagued by the revenant of a former patient. You see, Mr. Holmes, he once had to remove the hand of a fellow from some mountain tribe who was suffering from a tumorous growth. My uncle naturally wished to keep the specimen for his collection. However, after the man died, his ghost began to haunt Sir Dominick, forever requesting the return of his hand."

Holmes shrugged. "If he was so troubled by this supposed spirit, why did Sir Dominick not simply comply with its wishes?"

"I asked him the same thing, Mr. Holmes. It seems that much of his former collection was destroyed by a house fire."

"And you believe his story?"

"I do, Mr. Holmes. It was a simple thing you see. For when I slept that night in Sir Dominick's laboratory, I saw the hillman's ghost myself."

"Ah!" said Holmes, his eyebrows rising with interest. "Pray continue."

"Well, I considered this curious narrative which Sir Dominick had confided to me – a story that to many would have appeared to be a grotesque impossibility, but one – after my experience of the night before and my previous knowledge of such things – I was prepared to accept as an absolute fact."

I glanced over at Holmes, and saw him frown at this profound display of credulity. "What did you do next?" he asked.

"I thought deeply over the matter," continued Hardacre, "and brought the whole range of my reading and experience to bear upon it. After breakfast, I surprised my host and hostess by announcing that I was returning to London by the next train. 'My dear doctor,' cried Sir Dominick in great distress, 'you make me feel that I have been guilty of a gross breach of hospitality in intruding this unfortunate matter upon you. I should have borne my own burden.'

" 'It is, indeed, that very matter which is taking me to London,' I answered; 'but you are mistaken, I assure you, if you think that my experience of last night was an unpleasant one to me. On the contrary, I am about to ask your permission to return in the evening and spend one more night in your laboratory. I am very eager to see this visitor once again.'

"My uncle was exceedingly anxious to know what I was about to do, but my fears of raising false hopes prevented me from telling him. I was back in my own consulting-room a little after luncheon, and was confirming my memory of a passage in Alexandre Smiley's book, *Occultism and the Esoteric Currents*, which had arrested my attention when I read it."[160]

He paused and reached over to his bookshelf to take down the volume in question. Flipping through it, he paused on a page roughly a third of the way through. "Here it is." He turned the book about and handed it to me.

I read aloud the paragraph that he had indicated:

> *"In the case of earth-bound spirits, one dominant idea obsessing them at the hour of death is sufficient to hold them in this material world. They are the amphibia of this life and of the next, capable of passing from one to the other as the turtle passes from land to water. The causes which may bind a soul so strongly to a life which its body has abandoned are any violent emotion. Avarice, revenge, anxiety, love and pity have all been known to have this effect. As a rule it springs from some unfulfilled wish, and when the wish has been fulfilled the material bond relaxes. There are many cases upon record which show the singular persistence of these visitors, and also their disappearance when their wishes have been fulfilled, or in some cases when a reasonable compromise has been effected."*

"'A reasonable compromise effected'!" cried Hardacre. Those were the words that I had brooded over all the morning, and that I had now verified in the original. No actual atonement could be made here – but a reasonable compromise! That was perhaps possible."

"So you made your way to Shadwell Seaman's Hospital to talk to your old friend Jack Hewett," concluded Holmes. "You knew that his wards were likely to be full of Indians."

"Precisely!"

"And what did you do with your Lascar hand?"

"I promptly took it back to Rodenhurst. I arrived before dinner with this curious outcome of my day in town carefully concealed. I still said nothing to Sir Dominick, but after a cup of tea, I slept that night in the laboratory, and I placed the Lascar's hand in one of the glass jars at the end of my couch.

"So interested was I in the result of my experiment that sleep was out of the question. I sat with a shaded lamp beside me and waited patiently for my visitor. This time I saw him clearly from the first. He appeared beside the door, nebulous for an instant, and then hardening into as distinct an outline as any living man. The slippers beneath his grey gown were red and heelless, which accounted for the low, shuffling sound that he made as he walked. As on the previous night, he passed slowly along the line of bottles until he paused before that which contained the hand. He reached up to it, his whole figure quivering with expectation, took it down, examined it eagerly, and then, with a face which was convulsed with fury and disappointment, he hurled it down on the floor. There was a crash that resounded through the house, and when I looked up the mutilated Indian had disappeared. A moment later my door flew open and Sir Dominick rushed in.

" 'You are not hurt?' he cried.

" 'No – but deeply disappointed,' I answered.

"Sir Dominick looked in astonishment at the splinters of glass, and the brown hand lying upon the floor. 'Good God!' he cried. 'What is this?'

"I told him my idea and its wretched sequel. He listened intently, but shook his head.

" 'It was well thought of,' said he, 'but I fear that there is no such easy end to my sufferings. But one thing I now insist upon. It is that you shall never again upon any pretext occupy this room. My fears that something might have happened to you – when I heard that crash – have been the most acute of all the agonies that I have undergone. I will not expose myself to a repetition of it.'

"He allowed me, however, to spend the remainder of that night where I was, and I lay there worrying over the problem and lamenting my own failure. With the first light of morning there was the Lascar's hand still lying upon the floor to remind me of my fiasco. After a sombre breakfast, I bid adieu to the Holdens and slunk back home." He suddenly smiled. "However, I now have a new idea by which I might help my uncle."

"And what is that?" asked Holmes.

"I will entreat that you return with me to Rodenhurst, Mr. Holmes. If there is anyone who can determine a way by which this revenant might be dispelled, it is you!" he cried.

Holmes snorted and shook his head. "I think not, Dr Hardacre. My business is with the true and solid. Not the wisps and spirits of the mind."

"So you believe both Sir Dominick and I to be deluded?"

"I think you are mistaken in what you have seen."

"I saw the Indian hillman as clearly as I see you now."

"Then you have seen a living hillman."

"In Wiltshire?" said our visitor, his tone dubious.

Holmes smiled. "I admit that it is rather improbable, but that is still more likely than the impossible."

"If you come with me to Sir Dominick's estate, I am certain that you will be convinced otherwise," said Hardacre firmly. "I have little ready funds, but I will pay whatever fee you wish, should you successfully rid my uncle of this ghoul – whatever it may be."

§

In the end, Holmes refused Dr Hardacre's offer of payment. I knew that my friend's interest had been piqued by this outré and grotesque incident, and that he would not stop until he had learned the truth behind Sir Dominick's ghost. Holmes did not ask for my opinion, but if he had, I would have suggested that he should not, at the moment, prejudice himself by ruling out any possibility. Instead, I thought he should take heed of Hamlet's advice to Horatio. For I had seen and heard of some strange things during my travels through India – fakirs who could lie on beds of nails, walk through burning coals, and levitate themselves off the ground. Once the ancient mysteries of India entered into a case, I supposed that anything was possible, no matter how bizarre.

That is how we found ourselves travelling back to London in the company of Dr Hardacre. The doctor had wired ahead to his uncle to warn the old surgeon to expect us. From Waterloo, we caught the West of England main line to Salisbury, where we changed to the branch line to the village of Dinton. Holmes took advantage of the trip to inquire about Dr Hardacre's cousins.

The man appeared surprised by this request. "As I told you, Mr. Holmes, they have already been up to Rodenhurst. I doubt that Sir Dominick would have mentioned the ghost to any of them."

"Nevertheless," Holmes persisted, "I am interested."

"Well, I am the second youngest. The oldest are the three daughters of my aunt Nettie with Mr. Stephen Farmer. Their names are Norah, Rosalie, and Deborah. They are all married and live in Swindon. The youngest is Aunt Mabel's son Tom Crabbe. He was a lieutenant in the 35th Bombay Infantry, but has since sold his commission and is seeking to represent the constituency of Salisbury in the House of Commons.[161] Is this somehow relevant, Mr. Holmes?"

My friend shrugged. "Perhaps not. However, I like to have a lay of the land when I embark upon a difficult case."

The estate belonging to Dr Hardacre's uncle was situated where the arable land of the plains begins to swell upwards into the rounded chalk hills that are characteristic of the county. As we drove in a hired trap from Dinton Station in the slanting light of that autumn day, I was much impressed by the weird nature of the scenery. The few scattered cottages of the peasants were so dwarfed by the huge evidences of prehistoric life that the present appeared to be a dream and the past to be the obtrusive and masterful reality. The road wound through the valleys, formed by a succession of grassy hills, and the summit of each was cut and carved into the most elaborate fortifications, some circular, and some square, but all on a scale that has defied the winds and the rains of many centuries.

Hardacre noted my interest in the landscape. "Some call them Roman and some British," said he, "but their true origin and the reasons for this particular tract of country being so interlaced with entrenchments have never been made definitively clear."[162]

I pointed to other structures, which rose here and there on the long, smooth, olive-coloured slopes. "And those?"

"Ah, the small, rounded barrows? They are called tumuli. Beneath them lie the cremated ashes of the race that cut so deeply into the hills. But their graves tell us nothing save that a jar full of dust is all that represents the man who once laboured under the sun."

I was moved by this poetic description, though I heard Holmes snort in contempt. It was through this weird country that we approached Sir Dominick's residence of Rodenhurst, and I found that the house was in due keeping with its surroundings. Two broken and weather-stained pillars, each surmounted by a mutilated heraldic emblem, flanked the entrance to a neglected drive. A cold wind whistled through the elms that lined it, and the air was full of the drifting leaves. At the far end, under the gloomy arch of trees, a single yellow lamp burned steadily. In the dim half-light of the coming night, I saw a long, low building stretching out two irregular wings, with deep eaves, a sloping gambrel roof, and walls that were criss-crossed with timber balks in the fashion of the Tudors.[163]

The cheery light of a fire flickered in the broad, latticed window to the left of the low-porched door, and this, as it proved, marked the study of Hardacre's uncle, for it was thither that we were led by his Indian khitmutgar in order to make our host's acquaintance. This later individual was clad in an orange turban, white-loose fitting clothes, a green sash, and white gloves. Such an exotic figure of the tropics seemed rather out of place amongst the ancient grey stones of Wiltshire.

Sir Dominick was cowering over his fire, for the moist chill of an English autumn had set him shivering. His lamp was unlit, and I only saw the red glow of the embers beating upon a huge, craggy face, with a bright red nose and cheek, and deep furrows and seams from eye to chin, the sinister marks of hidden volcanic fires. He sprang up at our entrance with something of an old-world courtesy and welcomed us warmly to Rodenhurst. At the same time, I was conscious, as the lamp was carried in, that it was a very critical pair of light-blue eyes that looked out at us from under shaggy eyebrows, like scouts beneath a bush. I thought that this outlandish uncle of Hardacre's was carefully reading off our characters with all the ease of a practised observer and an experienced man of the world.

For my part, I looked at him, and looked again, for I had never seen a man whose appearance was more fitted to hold one's attention. His figure was the framework of a giant, but he had fallen away until his coat dangled straight down in a shocking fashion from a pair of broad and bony shoulders. All his limbs were huge and yet emaciated, and I could not take my gaze from his knobby wrists, and long, gnarled hands. However, his eyes – those peering, light-blue eyes – they were the most arresting of any of his peculiarities. It was not their colour alone, nor was it the ambush of hair in which they lurked; but it was the expression that I read in them. For the appearance and bearing of the man were masterful, and one expected a certain corresponding arrogance in his eyes, but instead of that I read the look which tells of a spirit cowed and crushed, the furtive, expectant look of the dog whose master has taken the whip from the rack. I formed my own medical diagnosis upon one glance at those critical and yet appealing eyes. I knew that he was stricken with some supernatural ailment, that he knew himself to be exposed to sudden death, and that he lived in terror of it. Such was the look that I read in his eyes.

Sir Dominick's welcome was, as I have said, a courteous one, and in an hour or so we found ourselves seated with him, his wife, and their daughter Victoria at a comfortable luncheon, with curious, pungent delicacies upon the table, and the stealthy, quick-eyed *khitmutgar* behind his chair. Lady Holden was a small, quiet woman with eyes that were clouded with age, and her expression as she glanced at him was a certificate of character to her husband. Yet, though I read a mutual love in their glances, I read also mutual horror, and recognized in her face some reflection of that stealthy fear which I had detected in his. Their talk was sometimes merry and sometimes sad, but there was a forced note in their merriment and a naturalness in their sadness that told me that a heavy heart beat upon either side of me.

Victoria, on the other hand, was blessed with the vivacity of youth. She was rather above the middle height, slim, with dark hair and intelligent eyes. She bantered rapidly with me about shared experiences in India. With the blessing of her generous parents, Victoria had – rather unusually for a young woman – enrolled in classes at Bombay University. She was especially interested in comparing the native architecture of India's temples and monuments to the neo-Gothic buildings that the British Empire was building in and around them. Her favourite was Stevens' Victoria terminus, which – though still incomplete – I had myself passed through upon my way to Kandahar.[164]

"How are you adjusting to life in England, Miss Holden?" asked Holmes.

She shrugged with remarkable aplomb. "It is completely different than India, of course. However, it has permitted a new angle to my hobby, in that I can now travel about and study the revived Gothic buildings against the remaining medieval structures."

"Which is your favourite?"

"I am partial to the Midland Grand.[165] I love its polychromatic bricks."

"And which original?"

She considered this for a moment. "York Minster."

"Not Salisbury?" asked Holmes.

She hesitated. "Well, the spire is magnificent, of course. The tallest building in the Empire must be impressive.[166] However, York's Great West Window is uniquely exquisite."

Holmes' gaze shifted to our host. "You have another nephew in Salisbury, do you not, Sir Dominick?"

"That is correct. Thomas Crabbe, my youngest sister's son," the old surgeon replied, somewhat stiffly.

"Does he come round often?"

"Not really. Just the once since our return, I believe – same as my other nieces and Dr Hardacre here. Lady Anne and I are not much for socializing."

"I see. But what about you, Miss Holden? Surely, you must wish for more company. I imagine that Lieutenant Crabbe must be about the same age as you?"

"A year or two older, I think," she replied, carelessly.

"And was Lieutenant Crabbe in the British Army?" Holmes asked our host.

"No, Indian Army."

"Ah, were you close while in Bombay?"

"No. His regiment was based at Lucknow. He rarely visited."

With this line of questioning at a close, we adjourned from Lady Holden and Miss Victoria to the drawing room, where we might talk of heavier things.

"I trust, Mr. Holmes," said Sir Dominick, after we were all seated with brandy glasses in our hands, "that you have already been briefed on the state of affairs at Rodenhurst by my nephew?"

"Indeed."

"And you believe that you can rid me of this problem?"

"I think it highly likely."

"Hardacre has tried his best to dispel the phantom, but his

fine efforts were in vain. However, from the little that I have seen of you, it appears to me, Mr. Holmes," said he, "that you are the very man I have wanted to meet."

"I am delighted to hear it, sir."

"Your head seems to be cool and steady. You will acquit me of any desire to flatter you, for the circumstances are too serious to permit of insincerities. Do you have some special knowledge upon these subjects?"

Holmes smiled. "Watson here can tell you of the time when we faced a Professor of History who had been possessed by the spirit of a Viking berserker. Or how a Wimbledon banker vanished aboard a phantom omnibus. And of course, Watson may someday relate to the world of how we brought down a diabolical hound upon the moors of Devon."[167]

"Ah!" cried Sir Dominick. "I can tell that you evidently view them from that philosophical stand-point which robs them of all vulgar terror. I presume that the sight of an apparition would not seriously discompose you?"

"I think not, sir."

"Would even interest you, perhaps?"

"Most intensely."

"As a psychical observer, you would probably investigate it in as impersonal a fashion as an astronomer investigates a wandering comet?"

"Precisely."

Sir Dominick gave a heavy sigh. "Believe me, Mr. Holmes, there was a time when I could have spoken as you do now. My nerve was a byword in India. Even the Mutiny never shook it for an instant.[168] Yet you see what I am reduced to – the most timorous man, perhaps, in all this county of Wiltshire. Do not speak too bravely upon this subject, or you may find yourself subjected to as long-drawn a test as I am – a test which can only end in the madhouse or the grave."

Holmes waited patiently until Sir Dominick should see fit to proceed in his confidence. His preamble had, I need not say, filled me with interest and expectation, and I thought that

Holmes must have felt the same.

"For some years, Mr. Holmes," he continued, "my life and that of my wife have been made miserable by a cause which is so grotesque that it borders upon the ludicrous. Yet, familiarity has never made it easier to bear. On the contrary, as time passes, my nerves become more worn and shattered by the constant attrition. If you have no physical fears, Mr. Holmes, I should very much value your opinion upon this phenomenon which troubles us so."

"For what it is worth, my opinion is entirely at your service," said Holmes. "May I ask the precise nature of the phenomenon?"

"It will suffice to give you an explanation of this extraordinary affair – so far as I can explain that which is essentially inexplicable. In the first place, when I tell you that for four years I have never passed one single night, either in Bombay or here in England – save aboard ship – without my sleep being broken by this fellow, you will understand why it is that I am a wreck of my former self. His programme is always the same. He appears by my bedside, shakes me roughly by the shoulder, passes from my room into the laboratory, walks slowly along the line of my bottles, and then vanishes. For more than five hundred times he had gone through the same routine."

"Dr Hardacre indicated that the revenant wants the return his hand?" asked Holmes.

"Yes, it came about in this way. I was summoned to the Army base hospital at Peshawar for a consultation some ten years ago, and while there, I was asked to look at the hand of a native who was passing through with an Afghan caravan. The fellow came from some mountain tribe living away at the back of beyond somewhere on the other side of Kaffiristan.[169] He talked a mangled Pushto, and it was all I could do to understand him.[170] He was suffering from a soft sarcomatous swelling of one of the right metacarpal joints, and I made him realize that it was only by losing his hand that he could hope to save his life. After much persuasion he consented to the operation, and he asked me, when it was over, what fee I demanded. The poor fellow was almost a beggar, so the idea of a fee was absurd, but I answered in jest that my fee should be his hand, and that I proposed to add it to my pathological collection.

"To my surprise he demurred very much to the suggestion, and he explained that, according to his religion, it was an all-important matter that the body should be reunited after death, and so make a perfect dwelling for the spirit. The belief is, of course, an old one, and the mummies of the Egyptians arose from an analogous superstition. I answered him that his hand was already off, and asked him how he intended to preserve it. He replied that he would pickle it in salt and carry it about with him. I suggested that it might be safer in my keeping than his, and that I had better means than salt for preserving it. On realizing that I really intended to keep it carefully, his opposition vanished instantly.

"I will never forget his words. 'But remember, sahib,' said he, 'I shall want it back when I am dead.' I laughed at the remark, and so the matter ended. I returned to my practice, and he no doubt in the course of time was able to continue his journey to Afghanistan.

"Unfortunately, I had a bad fire in my house at Bombay. Half of it was burned down, and, among other things, my pathological collection was largely destroyed. What you will see are the poor remains of it. The hand of the hillman went with the rest, but I gave the matter no particular thought at the time. That was three years ago.

"A year ago – two years after the fire – I was awakened one night by a furious tugging at my sleeve. I sat up under the impression that my favourite mastiff was trying to arouse me. Instead of this, I saw my Indian patient of long ago, dressed in the long, grey gown that was the badge of his people. He was holding up his stump and looking reproachfully at me. He then went over to my bottles, which at that time I kept in my room, and he examined them carefully, after which he gave a gesture of anger and vanished. I realized that he had just died, and that he had come to claim my promise that I should keep his limb in safety for him.

"Well, there you have it all, Mr. Holmes. Every night at the same hour for the last year and a half, this performance has been repeated. It is a simple thing in itself, but it has worn me out like water dropping on a stone. It has brought a vile insomnia with it, for I cannot sleep now for the expectation of his coming. It has poisoned my old age and that of my wife, who has been the sharer in this great trouble.

"So Lady Holden has also seen the spectre?" asked Holmes.

"Yes," said Sir Dominick, nodding.

"And your daughter?"

"Only once. In the very early days of my haunting, she wished to make certain that I was not losing my mind. Ever since then she has slept far away from my room, and the ghost appears content to leave her alone."

"And where did Dr Hardacre see it?"

"I will show you. Would you gentlemen mind following me this way?"

He led us out of the dining room and down a long passage until we came to a door. Inside was a large, bare room fitted as a laboratory, with numerous scientific instruments and bottles. A shelf ran along one side, upon which there stood a long line of glass jars containing pathological and anatomical specimens.

"You see that I still dabble in some of my old studies," said Sir Dominick. "These jars are the remains of what was once a most excellent collection, but as I told you, I lost the greater part of them when my house was burned down in Bombay in '92. It was a most unfortunate affair for me – in more ways than one. I had examples of many rare conditions, and my splenic collection was probably unique. These are the survivors. The only new addition is the one in the glass jar over at the near end, which holds my nephew's attempted contribution."

Holmes studied these with apparent interest. For my part, I glanced over them, and saw that they really were of a very great value and rarity from a pathological point of view: bloated organs, gaping cysts, distorted bones, and odious parasites – a singular exhibition of the products of India. However, I thought that it would take either a medical man or someone with Holmes' level of detachment to stomach the sight.

When I said as much, Sir Dominick nodded. "You are correct, Dr Watson. Neither my wife nor daughter will enter this room voluntarily. Of all the servants, only Keshav will clean in here."

"Is Keshav your only native servant?" asked Holmes.

"Yes, Mr. Holmes. He was the only one loyal enough to leave his home and come with us to England. The other servants are all local to the area."

I thought I understood what Holmes was asking. "Could Keshav be impersonating your ghost, Sir Dominick?" I asked.

The old surgeon chuckled. "That is absurd on many levels, Dr Watson. Keshav is a Marathi, native to Bombay, while the hillman was a Pushto. They look nothing alike."

"Perhaps coloured plaster?" I persisted. "I have seen men transform under such masks to such a degree that not even their own wives could recognize them."

Sir Dominick shook his head. "Even with the best of disguises Keshav could not fake the most distinctive feature of this ghost." He turned to Hardacre. "You have seen him, Phillip. Tell him."

"I concur with Sir Dominick," said his nephew. "The ghost has no hand. The stump is quite unmistakable."

"But Keshav always wears gloves," I noted. "Conceivably he does so to hide a prosthetic hand, which he removes whenever he is portraying the ghost?"

Holmes had listened to my theories with apparent interest. "It will not do, Watson. There is no prosthetic which is so advanced. Baliff's hand, while remarkable, is not yet natural enough to hide under gloves.[171] I observed Keshav while he was serving dinner. His actions would have been impossible with a fake hand. No, I think there must be a more reasonable explanation for his constant use of gloves."

"There is," said Sir Dominick. "Keshav attempted to rescue many of my specimens from the fire. Sadly, he would not desist until it was too late. His hands were horribly burned. He wears those gloves to hide his terrible scars. I would trust Keshav with my life. His loyalty is unquestioned."

"Precisely," said Holmes, before glancing at his pocket watch. "There are still many hours before the sun will set and your hillman will make his appearance, Sir Dominick. Watson here can tell you that the ancient mystery of places such as Wiltshire have always appealed to my imagination. I believe that I shall go for a nice, cheery country walk."

Dr Hardacre and Sir Dominick stared in amazement at Holmes' cavalier attitude, but my friend would not be dissuaded.

As he put on his travelling cloak and cap, I frowned at him. "You should take this more seriously, Holmes."

"I assure you that I am, Watson. Most seriously indeed."

He would say no more, and I watched Holmes stride away from the house, my brow furrowed in puzzlement about precisely how he intended to deal with the supernatural revenant that plagued this house.

§

"This is most fascinating, Sir Dominick," said Holmes upon his return. "I have been considering your predicament."

I had been thinking the same, but had come to little conclusion. During Holmes' absence, I had occupied myself by inspecting the house and interviewing Keshav and the local servants. The thought had come into my head that the house might have a priest hole, such as the one employed by Jack Douglas at Birlstone Manor. However, despite my repetitive rapping upon the various walls, fireplaces, and staircases, I found nothing remarkable. My discussions with Keshav were similarly unrevealing, as the man simply corroborated everything we had heard from Sir Dominick. The local servants were rather more lurid in their speculations about the revenant; however, I ultimately dismissed all of it as rampant nonsense conceived by minds lacking sufficient stimulation. In short, I had made no progress, and was therefore much interested in what Holmes could have possibly uncovered while strolling about in the surrounding hills.

"Do you have a solution?" asked the old surgeon.

"I have a plan," responded Holmes, "which is perhaps not the same thing, but I believe it has the potential to unravel the reasons for your haunting."

"I am most eager to hear it."

"Very well. First, Dr Hardacre will return to his own home. If we are to banish this spirit we will need to not clutter the *genius loci* of the house with too many new souls."

Hardacre appeared surprised by this request, but nodded his agreement. "Well, Mr. Holmes, if you believe that it will help."

"I do. And the same goes for me," said Holmes.

"What?" cried Sir Dominick. "You would desert me already?"

"Not at all. I merely believe that the ultimate elucidation to your problem must be sought outside of your estate."

The old surgeon appeared unconvinced. "I do not see how?"

"You must trust my methods, sir. Moreover, I shall not leave you alone. I propose that Watson here will spend the night in your laboratory."

"What?" I exclaimed.

"Surely you have no concerns, Watson?" asked Holmes.

I narrowed my eyes at Holmes, wondering what device he was employing. However, in the end, I knew from long experience that my friend would not reveal his stratagem until it was time for the dénouement, and I had to trust in his judgement. "Very well," I replied.

That is how, several hours later, I found myself back in Sir Dominick's laboratory. Holmes and Dr Hardacre had departed back to Dinton station in the surgeon's trap, leaving me alone with the Holden family. We had partaken of a light supper, and Sir Dominick and I had enjoyed an after-dinner cigar while reminiscing about our mutual adventures as medical men attached to the Army in India. His tales of journeys through the Himalayan foothills while occupied with the Mutiny competed with my stories of traversing the Hindu Kush during the second Afghan War. Eventually, the old surgeon led me back upstairs.

"Lady Holden and I are both much indebted to you for your gallantry, Dr Watson," said he, "for it takes something from the weight of our misfortune when we share it, even for a single night, with a friend. And it reassures us to our sanity, which we are sometimes driven to question."

"Do not concern yourself, Sir Dominick. I have waited in far worse conditions for various villains and spectres to appear. Fortunately, such vigils have typically been successful. If there is one man who can bring an end to your haunting, it is Holmes."

Sir Dominick smiled wanly. "I certainly hope so, Doctor. I fear my constitution can hardly take another week of this. There is, as you see, a small settee here," he continued. "It was far from our intention to offer a guest so meagre an accommodation, but since affairs have taken this turn, it is a great kindness upon your part to consent to spend the night in this apartment. I beg that you will not hesitate to let me know if the idea should be at all repugnant to you."

"On the contrary," I said, "it is most acceptable."

"My own room is the second on the left, so that if you should feel that you are in need of company, a call would always bring me to your side."

"I trust that I shall not be compelled to disturb you."

"It is unlikely that I shall be asleep. I do not sleep much. Do not hesitate to summon me."

When Sir Dominick had departed, I looked about my temporary abode. It was much as it had been during the afternoon, though the vanishing of the sun had taken with it any little cheer that such a place held. In the meagre light of my candle, it seemed just the place that might attract a vengeful ghost.

The only thing out of place was a bit of desiccation sand that someone had spilled upon the floor since our visit.

As I wondered about that, there was a rap upon the door, which I opened it to find the smiling face of Miss Victoria.

"Good evening, Doctor," said she. "You are doing a brave thing for my father. I trust that you might find a cup of rosehip tisane conductive to a restful sleep?"[172]

I thanked her for this kindness and she departed. It was no affectation upon my part to say that the prospect of my night's adventure was not an altogether disagreeable one. I have no pretence to greater physical courage than my neighbours do, but familiarity with a subject robs it of those vague and undefined terrors that are the most appalling to the imaginative mind. The human brain is capable of only one strong emotion at a time, and if it were filled with curiosity or scientific enthusiasm, there is no room for fear. It is true that I had Sir Dominick's assurance that he had himself originally taken this point of view, but I reflected that the breakdown of his nervous system might be due to his forty years in India as much as to any psychical experiences that had befallen him. I, at least, was sound in nerve and brain. Therefore, it was with something of the pleasurable thrill of anticipation with which the sportsman takes his position beside the haunt of his game that I shut the laboratory door behind me, and partially undressing, lay down upon the rug-covered settee.

It was not an ideal atmosphere for a bedroom. The air was heavy with many chemical odours, that of methylated spirit predominating. Nor were the decorations of my chamber very sedative. The odious line of glass jars with their relics of disease and suffering stretched in front of my very eyes. There was no blind to the window, and a three-quarter moon streamed its white light into the room, tracing a silver square with filigree lattices upon the opposite wall. When I had extinguished my candle this one bright patch in the midst of the general gloom had certainly an eerie and discomposing aspect. A rigid and absolute silence reigned throughout the old house, so that the low swishing of the branches in the garden came softly and smoothly to my ears. It may have been the hypnotic lullaby of this gentle susurrus, or it may have been the result of my tiring day, but after many dozings and many efforts to regain my clearness of perception, I fell at last into a deep and dreamless sleep.[173]

I was awakened by some sound in the room, and I instantly raised myself upon my elbow on the couch. Some hours had passed, for the square patch of light upon the wall had slid downwards and sideways until it lay obliquely at the end of my bed. The rest of the room was in deep shadow. At first, I could see nothing. Presently, however, as my eyes became accustomed to the faint light, I was aware – with a thrill that all my scientific absorption could not entirely prevent – that something was moving slowly along the line of the wall. A gentle, shuffling sound, as of soft slippers, came to my ears, and I dimly discerned a human figure walking stealthily from the direction of the door. As it emerged into the patch of moonlight, I saw very clearly what it was and how it was employed. It was a man, short and squat, dressed in some sort of darkgrey gown, which hung straight from his shoulders to his feet. The moon shone upon the side of his face, and I saw that it was chocolate-brown in colour, though it glowed with a red intensity. He had a ball of black hair, like a woman's, at the back of his head. He walked slowly, and his eyes were cast upwards towards the line of bottles that contained those gruesome remnants of humanity. He seemed to examine each jar with attention, and then to pass on to the next. When he had come to the end of the line, immediately opposite my bed, he stopped, faced me, threw up his hands with a gesture of despair, and vanished from my sight.

I have said that he threw up his hands, but I should have said his arms, for as he assumed that attitude of despair I observed a singular peculiarity about his appearance. He had only one hand! As the sleeves drooped down from the up-flung arms, I saw the left plainly, but the right ended in a knobby and unsightly stump. In every other way his appearance was so natural, and I had both seen and heard him so clearly, that I could easily have believed that he was an Indian servant of Sir Dominick's who had come into my room in search of something. It was only his sudden disappearance that suggested anything more sinister to me. As it was, I sprang from my couch, lit a candle, and examined the whole room carefully. The sand on the floor had been disturbed, but I had likely done so myself in my alarm. There were no signs of my visitor, and I was forced to conclude that there had really been something outside the normal laws of Nature in his appearance. I lay awake for the remainder of the night, but nothing else occurred to disturb me.

I am an early riser, but Sir Dominick proved to be an even earlier one, for I found him pacing up and down the lawn at the side of the house. Sir Dominick ran towards me in his eagerness when he saw me come out from the door.

"Well, well!" he cried. "Did you see him?"

"The Indian with one hand?" I cried.

"Precisely," said Sir Dominick nodding.

"Yes, I saw him!" I told him all that occurred.

When I had finished, he led the way into his study. "We have a little time before breakfast," said he. "I am most happy that you can confirm my account. However, I fail to see how Mr. Holmes plans to banish this revenant."

"I will admit, Sir Dominick, that a way forward seems unlikely. However, I have only seen Holmes beaten on a handful of occasions."

He shook his head sadly. "But those were men…"

"And, once a woman," I interjected.

"Can he possibly apply the same methods to something from beyond the rational world?"

I admitted that his concerns were valid. Holmes had before proven that various cases of the supposedly supernatural had, in fact, more earthly explanations, but did it follow that all such cases would invariably follow this pattern?

"But there is the breakfast gong," said Sir Dominick. "My

wife will be waiting impatiently to know how it fared with you last night."

I related my story again to Lady Anne and Miss Victoria, who were much interested to learn of it, despite the fact that I had made little headway in locating a solution to the problem that plagued Rodenhurst. I spent the rest of the morning wandering about the estate hoping to notice something of interest that might advance the case, though this task was in vain.

Eventually, about an hour after luncheon, Sir Dominick and I were resting when Holmes reappeared from his mysterious errand, a Gladstone bag in his hand.

"Holmes!" I cried. "Where have you been?"

"The Shadwell Seaman's Hospital."

"What could you have possibly needed there?"

In response, Holmes reached into his bag and removed an item that had been tightly wrapped in cloth bandages. These he proceeded to unwind until he exposed what lay inside.

"A hand!" I exclaimed.

"Not just any hand, Watson," said Holmes, setting it upon the table. "The mate to the one so recently obtained by Dr Hardacre."

"I do not understand, Mr. Holmes," said Sir Dominick, his brow furrowed. "Philip already tried his gambit with the Lascar's hand and failed."

Holmes smiled. "Indeed. However, there was a good reason for his failure. I admit that I did not see it at once." He turned to me. "What about it, Watson? You spent the night in the laboratory. Surely you see now the problem with Dr Hardacre's solution?"

I sat down and studied the hand that Holmes had brought. As I did so, suddenly an idea flew like a bullet through my head and brought me quivering with excitement out of my chair. I raised the grim relic from where it sat. Yes, it was indeed so. This was the right hand of the Lascar. The one which the hillman was missing. Which could only mean that the one packed by Travers for Dr Hardacre was the left hand!

"It was the wrong hand!" I cried.

"Capital, Watson," said Holmes, clapping. "I thought you would eventually see it." He turned to our host. "Yesterday, Sir Dominick, you told us that the hand you removed from the Pushto was the right. However, when I examined the jar that held the hand Dr Hardacre had brought with him from Shadwell, I immediately noted that it was the left. If your nephew's theory of a need for a reasonable compromise with the revenant is correct, surely the wrong hand does not fit that bill. No, your spirit will only be satisfied with a right hand.

"Therefore, as you know, I took the first train back to town, and hurried at once to the Seamen's Hospital. For I remembered Mr Travers noting that both hands of the Lascar had been amputated, but I was concerned that the precious remaining organ of which I was in search might have been already consumed in the crematory. Fortunately, my suspense was soon ended. It had still been preserved in the post-mortem room. And so I returned to Rodenhurst as soon as possible, with my mission accomplished and the material for a fresh experiment."

Sir Dominick was elated by this explanation, and consumed with excitement to try Holmes' approach. Unfortunately, the revenant would only manifest himself in the dead of night, so we were forced to wait with taught anticipation. For his part, Sir Dominick seemed convinced that we were on the right track and that his worries were over. Lady Anne gallantly supported her husband, though Miss Victoria seemed more circumspect, warning her father not to get his hopes up. She was plainly worried that another failed experiment would bring about an utter collapse of his fraying nerves.

When the time finally came for us to turn in, Sir Dominick would not hear of my occupying the laboratory again, nor would he permit Holmes to do so. To all our entreaties, he turned a deaf ear. It offended his sense of hospitality, and he could no longer permit it. If anyone would wait for the revenant's appearance, it would be his burden alone.

To my surprise, Holmes cheerfully acquiesced to this plan. I left the hand, therefore, in the same position of its fellow two nights before, and Holmes and I occupied a comfortable double-bedded room in another portion of the house, some distance from the scene of my adventure. We had shared a room before when engaged on cases, and my slumber was typically disturbed by Holmes' strange habits and apparent lack of the normal human requirement for sleep. Therefore, it was quite the reversal when Holmes – without any apparent ado about the peculiar happenstances of this house – lay in his bed, closed his eyes, and rapidly drifted off.

For my part, even after I had turned down the lamp, I was too excited to readily fall asleep. What was Holmes' game? Did he really believe that the simple provision of a right hand would solve Sir Dominick's problem? And if so, was it possible that Holmes had finally acknowledged the existence of a world beyond the one so coldly described in the scientific textbooks?

Eventually, the absolute darkness accomplished its charge and I fell asleep, though this was not destined to be uninterrupted. In the dead of night, Sir Dominick burst into our room, a lamp in his hand. His huge, gaunt figure was enveloped in a loose dressing gown, and his whole appearance might certainly have seemed more formidable to a weak-nerved man than that of the Indian of the night before. However, it was not his entrance so much as his expression that amazed me. He had turned suddenly younger by twenty years at the least. His eyes were shining, his features radiant, and he waved one hand in triumph over his head. I sat up astounded, staring sleepily at this extraordinary visitor. But his words soon drove the sleep from my weary eyes.

"We have done it! We have succeeded!" he shouted. "My dear Mr. Holmes, how can I ever in this world repay you?"

"You don't mean to say that it is all right?" I cried.

"Indeed I do. I was sure that you would not mind being awakened to hear such blessed news."

"Mind! I should think not indeed. But is it really certain?" I asked.

"I have no doubt whatever upon the point. I owe you such a debt, Mr. Holmes – and you too Dr Watson, not to mention to my dear nephew Phillip who brought you here – as I have never owed a man before, and never expected to. What can I possibly do for you that is commensurate? Providence must have sent you to my rescue. You have saved both my reason and my life, for another six months of this must have seen me in either a cell or a coffin. And my wife – it was wearing her out before my eyes. Never could I have believed that any human being could have lifted this burden off me."

He seized Holmes' hand and wrung it in his bony grip.

Holmes smiled wanly. "It was only an experiment – a sort of forlorn hope – but I am delighted from my heart that it has succeeded. However, how do you know that it is all right? Have you seen something?"

Sir Dominick seated himself at the foot of Holmes' bed.

"I have seen enough," said he. "It satisfies me that I shall be troubled no more. What has passed is easily told. You know that at a certain hour this creature always comes to me. To-night he arrived at the usual time, and aroused me with even more violence than is his custom. I can only surmise that his disappointment of two nights ago increased the bitterness of his anger against me. He looked angrily at me, and then went on his usual rounds. However, in a few minutes I saw him – for the first time since his persecution began – return to my chamber. He was smiling. I saw the gleam of his white teeth through the dim light. He stood facing me at the end of my bed, and three times he made the low, Eastern salaam, which is their solemn leave-taking. And the third time that he bowed he raised his arms over his head, and I saw his two hands outstretched in the air. So he vanished, and, as I believe, for ever."

The following morning was an early one for the entire household, for who could sleep after such a remarkable turn of events? Sir Dominick repeated the story for his wife, his daughter, even his servant Keshav. The latter in particular seemed particularly overwhelmed, his eyes flooded with tears of joy that his employer's curse had been lifted.

"Now, now, my good man," said Sir Dominick, uncomfortably. He awkwardly patted the man upon the back. "I never blamed you for the fire in Bombay, nor the fact that we were unable to salvage the Pushto's hand. You tried your best."

"I am most moved by this experience, father," said Victoria, suddenly. "We have witnessed something remarkable, and scarcely credible. I have been inspired to return to India and seek out the holy men there. I wish to learn from them."

"What?" cried Sir Dominick, shocked by this sudden announcement. "Are you serious?"

"My decision is made. I am completely resolved to see this through. In fact, I want you to alter your final will immediately, father. I am henceforth going to live a simple life, and will take a vow of poverty.[174] I wish for no money from you – ever."

The old surgeon seemed staggered by this turn of events. "If you insist, my dear," said he, hesitantly.

By the time Holmes and I were ready to depart Rodenhurst, I thought Sir Dominick had come to terms with the double shocks of the day. His terrible persecution had ended. Nevertheless, this happy event was counterbalanced by the sadness brought on by his daughter's resolve to return to India alone. As we drove away in his trap, I glanced back at the old couple standing side by side in the doorway to their melancholy estate. I thought that they had finally come round to that tragic imitation of the dawn of life when husband and wife, having lost or scattered all those who were their intimates, find themselves face to face and alone once more, their work done, and the end nearing fast. Perhaps those who have reached that stage in sweetness and love – those who can change their winter into a gentle, Indian summer – have come as victors through the ordeal of life?

§

"I cannot thank you enough, Mr. Holmes," said Dr Hardacre. "I, at least, will always have reason to bless the memory of the poor man with the amputated hands, and the day when I was fortunate enough to bring you with me to Rodenhurst and relieve my uncle of his unwelcome presence."

We had met him again in passing at Dinton Station, where he was disembarking from the London train, having been summoned by Sir Dominick's good news earlier that morning. Holmes and I shook his hand, and assured him that it was our great pleasure to be of assistance. As he promised to Travers, Holmes had taken no fee for his work on the Holden case. For him, the recherché nature of the work was plainly sufficient to meet his needs. Moreover, I had the pleasure of finally seeing Holmes confront and confirm the reality of the great unknown.

As for Dr Hardacre, many knew that there were at least five people between the inheritance of Rodenhurst and him, and to them, I supposed that Sir Dominick's selection appeared to be altogether arbitrary and whimsical. I can assure them, however, that they are quite mistaken, and that – although I only knew Sir Dominick in the closing years of his life – there were, none the less, very real reasons why he should show the majority of his goodwill towards his young nephew. In fact, one could venture to say, that no man – save only Mr. Sherlock Holmes – ever did more for another than Dr Hardacre did for his uncle. I cannot expect the story to be believed, but it is so singular that I should feel that it was a breach of duty if I did not put it upon record – so here it is, and your belief or incredulity is your own affair.

With this conclusion, I set down my pen on my sketch, which I thought to embody with the somewhat fantastic title of 'The Adventure of the Risen Revenant.' It was the morning after our return to Baker Street. I had quickly put down my recollections on paper, for I did not want time to dull the vividness of any of them. I was planning to send the manuscript off in the evening post to my literary agent, with instructions to forward to the editor of *The Strand.* I was certain that my readers would greatly enjoy reading of such a unique experience, even when compared to the many other singular cases that Holmes had undertaken throughout the course of his career.

I shook my head with astonishment as I thought over the case. "I really cannot believe that you banished a revenant, Holmes. I never thought I would see the day when you would even admit to their existence."

Holmes glanced up from his newspaper. "Whatever are you talking about, Watson?"

"Why, the hillman's ghost!" I cried.

"There was no ghost, Watson."

I was speechless. "But, I saw him."

"You saw a hillman, yes," said he, agreeably.

I stared at him, comprehension slowly dawning. "Do you mean to say that there was an actual Pushto hillman terrorizing Sir Dominick?"

"Capital, Watson!" said Holmes, with a smile. "You now understand."

"I understand nothing," I cried. "How could there have been a living Pushto, who – according to Sir Dominick himself – looked exactly like his former patient, terrorizing him?" I stopped for a moment and thought about it. "Wait! I know – the man never died!"

"Close, Watson. I will admit that I had considered that a likely explanation for some time. Until I met the hillman, of course."

"You what?"

"I met him. On my post-luncheon walk, which had a rather explicit purpose, besides the general opportunity to meditate in solitude."

"Which was?"

"I wished to inspect the ancient barrows. I had decided that if there was a Pushto hillman roaming about Wiltshire, he was hardly taking a room in town. He would have been instantly commented upon, and word would have eventually gotten back to Sir Dominick, who in turn would realize what was happening."

"What was happening?" I cried. "Who was this hillman?"

"I followed his steps into the hills behind Sir Dominick's estate, for there are not many in the area who commonly wears such a distinctive sandal. I found him nestled in one of those prehistoric chambered tombs that litter so much of our English countryside. The one in question was roughly rectangular in form, with a grassy tumulus enclosed by kerbstones. Some antiquarian must have long ago excavated it, and its current unremarkable nature meant that it is now little visited. It therefore formed a perfect little habitation for our friend, much like the one I once occupied on the Black Tor. I eventually learned that his name is Jamal. He is the brother of Sir Dominick's deceased patient, who was Khushkal, a Prince of the Khattak tribe. Hence their similar physical appearance."

"But his hand! How did he fake that?"

Holmes shook his head. "He did not, Watson," said he, gravely. "When his brother died, Jamal travelled all the way to Bombay to recover Kushkal's hand. For in their beliefs, the prince could not be properly sent off to the afterlife without it. Sadly, Jamal did not trust that Sir Dominick would willingly release the hand to him. At least not without a protracted discussion. So, rather than asking politely, Jamal determined to steal it back. Unfortunately, he tipped over his candle, and in so doing, set Sir Dominick's house on fire, thereby inadvertently destroying the very item that he sought. Jamal had only one recourse. When he returned to his tribe, Jamal had his own hand chopped off and laid it in the ground with Kushkal, making his deceased brother whole."

"What!" I cried. "That is madness! How could he do such a thing?"

"His belief in the afterlife and love for his brother were far stronger than any fear of personal harm. It is a rather remarkable level of detachment."

"But his face was glowing red!" I protested. "How did he accomplish that? Surely he was no chemist like Stapleton, to concoct an ingenious preparation of phosphorus?"

"He had no need to, Watson. He brought with him the red pigment from his home country. It is a powder called *gulal*, which they use for their festival of *Hoolee*.[175] It accomplished much the same thing as Stapleton's trick."

"But if he has made his brother whole, why was Jamal still terrorizing Sir Dominick?"

"After he recovered, Jamal realized that he must be made whole himself. He could not risk a future death without a right hand to accompany him into the long night beyond the grave. Therefore, he returned to Bombay and began to visit Sir Dominick while the old surgeon was attempting to sleep. Sadly, Jamal's command of English was insufficient to make plain for what exactly it was that he wished. Moreover, even if Sir Dominick had understood the hillman, he had by this time retired. He therefore no longer had a ready source of amputated extremities to simply turn over to Jamal."

"And Jamal nevertheless persisted?"

"He is a singularly determined man. To be honest, I rather admire him."

"But how did he get to England?"

"Excellent, Watson, you have finally come to the key question! This was the very problem which so troubled me. I had determined that Jamal was a living, breathing man, and a most resourceful one at that. He was also aided by the fact that Sir Dominick was in the habit of taking a nostrum laced with laudanum to aid in sleeping.[176] Anything he saw would be twisted by the visions produced by that tincture. Furthermore, as you have already observed, Lady Anne is nearly blind from cataracts and can hardly be counted upon to make out the true nature of any supposedly spectral forms that abruptly appear in her dark bedroom. However, I could hardly credit Jamal with the degree of cunning that would have been required to make his way aboard a ship and follow Sir Dominick all of the way to distant Wiltshire. In short, he needed an accomplice."

"An accomplice!" said I, stunned. "Who?"

"Well, surely this should be obvious, Watson. Who else saw the ghost and could therefore reinforce Sir Dominick's beliefs? Who else would have the opportunity to drug the bedtime cup of tea that was served to both Dr Hardacre and yourself – making it far easier for Jamal to make you believe that he was some terrible revenant that could vanish at will?"

"Do you mean his daughter Victoria? Is that why she suddenly decided to return to India?"

"Of course, Watson. A young, high-spirited woman like Miss Victoria Holden is not likely to conceive of such a path herself.[177] On the afternoon of my return to Rodenhurst, I took her aside and explained that I knew all. I gave her the option of refusing her inheritance voluntarily, or having her actions exposed; such that Sir Dominick would finally learn what she had being doing to him. Fortunately, she chose the less painful route."

"But why would she do such a thing?"

"Ah, there we have a sad but familiar tale. Do you recall, Watson, poor Mary Holder?"

"Of course. I can hardly forget the time that you saved England from a great public scandal."

"Well, Victoria Holden was similarly seduced by a great villain. The Sir George Burnwell of this case is none other than her cousin, Lieutenant Thomas Crabbe. While I was travelling up to London to obtain the other hand of the Lascar, I made some inquires and learned that – as sometimes is wont to happen in the tropics – Lieutenant Crabbe began to go wrong. Without any open scandal, he was dismissed from the Army. Sir Dominick must have sensed that something was not right with the man, and was dismayed to learn that his daughter had formed an attachment to him. He cut off all relations with Crabbe, under the guise of distancing his family from all of the cousins.

"However, Crabbe would not be content with that. He must have promised Victoria a life beyond the narrow confines of her father's estate. Perhaps he told her that they could travel the world together. Nevertheless, such a thing could never be, as long as Sir Dominick was opposed to their union. If only they had possession of her father's money, all might be well between them. Such is how I imagine Crabbe eventually won Victoria Holden over to his cruel scheme. Crabbe convinced Jamal that the only way to get something to replace his missing hand was to keep persecuting Sir Dominick until the old man died. Jamal admitted to me that Crabbe supplied him with food and sufficient money to build a small palace back home in Kaffiristan. Crabbe secured a passage for Jamal on the next mail-boat leaving Bombay after the one which carried the Holdens back to England – recall, Watson, that only aboard ship did Sir Dominick find himself free of his supposed revenant.

"In turn, I convinced Jamal that it would be better to desist his hauntings. Instead, I would supply him with his needs, both corporeal – in the form of passage back to Karachi, from where he could make the journey home – and spiritual – in the form of the Lascar's other hand. Similarly, I sent Lieutenant Crabbe a note that any further attempts to stand for Parliament would be promptly met with public revelation of his wrongdoings. We can hardly have such a ne'er-do-well sitting in Westminster."

I sat in stunned silence for a few minutes, absorbing all that he had just related. "I can hardly believe it, Holmes. But why did you not just tell Sir Dominick what had happened? Why the whole Mumbo Jumbo with the second hand?"[178]

"Come now, Watson. Surely, such a revelation of treachery by his own daughter might have killed the poor man. Do you not recall how devastated Mr. Alexander Holder was after he learned about his niece Mary? His spirit was broken, and he had to retire from the running of his banking firm. I would have spared Sir Dominick such pain."

I nodded slowly. "You are right, Holmes. It was a more elegant solution."

"Sadly, you can never write of it, Watson. For in so doing, you would in a moment dash away the careful fantasy which I have crafted."[179]

§

Several years have gone by, and I thought to add an afterword to some my notebooks of unrecorded cases. Sir Dominick and Lady Holden spent a very happy old age, unclouded, so far as I know, by any trouble, and they finally died during the great influenza epidemic within a few weeks of each other.[180] A few weeks after that sad news, we got a note from Dr Hardacre. As promised, their deaths had changed him in the span of an hour from a simple country doctor into a well-to-do landed proprietor. In his letter, Dr Hardacre reported that during Sir Dominick's lifetime, he had become a sort of son to the famous Indian surgeon and Lady Anne – replacing their absent daughter Victoria. Sir Dominick had always turned to his nephew for advice in everything concerning that English life of which he remembered so little. It seemed that Dr Hardacre also aided him in the purchase and development of his estates. It was then, perhaps, no great surprise when the man who had brought Sherlock Holmes to Rodenhurst found himself promoted over the heads of his exasperated cousins into the head of an important Wiltshire family. For Sir Dominick's anticipations were realised, and never again was he disturbed by the visits of the restless hillman in search of his lost hand.

As I laid down Hardacre's note, a thought suddenly occurred to me. "The sand!" I cried.

"What is that, Watson?"

"You spilled the sand on the floor to prove that the supposed one-handed revenant was actually a mortal man."

Holmes shook his head at the memory. "Almost correct, Watson. I did so in order to prove it to you. I had no such need. For, as I said from the beginning, surely such things are beyond the realm of the possible."

§

THE MANNERING TOWERS MYSTERY

It was a fine early September day in 1897 when Mr. Sherlock Holmes received a caller who set him upon the track of one of the cruellest foes of his career. I will likely never set this sketch before the public, for it is far more pleasing to dwell upon Holmes' many successes rather than one of his rare failures. Yet, there is something so remarkable about the events that transpired at Mannering Towers that I believe the details should not be completely forgotten, even if they are buried in my despatch box until some future day arrives.

The caller in question – who introduced himself as Mr. Gilbert Sampson – was about forty years of age, with a clean-shaven face, a sharp nose, and piercing blue eyes. He wore a well-cut suit and a bowler, which he removed at the door and hung upon the rack.

"How may I be of assistance, Mr. Sampson?" asked Holmes, after the man was settled in the basket chair. "Other than the fact that you are a left-handed solicitor from Devizes, with a wife who cares deeply for you, I know nothing of your particular problem."

The man's brown eyes widened in amazement. "How did you know all that, sir?"

Holmes waved his hand. "It is a trifle, Mr. Sampson. First,

your left cuff is very shiny, while your right sleeve has a smooth patch near the elbow. This suggests that you spend a considerable portion of your day sitting at a desk and writing with your left-hand. As for Devizes, I can see a return ticket from that town to Paddington protruding from your coat pocket."

"And my wife?"

"Your hat has been lovingly brushed this morning, and the shaving of your right cheek was touched up by a second hand, presumably because you trimmed by an uneven light and missed a patch of early whiskers."

The man nodded approvingly. "Very good, Mr. Holmes. It seems that I have come to the right man. I am indeed a solicitor of the public courts at Devizes, where I review petitions for all of Wiltshire. I can assure you that the vast majority of such pleas are frivolous, for the prisoners are almost always unquestionably guilty."

"Ah," said Holmes, "I see. However, you have recently come upon one case where a little mouse of doubt has entered your brain."

"Precisely. The man in question is one Harry Bertram, who is listed as convict no. B24 at Devizes Prison. He is serving life imprisonment for the murder of Lord Robert Mannering. Mr. Bertram has told his unwavering story so many times to Frank Kennedy – the prison's warden – that Kennedy finally began to wonder if there was something to it. In turn, Mr. Kennedy passed Bertram's petition along to me. However, as I am a lawyer, and not a private inquiry agent, I thought that you, Mr. Holmes, would be far more qualified than I to learn whether or not there is any truth to his story."

"Very well, pray proceed."

"I will start with describing the prisoner. Mr. Harry Bertram is a little wizened fellow of indeterminate age. His face is thin, and brown and deeply lined. He rarely smiled during our conversation, but when he spoke, you could tell that his teeth were an irregular line of yellow. When the guards showed him into the visitors' room, I noted that he had a shambling style of walking. In short, he could be an ill-used forty-year-old or a spry man of seventy. Bertram himself refused to talk much about his antecedents, though he made it plain that he was a wayward tramp who performed odd jobs as he went about the country, despite once possessing some training as a skilled mechanic. He had previously done a year in Exeter Gaol for some minor thieving down at Merton Cross. However, he claimed that he had enough of visiting Queen Victoria and that he was trying to stay upon the straight and narrow when he fell into the terrible misadventure at Mannering Towers. It seems that Bertram had been at Bristol in the summer seeking work, and then he had the notion to look for some employment at Portsmouth. He did some wood-cutting and stone-breaking, but was paid such a pittance for it that he could hardly afford sufficient food to sustain his body."

"Once the black mark is against a man's name, it can be cruelly hard to get honest work again," noted Holmes.

"That is true enough. In any case, this is how he found himself – on the night of the 13th of September three years ago – upon the road between Blandford and Salisbury. There, he stumbled upon an alehouse called 'The Willing Mind' in the village of Georges Parva.[181] With the few shilling left in his pocket, he begged a bed from the innkeeper – one Mr. Dick Allen.

"As Bertram tells the story, he was sitting alone in the tap-room nursing a mug of ale just about closing time when Allen came up and began telling yarns about the neighbourhood. Bertram took no great interest in what Allen was saying until he began to talk about the riches of Mannering Hall and its occupants. Do you recall the story, Mr. Holmes?"

"Vaguely," replied Holmes. "I will consult my commonplace book, if required. However, please omit no detail of what you know, in case it is of importance and was missed by the press."

Sampson nodded and continued. "At the time, the Hall was owned by Lord Robert Mannering, who was something of a notorious miser, and yet had recently won himself the prettiest wife in England. You see, shortly after he turned the age of sixty, old Lord Mannering decided that he would see the world. He was away for a year, and when he came home, he brought back with him a young wife – some five-and-thirty years younger than himself. It is a matter of public record that Lady Julia had once been on the stage in London. However, she had given all of this up in order to settle down with Lord Mannering. He was also famous for his great collection of gold medals, which some say was the most valuable in the world."

"Army Medals?" I asked.

"Yes, of course. But also those of the Royal Astronomical Society and the Royal Institute of British Architects. Rumour holds that the Mannering Collection includes medals that once belonged to the Earl of Uxbridge, General Sir James Chatterton, Charles Babbage, and Sir Charles Barry, amongst others."[182]

"So Mr. Allen told Bertram about Mannering Towers and the medals," said Holmes. "It seems obvious that Bertram was therefore tempted by these riches lying within his reach. What then was Bertram's excuse for being at the house in the first place?"

"He has none. He made no complaint as far as the burglary goes. In fact, Bertram freely confesses that after hearing about Lord Mannering's collection that he decided to avail himself of it."

"Fascinating. So, he admits to one crime but not the other?"

"Well, simple thieving has a far shorter sentence than murder, Mr. Holmes, so this is perhaps not surprising. He believes that the three years he has served thus far have gone to sufficiently pay for the conviction of attempted robbery."

"Certainly," said Holmes. "However, it establishes the frame of mind of the prisoner. He goes to Mannering Hall with the sole intention of robbing it. He has no personal grievance against Lord Mannering, nor would he purposefully want to commit a crime that might land him in gaol for life – or worse, a trip to the gallows. Yet, Lord Mannering is dead. So what happened next?"

"Well, as Mr. Bertram tells it, he took his time surveying the house until he found a promising window. Then, around one o'clock in the morning, he used his clasp knife to prize open the shutter and entered the building. However, as soon as he made his way into the room, he was surprised by a voice which bade him welcome."

"Oh?" said Holmes, his eyebrow raising with interest. "Someone surprised him as he broke into the house? Surely they would have raised a hue and cry, and not invited him in?"

"Of course, Mr. Holmes," said Mr. Sampson. "This is the part of Bertram's tale that I found so remarkable. As he tells it, he looked up only to find that Lady Mannering was standing before him in her dressing gown, a green taper in her hand. However, rather than calling for her husband, the butler, or some other servant, she instead instructed Bertram not to be frightened."

"That is preposterous!" said I.

The solicitor nodded. "So felt everyone in the courtroom, Doctor. However, Bertram claims that Lady Mannering then took him by the sleeve and drew him into the room. She instructed him to close the shutter and not concern himself for the light – as the servants all slept in the other wing. She then informed him that she hated her husband and had suddenly conceived of the idea to use Bertram to deprive Lord Mannering the one thing he prized most in the world – his gold medal collection. These could easily be melted down, and none would be the wiser from whence they came. She guided him to the room of the house – the door of which was locked, but the key was in it – where the medals rested in their case. She handed him a large leather sack-bag to hold as many of them as he could carry. He was about to pry the first case open with his knife, when she showed him how to unlock the secret spring to the lock. He proceeded to pick up the first medal, when she suddenly laid her hand upon his arm."

"She had changed her mind?" I interjected.

"On the contrary. Bertram testified that she tried to interest him in gold sovereigns instead. However, he balked when he learned that Lord Mannering kept these in a tin box under his bed. Bertram did not want to risk waking the man, for he wished no violence upon him – or so his story goes. For her part, Lady Mannering was scornful that Bertram would be afraid of an old man, and said that Bertram – who is a stout and sturdy-appearing man – could easily overpower her husband without harming him. She contemptuously called Bertram a faint-hearted fool, but Bertram grew wary about the path by which Lady Mannering sought to work her revenge upon her husband. He thought he saw a crafty, malignant look in her black eyes, before it suddenly vanished into a kindly smile. She mildly agreed that the loss of the medals, especially the rarest ones – the apples of his eye – would be a sufficient blow and encouraged Bertram to proceed.

"As Bertram tells it, after a minute or two of stuffing medals into the bag, Lady Mannering then sounded the alarm. She had heard her husband coming down the stairs, and pushed Bertram behind some curtains. In his haste, he soon realized that he had left his clasp knife laying atop one of the cases. Bertram remained in his hiding spot for some time, as he listened to two voices arguing about a man called Edward, whom Bertram assumed was Lady Mannering's lover. Then, he heard Lord Mannering cry out, followed by the sounds of blows being struck. Bertram sprang out from behind the curtain, only to find Lady Mannering holding his knife, now stained with the dripping blood of her husband."

"She killed him?" I cried.

"So claims Harry Bertram, Doctor," said Sampson, with a nod of his head. "He said that she convinced him that she was sorry for her action and asked Bertram to help set Lord Mannering back in his chair. In so doing, he got some of the man's blood upon him. Lady Mannering then told him to flee with as many medals as he could carry, which he proceeded to do. However, he had hardly cleared the shadow of the house when she raised a cry of murder. Bertram scarpered away as fast as his legs would carry him, but he was shut up in the park of the estate by the closed gates. He tried to hide, but he was soon roused from where he went to ground by a pack of dogs. Lady Mannering swore that she had seen Bertram strike the fatal blow and, while he tried to claim the opposite, the police ignored his pleas. For did he not have Lord Mannering's blood on his hand? Was it not his knife that had been used? Was he not in possession a sack of Lord Mannering's medals?"

Holmes nodded slowly. "Yes, I can see how it would have looked."

"Well, Mr. Holmes, when Bertram had finished his story he looked at me with imploring eyes. He asked if I would put his statement on one side, as did the constable at Mannering Towers, or the judge afterwards at the county assizes. Alternatively, would I – perhaps – see that there was a ring of truth in what he said and would I follow it up? I consider myself a man who does not grudge a bit of personal trouble where justice is to be done. I thought the least I could do was to come up to London to see if I could engage a private agent. Bertram has only me to look to in hopes of clearing his name of a possibly false accusation."

"So you agreed to help?"

"Well, to be honest with you, Mr. Holmes, he left me little choice."

"How is that?"

"He said that if I failed him, it was his solemn promise that he would rope himself up to the bar of his window."

Holmes' right eyebrow rose. "Ah! Anything else?"

Sampson swallowed deliberately. "He said that I would never lie easy in my bed again. That he would come to plague me in my dreams if ever yet a man was able to come back and haunt another. Not that I take stock in such things, of course," said he, laughing nervously.

"A most interesting tale," said Holmes, when the man had concluded. "I am surprised that Mr. Bertram did not get the gallows for such a crime."

The solicitor nodded. "Any judge but Sir James might have done so, Mr. Holmes, especially for a man with a previous conviction. However, life imprisonment is no minor matter, should he be an innocent man."

"What precisely do you wish for me to do?"

"What I ask is very simple, Mr. Holmes," said Sampson. "Make inquiries about this woman, watch her, learn her past history, find out what use she is making of the money that has come to her, and whether there is not a man Edward as Mr. Bertram has stated. If from all this, you should learn anything that shows you that her real character is something darker than she put about, or which seems to you to corroborate the story that Bertram has told me, then perhaps we can see the way to a repeat trial. He has the right to *Habeas corpus*,"[183]

"So you believe that his imprisonment has been unlawful?" asked Holmes. "It seems to me that he was duly tried."

"Well, perhaps not unlawful *per se*," admitted the solicitor. "However, there are certain peculiarities in the case. Of course, Mr. Bertram told his version of the story to the judge and jury, who declined to believe it. I have the files here. Sir James said at the time, and I quote, 'The prisoner put forward a rambling and inconsequential statement, incredible in its details, and unsupported by any shred of corroborative evidence.' It seems, Mr. Holmes, that the local police force accepted Lady Mannering's story without question, and made little effort to investigate Mr. Bertram's account of that night's events. I would hate to think that – knowing what I have now heard – we might repeat their mistake. It would be a shocking miscarriage of justice."

Holmes appeared unconvinced. I knew that pleas of reliance upon the goodness of his heart were likely to fall upon deaf ears. For Holmes was ever insisting that he never allowed emotions to dictate his judgment. I thought that it was likely he would refuse this case, and decided to intervene.

"We would be happy to come to the rescue of an innocent

man," I interjected.

Sampson looked at me gratefully. "You may keep this copy," said he, holding forth the case file.

"Possibly innocent," said Holmes. He pursed his lips and stared at me for a moment before turning back to the solicitor and reaching out to take the file. "How is the shooting on Cranborne Chase, Mr. Sampson?"[184]

"Excuse me?" asked Sampson, the expression on his face showing that he was plainly confused by this *non sequitur* of a question.

"The pheasants are now in season, are they not?"[185]

"I believe, so, sir," said the solicitor, weakly.

"That's good enough," said Holmes. "My friend here is a famous sportsman, are you not, Watson? He has coursed many creatures in many countries during his chequered career, but he has yet to traipse the downs of that mighty plateau. I believe we could put in an agreeable week there. Should you have any additional information for me, you may address us at Rodenhurst, the estate of Sir Dominick Holden. We should reach it tonight."

"So you will look into the matter?"

Holmes nodded. "Certainly. Once we have had the opportunity to inquire about the area of Mannering Towers, I will provide you with a considered opinion as to the veracity of Mr. Bertram's claims."

After Holmes had seen Mr. Sampson to the door, he turned to me. "As you seem inclined, Watson, to see this matter through, I require that you procure us some fowling pieces. Before we depart London, there are a few inquiries that I wish to make. I shall meet you at Waterloo Station in two hours."

§

I therefore went around to my club, for I knew that my friend Thurston was an avid shooter. After explaining the reason for my request, he gladly lent me two guns. I subsequently made my way round to Waterloo, where I found Holmes pacing up and down the platform. He had changed into a long grey travelling-cloak and close-fitting cloth cap, his typical attire for a rustic outing. He had already purchased two first-class tickets and escorted me to a private carriage.

"Ah, the Murcott Damascus Mousetrap," said he as we walked. The case I held was simply labelled with a 'T' and 'M.'[186] "A fine choice."

I recalled that Holmes carried the names of all of the gun makers in the world in his memory, and was therefore not surprised at his exact identification of what I had borrowed from Thurston. "Why Rodenhurst, Holmes?" I asked, once we had settled into our seats. "Why not stay at Georges Parva in the same inn as Bertram? 'The Willing-Mind,' I think it was called."

Holmes smiled. "Far too obvious, Watson. No, it must seem as if we are simply in need of a little change of scenery and are visiting a friend in the area. In fact, I had half a mind to drop in upon Miss Grace Dunbar – or should I say Mrs. Neil Gibson, as she is now known. Sadly, Thor Place is a bit too far away to be of a practical use to us as a base. Whereas, judging from Mr. Sampson's description that Abbas Parva is located on the Blandford Road, it seems that it will be only a few miles walk from Sir Dominick's estate to Mannering Towers. Surely, the old Indian surgeon owes us a favour or two after we relieved him of his ghost."[187]

"I do not understand why we are going to Cranborne Chase before we go to Devizes, Holmes? Would it not be wise to question Harry Bertram ourselves before proceeding any further? What if the man is simply confabulating the whole thing?"

Holmes shook his head. "Mr. Sampson's account of Prisoner B24's testimony was most thorough, Watson. I fear that there is little else to be learned there."

"And what did you learn while I was acquiring our hunting pieces?"

"I went around to Holborn. It appears that at least part of Mr. Bertram's story is accurate. Before she became Lady Julia

Mannering, the individual in question was formerly known as Miss Julie Merrilies of Poplar. She was once the star performer at Weston's Music Hall."

"That only makes her guilty of successfully moving up the social ladder," I observed.

"True enough, Watson. However, I furthermore uncovered the fact that Miss Merrilies was once a close acquaintance of Mr. Edward Glossin, also a performer at Weston's."

"Ah!" I cried. "The 'Edward' mentioned by Mr. Bertram!"

"Just so. It was said round Weston's that Miss Merrilies loved Mr. Glossin; however, the riches of Lord Robert Mannering tempted her to be false to her lover."

"And what does Mr. Glossin have to say for himself?"

"An excellent question, Watson, and one impossible to answer at the moment. For Mr. Glossin has not been seen in Holborn since October of three years ago."

"That is shortly after Lord Mannering's murder!" I exclaimed.

"Precisely," said Holmes, smiling. "It is a noteworthy coincidence that so soon after Mannering's death Lady Mannering's former lover absconded from his long-standing place of employment. Surely it will be rather interesting to see if Edward Glossin has turned up in Wiltshire, will it not?"

"So, you believe the story told by Mr. Bertram?"

"It is too soon to say anything for certain, Watson, but there is one detail in particular that made me wish to look into the matter."

"Which was?"

"The remarkable state of the locks upon the medal cases."

I frowned. "I don't recall hearing that anything was wrong with the locks?"

"That was what was so remarkable, Watson. Let us see what the official report has to say," said he, proceeding to flip through the file. "Here we go:

'The room where the accused hid is a small one, hung

all round with curtains which had pictures on them of a deer hunt. The only other thing in the room was a row of cases made of walnut, with brass ornaments. They had glass tops, and beneath this glass were displayed long lines of gold medals, some of them as big as a plate and half an inch thick, all resting upon red velvet. The cases were secured by a secret spring which opened only by pressing a brass knob.' "

He looked up at me. "Surely you see it now?"

I shook my head. "I am afraid not."

Holmes sighed. "Imagine yourself in Mr. Bertram's shoes, Watson. You are unshaven and grimed from a week on the roads. You have barely sufficient funds in your pocket to purchase food or drink. After vowing not to go back to gaol, you have succumbed to your desperation and decided to burgle the local manor. After using your perfectly good clasp knife to pry open the shutter covering the window, you are now confronted by a lock with a secret spring. Your fingers are itching to get a hold of those medals and escape from Mannering Towers as quickly as possible. Would you not immediately slip your knife under the lock of one of the cases and wrench it open?"

"I suppose so."

"And yet, according to the official report, that is not what Mr. Bertram course of action. Instead, he took the time to locate the secret brass knob that opened the cases without breaking any of the locks. Why, I ask you, would he do such a thing?"

"Because he thought it too loud to use his knife?"

Holmes shook his head. "Nonsense. Bertram has already used his knife to silently open the window. Why would this be any different?"

"I see. It is because Lady Mannering instructed him to do so!"

"Precisely, Watson. Bertram would only take that action if it seemed to be just as expeditious as the more violent option. Here, we find the first suggestion that there might be some truth to his tale."

"So we go to question Lady Mannering?"

He shook his head. "Not immediately. If she is – in fact – the cunning foe described by Mr. Bertram, she will have her guard up for a frontal attack. We must gather all relevant peripheral information before storming those towers."

"How so?"

"I wired to Sir Dominick and informed him not to expect us until close to dinner time, so we have a few hours to look about. I suggest that we hire a trap and first speak to Mr. Allen at 'The Willing Mind.' I have a few pressing questions for him."

"For the tavern keeper?" I asked. "Why?"

"Let me read to you from the excellent transcript recorded by Mr. Sampson after his interview with Mr. Bertram. The relevant part goes as follows:

> *"Allen was a man that liked to talk and to have someone to listen to his talk, so I sat there smoking and drinking a mug of ale that he had stood me; and I took no great interest in what he said until he began to talk – as the devil would have it – about the riches of Mannering Hall.*
> *"Now I had looked at it as I passed, and it had crossed my mind, as such thoughts will, that it was a very easy house to get into. I had put the thought away from me, and now here was this landlord bringing it back with his talk about the riches within. I said nothing, but I listened, and as luck would have it, he would always come back to this one subject.*
> *" 'He was a miser young, so you can think what he is now in his age,' said Allen. 'Well, he's had some good out of his money.'*
> *" 'What good can he have had if he does not spend it?' said I.*
> *" 'Well, it bought him the prettiest wife in England,' continued Allen, 'and that was some good that he got out of it. She has been at Mannering Hall ever since. She*

thought she would have the spending of his money, but she knows the difference now. Stephens, the butler, did tell me once that she was the light of the house when first she came, but what with her husband's mean and aggravating way, and what with her loneliness – for he hates to see a visitor within his doors; and what with his bitter words – for he has a tongue like a hornet's sting, her life all went out of her, and she became a white, silent creature, moping about the country lanes.

"Well, sir, you can imagine that it did not interest me very much to hear about the quarrels between a Lord and a Lady. What did it matter to me if she hated the sound of his voice, or if he put every indignity upon her in the hope of breaking her spirit, and spoke to her as he would never have dared to speak to one of his servants? The landlord told me of these things, and of many more like them, but they passed out of my mind, for they were no concern of mine. But what I did want to hear was the form in which Lord Mannering kept his riches. Title-deeds and stock certificates are but paper, and more danger than profit to the man who takes them. But metal and stones are worth a risk. And then, as if he were answering my very thoughts, the landlord told me of Lord Mannering's great collection of gold medals, and that it was reckoned that if they were put into a sack the strongest man in the parish would not be able to raise them. Then Allen's wife called him, and I went to my bed.

"I am not arguing to make out a case for myself, but I beg you, sir, to bear all the facts in your mind, and to ask yourself whether a man could be more sorely tempted than I was. I make bold to say that there are few who could have held out against it. There I lay on my bed that night, a desperate man without hope or work, and with my last shilling in my pocket. I had tried to be honest, but honest folk had turned their backs upon me. They taunted me for theft; and yet they pushed me towards

it. I was caught in the stream and could not get out. And then it was such a chance: the great house all lined with windows, the golden medals which could easily be melted down. It was like putting a loaf before a starving man and expecting him not to eat it. I fought against it for a time, but it was no use. At last, I sat up on the side of my bed, and I swore that that night I should either be a rich man and able to give up crime forever, or that the irons should be on my wrists once more. Then I slipped on my clothes, and, having put a shilling on the table – for the landlord had treated me well, and I did not wish to cheat him – I passed out through the window into the garden of the inn. There was a high wall round this garden, and I had a job to get over it, but once on the other side it was all plain sailing."

Holmes looked up at me. "What do you make of that, Watson?"

"The detail about the shilling was interesting. It hardly seems in character with the hardened criminal that Mr. Bertram is purported to be. Did Allen confirm this at the trial?"

Holmes smiled. "In fact, he did not. Mr. Allen testified that Harry Bertram left without paying his bill. It was another black mark upon his name as far as the jury was concerned."

"I fail to see the importance then?"

"Put yourself in the place of Mr. Allen, Watson. You have before you a coarse and grubby stranger who – as even the blindest innkeeper could tell by a single glance – had been living rough for weeks. He has taken your most modest room and paid for a small glass of your weakest ale. So what do you do with this poor stranger? Do you spin tales of the great riches that lay nearby? Why would you so tempt such a man as he?"

Now that Holmes had put it that way, it did seem odd. I shook my head. "I hardly know. What are you suggesting, Holmes?"

"What if Allen was in league with Lady Julia? As he described her, she was the most beautiful woman in England. If true, such a face might launch a thousand ships, or compelled one man to do her bidding. What if she coerced Allen to find a pawn – such as Mr. Bertram – to use as a tool in her scheme? For surely she could not kill her husband without a ready scapegoat to take the blame?"

"That is horrific, Holmes!"

He shrugged. "If Bertram is to be believed, and Lady Julia killed her husband, we are already well into the horrors, Watson. Surely, it is a matter of very small degree to go from thinking someone capable of killing a man in the heat of the moment and blaming a nearby innocent of the crime, to believing them able to coolly plot the man's death with premeditation? If she is capable of the first crime, she is capable of the second."

I shook my head. "So you think such a thing occurred?"

"In fact, Watson, I am increasingly sure of it."

"Why?"

"The shilling. As you noted, it appears to be such a minor thing. Why would Bertram insist upon it? Such an act would hardly save his neck from the crime of murder. Therefore, it is probable that it was the truth. In which case, why would Allen lie about it? The only plausible reason to do so would be if Allen was covering for his greater crime."

"And you think that you might get him to admit it?"

Holmes smiled. "I can be quite persuasive, Watson."

§

However, as fate would have it, Holmes would not get a chance to persuade Mr. Allen. At Salisbury, Holmes hired a trap to take us along the Blandford Road to 'The Willing Mind.' When we arrived at our destination, Holmes bade the driver wait for us, and we stepped down to the road. Before I could proceed inside, Holmes suddenly grabbed my upper arm. "There is something amiss, Watson."

"What do you mean?"

"How would you describe this building?"

I considered this. "Well, it is a tavern, of course. One may deduce that because it has the coarse glare and tawdry brilliancy typical of the public house."

Holmes shook his head. "You have missed the one noteworthy detail, Watson. This is hardly the wayside old-fashioned coaching inn of Jacobean times. In fact, I would wager it was constructed no more than two or three years ago."

"Since Mr. Bertram's visit?"

"Precisely. The timing of this is suggestive."

"How so?"

"Surely, Watson, you do not believe that Mr. Allen acted on behalf of Lady Mannering's plot without some form of recompense? I would think the funds to build a modern tavern might suffice to quell his conscience over his role in such a nefarious plot."

Yet, upon this occasion, Holmes' theory was dreadfully wrong, as we were soon to learn. Holmes pushed open the door of the private bar and ordered two glasses of cider from the ruddy-faced, white-aproned landlord.

"I was told to ask for Mr. Dick Allen," said Holmes.

The man shook his head. "You are about three years too late."

"What do you mean?"

"Allen is dead."

Holmes grey eyes narrowed. "How did it happen?"

"The poor sod burned up with the old building."

"The old building caught on fire?"

"Yes, sir. Course, it was a medieval firetrap, yes indeed. Just like Hindon before it burned."[188]

"Do you recall the date?"

"Sure enough. It was the 29th of September three years ago. I remember because it happened during Goose Day, and people said that Allen must have cooked his bird too long."[189]

Holmes nodded as if he expected this. "Did anyone else perish in the fire?"

The proprietor shook his head. "Just his wife. Therefore, there was no one left to rebuild. Nevertheless, 'The Willing Mind' has been a popular place over the years, and Lady Mannering provided the funds to rebuild it, so I took over the running of it."

"Did she now?" said Holmes. "That was most kind of Lady Mannering. What of Lord Mannering?"

"This was shortly after his lordship was killed by a passing tramp. Lady Mannering was in mourning, of course; however, she felt that it would be a fitting tribute to his lordship to sponsor the inn's rebirth. As you said, it was right generous of her. I took the keeping of it, and in my gratitude, I make sure that her ladyship's servants are treated right whenever they come by."

"Lady Mannering does not visit?"

"No, sir. Not likely. She is a proper lady."

"Say," said Holmes snapping his finger, "I think I once met Lady Mannering's butler. Stephens, is it not?"

"That is correct, sir."

"Yes, he had come into Salisbury to pick up some goods from the store. He was telling me about someone new at Mannering Towers. I think he said the name was Edward?"

The landlord nodded. "That would be Mr. Glossin. He is the factotum there now. Lady Mannering took him on after his Lordship's passing. Mr. Glossin runs the estate for her, which is hardly a task for a lady."

Holmes smiled. "Ah, it must be nice for her ladyship to have someone upon whom she can rely for such matters. Well, my good man, I thank you for the ciders, but we must be on our way."

When we emerged from the tavern, Holmes turned to me. "I fear, Watson, that Lady Julia is rather more ruthless than I first suspected. There was one weak link in her terrible scheme, and she made absolutely certain that her accomplice Allen could never betray her."

"But the wife too!" I cried.

He shook his head. "Lady Julia could hardly be confident that

Allen had not spoken to his wife of their deal. If the wife knew anything, and Allen died in mysterious fashion, she could have pointed a finger at Lady Julia. No, I can see her reasoning, Watson. In for a penny, in for a pound. If Allen was to die, so would his wife."

"Surely Lady Mannering did not kill them herself?"

"Most likely not. I suspect that Mr. Glossin took care of that grim business. Still, now that we know for certain that Lady Julia summoned Glossin to her side the moment she was free of her husband, it becomes more and more certain that Mr. Bertram is telling the truth. It now remains only for us to locate the evidence that will allow us to exchange Lady Julia's permanent residence from the Towers to that of Devizes Prison."

§

Holmes indicated that there was nothing else for us to accomplish on that evening, so he instructed the driver of the trap to take us to Rodenhurst. Sir Dominick and his wife welcomed us warmly, and the evening was spent in pleasant conversation. Although Holmes' temperament was typically suited for a melancholy evening wringing wailing notes from his Stradivarius, when he made the rare choice to reveal his effusive side, he could talk exceedingly well. He spoke on a rapid sequence of subjects, on Hippocrates' view of comparative pathology, on ancestral reversions, on the moral dilemma of the Gita, and on the diggings of Lane Fox.[190] His cheerful wit carried us effortlessly through the night until I gratefully collapsed into one of the guest beds. Unlike a prior haunted evening that I once spent in that abode, I slumbered dreamlessly until the crowing of the rooster announced that dawn was about to break, at which point I was awakened by Holmes' visit to my room.

"Good morning, Watson!" he cried, cheerfully. "Did you sleep well?"

"Tolerably so," I replied. "And you?"

"Oh, I did not sleep at all last night. I was too busy reconnoitring the site of our upcoming battle."

"You went to Mannering Towers!" I exclaimed.

"Oh yes, I thought it wise. After the clock struck midnight, I set out upon my errand. I did not meet a soul upon the road, and the iron gate of the avenue was open. No one was moving at the lodge. The moon was shining, and I could see the great house glimmering white through an archway of trees. I walked up it for a quarter of a mile or so, until I was at the edge of the drive, where it ended in a broad, gravelled space before the main door. There I stood in the shadow and looked at the long building, with moonlight shining in every window and silvering the high stone front. I crouched there for some time, and I wondered where Mr. Bertram would have decided was the easiest entrance. The corner window of the side seemed to be the one that was least overlooked, and a screen of ivy hung heavily over it. His best chance was evidently there. I worked my way under the trees to the back of the house, and then crept along in the black shadow of the building. A dog barked and rattled his chain, but I stood waiting until it was quiet, and then I stole on once more until I came to the window that I had chosen.

"It is astonishing, Watson, how careless they are in the country, in places far removed from large towns, where the thought of burglars never enters their heads. I suspect that Mr. Bertram would call it setting temptation in a poor man's way when he places his hand – meaning no harm – upon a door, and finds it swing open before him. In this case, it was not as bad as that, but the window was merely fastened with an ordinary catch, which I easily opened with a push from the blade of my knife. I pulled up the window as quickly as possible, and then I thrust the knife through the slit in the shutter and prized it open. They were folding shutters, and I shoved them before me and walked into the room."

"You broke in! Why?"

"I wished to see how much of Mr. Bertram's purported route

I could re-trace."

"And what did you learn?"

"It is as I suspected, Watson. The whole thing was a set-up, planned by Lady Julia from the first." He reached into his pocket and pulled out the file given to him by Mr. Sampson. Here is what Bertram said about what happened once he entered the building:

> " 'Good evening, sir! You are very welcome!' said a voice.
> "I've had some starts in my life, but never one to come up to that one. There, in the opening of the shutters, within reach of my arm, was standing a woman with a small coil of wax taper burning in her hand. She was dressed in some sort of white dressing-gown which flowed down to her feet, and what with this robe and what with her face, it seemed as if a spirit from above was standing in front of me. My knees knocked together, and I held on to the shutter with one hand to give me support. I should have turned and run away if I had had the strength, but I could only just stand and stare at her.
> "She soon brought me back to myself once more. 'Don't be frightened!' said she, and they were strange words for the mistress of a house to have to use to a burglar. 'I saw you out of my bedroom window when you were hiding under those trees, so I slipped downstairs, and then I heard you at the window. I should have opened it for you if you had waited, but you managed it yourself just as I came up.'

"Now, then, Watson," he continued, "this story of Lady Julia's is patent nonsense. I consulted the almanac, which assured me that the moon was in roughly the same place last night as it was on the night of Lord Mannering's murder. I slipped into the room next to her bedchamber and I gazed out of nearly the same windows from which she would have looked. There is no possible way that Lady Julia could have seen someone hiding under the trees by happenstance alone. Only if she had been warned by Allen to expect Bertram could she have conceivably spotted him."

"So you believe him?"

He nodded slowly. "I believe that there is an increasingly strong possibility that Bertram's version is the truth. Proving it will be an entirely different matter, however. Sir James Pleydell will hardly be willing to reverse his original judgement solely on the basis of my opinion."

"Then what is our next course of action?"

"We shall enact our original plan. As a pair of gentlemen hunters wandering the downs, I would hope that Lady Julia will be so kind as to invite us in to partake of some refreshments."

It was thus two hours later that I found myself dressed in my hunting garb and following Holmes along the winding country paths connecting Rodenhurst and Georges Parva. Eventually we broke out upon the Blandford Road, and after a short while, Holmes directed our steps towards the large house on the left as we came towards the village. This long white house, with pillars and a great row of ground windows and glass doors, stood in its own park. After chatting with the lodge keeper and passing the stables, we strode up the gravel drive, our guns broken over our shoulders to demonstrate our peaceful intent.

As we approached, a sturdy, middle-sized fellow stepped out of the front door. He was some thirty years of age, clean-shaven, and glowing-skinned, with a pair of wonderfully sharp and penetrating blue eyes. He was dressed in the attire of a country squire, and he clapped a straw boater over his light brown curls.

"What can I do for you gentlemen?" asked the man.

"I am Mr. Harris of Bermondsey," said Holmes, "and this is my great friend, Mr. Price of Birmingham. We are staying over at Rodenhurst with Sir Dominick for the start of the pheasant season. He said that if we were in the neighbourhood of

Georges Parva we should stop in at the estate of Lord Robert Mannering to look upon his medals. He heard that Lord Mannering might even possess the Iron Duke's Seringapatam Medal, which we would be mighty interested to look upon."[191]

The man shook his head. "I am afraid, gentlemen, that Sir Dominick's information is rather out of date. After Lord Mannering's passing, his widow donated his entire collection to the South Kensington Museum."[192]

"Ah, that is tragic!" cried Holmes.

"She knew that he would have wished to see it enjoyed by the world, not squirreled away in this remote estate."

Holmes nodded appreciatively. "That is most perceptive of her. Well, we shall have to seek out the collection next time we are up to London."

"You gentlemen are here for the hunt?" asked the man.

"Indeed. Price and I were partners in trade. Perhaps you have heard of our former import business – Harris & Price of Fenchurch Street? No? Well, no matter. We made a tidy sum operating several merchantmen on the Calcutta route; for things were wide open after the Company was disestablished.[193] We have since sold the name to the firm and retired to our respective birth cities, but we still get together every year for a grand shoot."

"And where is your gun dog?"[194]

"Ah, we prefer to hunt without a flusher," said Holmes. "It makes it more of challenge."

"I would say so," said the man, laughing. "For you appear to be short a bird or two."

Holmes smiled. "It is still early in the day. And to be honest, sir, the whole endeavour is more an excuse to get out and stretch our legs in some new corner of the Queen's beautiful realm. If we happen to catch a bird for our dinner, that is merely a welcome bonus."

"Well, I see you gentlemen are travelling light. I am certain that Lady Mannering would be glad if you were to join her for luncheon. By the way, I am Edward Glossin, Lady Mannering's factotum."

"Most kind," said Holmes, with a smile and small nod.

"If you will follow me," said Glossin, with a wave of his hand.

We stepped into the house's foyer, where a thin plump-faced, clean-shaven, balding fellow of sixty met us. He was dressed in a butler's suit.

"Stephens," said Mr. Glossin to the butler, "please let your mistress know that we have two gentlemen joining us."

"Very good, sir," the man replied, before setting off upon his errand.

Glossin led us into a comfortable parquet-floored drawing room, filled with leather-backed armchairs. Upon one of these, a woman was reading a Thackeray novel.[195] She looked up as we entered and rose to her feet. She was tall and straight and slender, with a beautiful white face that might have been cut out of clear marble, but her hair and eyes were as black as night.

Holmes introduced us under our assumed identities, and repeated the story he had related to Mr. Glossin about our reason for visiting Mannering Towers.

She smiled, but the warmth did not reach her eyes. "So, you are collectors?" she asked. "Of gold medals?"

"Oh no, Lady Mannering," said Holmes. "We are simply enthusiasts about all things connected to the Raj. The Duke is an especial interest, given how he got his start there, so to speak."

"I see. Well, we still have a few items from the Eastern Empire, which my late husband had collected. Would you care to see them, Mr. Harris?"

"Very much!" cried Holmes, enthusiastically.

She indicated that we should follow her. She swept on in front of us, until we found ourselves in a room that was long and low, with many rugs and skins scattered about on a polished wood floor. Small cases stood here and there, and the walls were decorated with spears and swords and paddles, and other such items that eventually find their way into museums after their original collector passes on. There were some queer clothes, too, which had been brought over from various exotic countries, and Lady Mannering pointed at a large leather sack-bag. "This is the only thing here purportedly once owned by the Sepoy General. I have heard that he slept in this sack during the Assaye Campaign."[196]

"I am most sorry that we missed seeing your late husband's medals, Lady Mannering," said Holmes. "We really must get up to London to look at them. How long ago did he pass?"

"Three years," said she, dabbing at the corner of her glistening eyes with a handkerchief.

"Ah, I see. Was he ill for some time or was it a sudden attack?"

"Most sudden, I would say," said Mr. Glossin. "Lord Mannering was murdered."

"No!" cried Holmes. "How terrible! In London, I assume?"

"Not at all," Glossin continued. "It was here in his own home. A passing tramp."

Holmes appeared astonished. "I am glad that you were not harmed, Lady Mannering."

"Yes," said she, tightly. "Fortunately, the tramp fled the house immediately after his crime. Sadly, I saw it with my own eyes. It was horrible. We heard the noise and we came down. My poor husband was in front. The man had opened one of the medal cases, and was hurriedly filling a black leather bag. When my husband cried out, the tramp rushed past us, and my husband seized him. There was a struggle, and the tramp stabbed my poor husband twice – leaving his knife in Lord Mannering's body – before he fled. When they arrested the tramp, you could still see the blood upon his hands. My mind was paralyzed at first, of course; however, before the villain had taken five steps out from the window and while he was still skirting down the shadow of the house, I screamed in a voice that might have raised the parish, and then again and again.

" 'Murder!' I cried. 'Murder! Murder! Help!' and my voice rang out in the quiet of the night time and sounded over the whole countryside. In an instant, lights began to move and windows to fly up, not only in the house, but also at the lodge and in the stables by the road. Like a frightened rabbit, the villain bolted down the drive, but the grooms had managed to shut the gate before he could reach it and escape. He then attempted to hide his bag of stolen medals under some dry fagots, and tried to get away across the park, but someone saw him in the moonlight. Eventually, the tramp had half a dozen of the stable lads with dogs upon his heels. He crouched down among the brambles, but those dogs were too many for him, and I suspect that he was glad enough when the men came up and prevented him from being torn into pieces. They seized the tramp, and dragged him back to the room where his crime had transpired.

"Stephens, our butler, asked me to identify him. I had been bending over the prostrate body of my poor husband, but I turned upon the villain with the face of a fury. 'Yes, yes, it is the very man,' I cried. 'Oh, you villain, you cruel villain, to treat an old man so!' Fortunately, by then, the village constable had arrived. He laid his hand upon the murderer's shoulder. The tramp tried to claim his innocence, but the constable and one of the men-servants struck at him with their fists. He kept trying to say that he had not done it, and I recall that the footman was about to strike him again."

"What did you do?" asked Holmes.

"I held up my hand and instructed them not to hurt him anymore," said Lady Mannering. "I thought that that the tramp's punishment would be safely left to the law. The constable said that he would see to it. Once the grooms came in with the sack that he had dropped during his flight, which was filled with my slain husband's gold medals, it was sufficient proof for the constable. He and Stephens kept the villain locked in the cellar under guard for the remainder of the night until the local inspector came round and took him into Salisbury.

"I was forced to testify at his trial. The poor creature," she continued. "For my own part, I forgave him any injury which he has done me. Who knows what temptation may have driven him to crime? His conscience and the law has delivered him punishment enough without any reproach of mine rendering it more bitter."

"That was most generous of you, Lady Mannering," said Holmes, a hint of appreciation in his voice.

§

As we strode back down the drive, after taking tea with Lady Mannering and Mr. Glossin, Holmes turned to me with a small smile. "Oh, what an actress that woman was, Watson! I have not seen her like in many a year."

"You sound as if you admire her, Holmes. If Bertram is correct, she is a cold-blooded murderer."

He shrugged. "The stage lost a fine performer when she decided to make the climb to a higher stratum of society. That does not excuse her exploits, of course, but still one must appreciate a fellow artist, even one who has turned their gifts towards an evil path."

I shook my head at Holmes' rare ability to separate the woman from her deeds. "What do you propose for our next course of action?"

"There is nothing more we can do here this afternoon. Now that I have both a lay of the land and the measure of my opponents, I suggest that we set our sights upon a pheasant or two, which will be a rather fine way to repay Sir Dominick's hospitality."

The rest of the afternoon and evening was spent as Holmes indicated, including an epicurean repast at Rodenhurst highlighted by my bagged bird. For much of the time, I was troubled by my unsuccessful attempts to conceive of a method by which we might prove Mr. Bertram's innocence. However, Holmes seemed confident that he could discover a solution to this vexing quandary. I assumed that – like so many times before – a night of seclusion and solitude, stocked with a sufficient supply of shag tobacco, would be sufficient for him to focus his intense mental concentration to the problem at hand. Therefore, I slept soundly, trusting in my friend's powers.

Over breakfast the following morn, a thought occurred to me. "It is a shame," said I, "that the inspector who investigated the case did not think to examine the medals passed to Bertram for Lady Mannering's thumb marks. I recall in the McFarland case you saying that no two are alike."[197]

"Indeed. Faulds is good on the matter, and I elaborated upon his proposal in a small monograph.[198] In this case, however, Watson, I am afraid that it would do little good. Lady Julia would simply claim to have touched them at some other point in the past. There is no way to prove that her marks were laid down when she handed the medals to Bertram, as he claimed. Furthermore, if Mr. Glossin is to be believed – which is a simple enough matter to verify – she has subsequently bequeathed the medals to the Kensington Museum. Where, I suspect, they would have been well cleaned prior to being put upon display. Truly, this action was a masterstroke upon her part. For who could accuse her of profiting from her husband's death when she gives away one of the most valuable parts of his estate?"

I was still pondering how we might use Lady Mannering's role in the halted theft of the medals against her when Sir Dominick's servant brought in a note for Holmes.

"It is from Mr. Sampson," said he, as he tore it open. "Ah! Those villains!"

"What is it, Holmes?"

His face was twisted with mute anger. I could see that he was deeply moved. Finally, he gathered himself and spoke calmly. "I have been beaten, Watson. Lady Julia and Edward Glossin have struck again. First, Mr. and Mrs. Allen had to be silenced. And now Bertram is dead. Our visit yesterday must have raised their misgivings as to his persistent denials."

"How was he killed?" I cried.

"It seems some sort of poison was used."

"Are you certain that it was Lady Mannering and Glossin? Perhaps Bertram believed that Mr. Sampson did not believe him and carried out his threat of suicide?"

Holmes shook his head. "No, it will not do, Watson. Bertram promised to hang himself from the bars of his window. That would be a far easier method than obtaining a poison while locked in prison."

"But this is a terrible mistake they have made!" I cried. "Unlike the long-past death of Mr. and Mrs. Adams, we can investigate this new murder, Holmes. Perhaps they made an error that will allow us to point the blame at them?"

He nodded, resignedly. "Yes, Watson, you are correct. I must go to Devizes Prison and see how it was done."

"I will go with you, of course," said I, standing.

"No, Watson. I require you to go to Mannering Towers. Make some excuse to speak to the butler Stephens. Find out if either Lady Julia or Edward Glossin was absent from the estate yesterday evening. Once we know which hand struck the fatal blow, it may be simpler to trace their movements."

§

Following Holmes' instructions, I donned my fowling attire and went round to Mannering Towers. On my way, I devised what I thought was a clever stratagem. At the lodge, I explained to the keeper that I had lost my prized hawk whistle, handed down by my father, and wondered if I could speak with Stephens to see if it had turned up in the house. The keeper waved me on, and my knock upon the front door soon summoned the man with whom I wished to converse.

I again explained the supposed reason for my visit, and the man nodded sadly at my story, before apologizing that the fictional whistle had not turned up. Decrying my supposed misfortune, I engaged the man in conversation for a bit longer and learned that Mr. Glossin had left the house shortly after our visit. He announced a sudden trip to London for some shopping and was absent from the estate for most of the evening, only returning late into the night.

When I returned to Rodenhurst, I was informed by the footman that Holmes was still away upon his errand. I therefore went around to the drawing room where I noted that Holmes had left behind the case file prepared by Mr. Sampson. Flipping through this, I became engrossed in the transcript the solicitor had made of Prisoner B24's depiction of the fateful night's events. The relevant portion ran as follows:

> "She had opened one of the cases, and the beautiful things all lay exposed before me. I had my hand upon the one that she had pointed out, when suddenly a change came over her face, and she held up one finger as a warning. 'Hist!' she whispered. 'What is that?'
> Far away in the silence of the house, we heard a low, dragging, shuffling sound, and the distant tread of feet. She closed and fastened the case in an instant.
> 'It's my husband!' she whispered. 'Alright. Do not be alarmed. I will arrange it. Here! Quick, behind the tapestry!'
> She pushed me behind the painted curtains upon the wall, my empty leather bag still in my hand. Then she took her taper and walked quickly into the room from which we had come. From where I stood, I could see her through the open door.
> 'Is that you, Robert?' she cried.
> The light of a candle shone through the door of the museum, and the shuffling steps came nearer and nearer. Then I saw a face in the doorway, a great, heavy face, all lines and creases, with a huge curving nose, and a pair of gold glasses fixed across it. He had to throw his head back to see through the glasses, and that great nose thrust out in front of him like the beak of some sort of fowl. He was a big man, very tall and burly, so that in his loose dressing gown his figure seemed to fill up the whole doorway. He had a pile of grey, curling hair all round his head, but his face was clean-shaven. His mouth was

thin and small and prim, hidden away under his long, masterful nose. He stood there, holding the candle in front of him, and looking at his wife with a queer, malicious gleam in his eyes. It only needed that one look to tell me that he was as fond of her as she was of him.

'What is this?' he asked. 'Some new tantrum? What do you mean by wandering about the house? Why don't you go to bed?'

'I could not sleep,' she answered. She spoke languidly and wearily. If she was an actress once, she had not forgotten her calling.

'Might I suggest,' said he, in the same mocking kind of voice, 'that a good conscience is an excellent aid to sleep?'

'That cannot be true,' she answered, 'for you sleep very well.'

'I have only one thing in my life to be ashamed of,' said he, and his hair bristled up with anger until he looked like an old cockatoo. 'You know best what that is. It is a mistake which has brought its own punishment with it.'

'To me as well as to you. Remember that!'

'You have very little to whine about. It was I who stooped and you who rose."

'Rose!'

'Yes, rose. I suppose you do not deny that it is promotion to exchange the music-hall for Mannering Hall. Fool that I was ever to take you out of your true sphere!'

'If you think so, why do you not separate?'

'Because private misery is better than public humiliation. Because it is easier to suffer for a mistake than to own to it. Because also I like to keep you in my sight, and to know that you cannot go back to him.'

'You villain! You cowardly villain!'

'Yes, yes, my lady. I know your secret ambition, but it shall never be while I live, and if it happens after my death, I will at least take care that you go to him as a beggar. You and dear Edward will never have the satisfaction of squandering my savings, and you may make up your mind to that, my lady. Why are those shutters and the window open?'

'I found the night very close.'

'It is not safe. How do you know that some tramp may not be outside? Are you aware that my collection of medals is worth more than any similar collection in the world? You have left the door open also. What is there to prevent anyone from rifling the cases?'

'I was here.'

'I know you were. I heard you moving about in the medal room, and that was why I came down. What were you doing?'

'Looking at the medals. What else should I be doing?'

'This curiosity is something new.' He looked suspiciously at her and moved on towards the inner room, she walking beside him.

It was at this moment that I saw something that startled me. I had laid my clasp knife open upon the top of one of the cases, and there it lay in full view. She saw it before he did, and with a woman's cunning she held her taper out so that the light of it came between Lord Mannering's eyes and the knife. Then she took it in her left hand and held it against her gown out of his sight. He looked about from case to case – I could have put my hand at one time upon his long nose – but there was nothing to show that the medals had been tampered with, and so, still snarling and grumbling, he shuffled off into the other room once more.

And now I have to speak of what I heard rather than of what I saw, but I swear to you, as I shall stand some day before my Maker, that what I say is the truth.

When they passed into the outer room I saw him lay his candle upon the corner of one of the tables, and he sat himself down, but in such a position that he was just out of my sight. She moved behind him, as I could tell from the fact that the light of her taper threw his long, lumpy shadow upon the floor in front of him. Then he began talking about this man whom he called Edward, and every word that he said was like a blistering drop of vitriol. He spoke low, so that I could not hear it all, but from what I heard, I should guess that she would as soon have been lashed with a whip. At first, she said some hot words in reply, but then she was silent, and he went on and on in that cold, mocking voice of his, nagging and insulting and tormenting, until I wondered that she could bear to stand there in silence and listen to it. Then suddenly I heard him say in a sharp voice, 'Come from behind me! Leave go of my collar! What! Would you dare to strike me?'

There was a sound like a blow, just a soft sort of thud, and then I heard him cry out, 'By the Lord Harry, it's blood!' He shuffled with his feet as if he was getting up, and then I heard another blow, and he cried out, 'Oh, you she-devil!' and was quiet, except for a dripping and splashing upon the floor.

I ran out from behind my curtain at that, and rushed into the other room, shaking all over with the horror of it. The old man had slipped down in the chair, and his dressing gown had rucked up until lie looked as if he had a monstrous hump to his back. His head, with the gold glasses still fixed on his nose, was lolling over upon one side, and his little mouth was open just like a dead fish. I could not see where the blood was coming from, but I could still hear it drumming upon the floor. She stood behind him with the candle shining full upon her face. Her lips were pressed together and her eyes were glowing. A touch of colour had come into each of her cheeks, and this was all that was needed to make her the most beautiful woman I had ever seen in my life.

'You've done it now!' said I.

'Yes,' said she, in her quiet way, 'I've done it now.'
'What are you going to do?' I asked. 'They will have you for murder as sure as fate.'
'Never fear about me. I have nothing to live for, and it does not matter. Give me a hand to set him straight in the chair. It is horrible to see him like this!'
I did so, though it turned me cold all over to touch him. Some of his blood came on my hand and sickened me.
'Now,' said she, 'you may as well have the medals as anyone else. Take them and go.'
'I don't want them. I only want to get away. I was never mixed up with a business like this before.'
'Nonsense!' said she. 'You came for the medals, and here they are at your mercy. Why should you not have them? There is no one to prevent you.'
I held the bag still in my hand. She opened the case, and between us, we threw a hundred or so of the medals into it. They were all from the one case, but I could not bring myself to wait for any more. Then I made for the window, for the very air of this house seemed to poison me after what I had seen and heard. As I looked back, I saw her standing there, tall and graceful, with the light in her hand, just as I had seen her first. She waved goodbye, and I waved back at her and sprang out into the gravel drive. I thank the Lord that I can lay my hand upon my heart and say that I have never committed a murder, but perhaps it would be different if I had been able to read that woman's mind and thoughts. There might have been two bodies in the room instead of one if I could have seen behind that last smile of hers. However, I thought of nothing save that I needed to get myself safely away, and it never entered my head how she might be fixing the rope round my neck."

I set the account down and considered what I had learned. If this was a fiction, I thought that Prisoner B24 had missed his true calling in life. It was a vivid story. Then a thought occurred to me. I inquired of Keshav, Sir Dominick's *khitmutgar*, whether the estate kept old copies of the daily paper. A slight frown creased his forehead at this unusual request, however, his imperturbable nature won out, and he bid me follow him to the lumber-room. There, I was gratified to find that our host was as an avid a magpie as my suite-mate, for I was shown an enormous stack of the *Salisbury and Winchester Journal* going back several years.[199]

Sorting through this pile was the work of many hours; however, I was finally rewarded with an article of some interest. I was pondering its implications, when Keshav announced that Holmes had finally returned.

My friend immediately inquired as to what I had learned, so I shared the details of my brief visit to Mannering Towers. "If your theory is correct, Holmes, and Edward Glossin killed Mr. Bertram, we should be able to prove that he never went to London," I concluded.

Holmes shook his head. "Tricky, Watson. I suspect that Glossin is far too clever to have made a simple mistake such as travelling directly from Mannering Towers to Devizes. No, I wager that he not only went up to London as he put about, but that he made an especial effort to be noticed by either a station manager or train attendant, who would be able to testify to his presence if needed."

"But then if he went straight from London to Devizes, surely his presence would also have been noted during that leg of his trip?"

"Not if he disguised his appearance. Do not forget, Watson, that we are dealing with a pair of trained actors. I suspect that Mr. Glossin's skill with costumes and face-paint likely rivals that of Mr. Neville St. Clair."

"Well, if he did not actually do any shopping in London as he claimed – because he immediately made his way to Devizes – we should be able prove to that."

"It is much harder to prove a negative, Watson. Absence of

evidence is not evidence of absence. Simply because no one recalled him at the shops where he asserts to have visited does not prove beyond a shadow of a doubt that he was not there and was simply overlooked."

"Well, can they identify him at Devizes Prison?"

"Unfortunately not. I spoke with Mr. Kennedy, the warden, and was allowed to consult the visitor log. Only one individual called upon Prisoner B24 yesterday afternoon. He called himself Charles Hazelwood, and claimed to be a mechanic who once worked with Mr. Bertram at Exeter."

"That must be Glossin!"

"Undoubtedly, Watson. However, I questioned the guard who escorted the supposed Mr. Hazelwood in to see the prisoner. The guard described him as a man of fifty, with pale skin and red hair and whiskers."

"That sounds nothing like Glossin," said I, frowning.

"As I would have expected. The supposed Mr. Hazelwood had blue eyes, which is the one thing that Glossin could not disguise, given the prison's prohibition against tinted lenses. However, beyond that sole shared characteristic, I am afraid that the guard would never be able single out Glossin upon the stand."

I groaned in frustration at the thought that Glossin would get away with his crime. "How did they poison Bertram?"

"The medical examiner believes that Bertram ingested corrosive sublimate. A rare choice, but hardly one unheard of in the annals of crime. The cases of Bille in Copenhagen, and of course Desrues in Paris, come to mind."[200]

I shuddered to think what that treatment – which was intended only to be applied topically – would do to the interior of a man. "But how did Glossin get it past the guards?"

"I cannot say for certain, Watson, though I have a theory that a most diabolical device was utilized. As I can will attest, all visitors to the prison are meticulously searched. Even their cigar cases or tobacco pouches are confiscated. They are not permitted to bring anything with them into the room where they can speak to the prisoners."

I frowned. "Then how did he do it?"

"I wondered the same thing for a while. Then an idea occurred to me. Do you recall, Watson, when we attended Covent Garden after we recovered the Duchess of Ferrers' Topaz Pendant?"[201]

"Of course, we saw Adelina sing in 'The Troubadour.' "[202]

"And as Leonora, she sang, *'Mira, d'acerbe lagrima.'* "

" 'See the bitter tears I shed,' " I translated, automatically.[203] "Ah! The poison ring!" said I, recalling the scene.

"Precisely, Watson. Rather than allowing Count di Luna to possess her, Leonora swallows poison concealed in a hollow of her ring. Edward Glossin would be familiar with such a device from his days striding the boards. He may have pilfered it from Lord Mannering's collection of exotic items."

"Then if we are able to locate the ring, we can prove that Glossin killed poor Bertram."

Holmes shook his head. "He would have no reason to keep such damning evidence. If I were Glossin, I would have ditched in the River Colne as the train passed over its bridge upon its return to Paddington."

"So what will you do now?"

"I have been pondering this exact question during my trip back from Devizes. I cannot allow such a thing to pass unpunished, Watson. I intend to ensure that justice has been done."

"How?"

"You know what Mr. Franklin says, Watson," said Holmes, his lip curled up cruelly. "Two may keep a secret if one of them is dead."[204]

"What do you mean?"

"I intend to convince Lady Julia that her lover has suddenly developed a terrible remorse for his actions and is planning to confess to his crimes, as well as her own. Simultaneously, I will persuade Edward Glossin that Lady Mannering has decided that she can only be wholly safe from prosecution if no one living knows her secrets, and intends to have Glossin perish in an apparent accident. The two of them will then gladly betray each other."

I frowned. "That sounds rather complicated, Holmes."

"Indeed. Nevertheless, it will be a great pleasure to plan. I have a few ideas along this route already."

"Perhaps there is an easier way?"

He frowned at me. "What do you mean?"

I showed him the testimony of Harry Bertram, as carefully recorded by Mr. Sampson. "Do you see, Holmes?" said I, my finger pointing to the key passage. "How did Lord Mannering intend to prevent his wife and Edward from squandering his savings after his death? He must have prepared a will that left her with nothing! But after he told her of this fact in the moments before his death, Lady Mannering somehow managed to forge a replacement will prior to the formal reading of her husband's last testament."

Holmes shook his head. "It won't hold, Watson. Lord Mannering's solicitor would have pointed out this discrepancy."

"Not if he were dead."

I had the rare pleasure of seeing Holmes surprised. He rocked back upon his heels. "What?" he cried.

I showed him the newspaper paragraph I had located. His eyes ran over it quickly, and a gleam of excitement shone in his grey eyes.

"By Jove, Watson!" he cried. "The official force has much to answer for! Not two days after Lord Mannering is supposedly stabbed to death by Harry Bertram, his Salisbury solicitor, Mr. Gabriel Mervyn, was trampled to death by a runaway carriage."

"It seems that the driver was a habitual drunkard. He had left his carriage unattended and the horses slipped their ties. As there was no evidence of foul play, the jury brought a verdict of 'death from accidental causes.'"

Holmes shook his head. "The timing of this should have raised a suspicion. Nevertheless, we have them now. I wager that Edward Glossin absented himself from London as soon as he got the news of Lord Mannering's death. He may have slipped away unnoticed when he burned down 'The Willing Mind;' however, I wager that Glossin will have no alibi for either the prior death of Mr. Mervyn or the recent murder of Mr. Bertram."

"My only concern is that it is all rather circumstantial."

"True enough, Watson. However, Lord Mannering's testament would have been recorded. We can request that Sir Daniel Philbrick, the celebrated barrister and philatelist, examine it. His testimony has regularly been considered by the Law Courts to be the final word on matters of forgery.[205] Philbrick has pronounced the verdict upon some of the very heads of that profession, including John Clay, Archie Stamford, Arthur H. Staunton, and Victor Lynch. Lady Julia may be a ruthless foe and a most skilled actress, but she cannot possibly hold a candle to those individuals' skill with a pen. Sir Daniel will prove to be the instrument of her downfall, and I have little doubt that – in the hopes of saving her own skin – Lady Julia will eagerly pin upon her accomplice Mr. Glossin the deaths of the Allens, Mr. Mervyn, and Harry Bertram."

§

The rest of the case played out just as Holmes predicted. He prevailed upon Sir Daniel to come down to Salisbury, where the final will and testament of Lord Robert Mannering was found to be a rank forgery. Inspection of the files of the deceased Mr. Gabriel Mervyn unearthed a true copy of the will, in which Lord Mannering explicitly bequeathed his entire estate to a second cousin upon his mother's side. To his wife, he had left nothing, save only his 'third best bed.'[206]

This evidence was brought before Sir James Pleydell – the Assize Court judge who had mistakenly sentenced Harry Bertram to prison at Devizes – and his faced clouded like a storm as he listened. When the story was over, Sir James considered the situation for a moment and – while no man prefers to admit his faults – magnanimously agreed that justice had not been served in the case of Harry Bertram. Sir James made it clear that he would not be repeating this error when ruling upon Lady Julia Mannering and Mr. Edward Glossin.

Suddenly dragged into court, and faced with this damning evidence, Lady Mannering's imperturbable façade broke under the withering glare of Sir James. Sobbing, she admitted to stabbing her husband in a rage, framing Bertram as a spontaneous act, and altering the will in her favour. Lady Mannering had been eating her heart out because she had lost her lover Glossin, and yet her husband kept from her any access to his wealth. She said that Lord Mannering made her feel like the poorest woman in the parish for all the money of which she had the handling. When it became apparent that Sir James intended to also charge her for the premeditated deaths of three more men – a hanging offense – she gladly volunteered to testify that all of those murders were conceived and carried out by Edward Glossin. In the end, it was Glossin who faced the long drop, while the former Lady Julia Mannering, now plain Julie Merrilies again, was sentenced to live out the rest of her natural life in Devizes Prison, the same gaol to which she once coolly sent Harry Bertram. I thought she would be little missed, and got off rather easy for her role in all these horrors.

Mr. Gilbert Sampson had come round for the sentencing of Glossin and Merrilies, and after they had been led away, he expressed his gratitude to Holmes for looking into the case. He noted that he would ensure that the county forward the sum of Holmes' professional charges. Holmes merely shook his head and waved his right hand, noting that he wished to remit them altogether. Glossin protested weakly; however, in the end Holmes had his way.

I could tell from his manner that Holmes was displeased with the outcome of the case. He spent the entire ride back to London gazing out of the carriage window and puffing at his long pipe. Not another word did he speak until our train was pulling back into Paddington. Before we alighted, he shook himself from his meditations and reached out to grab hold of my arm.

"This was hardly my finest hour, Watson. I almost refused the case, and even when I did so, I was painfully slow. I should have acted in time to prevent Bertram's death. I am afraid that you will have to file this with some of my other great failures. If it should ever strike you that I am getting a little sure of my own cleverness, or giving less pains to a case than it deserves, I beg you to whisper 'B24' in my ear, and I shall be considerably indebted to you."

Consequently, for the sake of his vanity, I shall refrain from ever putting this case before my readers.[207] However, I record it here for posterity, in order to set the record straight upon the rumour that Mr. Sherlock Holmes was not infallible. He had fallen short with clients before Harry Bertram, such as poor Mr. John Openshaw of Horsham. And he would do so again, as Mr. Hilton Cubitt of Ridling Thorpe Manor sadly learned. Yet, despite Holmes' protestations that all emotions were abhorrent and played no role in his calculations, each time he failed someone who had come to him for help, I think a small piece of him died inside. For he was a man, take him for all in all. And we shall not look upon his like again.[208]

§

THE ADVENTURE OF THE TWELFTH HOUR

For as long as I had known him, Mr. Sherlock Holmes held a peculiar conviction regarding which of his cases would be of interest to the general reading public. Upon occasion, he would be spot-on, and might specifically suggest that I tell my readers of certain remarkable events, such as those that transpired during the Cornish Horror or at the Camford home of Professor Presbury. However, much more frequently, Holmes would dismiss my writings as – if I recall his words correctly – 'superficial embellishments that were overly tinged with romanticism.' Therefore, many extraordinary cases languish in my tin despatch box due to his outright prohibition against proceeding with their publication.

Perhaps the most striking example of Holmes' discrepant opinion from mine own transpired at the conclusion of one of my occasional weekend visits from Southsea to his little Sussex home. The visit included the fascinating investigation of a death that had occurred in his figurative back yard. Tragically, however, Holmes refused permission for me to include any mention of his role in the conclusion of that case in my next communication with my literary editor. Instead, Holmes handed me a precisely typewritten manuscript, which he had entitled 'The Lion's Mane.' He plainly believed that it was an abstruse and unusual problem; however, after reading through it in ever-growing dismay, I did not have the heart to inform Holmes that it was not much of a crime.[209] I duly forwarded it on to my literary editor, who agreed with my assessment that Holmes' account of the accidental death of Fitzroy McPherson was hardly worthy of publication, and instead brought forward the far more interesting cases of Mr. John Scott Eccles and Mr. Cadogan West. It was not until many years later that my editor decided that the release of any adventure of Sherlock Holmes was better than none. Very few such tales were forthcoming in those difficult and weary days in the immediate aftermath of the general strike and the lingering effects of the Great War – so my editor finally sent it on to Mr. Smith for his consideration.[210] Here, however, I shall set down the details of this other case, in hopes that someday Holmes shall relent and allow me to bring it forth.

It was a fine early September day when I went round to visit Holmes. Enough has been said of my friend's retirement hermitage that I shall refrain from providing further details concerning its location, as he is exceptionally adverse to entertaining visitors and abhorrent regarding the idea of anyone making the journey to consult with him regarding any trivial matters. Nevertheless, many members of the local constabulary were well aware that the world's greatest consulting detective happened to be residing nearby, and were not happy to call upon him whenever they found themselves over their heads regarding some obscure matter or another. Much of the time, Holmes sent them on their way with either an irritated wave of his bee smoker or – if he was in one of his rare garrulous moods – a helpful suggestion.

Upon the occasion of my visit, Holmes and I were partaking of our early cups of tea and reminiscing about my ignominious attempts at impersonations during various past investigations. I was of the opinion that I was the poorest connoisseur of Ming pottery in all of London, while Holmes maintained that I was least successful while attempting to pass for my friend in the wilds of California.[211] We had not come to an agreement regarding this matter when Inspector Bardle appeared at my friend's door. Our old housekeeper showed in this gentleman, who had a steady, solid build and thoughtful brown oxen eyes.

"I am sorry to trouble you, Mr. Holmes," said he. "But there is something amiss over at Alfriston, and none of us can determine the best course of action. I was about to summon someone from the Yard, and then recalled your recent assistance with the McPherson case. I was hoping that you would be willing to consider this matter?"

"I am retired, Inspector," replied Holmes, with a slow shake of his head. "As the *Cyanea capillata* very nearly proved, my powers have been dulled by the torpor of the Downs. I am afraid that I would be of little use in your investigation."

I spluttered in disagreement. "I hardly think that is true, Holmes. Why it was only last month that we met with the Marquis...."[212]

He held up his hand to forestall my divulgement of any further details regarding that sensitive case before an official member of the police force. "What would you have me do, Watson?"

"At the very least we can hear what has transpired in Alfriston, Holmes. With your immense knowledge of the annals of crimes, it seems likely that you might be able to assist Inspector Bardle without ever leaving your armchair and cup of tea."

"Very well," said Holmes, waving the inspector to an empty chair. "Pray tell what has occurred in Alfriston, Bardle. It is hardly the local epicentre of crime. In fact, I would wager nothing more serious than a stolen pie has happened in Alfriston since Stanton Collins was convicted of sheep rustling in 1850."

Inspector Bardle chuckled. "Well, sir, as I understand things, fortunately that notorious smuggler – along with his entire violent gang – was transported to Australia, so it seems unlikely that he is the culprit in the current matter. In fact, I am unsure that there is even a criminal at work."

"What do you mean?"

"Well, at first blush it appears as if Professor Mercer has died of natural causes; much like what happened to poor Mr. McPherson. However, there is an irregularity."

"We shall get to that in a moment, Bardle. First, who precisely was Mercer?"

"He was an American, about seventy years of age. According to Joseph Tilson, the landlord of the Half Moon Inn, the professor was walking the Downs and looking for insects to collect."[213]

"An entomologist," said Holmes.

"Yes, that's just the word," said Bardle, consulting his notepad. "He had been at the inn for the last six nights and was due to depart in the morning for Battle. Last night, he was taking his dinner alone in the main dining room – surrounded by the other guests of the inn – when he suddenly collapsed."

"So his death was witnessed by several of the other guests?"

The inspector shook his head. "That is just the thing, Mr. Holmes. No one actually saw him collapse. You see, there was a commotion in the road right outside the inn and everyone's attentions were turned to the windows."

"What about the inn's staff?"

"They had gone out into the road to help. A delivery wagon had overturned and had spilled its contents everywhere."

"What did the local physician conclude?"

"Dr Gade looked over the body and noted that Professor Mercer's face was constricted in a rictus of horror. However, Gade said that finding was not in and of itself unusual when someone has died of an infarct of the heart."

"It seems to me, Inspector, that Dr Gade has pronounced a verdict of natural causes. I fail to see how I may be of assistance?"

The policeman shook his head. "I agree, Mr. Holmes, and was about to close the book on the case myself. However, there was one thing that was out of place. You see, on the Professor's plate was a pot of caviare."

"Was it poisoned?"

"Not so far as we can tell. All of the standard tests have been negative. In any case, the pot did not appear to have been opened prior to the Professor's death. The metal clasp was still intact."

"That is not conclusive, of course, as there are many poisons that are missed by the standard tests. Blyth is good on the matter.[214] However, introducing a toxin while maintaining the integrity of the metal clasp would be significantly harder to manage," said Holmes with a shrug. "What then is so unusual about the pot?"

"The Half Moon Inn does not serve caviare, Mr. Holmes."

My friend's lip curled up in a smile. "Ah, very good, Inspector!" he cried. "I shall be forced to desist in chaffing you gentlemen of the force if you persist in making such perspicacious observations. However, I have one possible explanation for you – the professor brought the pot of caviare with him."

"I thought of that, Mr. Holmes. I asked the maid who cleaned the professor's room for the last few days and she denied having seen it. Now, Miss Frances Playstead is no Oxford don, but she is a sharp enough lass. I admit that there is a small possibility that she may have overlooked the pot. However, when you see it, you will agree that it is a rather distinctive piece."

Holmes looked unconvinced, so I decided to intervene. "Why not go round to Alfriston, Holmes? Even if it turns out to be nothing, it will prove to be a nice roam about the countryside."

He sighed and then nodded slowly. "I suppose that I have little to do at the moment, Inspector. Let us see what we can make of your mysterious pot of caviare."

§

It was a half hour ride in the Inspector's trap to the ancient village of Alfriston, which lay in the valley between two of the down-land hills. As we rode along, the inspector continued to relate the details of the scene.

"I asked the guests to remain at the Half Moon until further notice and for Mr. Tilson to keep the Professor's table untouched – as I hoped you would be willing to look it over. And here is a list of all of the guests who were present in the dining room at the time of Professor Mercer's death," said Bardle, handing a paper to Holmes.

My friend ran his eyes down this, and then handed it to me, which I reproduce here:

> *Ainslie, John. Foreign Office, London.*
> *Anderson, Mary. Poet, Edinburgh, Scotland.*
> *Dresler, Klaus. Author. German.*
> *Ralston, Hetta. Painter, Paisley, Scotland.*
> *Rameau, Colonel Henri: Retired. French.*
> *Sinclair, Arthur. Retired solicitor. Glasgow, Scotland.*

"Very good, inspector," said Holmes. "I commend your thoroughness. However, you mentioned a commotion outside the inn, which distracted all of their attention."

"Yes, sir. What of it?"

"Do you not think it a coincidence that such a thing transpired at the very moment when Professor Mercer met his end?"

Bardle looked thoughtful. "I suppose so, Mr. Holmes. Now that you mention it, it does seem a bit funny."

"What was the nature of this commotion?"

"If you would be so kind as to take control, Doctor," said he, "I shall consult my notes." Having handed the reins to me, Bardle pulled his notebook from his pocket and flipped through it. "Ah yes, I have it here. A tourist, one Commodore Robert Wyndham, was riding through town on a trap when he lost control of his horse. It ran into one of the local farmer's apple carts, spilling them all over the roadway and blocking traffic in both directions. Both Joseph Tilson and Frances Playstead ran out to help restore order, while the other guests watched from the windows."

"What do you know of Commodore Wyndham?"

"I spoke with him myself. He was a stern man, retired from the Royal Navy after many years of service and now living in Sheerness. He was merely passing through town on his way to Portsmouth to attend a ceremony of some sort."

"Very good," said Holmes. "The Commodore's purposeful involvement in Professor Mercer's passing seems improbable. Ah, here we are," he noted, as we drew up to Alfriston.

Bardle tied up the trap at the southern edge of town. We disembarked and walked slowly along the High Street. The morning sun shone on the old houses, leaving those upon the right side in deep shade, while those the left side glowed. The tree in the middle of the little square threw a pleasant shadow over a funnel-shaped stone lock-up. The Half Moon Inn was a half-timbered structure built during the days of Elizabeth. Protruding lead-cased bow windows lined the first floor, while hanging baskets filled with white flowers enlivened the ground floor and carved wooden figures looked down upon passing travellers.

We entered the dimly lit dining room, which was dominated by a massive fireplace that was currently cold. Hearing the bell tinkle as the door opened, a stocky middle-aged man came out of the kitchen doorway. By his dress, and the dirty towel tucked into his waist, he was plainly the innkeeper.

"Hello, Inspector Bardle," said he. "May I be of some assistance?"

"Mr. Tilson, this is Mr. Sherlock Holmes and Dr Watson. You may have heard of them. I have asked them round to look into the matter of the Professor's death."

"Very good, sir," said the innkeeper.

"A lovely place you have here," said Holmes. "It looks rather old."

"Old? Yes, you could say that. The Abbot of Battle built the current structure in the 1300's as a hostel. He placed it on the site of a Saxon peasant's hut. For this area goes back to the days even before the Normans. In fact, it was on this very spot that Alfred burnt the cakes."[215]

"Truly?" said I. "I had heard that story occurred in the Somerset Levels as Alfred fled from Chippenham."[216]

"Pshaw!" cried the man. "Somerset Levels, indeed. Alfred had a naval base and palace at West Dean. That is where he was headed. Not some swamp." Tilson shook his head. "Those fools know not of what they speak!"

"While Ancient British history is an especial interest of mine, Mr. Tilson," said Holmes, "and I may return to talk with you more regarding such matters, at the moment I am more interested in what you can tell me of Professor Mercer? I understand that he was an entomologist who had stayed with you for the last six nights and was due to depart today. Is there anything else?"

The man shook his head. "Not really, Mr. Holmes. He was a nice enough old chap, if a little hard of hearing. He spent most of his days traipsing about the downs with his walking stick, a satchel filled with some lunch items that we packed for him, and the tools of his peculiar trade. In the evenings, he was a quiet sort, seemingly content to let others do the talking. I did hear him say that he was originally from California, and it was evident that he was well travelled."

"Indeed?" said Holmes. "Did he mention where precisely?"

"Not that I recall. But I got the impression that it was somewhere in the Far East."

"Thank you, Mr. Tilson. I shall let you know if I have any further questions for you. Now then, Bardle, let us see where the Professor passed on."

Bardle guided us over to a plain wooden table, set for one. Upon the plate was a clay pot, about three inches high, with a lid that had once been secured by a metal clasp, now broken during the police investigation. The pot was inscribed:

THE ASTRACHAN CAVIARE

REAL RUSSIAN PRESSED CAVIARE
AS SUPPLIED TO HIS MAJESTY
THE CZAR OF RUSSIA
AND THE RUSSIAN IMPERIAL COURT

"Fascinating," said Holmes. "This is not the caviare pot by Misters Fortnum and Mason of Piccadilly West London that one typically sees in the homes of the upper class."[217]

"What does that tell you, Mr Holmes?" asked Bardle.

"That someone went out of their way to procure this specific brand in order to set it before the Professor. Presuming that the negative toxicology tests are accurate, it is most singular. Let us see what other items of interest can be found here." Holmes proceeded to inspect Mercer's satchel, butterfly-net, and walking stick. The former contained a book on entomology, a notebook and pens, as well as various tweezers, collecting-boxes, and glass jars, while the latter seemed mainly unremarkable to my eyes. Holmes spent a few minutes flipping through the insect book, before turning his attention to the stick.

"Anything of note?" I asked. "Did the Professor have a curly-haired spaniel?"

Holmes glanced over at me for a moment. "Your pawky attempts at humour aside, Watson, we may conclude a few things from the Professor's possessions. First, the man was an acknowledged expert in his field. Here is a copy of the Entomological Society's *Transactions*, in which they list the *Lepidus Mercerensis*, named for its discoverer.[218] As for the Malacca walking stick, its thick-iron ferrule is considerably worn down and it has been knocked about a great deal. From this, we may conclude that Professor Mercer was just as he appeared, an entomologist much given to long rambles about the countryside."

Holmes set down the cane and flipped through the man's notebook. He paused for a moment and raised it to his nose. "Fascinating. I think there may have been more to Professor Mercer than meets the eye." He then removed his glass from his pocket and looked over the table. "Ah!" he cried. "What have we here?" He lifted a long blond hair from the seat across from the professor and displayed it for us to see. "What colour is Miss Playstead's hair, Inspector?"

"Dark brown."

"And the two lady guests? Miss Anderson and Miss Ralston?"

"Much of the same."

"Mr. Tilson's hair is not of sufficient length to claim this strand. I presume that the same can be said of the other male guests?"

The inspector nodded. "That is correct, Mr. Holmes."

"Then to whom does this hair belong?"

Bardle shrugged. "Perhaps a prior guest?"

"You have a poor opinion of Miss Playstead's cleaning skills, Inspector."

"What is your theory, then?" asked the inspector, his tone rankled.

"I do not have one as of yet," said Holmes, mildly. "However, there is certainly something interesting occurring here, and I wager there is a woman involved in some fashion. Shall we see if any of the other guests can illuminate what transpired last evening? Let us begin with Colonel Rameau."

§

Inspector Bardle stomped upstairs to ask the colonel to step down to the dining room, where Holmes arranged a set of chairs in such a way that the afternoon light would illuminate the faces of those he was questioning. Colonel Rameau proved to be a spry man of some five-and-sixty years, with the ramrod straight back of someone who had served most of his life in the military. He had light blue eyes and thinning brown hair, though his pike-devant beard was full. He wore a pair of casual trousers, with a light blue shirt and hacking jacket.

"You are Colonel Henri Rameau?" asked Holmes.

"I am," answered the man, his French accent plain in his

words.

"You are a long way from Brest, Colonel," said Holmes.

The man frowned. "You have been investigating me, sir. Am I under some suspicion?"

"Not at all, Colonel," said Holmes. "I merely recognized your accent. I also note that you served in Algiers."

"You are most perceptive, Monsieur Holmes," said Colonel Rameau. He paused and considered this for a moment. "I presume you deduced this from my penchant for wearing light blue? Yes, until my retirement last year, I commanded the seventh regiment of the Chasseurs d'Afrique."[219]

"And your beard," said Holmes. "The style is most distinctive of your colonial forces. Did you serve beyond Africa? If I understand correctly, the chasseurs fought at Sevastopol, during the War of 1870, even during the Mexican Adventure."[220]

Colonel Rameau smiled wryly and shook his head. "No, I was never deployed elsewhere. My regiment remained to keep the peace in the Protectorates."[221]

"And what is your business in Alfriston?"

"After my return to Brittany, I developed an amateur interest in the Celtic lore of my homeland. Therefore, I came to see the Wilmington Giant," said he, "or the 'Green Man,' as the locals call him."[222]

"Not the White Horse?"[223]

The Frenchman nodded his head. "That too. Litlington's horse is nice, though I have read that Uffington is the oldest of its kind."

"And what was your impression?"

"*Magnifique.* They are most distinct from the megaliths of Brittany. We have no such representations of men or beasts."

"And what do you intend to do next?"

"I will continue my holiday. I am working my way westwards. I hope to next gaze upon the standing stones of Stonehenge and Avebury, as well as King Sil's hill."

"Very good, colonel," said Holmes. "I wonder if you can relate your impressions of Professor Mercer's death?"

"There is little to say, monsieur. I was sitting at my table, just there," he pointed to a table by the window. "Herr Dresler had joined me, for he has a great interest in all things related to Napoleon, and wished to discuss the French viewpoint of our former Emperor. We both witnessed the commotion outside and our attention was focused upon the fiasco with the apples. I then heard a noise behind me. When I turned, the Professor had already slumped out of his chair. I sprang up to help him, as did Miss Ralston, but we were too late. It was plain that the man's heart had given out."

"And was anyone near Professor Mercer when you turned?"

"No, monsieur."

"Did you note the pot of caviare? Was it already sitting before the Professor when you turned to see what had transpired?"

The Frenchman considered this and nodded slowly. "I believe so. It was not at the forefront of my attention, you understand. But it is my impression that the pot was there when I rushed to attend to him."

"Very good, Colonel. May I ask when you met Herr Dresler?"

"Three days ago."

"Oh, I understood that you were longer acquaintances," said Holmes.

"No, monsieur. We met here for the first time."

"Ah, and the other guests? Did you know any of them before your visit to the Half Moon?"

"No."

"Does that include Professor Mercer?"

"Yes, monsieur. I had never met the Professor. In fact, I did not even have the opportunity to speak to him before his unfortunate passing."

Holmes thanked the colonel for his time and dismissed him. Once the man had departed, he turned to the policeman. "Shall we speak with the German guest next, Inspector?"

Bardle stepped out to fetch Herr Dresler. The German looked to be roughly five and thirty years of age, with short black hair and an imperturbable face. He was powerfully built, and when Holmes held out his hand, Dresler's broad red palm seemed to engulf that of my friend.

"*Guten Tag*, Herr Dresler," said Holmes.

"*Guten Tag*," the man replied.

"May I inquire from where you hail?"

Dresler nodded. "A small town near Hannover."

"I see that you are a military man."

The man frowned. "No, sir. What makes you think that?"

"I have been told that you have a passion regarding Napoleon. Furthermore, your accent is not typical of the Saxon. I hear hints of Bavarian, and even some Alsatian."

"That does not make me a soldier, Herr Holmes. Merely someone who has moved about frequently – which I have done in pursuit of my planned history of the Napoleonic Wars."

"A topic of which much has already been written."

Dresler snorted in amusement. "Ah yes, Gifford. Well, if you would take him at his word, the Iron Duke seems to have personally defeated the entire Grande Armée.[224] I hope to restore the importance of the Prussian Army under Prince Blücher to the public consciousness. *Mein Gott!* If he had not kept his promise to Wellington, and ensured that the Prussian vanguard drew off Napoleon's reserves, Waterloo would have been lost, and we might all be speaking French today."[225]

"You are a long ways from Wavre."[226]

The German smiled at this display of Holmes' knowledge regarding the role of the Prussian troops at Waterloo. "Yes, this is admittedly a bit of a side project. The issue of defence, and how it influenced the course of the war, fascinates me. I plan to write about the various preparations you British made in the event of Napoleon's invasion from Boulogne. I have looked over your Martello towers, and been to Dymchurch. Now that I have seen the Eastbourne Redoubt, I finally understand how he was dissuaded from launching his flat-bottomed boats.[227] Of course, the Emperor then turned his attention away from Great Britain towards the Austrians, Russians, and eventually the Prussians. Jena and Auerstedt were disasters for us.[228] But if we could create our own defences, modified for land assaults, rather than sea, it could result in a great peace for Germany."[229]

"Fascinating," said Holmes. "And did you know Professor Mercer?"

Dresler shook his head. "No, Herr Holmes. We exchanged greetings; that is all."

"Very good. I may have a few more questions for you later."

When Dresler had left the room, Holmes instructed Inspector Bardle to summon Mr. John Ainslie. This individual proved to be a young man, rather shy of thirty, with a sombre face. He wore a Norfolk jacket and knickerbockers, looking prepared for a leisurely walk.

"You are John Ainslie of London," asked Holmes.

"Yes, sir."

"Your occupation, Mr. Ainslie?"

"I work for the Foreign Office."

"Crown service or Civil?"

"Civil, based at St. James's."

"And your reason for staying in Alfriston?"

"I am on holiday, indulging in my hobby."

"Which is?"

"I am writing a book about ghosts, Mr. Holmes, and prefer to do local research whenever possible."

Holmes' face took on a sceptical look, so I hastened to maintain the conversation. "And Alfriston has a ghost, Mr. Ainslie?"

"Not anymore," said he.

"I am afraid that I am not following you, sir," said I.

"You see, Doctor, towards the middle of the 1700's, the young son and heir of the Chowne family – who owned the nearby Place House Estate – was walking with his dog when they were attacked by thieves. A blow to the head killed him, and the thieves buried the body. Seven years later, a couple were walking along the road, when they saw the lad's small white dog."

Holmes shrugged. "It may have been the same dog."

"Ah, true! However, as the couple watched," continued Ainslie, "the dog walked into the bank of the road and vanished. It was not seen again for seven years, and every seven years thereafter, the phantom dog returned. Finally, in 1824, the skeleton of a boy was discovered when the road was being widened. His bones were moved to the church, and the ghost of his loyal dog was finally able to rest. It has not been seen since."

"So why include it in your book?" asked Holmes.

"Because it is such a perfect tale, Mr. Holmes," said the man, spreading his hands wide before him. "You have both the reason for the ghost and how it was set to rest. Few stories have such a tidy ending."

Holmes nodded slowly, as if this were a profound statement. "And did you know Professor Mercer?"

"I talked with him briefly the other night," said Ainslie, "but our interests had little overlap. I know almost nothing about insects, and he seemed indifferent to the prospect of the supernatural."

"And his death?" asked Holmes. "Did you witness this?"

"No sir," said the man, shaking his head. "I was distracted by the accident with the apple cart."

"Do you know who placed the pot of caviare on his plate?"

"The pot of caviare?" asked Ainslie, his brow contracted in puzzlement. "What does that have to do with anything?"

"Perhaps nothing," said Holmes, mildly. "Well, I thank you for your time. If you would be so kind to remain at the Inn, I have hopes of settling this matter soon."

"Oh yes?" said Ainslie, his eyes opening with interest. "Do you think the Professor was killed?" He straightened his face. "I ask for professional reasons, of course. A violent death may leave a psychic impact upon a place, and thereby spawn an earthly remnant of the deceased. I have never been present at the creation of a ghost, so this would be of great interest for my book."

Holmes shook his head. "I have no reason to doubt Dr Gade's

verdict of an arrest of the heart."

Ainslie looked somewhat disappointed at this news, and departed. Holmes stared after him for a moment, his face pensive. He then glanced at me for a moment, with a smile and a slight shake of his head, before asking Inspector Bardle to bring in Miss Ralston.

She was a keen, bird-like woman in her mid-thirties, unless I missed my guess, with dark hair, bright eyes, and a long, projecting nose. She wore a blue dress, covered with a paint-spattered smock-frock.

"Good afternoon, Miss Ralston. I understand you are from Paisley."

"Yes, Mr. Holmes."

"Did you know Dr Archie MacDonald?"

Her eyebrows rose in alarm. "The murderer?" she exclaimed. "Oh no, sir! He was locked up some twenty years ago. I was just a child."[230]

"Of course. I see that you are a painter."

She glanced down at her clothes. "I hope that is obvious, sir."

"Landscapes, I presume."

"Indeed," she smiled.

"You have come a long ways to paint. I am an amateur painter myself, and found that the scenery of the Isle of Arran to be exceptionally dramatic."

"Certainly, but our isle has infinite variety. The light here in Sussex is vastly different from what we have up at the Firth of Clyde. I have an especial interest in its interplay with the water and waves."

"Ah, like Haughton?"[231]

She shook her head. "I have not seen his ocean work. I know that he was through here and the Weald a few years ago, but thought that he was focused on the downlands."

"Ah, yes, my mistake," said Holmes, mildly. "May I ask if you knew Professor Mercer?"

"A bit. I knew that he was an avid walker, and wondered if he had seen any particularly promising views while out searching for his bugs."

"And did he?"

"I am afraid not, Mr. Holmes. It seems that his gaze was solely focused on the small and narrow. He had little time for the broader perspective."

"I understand that you were in the dining room when he passed?"

Miss Ralston nodded. "That is correct, but my gaze was distracted by the mishap in the road. When I turned at the sound of his gasp, he had already collapsed to the floor. The Frenchman – Colonel Rameau – and I sprang up at the same time to see if we could help, but the professor was already dead."

"Can you think of any reason why someone would wish him harm?"

"Not at all!" she exclaimed, a look of surprise upon her face. "Of course, I hardly knew anything about him. I think he said that he was from California, but that is all, really. He didn't appear overly friendly with any of the guests, if truth be told."

Holmes dismissed Miss Ralston in a fashion similar to the others. I saw a dissatisfied look cross his face, as if he had not found in her testimony the answer he was seeking. He indicated that Inspector Bardle should ask Mr. Arthur Sinclair to step in.

The man in question was pale, with a sickly look upon his face. A few wisps of hair clung to his balding pate, and his light blue eyes seemed dull. A brief glance would have placed him close to seventy years of age, but my professional eye suggested that he was closer to fifty. It was readily apparent that he was not long for the world.

"You are from Glasgow, Mr. Sinclair?" asked Holmes.

"That is correct, sir."

"You are on holiday?"

"Of a sort. I was a solicitor, but have been retired for the last few years. However, I was recently told that I have a growth in my chest. My physician believes that I have only a handful of good months left."

"I am most sorry to hear that, Mr. Sinclair," said Holmes. "But in that case, why spend your days here, rather than with your friends and family?"

The man smiled sadly. "My wife, Maud, passed on a few years back. When we were young, Maud and I had visited the Seven Sisters and it was at Birling Gap where I proposed to her. I suppose that I wanted to see it one last time."

"Do you have any children, Mr. Sinclair?"

The Scotsman's face clouded. "We did," said he huskily. "But Dorothea died seven years ago."

Holmes shook his head again. "Again, my condolences for your loss. It is tragic for a parent to see their children pass before them. The workings of a cruel and uncaring world."

"Aye," said Sinclair, nodding his head slowly. "You could say that again, Mr. Holmes."

"If you will forgive me for dredging up painful memories, Mr. Sinclair, may I ask how Dorothea died?"

"A plague."

Holmes's eyebrows rose with interest. "Indeed! In England?"

"Nay," said the Scotsman. "She was a missionary in China."

"Ah, I see. Well, I will trouble you with only one more question, Mr. Sinclair. Did you know Professor Mercer?"

"No."

"Surely you spoke to him?"

"No, Mr. Holmes. At this juncture in my life, I have little interest in making new acquaintances. I am content with my memories."

"Well, then. I shall not detain you any longer. I hope to release you from the hotel later this evening."

"Very good, sir. I am thinking that it is time to get on home before I am called to a far better world than this one."

As the old man shuffled from the room, I gazed after him sadly. Now that Holmes and I were both past the midway point of our lives, I wondered how soon it would be before the two of us would come to resemble the worn and broken Mr. Sinclair?

Holmes, for his part, had little time for such melancholy

musings, and had already turned to Bardle. "It is time for our final guest, Inspector. Let us speak with Miss Mary Anderson."

When the lady in question appeared, I noted that she possessed a bright face, lined by a shock of short, dark hair. Tortoise-shell glasses covered her green eyes. She had a sunny boyish smile, which was complemented with a vibrant yellow dress.

"Good afternoon, Miss Anderson," said Holmes. "You are from Edinburgh?"

"Correct."

"There is quite the gathering of Scotsmen here in Alfriston," Holmes remarked. "Do you know Miss Ralston or Mr. Sinclair?"

"Not prior to this visit, Mr. Holmes, but I since have become friendly with Miss Ralston. As we have many things in common, we have been taking our meals together. Mr. Sinclair is more reserved and appears content to eat alone."

"Miss Ralston is a painter, and you are poet, I understand?"

"Indeed. I had read Swinburne's *South Coast*, and decided that I would take in its sights to see if I was similarly moved."[232]

"And have you been?" asked Holmes. "May I hear your verses?"

She shook her head. "I have nothing so solid as a complete poem, Mr. Holmes. More like images that are roiling about in my brain, where I hope that they might coalesce into something worthy. This is what I have thus far:

> "On the back of that great bow-headed beast,
> A white whale of rugged land and diaphanous sky,
> The emerald swells surge in an unending dance.
> At the pinnacle of the realm, soaring to the hidden places,
> A step in the ancient journey of divine man
> To crown that long ago promised peace."

Holmes nodded his head appreciatively. "Very nice, Miss Anderson."

I glanced at him, for Holmes was never one for poetry, but he seemed sincere.

"May I ask you a question, Mr. Holmes?" said the poetess.

"Certainly."

"You are a consulting detective, are you not? What is it about Professor Mercer's death that has warranted you coming down from London?"[233]

Holmes smiled. "I was already in the area. In point of fact, it appears that the professor's death was nothing more than an infarction of the heart. Before he officially closed the case, Inspector Bardle merely wished for me to question the guests in order to ensure nothing untoward had occurred."

"Ah, I see," said Miss Anderson. "Well, please let me know if there is anything else where I may be of assistance."

Holmes watched her go, and continued to stare at the swinging door until it came to a complete stop. He drummed his long, thin fingers upon the arm of his chair for another half minute before finally turning to me.

"Well, Watson, what do you think? Does the testimony of any of the guests suggest anything of note?"

I shook my head. "As you said to Miss Anderson, it is difficult to imagine how the professor's death could be anything other than a natural event. Colonel Rameau and Mr. Dresler were seated together, as were Miss Ralston and Miss Anderson. Surely, even with the distraction outside the window, they would have noted if their companion rose and tampered with Professor Mercer's meal. Similarly, it is implausible to think that Mr. Sinclair – who is hardly the picture of health – bounded from his seat to poison the professor. I suppose that it is conceivable that Mr. Ainslie could have done so – but he is the only one."

"Very good, Watson," said Holmes. "You have established opportunity. It now remains for us to determine means and motive. Let us set means aside for the moment, as it is unclear whether or not poison was involved. What of motive?"

"I can hardly think of one."

"Well, if we hypothesize that the professor's death was unnatural, then it stands to reason that one of the guests must be lying. For none of them claim to have known him prior to this visit."

A thought occurred to me. "What if the professor was killed because of something he learned?"

"What do you mean?"

"Well, Mr. Dresler might be a spy. He admitted that he has been inspecting our coastal defences. What if this was not for some book, but instead on behalf of a foreign power?"

Holmes laughed. "I have in the past chided Inspector Lestrade with too little imagination, Watson, but I am afraid that you have a surfeit. While our relations with the Imperial State of Germany are currently exceptionally strained, it seems clear that the recent launch of the *Dreadnought* has put the Royal Navy in a vastly superior position when it comes to the naval arms race.[234] Even the most feverish dreams of the Kaiser do not include a seaborne invasion of our isles. No, I doubt that Mr. Dresler is engaged in espionage."

"What is your theory then?" said I, annoyed at this flat-out dismissal of my notion.

"I have but a few threads at the moment, Watson, and am attempting to weave them together into a tapestry. First, we have an entomologist who is well travelled in the Far East. In fact, he has a species of Lepidoptera named after him – a rare feat that the late-lamented Jack Stapleton would have envied. The proceedings note that this particular butterfly is native only to the coasts of China. Second, we have a man whose daughter died in China seven years ago."

"Mr. Sinclair? But she died of the plague," I protested. "Wait, do you think that the plague was transmitted by one of Professor Mercer's insects?"

"Ah, a fascinating thought, Watson! Due to the work performed in Hong Kong during the recent pandemic, we now know that terrible microbe's vector.[235] However, we have no evidence that the professor was interested in rat fleas. He appeared to confide himself to butterflies and moths, which we believe to be innocent of such transmission. However, Mr. Sinclair did not say 'the plague.' He said 'a plague.' Upon such a small article may rest a world of difference, a transmutation of the literal for a metaphor."

"So you believe that Mr. Sinclair blames Professor Mercer for the death of his daughter? In what way?"

"Recall the date in question, Watson. Seven years ago was during the Insurrection. What if Mr. Sinclair's plague was a reference to the Boxers?"[236]

"The Boxers!" I cried. "They cannot possibly be involved, Holmes! This is Sussex, not Limehouse.[237] I hardly think a group of Boxers could stroll about the streets of Alfriston without being noticed."

He shook his head. "Do not be so dramatic, Watson. I did not intend to suggest that the Boxers were directly implicated in the Professor's passing, merely that they might be peripherally related. At the moment, the connection to China is the only apparent link between one of the guests and Professor Mercer."

"So Mr. Sinclair had both opportunity – however challenging it would have been for him to act during the window of time when the other occupants of the dining room were distracted – and now motive. But what of means?"

Holmes shook his head. "Too soon, Watson. You are forgetting something."

"What?" said I, with a frown.

"The strand of blond hair."

I waved my hand. "That could have come from anywhere, Holmes. It hardly needs to be a clue."

"Ah, but it is," said he, with a small smile.

"How can you be certain?"

"Because one of the guests is wearing a postiche."[238]

"What!" I cried.

"Oh, yes. I saw through it right away. As old Baron Dowson said to me the night before he was due to be hanged, the stage lost a fine actor when I decided to pursue the law instead. It is the first quality of the criminal investigator to be able to see through a disguise."[239]

"Who?"

"You must allow me my small surprises, Watson. I shall let you know soon enough."

"Then you know what happened to Professor Mercer?"

He shook his head. "Not as of yet. I have hopes; however, I first require something of our host."

"What do you need, Mr. Holmes?" asked Bardle.

"Would you kindly ask Mr. Tilson to bring in a pot of hot tea and a bowl of red cabbage?"

Bardle stared at Holmes as if my friend had lost his mind, an estimation I would have considered myself if not so accustomed to Holmes' dramatic touches. I knew better to ask him what he had in mind. Retirement had not lessened his curious secretive streak.

Once the inspector returned from this strange mission, Holmes waved his hands about the room. "I realized, Bardle, that there is one player in this scene from whom we have yet to hear."

The inspector frowned. "Oh?"

"Would you please summon Commodore Wyndham? Moreover, while you are at it, we might as well ask the other guests to join us here in the dining room. I am certain that everyone shall be most interested in the story we are about to hear."

§

Fortunately, the Commodore had remained in Alfriston while awaiting the repair of his trap, so it was only a matter of a quarter-hour before Bardle had assembled everyone as per Holmes' request. During this time, Holmes sat quietly in one of the chairs, smoking his old briarroot pipe and flipping through one of the London morning papers. He seemed so engrossed in the news from the Empire that he failed to even touch the teapot or bowl of cabbage brought in by Mr. Tilson.

It was only the arrival of an active man of roughly sixty years that finally shook Holmes from his torpor. This individual, whose creased face and white hair and beard suggested a lifetime upon the sea, looked about with confusion in his intense blue eyes.

"Have a seat, Commodore. Yes, that one is fine," said Holmes, indicating the chair where the man had died. "I can assure you that Professor Mercer will not be joining us."

The man frowned, but did as Holmes requested. Sitting up straight as a mast in the chair, the commodore turned to Inspector Bardle. "May I ask, sir, what I am doing here?"

The policeman appeared troubled. "I have asked Mr. Sherlock Holmes – whose immense experience with crime is well known – to look into the matter of Professor Mercer's death."

"The man who died during my accident outside?"

"That is correct," said Bardle.

The commodore shrugged. "I fail to see what I can add to your inquiries?"

Bardle cast an imploring gaze upon Holmes, who rose to his feet with a swift nod and began to pace about the room. "We shall return to you in a moment, Commodore Wyndham, if you will be patient with me. First, I suggest that we turn our attention to the most remarkable part of this tableau – the pot of Russian caviare. I asked myself what possible role could it have played in Professor Mercer's death?"

"Are you suggesting that it was poisoned?" asked Mr. Ainslie.

"No sir, although it has subsequently been opened by the police," said Holmes, "at the time of the professor's death, I have been assured that it remained sealed."

The diplomat shrugged. "Could it not have been re-sealed? A clever man could accomplish that by melting the metal."

"Ah, that is an excellent point, Mr. Ainslie," said Holmes, as if this thought had just occurred to him. "Certainly the salty, pungent taste of caviare would be an excellent medium to hide the perception of a poison with a distinctive smell – such as, say, the bitter almonds of cyanide."

"But, Mr. Holmes," said Bardle. "The caviare was tested for poison. We would have found something as common as cyanide."

"Very well, we shall dispose of my poison theory. So what then was it doing there, and more importantly, who placed it in front of Professor Mercer during the Commodore's incident with the apple cart?"

Colonel Rameau shrugged. "It could have been any of us."

"Indeed," said Holmes. "It could have been any of you. And in fact, unless we suppose the professor placed it there himself, it must have been one of you. So, what possible reason could one of you have had for carrying out such a prank?"

"Why does it matter, if it was just a prank?" asked Mr. Dresler.

"Because, Herr Dresler, I do not believe that it was a harmless joke. At least not one intended to be amusing. Professor Mercer had an appearance of horror upon his face when he died." He turned to me. "Watson, as a medical man, would you say it possible for a man with a weak heart to have had his final breaths hastened by the sight of an object of unmistakable horror?"

"Of course, Holmes," I replied, "but why would a simple pot of caviare cause such terror?"

"That is what I wish to know. Moreover, I expect that someone in this room will provide us with the answer. I think that everyone has been less than forthcoming with me. I asked many of you if you knew Professor Mercer...."

"Are you calling me a liar, sir?" said John Ainslie, heatedly, as he jumped up from his chair.

Holmes turned to face him. "Not precisely, sir. You claimed that you only talked with the professor briefly. However, I wonder if someone else in your family knew him? Civil service is often a family calling. Did you have a father, or a brother, who served overseas? In China, for example?"

Ainslie's animated face hardened into stone. "What if I did? How could that be relevant?"

But Holmes had moved on. He turned to Mr. Dresler. "And China once had many former German military officers advising its armies, did it not? Did a relative of yours find employment in the Middle Kingdom?"

The German did not respond, so Holmes continued to look about the room. "And China also engaged many railway men – for which Scotland is so well known – to modernize its system of transport. I wonder if you, Miss Ralston, have a relative who worked for the railway?"

The painter sat mute through this questioning, though I thought I detected a glimmer of tears come into her eyes.

"And of course," persisted Holmes "we already know from Mr. Sinclair that his daughter was a missionary in China, where she met a tragic end some seven years ago. I wonder if he is the only one in the room who had a family member that was a missionary?" His gaze travelled over to Mary Anderson and Colonel Rameau, where it paused for a moment.

"Finally," said Holmes, "we have Commodore Wyndham, without whom the entire scheme could not have been carried off."

The naval officer appeared outraged. "What do you mean, sir?"

"I wondered from the start, Commodore, about your role in this matter. Surely, it is rather unusual for a steady naval officer to lose control of his horse? And to do so at the precise moment when a man drops dead strains credibility. I submit that you staged the so-called accident with the apple cart to induce Mr. Tilson and Miss Playstead to vacate the dining room."

"And why would I do such a thing?"

Holmes smiled. "May I ask what ship you commanded?"

"The HMS *Tribune*, a Centurion-class battleship."[240]

"And where was it stationed, Commodore?"

"I served in a great many places, Mr. Holmes. As you well know, the sun never sets upon our great Empire. I went wherever my fleet was needed."

"Such as China Station?" asked Holmes.[241]

"Yes, for a time."

"Very good." He turned from the commodore to the poetess. "Now, all that remains is for Miss Mary Anderson to tell us her complete story. I would begin with your true name. Unless you wish to persist with this fiction? I assure you that it will not be difficult for Inspector Bardle to wire to Edinburgh, where I am certain no one will be able to confirm the existence of such an individual as you claim to be."

The young poetess stared at Holmes grimly. "Why do you single me out, Mr. Holmes?"

He shook his head. "Come now, Miss Anderson. The postiche you wear is exceptional, made by Jourliac of Paris, I believe.[242] I wore one of their faux coiffures myself when I was following Count Sylvius about London. It would fool most people, but I am not most people. I asked myself why a woman of your age, who surely still possesses most of her natural hair, would wish to adopt such a disguise? If you wished to change the colour, you simply could have died it. Therefore, it could only have been to ensure that Professor Mercer did not recognize you until the moment you were ready to reveal yourself to him – at the time you placed the pot of caviare before him."

"The strand of blonde hair!" I cried.

"Very good, Watson," said Holmes. "That strand must have fallen when Miss Anderson – or whatever her name is – removed her wig and disclosed her true self to the professor."

She nodded. "I will not deny it. I placed the pot of caviare before Mercer. I did so on my own account, taking the advantage of the commotion outside."

"Do not insult my intelligence, Miss Anderson. It is obvious that you could not have acted without the collaboration of the others in this room. I require the truth."

"You wish to hear the truth?"

"I have said so."

She shook her head. "Little good it will do you, Mr. Holmes. There is not a jury in all of England who would convict us for our actions. Did I intend to give Professor Mercer the fright of his life? Yes. But how could I know that his heart would give out?"

"Constructive manslaughter would cover such an act," said Holmes, with a shrug.

"Provocation," she replied, simply.[243]

"Indeed? How so?"

The lady sighed and reached up to her head. With a swift motion, she removed the postiche from her head, revealing a swath of blonde hair. "My name, Mr. Holmes, is Jessie Patterson. I am the only one in this room – save Commodore Wyndham, whom all witnesses will place outside upon the street – who was directly acquainted with Professor Mercer. And when I tell you of the day when I last laid eyes upon the man, you may judge whether I was unjust in my final gift to him."

"Pray continue," said Holmes.

The woman we had known as Miss Anderson sighed and then nodded her head. "Very well. It was the fourth day of the siege," said Miss Patterson, quietly. "Ammunition and provisions were both nearing an end. When the Boxer insurrection had suddenly flamed up, and roared, like a fire in dry grass, across Northern China, us few scattered Europeans in the outlying provinces had huddled together at the nearest defensible post of Ichau and held on for dear life, hoping for rescue to come.

"In addition to the native converts, there were eight of us Europeans. For the most part, only a few sorts of people go out to China – diplomats, soldiers, railway men, and missionaries. Regarding the latter, my parents – Craig and Mary – led the Scottish Presbyterian Mission, supported by Dorothea Sinclair, a nurse of exceptional skill. I was seventeen at the time, and accompanied them when they left Edinburgh. Father Jacques Pierre led the French Mission. Mr. Herbert Ralston was an engineer on the Northern China Railway, while Mr. James Ainslie was from the Diplomatic service. Colonel Rudolf Dresler, late of the 114th Hanoverian Infantry, commanded the absurd little garrison."

As she spoke these names, I saw Holmes nod along, as if he suspected the connection to Mr. Arthur Sinclair, Miss Hetta Ralston, Mr. John Ainslie, and Mr. Klaus Dresler. "Father Pierre was a particular friend of yours, Colonel Rameau?" he asked.

The Frenchman nodded in confirmation. "Since we were children, we were as close as brothers," said Rameau, his voice tight with emotion. "He chose the path of peace and I the path of war, though from those selections, one could hardly foretell our ultimate fates."

"Pray continue, Miss Patterson," said Holmes.

"Of course, there was at Ichau one exception to this rule – Professor Stratton Mercer, the old California entomologist who had arrived at that tinderbox of a country with a plan of seeking after his rare and innocent butterflies. Ichau was only fifty miles from the coast, and there was a European squadron in the Gulf of Liantong.[244] Therefore, when the Boxers rose up, we held on bravely with the conviction that help must soon come sweeping down to them from the low hills to eastward. The sea was visible from those hills, and on the sea were our armed countrymen. Surely, then, we could not feel deserted. With brave hearts, the men manned the loopholes in the crumbling brick walls outlining the tiny European quarter, and they fired away briskly, if ineffectively, at the rapidly advancing sangars of the Boxers.[245] It was certain that – in another day or so – we would be at the end of our resources, but then it was equally certain that in another day or so we must be relieved. It might be a little sooner or it might be a little later, but there was no one who ever ventured to hint that the relief would not arrive in time to pluck us out of the fire. Up to Tuesday night, there was no word of discouragement.

"It is true that on Wednesday our robust faith in what was going forward behind those eastern hills had weakened a little. The grey slopes lay bare and unresponsive, while the deadly sangars pushed ever nearer, so near that every feature of the enemy faces – which shrieked imprecations at us from time to time over the top – could be clearly seen. There was not so much of that after young James Ainslie had settled down in the squat church tower – with his neat little .303 sporting rifle – and devoted his days to abating the nuisance. However, a silent sangar is an even more impressive thing than a clamorous one, and steadily, irresistibly, inevitably, the lines of brick and rubble grew closer. Soon they would be so near that one rush would assuredly carry the frantic swordsmen over our frail entrenchment. It all seemed very black upon the Wednesday evening.

"Colonel Dresler, the German ex-infantry soldier, went about with an imperturbable face. Ralston, of the railway, was up half the night writing farewell letters. Professor Mercer, the old entomologist, was even more silent and grimly thoughtful than ever. Ainslie had lost some of his flippancy. On the whole, I think it fair to say that the ladies – Miss Sinclair and my mother – were the most composed of the party. Father Pierre, of the French Mission, was also unaffected, as was natural to one who regarded martyrdom as a glorious crown. I heard my father – with whom for years Father Pierre had wrangled over the souls of the natives – say half-jokingly that the Boxers yelling for his blood beyond the walls disturbed the Frenchman less than his forced association with us Scottish Presbyterians. My father and Father Pierre passed each other in the corridors as dog passes cat, and each kept a watchful eye upon the other lest even in the trenches his rival might filch some sheep from the opposite fold, whispering in his ear what the other called heresy.

"But Wednesday night passed without a crisis, and at the dawn of Thursday all was bright once more. It was Ainslie, up in the clock tower, who had first heard the distant thud of a gun. Then Dresler heard it, and within half an hour, it was audible to all of us — that strong iron voice, calling to us from afar and bidding us to be of good cheer, since help was coming. It was clear that the landing party from the squadron was well on its way. It would not arrive an hour too soon. The cartridges were nearly finished. Our half-rations of food would soon dwindle to an even more pitiful supply. However, what need was there to worry about all that, now that relief was assured? There would be no attack that day, as most of the Boxers could be seen streaming off in the direction of the distant firing, and the long lines of sangars were silent and deserted. We were all able, therefore, to assemble at the lunch-table – a merry, talkative party, full of that joy of living which sparkles most brightly under the imminent shadow of death. I can still remember every word, as clear as if they were spoken yesterday.

" 'The pot of caviare!' cried John Ainslie. 'Come, Professor, out with the pot of caviare!'

" '*Potz-tausend!* Yes,' grunted old Dresler.[246] 'It is certainly time that we had that famous pot.'

"We ladies joined in, and from all parts of the long, ill-furnished table there came the demand for caviare. It may seem a strange time to have asked for such a delicacy, but the reason is easily told. Professor Mercer had received a jar of caviare in a hamper of goods that had arrived a day or two before the outbreak. In the general pooling and distribution of provisions, this one dainty provision, as well as three bottles of Lachryma Christi from the same hamper had been excepted and set aside.[247] By common consent, these items were to be reserved for the final joyous meal when the end of our peril should be in sight. Even as we sat at the table, the thud-thud of the relieving guns came to our ears – more luxurious music to our lunch than the most sybaritic restaurant of London could have supplied. Before evening, the relief would certainly arrive at Ichau. Why, then, should our stale bread not be glorified by the treasured caviare?

"But the Professor shook his gnarled old head and smiled his inscrutable smile. 'Better wait,' said he.

" 'Wait! Why wait?' cried the company.

" 'They have still far to come,' he answered.

" 'They will be here for supper at the latest,' said Mr. Ralston. 'They cannot be more than ten miles from us now. If they only did two miles an hour it would make them due at seven.'

" 'There is a battle on the way,' remarked Colonel Dresler. 'You will grant two hours or three hours for the battle.'

" 'Not half an hour," cried James Ainslie. 'They will walk through them as if they were not there. What can these rascals with their matchlocks and swords do against modern weapons?'[248]

" 'It depends on who leads the column of relief,' said Colonel Dresler. 'If they are fortunate enough to have a German officer....'

" 'An Englishman for my money!' cried Mr. Ralston.

" 'The French commodore is said to be an excellent strategist,' remarked Father Pierre.

" 'I do not see that it matters a toss," cried the exuberant James Ainslie. 'Mr. Mauser and Mr. Maxim are the two men who will see us through, and with them on our side no leader can go wrong.[249] I tell you they will just brush them aside and walk through them. So now, Professor, come on with that pot of caviare!'

"But the old scientist was unconvinced. 'We shall reserve it for supper,' said he.

" 'After all,' said my father, in his slow, precise Scottish intonation, 'it will be a courtesy to our guests – the officers of the relief – if we have some palatable food to lay before them. I am in agreement with the Professor that we reserve the caviare for supper.'

"This argument appealed to our sense of hospitality. There was something pleasantly chivalrous, too, in the idea of keeping our one little delicacy to give a savour to the meal of their preservers. There was no more talk of the caviare.

" 'By the way, Professor,' said my father, 'I have only heard to-day that this is the second time that you have been besieged in this way. I am sure we should all be very interested to hear some details of your previous experience.'

"The old man's face set very grimly. 'I was in Sung-tong, in South China, in 'eighty-nine,' said he.[250]

" 'It is a very extraordinary coincidence that you should

twice have been in such a perilous situation,' said the missionary. 'Tell us how you were relieved at Sung-tong.'

"The shadow deepened upon the weary face. 'We were not relieved,' said Mercer.

" 'What!' cried my father. 'The place fell?'

" 'Yes, it fell.'

" 'And you came through alive?'

" 'I am a doctor as well as an entomologist. The Boxers had many wounded; they spared me.'

" 'And the rest?'

" '*Assez! assez!*' cried the little French priest, raising his hand in protest.[251] He had been twenty years in China. The professor had said nothing, but there was something – some lurking horror – in his dull, grey eyes that turned my mother and Miss Sinclair pale.

" 'I am sorry,' said my father. 'I can see that it is a painful subject. I should not have asked.'

" 'No,' the Professor answered, slowly. 'It is wiser not to ask. It is better not to speak about such things at all. But surely those guns are very much nearer?'

"There could be no doubt of it. After a silence, the thud-thud had recommenced with a lively ripple of rifle-fire playing all round that deep bass master-note. It must be just at the farther side of the nearest hill. We pushed back our chairs and ran out to the ramparts. However, there was little to see. The sangars were in their same location, seemingly deserted. As we gazed out at the hope of our relief, the guns finally ceased. I turned to the Commandant. There was a complacent smile upon his broad German face.

" 'The Kaiser will be pleased,' said he, rubbing his hands. 'Yes, certainly it should mean a decoration. I can see the headlines now. *Defence of Ichau against the Boxers by Colonel Dresler, late Major of the 114th Hanoverian Infantry. Splendid resistance of small garrison against overwhelming odds.* It will certainly appear in the Berlin papers.'

" 'Then you think we are saved?' I asked him.

" 'Well, my dear,' said the Colonel, lighting his long pipe, and stretching his gaitered legs upon a nearby bamboo chair, 'You should not concern yourself with such matter. However, I will stake my military reputation that all is well. They are advancing swiftly, the firing has died down to show that resistance is at an end, and within an hour, we shall see them over the brow of the hill. Ainslie is to fire his gun three times from the church tower as a signal, and then we shall make a little sally on our own account.'

" 'And you are waiting for this signal?'

" 'Yes, we are waiting for Ainslie's shots,' replied Colonel Dresler.

"I was reassured by the Colonel's confidence and we returned to our quarters. I spent some time in quiet contemplation, before my mother summoned me. As she dragged me by the arm to the dining room that had become the focal point of our group, she explained that Colonel Dresler had recently received a message. When we arrived, the outside door flew open and James Ainslie rushed into the room. Behind him crowded Mr. Ralston and my father, who had been manning their posts upon the wall.

" 'You have had news, Colonel?" he asked the German officer. 'The relief force is coming?'

"The Colonel opened his mouth, as if to speak; however, it was Professor Mercer who answered for him, pushing himself up from his chair. 'Colonel Dresler has just been telling me. It is all right. They have halted, but will be here in the early morning. There is no longer any danger.'

"A cheer broke from the group in the doorway. Every one of us was laughing and shaking hands.

" 'But suppose they rush us before to-morrow morning?' cried Mr. Ralston. 'What infernal fools these fellows are not to push on!'

" 'It's all safe,' said Ainslie, his voice filled with elation. 'These fellows have had a bad knock. We can see their wounded being carried by the hundred over the hill. They must have lost heavily. They won't attack before morning.'

" 'No, no,' said the Colonel; 'it is certain that they won't attack before morning. You shall see.'

"The afternoon wore away without the Boxers making any sort of attack. It appeared that the siege was indeed over, and that the assailants had been crippled by the losses that they had already sustained. The relief force would arrive at the eleventh hour and save us all.[252] It was a joyous and noisy party, therefore, which met at the supper-table, when the three bottles of Lachryma Christi were uncorked and the famous pot of caviare was finally opened. It was a large jar, and, though each of us was given a tablespoonful of the delicacy, it was by no means exhausted. Mr. Ralston, who was an epicure, had a double allowance. He pecked away at it like a hungry bird. Ainslie, too, had a second helping. The Professor took a large spoonful himself, and Colonel Dresler did the same. Both my mother and Miss Sinclair ate freely. Only I refused to take more than a nibble, for I disliked its salty, pungent taste. In spite of the hospitable entreaties of the Professor, my portion lay hardly touched at the side of my plate.

" 'You do not like my little delicacy, my dear? It is a disappointment to me when I had kept it for your pleasure,' said the old man. 'I beg that you will eat the caviare.'

" 'I have never tasted it before,' I replied. 'No doubt I should like it in time.'

" 'Well, you must make a beginning. Why not start to educate your taste now? Do, please!' said Mercer.

" 'Why, how earnest you are!' I laughed. 'I had no idea you were so polite, Professor. Even if I do not eat it I am just as grateful.'

" 'You are foolish not to eat it,' said the Professor, with such intensity that the smile died from my face. I have no doubt that, in that moment, my eyes reflected the earnestness of his own. 'I tell you it is foolish not to eat caviare tonight,' he continued.

" 'But why – why?' I asked.

" 'Because you have it on your plate,' said Mercer. 'Because it is sinful to waste it.'

" 'There! There!' said my stout mother, leaning across the table. 'Don't trouble her anymore. I can see that she does not like it. But it shall not be wasted.' She passed the blade of her knife under it, and scraped it from my plate on to her own. 'Now it won't be wasted. Your mind may be at ease, Professor.'

"But it did not seem at ease. On the contrary, his face was agitated like that of a man who encounters an unexpected and formidable obstacle. He was lost in thought. The conversation buzzed cheerily. Everyone was full of his or her future plans.

" 'No, no, there is no holiday for me,' said Father Pierre. 'We priests do not get holidays. Now that the mission and school are formed, I am to leave it to Father Amiel, and to push westwards to found another.'

" 'You are leaving?' said my father. 'You do not mean that you are going away from Ichau?'

" Father Pierre shook his venerable head in waggish reproof. 'You must not look so pleased, Mr. Patterson.'

" 'Well, well, our views are very different,' said my father, 'but there is no personal feeling towards you, Father Pierre. At the same time, how any reasonable educated man at this time of the world's history can teach these poor benighted heathen that....'

"A general buzz of remonstrance silenced the theological debate before it could begin.

" 'What will you do yourself, Mr. Patterson?' asked someone.

" 'Well, I will take three months in Edinburgh to attend the annual meeting. You will be glad to do some shopping in Princes Street, I am thinking, Mary. And you, Jessie, you will finally see some folk your own age. Then we can come back next autumn, when your nerves have had a rest.'

" 'Indeed, we shall all need it,' said Miss Sinclair. 'You know, this long strain takes me in the strangest way. At the present moment I can hear such a buzzing in my ears.'

" 'Well, that's funny, for it's just the same with me,' cried

John Ainslie. 'An absurd up-and-down buzzing, as if a drunken bluebottle fly were trying experiments on his range. As you say, it must be due to nervous strain. For my part, I am going back to Peking, and I hope I may get some promotion over this affair.[253] I can get a good game of polo here, and that is as fine a pastime as I know.[254] How about you, Ralston?'

" 'Oh, I don't know. I have hardly had time to think. I want to have a real good sunny, bright holiday and forget it all. It was funny to see all the letters in my room. It looked so black on Wednesday night that I had settled up my affairs and written to all my friends. I do not quite know how they were to be delivered, but I trusted to luck. I think I will keep those papers as a souvenir. They will always remind me of how close a shave we have had.'

" 'Yes, I would keep them,' said Colonel Dresler. His voice was so deep and solemn that every eye was turned upon him.

" 'What is it, Colonel? You seem in the blues tonight.' It was James Ainslie who spoke.

" 'No, no; I am very contented.' Colonel Dresler replied.

" 'Well, so you should be when you see success in sight. I am sure we are all indebted to you for your science and skill. I do not think we could have held the place without you. Ladies and gentlemen, I ask you to drink to the health of Colonel Dresler, of the Imperial German Army. *Er soll leben – hoch!*'[255]

"They all stood up and raised their glasses to the soldier, with smiles and bows.

"Dresler's pale face flushed with professional pride. 'I have always kept my books with me. I have forgotten nothing,' said he. 'I do not think that more could be done. If things had gone wrong with us and the place had fallen you would, I am sure, have freed me from any blame or responsibility.' He looked wistfully round him.

"I'm voicing the sentiments of this company, Colonel Dresler,' said my father, 'when I say – but, Lord save us! What's amiss with Mr. Ralston?'

"The railway man had dropped his face upon his folded arms

and was placidly sleeping.

" 'Don't mind him,' said the Professor, hurriedly. 'We are all in a stage of reaction now. I have no doubt that we are all liable to collapse. It is only tonight that we shall feel what we have gone through.'

" 'I am sure I can fully sympathize with him,' said my mother. 'I do not know when I have been sleepier. I can hardly hold my own head up.' She cuddled back in her chair and shut her eyes.

" 'Well, I have never known Mary to do that before,' cried my father, laughing heartily. 'Gone to sleep over her supper! Whatever will she think when we tell her of it afterwards? But the air does seem hot and heavy. I can certainly excuse anyone who falls asleep tonight. I think that I shall turn in early myself.'

"Meanwhile, James Ainslie was in a talkative, excited mood. He was on his feet once more with his glass in his hand. 'I think that we ought to have one drink all together, and then sing *'Auld Lang Syne,'* ' said he, smiling round at the company. 'For a week we have all pulled in the same boat, and we have gotten to know each other as people never do in the quiet days of peace. We have learned to appreciate each other, and we have learned to appreciate each other's nations. There is the Colonel here stands for Germany. And Father Pierre is for France. Then there is the Professor for America. Ralston, Patterson, and I are Britishers. Then there are the ladies, God bless 'em! They have been angels of mercy and compassion all through the siege. I think we should drink the health of the ladies. Wonderful thing – the quiet courage, the patience, the – what shall I say? – the fortitude – the – the – by George, look at the Colonel! He's gone to sleep, too – most infernal sleepy weather.'

Ainslie's glass crashed down upon the table, and he sank back, mumbling and muttering, into his seat. Miss Sinclair had dropped off also. She lay like a broken lily across the arm of her chair. My father looked round him and sprang to his feet. He passed his hand over his flushed forehead.

" 'This isn't natural, Jessie,' he cried to me. 'Why are they all asleep? There's Father Pierre – he is off too. Jessie, Jessie, your mother is cold. Is it sleep? Is it death? Open the windows! Help! help! help!' He staggered to his feet and rushed to the windows, but midway his head spun round, his knees sank under him, and he pitched forward upon his face."

Jessie Patterson paused her recitation for a moment, her voice raw and tears streaming down her face. I admired the courage it must have required to articulate the moment of her parents' deaths. Then, having gathered herself, she continued.

"I had also sprung to my feet. I looked round with horror-stricken eyes at my prostrate father and the silent ring of figures. 'Professor Mercer! What is it? What is it?' I cried. 'Oh, my God, they are dying! They are dead!'

"The old man had raised himself by a supreme effort of his will, though the darkness was already gathering thickly round him. 'My dear young lady,' he said, stuttering and stumbling over the words, 'we would have spared you this. It would have been painless to mind and body. It was cyanide. I had it in the caviare. But you would not have it.'

" 'Great Heaven!' I shrank away from him, my eyes dilated with revulsion. 'Oh, you monster! You monster! You have poisoned them!'

" 'No! no! I saved them. You do not know the Boxers. They are horrible. In another hour, we should all have been in their hands. Take it now, child.' Even as he spoke, a burst of firing broke out under the very windows of the room. 'Hark! There they are! Quick, dear, quick, you may cheat them yet!'

"But his words began to fall upon deaf ears. I sank back senseless in my chair. When I awoke, it was not a Boxer standing over me."

"It was Commodore Wyndham," said Holmes, gravely.

"That is correct, sir," said the naval man, taking up the tale. "I was the first – after our desperate and successful night attack – to burst into that terrible supper-room. Round the table sat the white and silent company. Only in the young girl, who moaned and faintly stirred, was any sign of life to be seen. Yet, there was one in the circle who had the energy for a last supreme duty. As I stood, stupefied, at the door, I saw a grey head slowly lift from the table, and the tall form of the Professor staggered for an instant to its feet. 'Take care of the caviare! For God's sake don't touch the caviare!' he croaked. Then he sank back once more and the circle of death was complete."

"But it was not complete, it seems," said Holmes. "For Professor Mercer lived, did he not, Commodore?"

Wyndham nodded. "Indeed. I have long suffered from angina. It is what forced me to retire from the Navy. In case of an attack, I always carry with me some pearls of amyl nitrate. A friend once laughingly told that they might be of use as an antidote against cyanide. It was such an interesting titbit that I remembered it, though at the time I never imagined I would have an opportunity to test such a function. I administered some to the Professor, and after he turned an impressive shade of blue, he began to slowly recover."[256]

"But you were unaware of the fact that Professor did not die with the others, Miss Patterson?"

"No," said she, heavily. "Until last year, I believed that I was the lone survivor of Ichau. I had been in contact with the relatives and friends of those who had perished. And when I learned that the Professor had survived, I persuaded them to join me in condemning him. He would face his crime, and we might learn the truth."

"Instead, his heart gave out."

She smiled bitterly. "No more than he deserved."

"But why did he do it?" I asked. "Why would he murder all of those people?"

"Perhaps this will clear up matters, Watson," said Holmes, holding out the professor's notebook.

"His notebook?" said I, with a frown. "We have already looked through it, Holmes. It is filled with various observations about *Cyclopedes* and *Pyralis vandeleuria*, of interest only to the most dedicated entomologist."[257]

Holmes smiled. "This is an example, Watson, where my abnormally acute sense of smell comes in handy. Here, take another whiff of this page, where the lines of writing are set far apart."

He handed it to me, and I brought it to my nose. There was a faint but incisive scent of vinegar, and I said as much.

"Very good, Watson. Now, vinegar – along with the juice of a lemon – is one of the most readily accessible of the invisible inks."

"Invisible ink!" I cried.

"Yes, now, as any chemist worth his salt will tell you, words written in vinegar are best revealed using the pigment flavin. While I do not have access to my old chemical bench, a simple solution of red cabbage boiled in water will typically suffice."

All of the room's occupants watched in fascination as Holmes proceeded to pour steaming water from the kettle into the bowl of cabbage.

He then turned to Miss Ralston. "May I borrow one of your brushes?"

She nodded and pulled one from the pocket of her smock-frock. Holmes dipped this in the red cabbage water and then painted this into the empty space upon the page. Like magic, words began to appear. As he went, I leaned over his shoulder and read aloud:

> *This will be my final testament. I can feel the cold breath of the end drawing near. I have cheated death twice. I doubt that I shall get a third opportunity. However, I have seen so many strange turns of Fate in my long life that I do not grieve, nor do I rejoice, until I know that I have cause. But I must put these words down, so that after I am gone, people will know that I am a great fool, but not a monster.*
>
> *I must go back to that moment when Colonel Dresler asked me about the siege of Sung-tong. I am certain the man was earnest when he wished to discuss it, for it*

appealed to his professional point of view. He wished to know if he had conducted as wise and good defence as at Ichau, one worthy of the traditions of the German army.

I objected and told him that it was not a pleasant subject. However, I said that I thought he could have done no more. He persisted in asking me if Sung-tong was ably defended. Could it have been saved? I told him that everything possible was done – save only one thing. The one omission was that no one – above all, no woman – should have been allowed to fall alive into the hands of the terrible Boxer mob.

Colonel Dresler knew at once that I was right. He thought that Ralston and Ainslie would die fighting, as he would himself, but that the missionaries would not lay hands upon their own lives. Their consciences would not permit it. So, in mercy, I resolved to kill them, if it came to the point where all hope was lost.

For I have been through it. I have seen the death of the hot eggs; I have seen the death of the boiling kettle; I have seen the women – my God! I wonder that I have ever slept sound again. At Sung-Tong, I was strapped to a stake with thorns in my eyelids to keep them open, and my grief at their torture was a smaller thing than my self-reproach, when I thought that I could – with one tube of tasteless tablets – have snatched them at the last instant from the hands of their tormentors. I am ready to stand at the Divine bar and answer for a thousand deaths such as that! Why, it is such an act as might well cleanse the stain of real sin from the soul. But if – knowing what I do – I should have failed this second time to do it, then, by heaven, there is no hell deep enough or hot enough to receive my guilty craven spirit.

Colonel Dresler shook my hand and went out again to check upon Ainslie, whose promised shots signalling the arrival of the relief force were long overdue. When Dresler staggered back into the room, his face a ghastly yellow-white, and his chest heaving like that of a man exhausted by running, I knew that the relief force was not coming. Dresler had been standing at the wall near the wooden postern gate, which opened on the rose garden, when a knock came upon the door. Opening it, he found a Tartar, badly cut about with swords.[258] *This messenger had come from the battle, sent by Commodore Wyndham. The relieving force had been checked. They had shot away most of their ammunition. They had entrenched themselves and sent back to the ships for more. Three days must pass before they could come. However, in the Colonel's opinion, we could hold out for an hour or two at the most. He pledged his credit as a soldier upon it. We must fall. There was no hope.*

When the others came back into the room, seeking news, I told them what they wished to hear – that all was well. The Boxers had been halted; they were carrying their scores of wounded back over the hill. They would not attack again before morning. It was a lie, of course. But why torture them with the truth, when it would make no difference regarding the ultimate outcome?

The afternoon was quiet. But to my ears, it was clear that the unwonted stillness meant only that the Boxers were reassembling their forces from their fight with the relief column, and were gathering themselves for the inevitable and final rush. We were doomed. So, we would have a final feast. And the main course would be my caviare, carefully prepared with cyanide. Everything went as planned, save only that Jessie Patterson would not partake. Well, I did what I could for the girl.

And then I heard the most terrible sound of all. The firing had resumed outside. But what was that? Merciful Father, what was that? Was I going mad? Was it the effect of the drug that I had consumed with the others? Surely it was a European cheer? Yes, there were sharp orders in English. There was the shouting of sailors. I

> *could no longer doubt it. By some miracle, the relief had come after all. I threw my arms upwards in despair. What have I done? Oh, good Lord, what have I done?*

The words ended and Holmes set down his brush. "Did you send that man, Commodore, with the message that your forces were checked?"

Wyndham shook his head gravely. "I sent no such messenger."

"A most cruel stratagem," said Holmes, nodding slowly. "Some fanatical Boxer sacrificed himself, hoping that his words might cause the garrison to lose hope and surrender itself before the relief force could arrive. And he was correct. That false message hastened the fatal twelfth hour."

I looked about the room. Miss Ralston and Mr. Sinclair quietly wept in their seats. Mr. Ainslie silently regarded at his balled fists, his face contorted with anger. Mr. Dresler appeared in shock, perhaps staggered that his father's masterful defence had been undone to the point where he actively colluded with Professor Mercer to bring about the deaths of those under his care. Colonel Rameau stood up and stepped over to the window, his eyes trained at the building across, but his soul seemingly staring into infinity.

Only Miss Jessie Patterson met Holmes' gaze. An indescribable emotion washed over her face. "It seems that I misjudged Professor Mercer, Mr. Holmes. I thought his monstrous act was some fit of madness. For why would he have done such a thing when the relief was so close? But now I understand, and I am prepared to face my fate."

Holmes nodded slowly. "And it seems that I misjudged you, Miss Patterson. Now I understand why you felt that your actions were a just condemnation of his past crime. But the past is now past. You were spared, perhaps for some larger purpose. You have a wide future before you – I urge you to seize it. I bid you *adieu*."

He turned and strode out of the inn. Inspector Bardle and I

looked at each other, and then raced after him. We caught up to Holmes at the end of High Street, as he was stepping into the policeman's trap.

"Mr. Holmes!" cried the inspector. "What are you doing?"

"I am ready to go home, Bardle."

"But what of Miss Patterson and the others?" said the policeman. "Surely they must be charged with a crime?"

"To what end, Inspector?" said Holmes, solemnly. "The circle of misery must be broken by someone. Let it be us. Dr Gade reported that Professor Mercer died of natural causes. Put that in your report."

"But that is not the truth!" Bardle protested.

"And did learning the truth change anything, Bardle? Put yourself in the place of Miss Patterson and the others, hoping against all odds that rescue would come in time – until it did not. For those whom it did not, the less said about their fate, the better. And while Miss Patterson was technically in the former camp, you have seen her face and looked into her eyes, Inspector. What did you see there? I, for one, fear that she has come back into the world of men having gazed very closely upon such an end as will ever haunt her dreams. I think that is punishment enough for her actions. Now we must hope that the road of destiny leads her to sunnier shores."

§

APPENDIX: ON DATES

A CHRONOLOGIC ORDER OF SHERLOCK HOLMES ADVENTURES (CANONICAL & NON-CANONICAL)

How best to read the various tales of Sherlock Holmes? The most obvious answer to that question is "the order in which they were written and published, beginning with A Study in Scarlet." However, Sir Arthur Conan Doyle, the first literary agent for Dr John H. Watson, did not publish the stories in a strict chronologic order, with many stories told primarily as flashbacks. Therefore, for the reader, either new to these wondrous tales or seeking to read them all again, I present the following option. By following this list, the reader is able to see for themselves the maturation of Holmes and Watson, from relatively young lads with all of London at their fingertips, to the mature gentlemen reflecting upon a lifetime of adventure.

I generally follow the dating laid out by the great Sherlockian editors William S. Baring-Gould in *The Annotated Sherlock Holmes* (1967) and Leslie S. Klinger in *The New Annotated Sherlock Holmes* (2005-6), which are themselves the product of consensus of other Sherlockians. These have often followed the vaguest of clues in the stories themselves in order to come to their conclusions. Dr Watson, for all his excellent qualities, was never his best with dates (he was known, from time to time, to even be off by a year or more). For point of reference, it is generally considered that Sherlock Holmes was born in 1854 (6 January, to be precise) and John Watson in 1852 (7 August, to be precise), making them at the time of their meeting in January 1881 twenty-seven and twenty-nine years of age, respectively.

At the risk of being accused of vanity, into the list this literary agent interjects the timing for those stories (in bold) that I have been so fortunate as to unearth and publish.

Before 221B Baker Street (1874 – 1880)
- July 12 – September 22, 1874: The *'Gloria Scott'* (from *TMSH*). Recounted to Watson c. February 1888.
- April 4–22, 1875: **The Lost Legion** (from *TTI!*). Recounted to Watson c. December 1894.
- December 28 – January 7, 1875-76: **The Father of Evil** (from *TSS*). Recounted to Watson January 6, 1903.
- October 2, 1879: The Musgrave Ritual (from *TMSH*). Recounted to Watson c. February 1888.
- July 27 – December 4, 1880: **The Isle of Devils**

A Suite in Baker Street (1881 – 1889)
- March 4–7, 1881: A Study in Scarlet
- August 25, 1881: **The Adventure of the Tragic Act** (from *SAO*)
- December 3, 1881: **The Adventure of the Double-Edged Hoard** (from *FMFL*)
- December 5-6, 1881: **The Adventure of the Fallen Desperado** (from *TAP*)
- August 21 – September 30, 1882: **The Adventure of the Most Dangerous Man** (from *TDC*)
- April 6, 1883: The Adventure of the Speckled Band (from *TASH*)
- May 5-12, 1883: **The Adventure of the Monstrous**

- **Blood** (from *TFC*)
- November 2, 1883: **The Adventure of the Haunted Grange** (from *TDC*)
- August 23 – September 10, 1884: **The Gate of Gold**
- October 6–7, 1885: The Resident Patient (from *TMSH*)
- November 3–4, 1885: **The Adventure of the Mad Colonel** (from *TFC*)
- October 8, 1886: The Adventure of the Noble Bachelor (from *TASH*)

The Well-Remembered Door (The First Desertion) (1886 – 1888)[259]
- January 23, 1887: **The Adventure of the Fabricated Vision** (from *TDC*)
- April 14–26, 1887: The Reigate Squires (from *TMSH*)
- May 20–22, 1887: A Scandal in Bohemia (from *TASH*)
- June 2–4, 1887: **The Adventure of the Dawn Discovery** (from *FMFL*)
- June 18–19, 1887: The Man with the Twisted Lip (from *TASH*)
- June 19-21, 1887: **The Adventure of the Missing Mana** (from *APRT*)
- September 29–30, 1887: The Five Orange Pips (from *TASH*)
- October 18–19, 1887: A Case of Identity (from *TASH*)
- October 21–22, 1887: **The Adventure of the Queen's Pendant** (from *TTI!*)
- October 29–30, 1887: The Red-Headed League (from *TASH*)
- November 19, 1887: The Adventure of the Dying Detective (from *HLB*)
- December 27, 1887: The Adventure of the Blue Carbuncle (from *TASH*)

The Return to Baker Street (1888 – 1889)
- January 7–8, 1888: The Valley of Fear

- April 7, 1888: The Yellow Face (from *TMSH*)
- April 14–15, 1888: **The Red Leech** (from *Assassination*)
- August 30-31, 1888: **The Adventure of the Loring Riddle** (from *TAP*)
- September 12, 1888: The Greek Interpreter (from *TMSH*)
- September 18–21, 1888: The Sign of Four
- September 25 – October 20, 1888: The Hound of the Baskervilles
- November 3-4, 1888: **The Adventure of the Imprisoned Monarch** (from *TAP*)
- March 24, 1889: **The Adventure of the Pirate's Code** (from *TTI!*)
- April 5–20, 1889: The Adventure of the Copper Beeches (from *TASH*)

The Second Desertion (1889 – 1891)[260]
- June 15, 1889: The Stockbroker's Clerk (from *TMSH*)
- July 30 – August 1, 1889: The Naval Treaty (from *TMSH*)
- August 31 – September 2, 1889: The Cardboard Box (from *TMSH*)
- September 7–8, 1889: The Adventure of the Engineer's Thumb (from *TASH*)
- September 11–12, 1889: The Crooked Man (from *TMSH*)
- September 21–22, 1889: **The Adventure of the Fateful Malady** (from *TFC*)
- March 24–29, 1890: The Adventure of Wisteria Lodge (from *HLB*)
- May 30 – June 1, 1890: **The Adventure of the Hallowed Ring** (from *TAP*)
- June 8–9, 1890: The Boscombe Valley Mystery (from *TASH*)
- June 20 – July 4, 1890: **The Oak-Leaf Sprig** (from *ARW*)
- September 25–30, 1890: Silver Blaze (from *TMSH*)
- December 19–20, 1890: The Adventure of the Beryl Coronet (from *TASH*)

- December 25, 1890: **The Adventure of the Spanish Sovereign** (from *TSF*)
- April 24 – May 4, 1891: The Final Problem (from *TMSH*)

The Great Hiatus (1891 – 1894)
- August 1-8: 1891: **The Harrowing Intermission** (from *FMFL*)

The Great Return (1894 – 1902)
- April 5, 1894: The Adventure of the Empty House (from *TRSH*)
- October 7-9, 1894: **The Adventure of the Boulevard Assassin** (from *APRT*)
- October 20 – November 7, 1894: **The Adventure of the Double Detectives** (from *RTW*)
- November 14–15, 1894: The Adventure of the Golden Pince-Nez (from *TRSH*)
- September 18–22: 1894: The Adventure of the Second Stain (from *TRSH*)[261]
- September 22–25, 1894: **The Adventure of the Third Traitor** (from *AEW*)
- December 23, 1894: **The Adventure of the Manufactured Miracle** (from *TSF*)
- January 13-14, 1895: **The Adventure of the Dishonourable Discharge** (from *TSS*)
- February 13-15, 1895: **The Adventure of the Secret Tomb** (from *APRT*)
- April 5–6, 1895: The Adventure of the Three Students (from *TRSH*)
- April 13–20, 1895: The Adventure of the Solitary Cyclist (from *TRSH*)
- June 23-25, 1895: **The Problem of the Black Eye** (from *SAO*)
- July 3–5, 1895: The Adventure of Black Peter (from *TRSH*)
- August 20–21, 1895: The Adventure of the Norwood

- Builder (from *TRSH*)
- October 4-6, 1895: **The Adventure of the Wrong Hand** (from *TDC*)
- November 21–23, 1895: The Adventure of the Bruce-Partington Plans (from *HLB*)
- December 22, 1895: The Adventure of the First Star (from *TSF*)
- October 28, 1896: The Adventure of the Veiled Lodger (from *TCBSH*)
- November 19–21, 1896: The Adventure of the Sussex Vampire (from *TCBSH*)
- December 8–10, 1896: The Adventure of the Missing Three-Quarter (from *TRSH*)
- January 23, 1897: The Adventure of the Abbey Grange (from *TRSH*)
- March 16–20, 1897: The Adventure of the Devil's Foot (from *HLB*)
- May 2–3, 1897: **The Adventure of the Fatal Fire** (from *TSS*)
- July 7, 1897: **The Adventure of the Sunken Indiaman** (from *FMFL*)
- September 4-5, 1897: **The Mannering Towers Mystery** (from *SAO*)
- July 27 – August 13, 1898: The Adventure of the Dancing Men (from *TRSH*)
- July 28–30, 1898: The Adventure of the Retired Colourman (from *TCBSH*)
- January 5–14, 1899: The Adventure of Charles Augustus Milverton (from *TRSH*)
- February 2, 1899: **The Adventure of the African Horror** (from *RTW*)
- June 8–10, 1900: The Adventure of the Six Napoleons (from *TRSH*)
- October 4–5, 1900: The Problem of Thor Bridge (from *TCBSH*)
- November 4, 1900: **The Adventure of the Awakened**

Spirit (from *TSS*)
- May 16–18, 1901: The Adventure of the Priory School (from *TRSH*)
- June 20-23, 1901: **The Adventure of the Fair Lad** (from *RTW*)
- May 6–7, 1902: The Adventure of Shoscombe Old Place (from *TCBSH*)
- June 26–27, 1902: The Adventure of the Three Garridebs (from *TCBSH*)
- July 1–18, 1902: The Disappearance of Lady Frances Carfax (from *HLB*)
- September 3–16, 1902: The Adventure of the Illustrious Client (from *TCBSH*)
- September 24–25, 1902: The Adventure of the Red Circle (from *HLB*)

The Final Desertion (1903)[262]
- January 7–12, 1903: The Adventure of the Blanched Soldier (from *TCBSH*)
- May 26–27, 1903: The Adventure of the Three Gables (from *TCBSH*)
- June 28, 1903: The Adventure of the Mazarin Stone (from *TCBSH*)
- August 2, 1903: **The Adventure of the Silent Drum** (from *TTI!*)
- September 6–22, 1903: The Adventure of the Creeping Man (from *TCBSH*)
- December 20-21, 1903: **The Adventure of the Barren Grave** (from *TFC*)

Retirement (1904 – 1918)
- January 6-18, 1904: **The Adventure of the Dead Man's Note** (from *APRT*)
- July 3–5, 1907: **The Cold Dish** (from *TSS*)
- September 2, 1907: **The Adventure of the Twelfth Hour** (from *SAO*)

- July 25 – August 1, 1907: The Lion's Mane (from *TCBSH*)
- June 21, 1909: **The Adventure of the Unfathomable Silence** (from *AEW*)
- October 31 – November 1, 1909: **The Adventure of the Pharaoh's Curse** (from *Assassination*)
- November 2–5, 1909: **The Problem of Threadneedle Street** (from *Assassination*)
- November 30 – December 1, 1909: **The Falling Curtain** (from *Assassination*)
- August 2, 1914: **The High Mountain** (from *AEW*)
- August 2, 1914: His Last Bow: The War Service of Sherlock Holmes (from *HLB*)
- March 19-22, 1915: **The Adventure of the Defenceless Prisoner** (from *AEW*)
- September 17, 1915: **Their Final Flourish** (from *AEW*)
- October 22, 1917: Preface (from *HLB*)
- December 22, 1918: **The Grand Gift of Sherlock** (from *TSF*)

§

THE COLLECTIONS

Literary Editor, Sir Arthur Conan Doyle (56 cases & 4 novels)
- *TASH: The Adventures of Sherlock Holmes* (12 cases; published 1891-92)
- *TMSH: The Memoirs of Sherlock Holmes* (12 cases; published 1892-93)
- *TRSH: The Return of Sherlock Holmes* (13 cases; published 1903-4)
- *HLB: His Last Bow: Some Reminiscences of Sherlock Holmes* (7 cases & 1 preface; published 1917)
- *TCBSH:* The Case-Book of Sherlock Holmes (12 cases; published 1921-27)

Literary Editor, Craig Janacek (53 cases & 2 novels)
- *The Assassination of Sherlock Holmes* (4 cases; published 2015)
- *Light in the Darkness,* comprising:
  - *TSF: The Season of Forgiveness* (3 cases & 1 letter; published 2014)
  - *TFC: The First of Criminals* (4 cases; published 2015-16)
- *The Treasury of Sherlock Holmes,* comprising:
  - *TTI!: Treasure Trove Indeed!* (4 cases; published 2016)
  - *FMFL: Fortunes Made & Fortunes Lost* (4 cases; published 2018)
- *The Gathering Gloom,* comprising:
  - *TSS: The Schoolroom of Sorrow* (5 cases; published 2018)
  - *AEW: An East Wind* (5 cases; published 2019)
- *The Travels of Sherlock Holmes,* comprising:
  - *APRT: A Prompt and Ready Traveller* (4 cases; published 2019)
  - *RTW: Round the World* (4 cases; published 2020)

- *The Chronicles of Sherlock Holmes,* comprising:
    - *SAO: Seen & Observed* (4 cases; published 2020)
    - *TDC: Their Dark Crisis* (4 cases; published 2021)
- *The Histories of Sherlock Holmes,* comprising:
    - *TAP: Thrust & Parry* (4 cases; coming soon)
    - *TFO: The Faculties of Observation* (4 cases, coming soon)

§

ALSO BY CRAIG JANACEK

THE DOCTOR WATSON TRILOGY
THE ISLE OF DEVILS
THE GATE OF GOLD
THE RUINS OF SUMMER*

THE MIDWINTER MYSTERIES OF SHERLOCK HOLMES (alternatively known as THE SEASON OF FORGIVENESS)[263]
THE ADVENTURE OF THE MANUFACTURED MIRACLE
THE ADVENTURE OF THE FIRST STAR
THE ADVENTURE OF THE SPANISH SOVEREIGN
THE GRAND GIFT OF SHERLOCK

THE FIRST OF CRIMINALS[264]
THE ADVENTURE OF THE MONSTROUS BLOOD
THE ADVENTURE OF THE MAD COLONEL
THE ADVENTURE OF THE BARREN GRAVE
THE ADVENTURE OF THE FATEFUL MALADY[265]

TREASURE TROVE INDEED![266]
THE LOST LEGION
THE ADVENTURE OF THE PIRATE'S CODE
THE ADVENTURE OF THE QUEEN'S PENDANT
THE ADVENTURE OF THE SILENT DRUM

FORTUNES MADE & FORTUNES LOST[267]
THE ADVENTURE OF THE DOUBLE-EDGED HOARD[268]

THE ADVENTURE OF THE DAWN DISCOVERY
THE HARROWING INTERMISSION[269]
THE ADVENTURE OF THE SUNKEN INDIAMAN[270]

THE SCHOOLROOM OF SORROW[271]
THE FATHER OF EVIL
THE ADVENTURE OF THE FATAL FIRE
THE ADVENTURE OF THE DISHONOURABLE DISCHARGE[272]
THE ADVENTURE OF THE AWAKENED SPIRIT[273]
THE COLD DISH

AN EAST WIND[274]
THE ADVENTURE OF THE THIRD TRAITOR[275]
THE ADVENTURE OF THE UNFATHOMABLE SILENCE[276]
THE HIGH MOUNTAIN
THE ADVENTURE OF THE DEFENCELESS PRISONER
THEIR FINAL FLOURISH

A PROMPT AND READY TRAVELLER[277]
THE ADVENTURE OF THE MISSING MANA
THE ADVENTURE OF THE BOULEVARD ASSASSIN
THE ADVENTURE OF THE SECRET TOMB
THE ADVENTURE OF THE DEAD MAN'S NOTE

ROUND THE WORLD[278]
THE OAK-LEAF SPRIG
THE ADVENTURE OF THE DOUBLE DETECTIVES
THE ADVENTURE OF THE AFRICAN HORROR
THE ADVENTURE OF THE FAIR LAD[279]

SEEN & OBSERVED[280]
THE ADVENTURE OF THE TRAGIC ACT
THE PROBLEM OF THE BLACK EYE
THE MANNERING TOWERS MYSTERY
THE ADVENTURE OF THE TWELFTH HOUR

THEIR DARK CRISIS[281]

THE ADVENTURE OF THE MOST DANGEROUS MAN
THE ADVENTURE OF THE HAUNTED GRANGE
THE ADVENTURE OF THE FABRICATED VISION[282]
THE ADVENTURE OF THE WRONG HAND

OTHER STORIES OF MR. SHERLOCK HOLMES
THE ADVENTURE OF THE FALLEN DESPERADO[283]
THE ADVENTURE OF THE LORING RIDDLE[284]
THE ADVENTURE OF THE IMPRISONED MONARCH[285]

THE ASSASSINATION OF SHERLOCK HOLMES
THE ADVENTURE OF THE PHARAOH'S CURSE
THE PROBLEM OF THREADNEEDLE STREET
THE FALLING CURTAIN
THE RED LEECH

SET EUROPE SHAKING: Volume One of 'The Exploits and Adventures of Brigadier Gerard'
(Compiled and Edited by Craig Janacek, with Three New Tales)
HOW THE BRIGADIER WRESTLED THE BEAR OF BOULOGNE
HOW THE BRIGADIER FACED THE FIRING SQUAD
HOW THE BRIGADIER DUELLED FOR A DESPATCH

A MIGHTY SHADOW: Volume Two of 'The Exploits and Adventures of Brigadier Gerard'
(Compiled and Edited by Craig Janacek, with One New Tale)
HOW THE BRIGADIER COMMANDED THE EMPEROR

OTHER NOVELS
THE OXFORD DECEPTION
THE ANGER OF ACHILLES PETERSON

EDITED BY
The Complete and Annotated SIR NIGEL & THE WHITE COMPANY
EXIT, SHERLOCK HOLMES: Sixteen Tales by Sir Arthur Conan Doyle *NOT* Featuring the World's Greatest Detective

*Coming soon

§

FOOTNOTES

---

[1] Excepting the two adventures narrated directly by Holmes (*The Adventure of the Blanched Soldier* and *The Adventure of the Lion's Mane*), as well as the adventure written in the omniscient third person (*His Last Bow*).

[2] There is some evidence, as noted in the non-Canonical tale *The Adventure of the Loring Riddle*, that two of Conan Doyle's most famous historical novels – *The White Company* (1891) and *Sir Nigel* (1906) – were in fact derived from a contemporary chronicle entitled the 'Gestes due Sieur Nigel,' possibly by Henry Knyghton (d.1396). If so, in a fashion similar to the works included in the present collection, Sir Arthur was likely passed a copy of this ancient narrative by his friend, Dr Watson.

[3] *The War in South Africa: Its Cause and Effect* (1902). In fact, there is no official reason listed for Conan Doyle's Honours, but it was his belief that this work justifying the United Kingdom's role in the Second Boer War was the reason for it.

[4] There is some evidence, as noted in the non-Canonical tale *The Adventure of the Boulevard Assassin*, that several of Conan Doyle's short stories and novels regarding the Napoleonic War, mainly featuring Brigadier Etienne Gerard, were derived from oral accounts transcribed by Joseph Lacour. The full details can be found in the introduction to the two-part collection *Set Europe Shaking* (2018) and *The Mighty Shadow* (2018).

[5] The popular notion of the vampire was only introduced to Victorian England by the publication of *Dracula* (1897) by Bram Stoker, a great friend of Sir Arthur Conan Doyle.

[6] There is no such dukedom, suggesting that Watson is here obscuring the true name of John Clay's grandfather. Six years later Clay

would reappear in *The Red-Headed League*.

[7] A misquotation from *Macbeth* (Act V, Scene VIII). The actual phrase is: 'Lay on, Macduff."

[8] The number of plays written by Shakespeare remains a subject of debate to this day. During the Victorian era, very few scholars considered *Edward III* for inclusion in this list. However, it is now generally accepted as such, bringing the total to thirty-nine, not including some of the lost plays.

[9] A thane is an archaic medieval Scottish title for a royal official who administers a portion of the king's land.

[10] I am unable to trace a Jake Brandin associated with the Lyceum Theatre in 1881, though he may have been a sub-manager. From 1878-1905, the business manager of the Lyceum was none other than Bram Stoker, whose most famous work, *Dracula*, was not published until 1897.

[11] William Macready (1793-1873) was such a great Shakespearean actor that Alfred Lord Tennyson wrote a poem to celebrate his retirement from the stage, which ends with: "Farewell, Macready; moral, grave, sublime, / Our Shakespeare's bland and universal eye / Dwells pleased, through twice a hundred years on thee." Edmund Kean (1787-1833) was another famous Shakespearean actor, who had plays written about his eccentric life by both Alexandre Dumas and Jean-Paul Sartre. We must forgive Mr. Brandin some artistic license here, as both actors either were dead or retired when he was still a youth.

[12] Johann Spurzheim (1776-1832) was a German physician and one of the chief proponents of phrenology, the pseudo-science of measuring the skull in order to predict mental traits.

[13] As noted in *The Adventure of the Naval Treaty*, Inspector Dubuque of the Paris Police was later instrumental in the non-Canonical tale *The Adventure of the Third Traitor*.

[14] Designed by George Gilbert Scott, the Midland Grand at St. Pancras Station opened in 1873. It is one of the great railway hotels of the world.

[15] Perhaps the most famous member of the Third Hussars was Brigadier Etienne Gerard, whose exploits were recounted by Sir Arthur Conan Doyle in seventeen short stories later collected in the volumes *Set Europe Shaking* and *A Mighty Shadow, The Exploits and*

Adventures of Brigadier Gerard.

[16] Much like the Fortescue Scholarship at the College of St. Luke's, details of the Beaumaris Scholarship have been lost to history.

[17] Field Marshal Lord Raglan (1788-1855) and Admiral Lord Lyons (1790-1858) were the commanders of the British Army and Navy during the Crimean War.

[18] The Battle of Inkerman (5 November 1854) was a victory by the allied armies of Britain and France against the Imperial Russian Army, shortly before the Siege of Sevastopol, near the finale of the Crimean War.

[19] The Theatre de Variétés has been operating at the passage des Panoramas since 1807.

[20] The Theatre de la Gaieté operated on the rue Papin from 1862-1989.

[21] A fusee, of flare, is a pyrotechnic device that produces a brilliant light of intense heat without an explosion.

[22] A 'roué' is a man devoted to a life of debauchery.

[23] Converting foreign currency from 1881 into today's values is a difficult equation, but ten thousand francs is worth roughly $480,000 in 2020 terms. In other words, this was an outrageous wager.

[24] The Bois de Boulogne is a large public part in the west of Paris built by Napoleon III in 1857.

[25] There is no such Countess. 'Sang-pur' translates as 'pure blood,' so this should be taken as a little joke by the Lieutenant.

[26] Persiennes are exterior window shutters with adjustable horizontal slats or louvers fixed at an angle to admit light but exclude sun and rain.

[27] The Jardin Mabille was an evening promenade notorious for being frequented by ladies of the night. A 'Café Chantant' was an outdoor café where small groups of performers played light-hearted and bawdy popular music.

[28] The third and fourth parries in the classical system of fencing.

[29] A 'cicerone' is an archaic term for a guide, especially one who conducts visitors and sightseers to museums, galleries, etc., and explains matters of archaeological, antiquarian, historic, or artistic interest. It derives from the name 'Cicero,' as Marcus Tullius (106 –

THE CHRONICLES OF
SHERLOCK HOLMES

c/o

Amazon EU SarL

£12-99

PRIVATE

SUBSCRIPTION NUMBER: 400
Mr Barry Jones
6 Nelson Place
Welshpool
SY21 7PQ

Return address:
Private Eye
3 Queensbridge
Northampton
NN4 7BF

43 BCE) was a paragon of learning and eloquence.

[30] It is well that Henry Latour was not playing Hamlet, for the Prince of Denmark never speaks this line. The closest is: 'Yet have I something in me dangerous' (Act V, Scene I).

[31] Presumably, Jack Latour is referring to the Hotel d'Angleterre, the former site of the British Embassy.

[32] A 'Cribb's hit' is a boxing term, named after Tom Cribb (1781-1848).

[33] *Savate*, or French foot-fighting, is a combat sport using both the hands and feet, from the French word for 'old shoe or boot.' It evolved from Paris street-fighting techniques beginning in the early 19th century.

[34] Evaporating lotions were mixtures of rectified spirit (a highly concentrated ethanol) and scented water, typically used for nervous headaches, restlessness, and skin irritability.

[35] The last official duel in France took place in 1547, but attempts to police the ban on this romantic escapade were usually in vain. Dying in a duel was prized very highly and commanded great respect for the brave hero duellist who danced with death and died with their weapon in hand and their head raised high. Even judges usually acquitted duellists.

[36] James Purdey & Sons is a London gun manufacturer founded in 1814.

[37] A rough paraphrase of Cassius from *Julius Caesar* (Act I, Scene II): "Men at some time are masters of their fates / The fault, dear Brutus, is not in our stars, But in / ourselves, that we are underlings."

[38] Cochin-China was a French colony in southern Vietnam from 1858-1949.

[39] The headquarters of the *Légion étrangère*, or French Foreign Legion, was in French Algeria until 1962.

[40] Although the events of the Jefferson Hope case transpired in 1881, *A Study in Scarlet* was not published until 1887.

[41] The careful reader will note that Holmes' words here are a rough paraphrase of the conclusion of *Hamlet* (Act V, Scene II), as spoken by Prince Fortinbras.

[42] Watson obeyed Holmes' order and never published this case during either of their lifetimes, though he must have felt compelled

to record it for the sake of posterity, finally allowing it now to be unearthed from amongst his journals. Furthermore, it seems that Watson described much of the backstory of Henry Latour's escapades in Paris to his first literary agent, Sir Arthur Conan Doyle, who crafted it into a straightforward story narrated by Mr. Barker and omitting all mention of Holmes' role in the matter. Conan Doyle entitled it *The Tragedians*, and sent it to *Blackwood's Magazine* in 1882, who rejected it. However, it was eventually accepted by the editor John Dicks at the literary magazine *Bow Bells*, who published it on 20 August 1884. It was later re-published under the alternate title *An Actor's Duel*.

[43] Here we see evidence that Watson purposefully refrained from telling of Holmes involvement in this case. Instead, his first literary editor, Sir Arthur Conan Doyle, published it anonymously in *Bow's Bells* magazine as *The Winning Shot* (1883).

[44] Interestingly, this list corresponds identically with one put forth by Sir Arthur Conan Doyle in a 1927 article in *The Strand Magazine* entitled *A Sherlock Holmes Competition. Mr. Sherlock Holmes to his Readers.*

[45] The careful reader may wonder if Holmes cheated a bit here, as he also may have simply observed the postmark of her preceding letter.

[46] The 'Long Vacation' was the period from July to October between the Trinity and Michaelmas Terms at school. The other three vacations are at Christmas, Easter, and Whit.

[47] There was no HMS *Shark* at this time. The prior ship by that name was lost to the French in 1795, while the next one would not be launched until 1894. Watson has changed the name, presumably for the sake of privacy.

[48] This would be the River Tavy.

[49] *Savoir faire* is French for the ability to act or speak appropriately in social situations.

[50] Jack Daseby must have swung by South America on his way back from Japan, for all three species of vampire bats are endemic to that area. None are found in Japan. A 'bugbear' is a folkloric bogeyman or hobgoblin. It was a described as creepy bear-like creature that lurked in the woods in order to scare children.

[51] Cape Blanco is a peninsula on the western edge of the Sahara, now known as Ras Nouadhibou. It is located some five hundred miles south of the Canary Islands. A sailboat running downwind can

travel up to 115 miles a day, but it is unclear precisely how long it would take to drift that distance without sails.

[52] While astral projection is described in the legends of numerous cultures, it did not occur in the accounts of mystical Islam or even pre-Islamic Arab pagans. One theory is that Gaster was reading an Arabic translation of a more ancient text – perhaps from Pharaonic Egypt – that had been preserved in an Abbasid library in Baghdad during the Golden Age of Islam.

[53] The reader will note that this tale was published fourteen years prior to the appearance of Bram Stoker's great novel *Dracula* (1897), so Lottie was probably familiar with the legend of the vampire from Sheridan Le Fanu's Gothic novella *Carmilla* (1872).

[54] The reader is tempted to identify the major as Prendergast of the Tankerville Club (*The Five Orange Pips*) and the substituted painting as one belonging to the Darlington family (*A Scandal in Bohemia*), but who the duke is remains unclear, and this may represent an unrecorded case.

[55] Lincoln's Inn is one of the four Inns of Court (along with Middle Temple, Inner Temple, and Grey's Inn), to which barristers belong, and where they are called to the Bar.

[56] The careful reader may wonder if Watson speaks of the Black Tor, upon which Sherlock Holmes later made his base while investigating the death of Sir Charles Baskerville?

[57] Crockford's was the popular name for the St James's Club founded by William Crockford in 1823. It was famous for its gambling closed in 1970. Tattersall's is an auctioneer of race horses, based near Hyde Park Corner, two rooms of which were reserved for members of the Jockey Club.

[58] Octavius Gaster, whose tale was first published in 1883, may be the inspiration for some fictional hypnotists, including those found in *The Realm of the Unreal* (1890) and *The Hypnotist* (1893) by Ambrose Bierce. The most famous was Svengali – introduced in George du Maurier's novel *Trilby* (1894) – who gave his name to a type of person who, with evil intent, dominates, manipulates, and controls another.

[59] A 'Cantab,' or Cantabrigian, is someone who received a degree from the University of Cambridge, though Trevor Hall had not quite yet earned that title.

[60] While odd to the modern reader used to the relatively calm temperament of the modern bulldog, the purebred Victorian era English bulldog – similar to their descendants the Pit bull – had a reputation for being pugnacious and combative, as they originally were bred for the baiting of bulls. Upon the Continent, they were considered the national animal of England. It seemed that college students were fond of keeping such animals, for Sherlock Holmes first met Victor Trevor when the latter's bull terrier froze onto Holmes ankle one morning (*The* 'Gloria Scott').

[61] *The Posthumous Papers of the Pickwick Club* (1836), commonly known as *The Pickwick Papers*, was the massively popular first novel of Charles Dickens. In Chapter 23, Sam Weller says: "It's over, and can't be helped, and that's one consolation, as they always say in Turkey, when they cuts the wrong man's head off."

[62] French for a 'pastoral festival or 'country feast.'

[63] There is a Norman era church at Bere Ferris, but no abbey, so they may have meant the nearby ruins of Tavistock Abbey instead.

[64] *Chef-d'oeuvre* is French for a 'masterpiece.'

[65] The identities of Steinberg and Gustav von Spee are uncertain, though the latter may have been a cousin of the famous Admiral von Spee. Madame Catherine Crows (1803-1876) was an English writer of supernatural stories, her most famous being *The Night-side of Nature* (1848). Gaster appears to take these fictions as truths. Daniel Dunglas Home (1833-1886) was perhaps the most famous medium of the Victorian era. In 1887, he supposedly levitated himself at Ashley Place, Westminster, though there is no record of a similar exploit in Paris.

[66] The 'Eddystone' refers to the Eddystone Rocks, a heavily eroded group of rocks off the coast of Plymouth that have long been a hazard for ships, and where a series of lighthouses have been erected over the years. The 'Start' refers to Start Point, a promontory also marked by a lighthouse.

[67] Telescopic sights, commonly called scopes, are magnifying tubes mounted above a rifle. They were invented c.1835. Clearly, the rules of the competition forbade their use.

[68] This conversation in the Devon dialect – which is heavily influenced by Cornish – is a bit challenging to follow. A rough translation would be: "Man's a rare ugly one." / "He is that." / "See the man's

eye?" / "Eh, Jock, see to the man's mouth, rather! Blessed if he is not foaming like Farmer Watson's dog – the bull pup that died mad from hydrophobia (an archaic term for rabies)."

[69] Martell Cognac was founded in 1715 and continues to this day. The 'devils' is plainly a reference to the delirium tremens – the rapid onset of confusion caused by withdrawal from chronic massive alcohol consumption.

[70] The Battle of Inkerman (5 November 1854) was an Anglo-French victory over the Russian Army immediately prior to the Siege of Sevastopol.

[71] During the Crimean War, the first British troops landed near the town of Eupatoria (modern Yevpatoria) on 13 September 1854. The Siege of Sebastopol (modern Sevastopol) lasted from 17 October 1854 to 9 September 1855, and was the decisive victory of the war.

[72] The Irish Home Rule movement arose c.1870, championed by the Liberal government of William Ewart Gladstone, and opposed by the Conservative Party.

[73] The Enfield rifle was introduced in 1853 just as hostilities began in the Crimean War. They were also used during the Sepoy Mutiny, and were eventually replaced by the Martini-Henry rifle in 1871.

[74] One of the most prestigious medical universities in the world, the Karolinska Institute was founded in 1810. This editor has been unable to trace any details regarding Professor Retzius's sudden death.

[75] The *Western Morning News* was founded in 1860 in Plymouth and to this day covers the West Country, including Devon.

[76] There is no town of Tromsberg in Sweden. It may refer to Gothenberg, the largest port in the country.

[77] *The Facts in the Case of M. Valdemar* (1845) is a short story written by Edgar Allen Poe. Published without a note that it was fictional, the prose was so powerful that it was taken to be true for some time.

[78] Technically known as erethism, but popularly called 'Mad Hatter' syndrome after the famous character from Lewis Carroll's novel *Alice's Adventures in Wonderland* (1865).

[79] Harry Pillar had plainly not heard the legend of the Curse of the Baskervilles, or he might have exercised more caution!

[80] A 'leat' is an artificial watercourse dug into the ground. The Ply-

mouth leat (completed 1591) is commonly referred to as 'Drake's,' for it was organized and partially paid for by Sir Francis Drake. Holmes would later walk its course in the non-Canonical tale *The Adventure of the Silent Drum.*

[81] The so-called 'Roman graves' are actually kistvaens, burial tombs from the late Neolithic and Early Bronze Ages. Tin mines have been worked on Dartmoor from pre-Roman times. Lover's Leap is a rock that projects from a steep hillside over a set of moderate rapids in the River Dart. It was named for a pair of lovers who allegedly leapt to their deaths from the spot.

[82] Longhouses, or housebarns, are traditional homes of western Britain, especially around Dartmoor. Holmes would later learn that the stone huts upon Black Tor are also suitable for a temporary habitation. Historians who fail to recognize that Sir Arthur Conan Doyle was merely Watson's literary editor often suggest that Conan Doyle's June 1901 visit to Hound Tor was the inspiration for *The Hound of the Baskervilles.*

[83] Ettan, founded in 1822, is the most popular brand of Swedish snus – a product similar to American dipping tobacco.

[84] Saint-Malo was infamous for being the base of French privateers and corsairs that forced English ships passing up the Channel to pay tribute. This notoriety lasted into the Victorian era, for César Cui's opera *Le flibustier* (*The Pirate*) premiered in 1888.

[85] The GRO, or General Register Office, was founded in 1836 and is responsible for the civil registration of births, adoptions, marriages, civil partnerships and deaths in England and Wales.

[86] A 'Black Maria' is a term used for a police van that originated in the mid 1800's, though the origin of the name is debated. Emile Gaboriau used the term in his tale of that 'miserable bungler' *Monsieur Lecoq* (1869).

[87] In many ways, it sounds as if Lottie Underwood was suffering an early case of Stockholm syndrome. Although the events that triggered the description of that disorder did not transpire until 1973, it is a rather strange coincidence that Dr Gaster originally hailed from that city.

[88] The Regency era officially ended with the death of George III in 1820.

[89] The astute reader will note that many of the details of this case

were first told by Sir Arthur Conan Doyle, Watson's first literary editor, in a tale entitled *Selecting a Ghost* (1883). Holmes must have forbidden publication of the tale, such that Watson gave permission for Conan Doyle to re-work the story, omitting all mention of Holmes' role in the matter.

[90] While the surname 'Dodd' is Anglo-Saxon in origin, meaning 'round' or 'plump,' the name with an apostrophe suggests the entomology of someone from a location called 'Odd.' As there are very few such recorded places, we may instead presume that Mr. Silas D'Odd added the apostrophe in a rather unsuccessful attempt to make his name sound more aristocratic.

[91] Bogles are creatures prone to causing vexation, but not active harm, in Northumbrian and Scots folklore.

[92] The word *'lucoptolycus'* appears to have been invented by Abrahams to suggest the name of a sacred insect – perhaps with an Egyptian feeling – as 'luco' means a 'grove sacred to the gods,' while 'ptolycus' is a species of beetle.

[93] The cotillion was a social dance popular in the 18th century. An epergne is an ornamental centerpiece for a dining table, typically used for holding fruit or flowers.

[94] Mr. D'Odd refers not to a single plate, but rather the entire collection of tableware and decorations used for formal dining, including plates, chargers, side-plates, bowls, saucers, cups, cutlery, pitchers, trays, salvers, platters, casserole dishes, tureens, sauce boats, salt cellars, candlesticks, and place markers. Cast in solid silver, this collection would be enormously valuable.

[95] A bill is a polearm weapon used by infantry in medieval Europe. It is similar to a halberd, but with a hooked blade, and was favoured by English troops.

[96] The Hellespont is the classical names for the Dardanelles, the narrow strait that serves as the continental boundary of Europe and Asia and connects the Aegean Sea to the Sea of Marmara. Mr. D'Odd is referring to the myth, exceptionally popular during the Victorian era, of Hero and Leander. Hero, a priestess of Aphrodite, dwelt in a tower on the European side of Hellespont, while her lover Leander dwelt on the other. He would swim the Hellespont every night through the warm summer, but drowned when a winter storm blew out the lamp lit by Hero to guide his way.

[97] The agent in the East End suggests Mercer, while Mr. Pike is likely

the same as Langdale Pike. Both were employed by Holmes in late Canonical tales, though herein we find evidence that they were part of Holmes' network much earlier in his career.

[98] Roughly, 'I believe what I can touch.'

[99] Sir Anthony de Rothschild, of the rich but common banking family, was created 1st Baronet Rothschild by Queen Victoria in 1847.

[100] This literary editor has been thus far unable to trace the location of the Morsely and Alton roads in Norfolk, suggesting that Watson must have changed the names.

[101] A virginal is a keyboard instrument of the harpsichord family, popular during the early Baroque era, which ended c.1750.

[102] Casque is a French word for helmet. Chesterfieldian is a description of a man who dresses like George Stanhope, the 6th Earl of Chesterfield (1805-1866), a leader in English fashion. A maiden MS. is a first manuscript.

[103] Sack is an antiquated term for a fortified white wine imported from the Canary Islands or Spain, once favoured by Sir John Falstaff.

[104] A jemmy is a short crowbar used by a burglar to force open windows or doors, while centre-bits are drills to bore a hole in locks.

[105] George II (1683-1760) was the last English king to lead an army in battle at Dettingen (27 June 1743), located in an area of the Holy Roman Empire that became part of modern Bavaria. It was a victory of combined British, Hanoverian, and Austrian troops over a French army during the War of the Austrian Succession.

[106] Interestingly, the story of the haunting of Goresthorpe Grange by the ghost of Godfrey Marsden was first set down on paper by Arthur Conan Doyle c.1877, well before he became the first literary editor for Dr John H. Watson. The saga of that tale is a fascinating one. Conan Doyle, who at the time was merely eighteen years of age, had yet to have anything of significance published as his first story, *The Mystery of Sassassa Valley*, was not published in *Chambers's Journal* until September 1879. He sent *The Haunted Grange of Goresthorpe – A True Ghost Story* to *Blackwood's Magazine* in Edinburgh. That journal neither published it, nor returned it, and Conan Doyle believed it to have been lost. In 1942, Blackwood's archives were sent to the National Library of Scotland, and sometime afterwards, the manuscript was unearthed. The now-defunct Arthur Conan Doyle Society finally published it in 2000. Where exactly Conan Doyle heard the

details of this tale is uncertain, though we must presume it was directly from Jack Brocket, or possibly his friend Tom Hulton.

[107] Chloral hydrate is a sedative and hypnotic invented in 1832 and widely used to treat insomnia and anxiety during the Victorian era. Dr John Seward – one of the protagonists of Bram Stoker's *Dracula* (1897) – used it, but this may be one of the earlier references to it in the literature of the time.

[108] A toper is a heavy drinker, someone who is frequently intoxicated.

[109] Lord Byron (1788-1824) was a leading Romantic poet. Henry Kirke White (1785-1806) was an English poet famous for dying young, likely of consumption. Joseph Grimaldi (1778-1837) was the most popular English entertainer of the Regency era. Tom Cribb (1781-1848) was a world-champion bare-knuckle boxer. Inigo Jones (1573-1652) was the first English architect to design in the classical style of ancient Rome and the Italian Renaissance.

[110] The Pretender was James Francis Edward Stuart (1688-1766), the son of the deposed James II, who led the Jacobite Rising of 1715 in an attempt to regain what he considered his rightful throne.

[111] 'Crackster' is a term in underworld cant to indicate a burglar, similar to 'cracksman' – one of the most famous being Beddington (*The Adventure of the Stock-Broker's Clerk*). 'Jemmy' is presumably a nickname.

[112] This phrase dates to at least 1833, as Edward Fitzgerald wrote in his *Letters*: "A genius with a screw loose, as we used to say."

[113] Sadly, Watson never officially related the details of this case, first mentioned in *A Study in Scarlet*.

[114] Lady Anne Neville was the wife of King Richard III. In Shakespeare's eponymous play (c.1593), Richard poisons her so that he could wed Elizabeth of York. She later appears to him as a ghost before the Battle of Bosworth Field (22 August 1485). The Theatre Royal at Drury Lane reputed to be haunted by several ghosts, including that of Joseph Grimaldi.

[115] A 'fly' is a light horse-drawn covered vehicle, similar to a carriage or cab.

[116] Electroplating, the process of creating a metal coating on a solid substrate through the means of a direct electric current, was patented in 1840 in England by George Elkington of Birmingham.

However, the ability to electroplate with silver created an illusion that people owned finer things than they could actually afford, and it therefore became a synonym for vulgarity.

[117] The astute reader will recognize many aspects of this case correspond with a story called *The Silver Mirror*, published in *The Strand Magazine* in August 1908 by Sir Arthur Conan Doyle, Watson's first literary editor. It is unclear why Conan Doyle did not submit it in its original form, but felt compelled to remove all mention of Holmes and instead publish it solely as the purported report of Mr. Darnley's strange experience.

[118] Dr Watson did not meet and wed Mary Morstan until 1888, so this is plainly a reference to his first wife, whom he married in (approximately) the autumn of 1886.

[119] The post-nominal 'ACA' indicates that Mr. Johnson is a member of the Institute of Chartered Accountants in England and Wales, established by royal charter in 1880.

[120] An alderman is a member of a county or borough council, next in status to the Mayor. Cordwainer is one of the 25 ancient wards of the City of London, named for the professional shoemakers whose guildhall is located in that area.

[121] 'Defalcation' is a crime in which there is misappropriation of funds by a person entrusted with its charge.

[122] A doctor or group of physicians established private hospitals in the nineteenth century for the care of paying patients. They employed trained nurses, and were considered cleaner, less crowded, and more respectable than the 'voluntary' hospitals that served patients free of charge and that ran solely upon voluntary contributions.

[123] Brachygraphy is a synonym for stenography, or the process of writing in shorthand – the abbreviated symbolic writing method that increases speed and brevity of writing. Several different systems existed in England, starting from 1588, and Samuel Pepys, who used it for his *Diary* (1825), popularized the art.

[124] Bromine-based compounds, especially the salt-form potassium bromide, were commonly used as sedative and headache remedies in the 19th and early 20th centuries; until evidence began to emerge that long-term consumption can lead to neurologic symptoms. Chloral hydrate was another widely used sedative and hypnotic after its discovery in 1832. It fell out of favour due to its addictive

nature and the identification of safer agents.

[125] The word 'slot' is here used in the archaic sense of 'trail,' as in a 'slot-hound.' The term eventually evolved into the word 'sleuth-hound,' from which the modern 'sleuth' derives.

[126] These volumes are not identified, but may have included Lord Patrick Ruthven's *Some Particulars of the Life of David Riccio, Chief Favourite of Mary Queen of Scots* (unpublished until 1815), or Sir John Hawkins' *History and Character of Scots Music, including Anecdotes of the Celebrated David Rizzio* (1778).

[127] David Rizzio (c.1533-1566) was an Italian courtier and singer from Turin. He travelled to Scotland with the ambassador from the Duke of Savoy, where he ingratiated himself with the Queen's musicians, eventually rising to the post of her secretary. Rumours whispered that he became her lover and was the true father of her son, the future James VI of Scotland and James I of England (1566-1625).

[128] Henry Stuart (1545-1567), Lord Darnley, was the first cousin and second husband of Mary, Queen of Scots. He was later murdered, likely by James Hepburn (c.1534-1578), the Earl of Bothwell, who wed Mary a few months later.

[129] Patrick Ruthven (c.1520-1566) was a Scottish nobleman who led the conspiracy of Protestant lords – likely at the behest of Lord Darnley – who murdered David Rizzio at Holyrood Palace, partly out of concerns for the Catholic courtier's influence over the queen.

[130] Mary Stuart (1542-1587) had wed the fourteen year-old Francis II, then Dauphin of France, in 1558. Francis ascended to the throne in July 1559 upon the death of his father Henry II. Francis died seventeen months later, likely from invasive mastoiditis. The throne passed to his younger brother, Charles IX, and Mary returned to Scotland.

[131] The Palace of Holyroodhouse is the official residence of the British monarch in Scotland, located at the downhill eastern end of the Royal Mile in Edinburgh. Built from 1671-78 to serve as the principal residence for the Kings and Queens of Scots, it derives its name from the now-ruined Holyrood Abbey situated on its grounds, which once contained a fragment of the supposed 'True Cross.'

[132] Diseases of the temporal lobe, including epileptic foci and tumours, can lead to auditory and visual hallucinations.

[133] Mania, now referring to a state of elevated arousal and

emotional lability, had a broader sense in the past. Ewald Hecker (1843-1909) was a German psychiatrist who coined the term 'hebephrenia' to describe the adolescent onset of what would later (in 1908) be termed schizophrenia, the modern word for an affliction characterized by hallucinations, delusions, and disorganized thinking.

[134] Ergotism, a poisoning by the ergot fungus in rye, can lead to psychosis and is one theory advanced for Joan of Arc's supposed 'visions.' It was also proposed as a potential cause for Colonel Warburton's madness in the non-Canonical tale *The Adventure of the Mad Colonel*, from the collection *The First of Criminals* (2016).

[135] The story of Professor Sidney was reported in the non-Canonical tale *The Adventure of the Double-Edged Hoard*, from the collection *Fortunes Made & Fortunes Lost* (2018).

[136] Samuel Taylor Coleridge (1772-1834) was addicted to opium for most of his life, and he reported that his great work, *Kubla Khan, or a Vision in a Dream*, was written immediately after emerging from the drug's influence.

[137] Although rarely used since bromine agents were withdrawn from general use, bromine is radiopaque and can be seen on an abdominal radiograph. However, Wilhelm Roentgen did not discover the utility of his so-called 'X-rays' for such purposes until 1895.

[138] Perhaps from his *Symphonie fantastique* (1830)?

[139] Given Watson's later comments, it seems unlikely that he was completely unaware of at least some of the details. We must assume that this is creative license for the sake of telling the story to his readers.

[140] It is unclear what paper Holmes is referring to here. There was a *Lancaster Observer*, which ran from 1860-1944, while the *Lancashire Evening Telegraph* and *Lancashire Evening Post* were both founded in 1886.

[141] Liverpool was part of Lancashire until 1974, when it was incorporated into the newly created county of Merseyside. The area southwest of Liverpool is the Wirral Peninsula, originally part of Cheshire. There is no village of Bishop's Crossing on the Wirral Peninsula, suggesting that Watson must have changed the name. If his directions of ten miles southwest of Liverpool are to be believed, then the village of Thornton Hough is a likely candidate.

[142] In Homer's *Odyssey*, true dreams pass through the gates of horn, while false dreams pass through the gates of ivory.

[143] Presumably the farcical *A Comedy of Errors* (c.1594), which is set in the Greek city of Ephesus (now in modern Turkey), and which was derived from the Latin play *Menachmi* by the great Roman playwright Plautus.

[144] Designed by William Baker and Francis Stevenson, the 200-foot spanned roof of Lime Street Station's train shed was the largest such structure in the world at the time of its completion in 1867.

[145] Holmes is slightly misquoting the lines of William Congreve from the 1697 play *The Mourning Bride* (Act III, Scene II): 'Heaven has no rage like love to hatred turned, Nor hell a fury like a woman scorned.'

[146] Capital punishment was not abolished in the United Kingdom until 1965.

[147] William Ewart Gladstone (1809-1898) was Prime Minister for twelve years spread out over four terms from 1868 to 1894. He was known affectionately to his followed as the 'G.O.M.' or 'Grand Old Man.'

[148] The 'Three Kingdoms' would be England, Scotland, and Ireland. Victoria was Queen of the United Kingdom of Great Britain and Ireland (formally established in 1800), with Great Britain being the Kingdoms of England and Scotland (formally established in 1706). Wales is a principality that was formally incorporated into the Kingdom of England in 1536.

[149] Watson is engaging in a bit of poetic license here. Public executions in the Hanging Corner ended in 1868, though private executions continued at Lancaster Castle until 1910.

[150] Strangely, despite the fact that we have no evidence that Holmes expressly forbade it, Watson never published this case in its complete form. Instead, he gave it to his first literary editor, Sir Arthur Conan Doyle, who omitted all mention of Holmes and Watson, and published it in *The Strand* as 'The Story of the Black Doctor' (1898).

[151] Women were excluded from sitting on juries until 1919.

[152] In December 1860, an armed band, instigated by a local prominent merchant, attacked the residence of the Federalist governor, José Antonia Virasoro, killing him and fourteen of his followers. We may presume that Don Alfredo Lana was one of these men.

[153] Corunna, now known as A Coruña, is a port on the northern coast of Spain. To the British, it was famous as the site of the Battle of Corunna (16 January 1809) during the Peninsular War, where Napoleonic troops under Marshal Soult temporarily drove British forces from Spain.

[154] Holmes makes it sound like the exile of Dr Rowe was a form of punishment; however, from 1880 to 1930 Buenos Aires became a leading destination for immigrants from Europe, particularly Italy and Spain, who turned it into a multicultural city that ranked itself with the major European capitals.

[155] There is no record in the Canon as to what precisely Watson is referring to here, since Holmes' famous statement in *The Adventure of the Sussex Vampire* had not yet transpired.

[156] There was a Seamen's Hospital at Greenwich, originally aboard converted warships and, after 1870, on land. There was also a British and Foreign Sailors' Institute in Shadwell, which was erected in 1855. However, this editor has been unable to trace the precise location where Travers and Dr Hewett worked.

[157] Sadly, Sir Dominick's textbook appears to have gone out of print. This editor has been unable to locate a extant copy.

[158] C.B. indicates a Companion of the Most Honourable Order of the Bath, an order of chivalry founded in 1725. The other C.B. in the Canon was Sir Augustus Moran, father of Colonel Sebastian. K.C.S.I. indicates the Most Exalted Order of the Star of India, an order of chivalry founded in 1861, now dormant.

[159] This editor has been unable to locate this hospital, which appears to have vanished during the massive expansion of independent India beginning in 1947.

[160] I have been unable to locate a copy of this book, so Watson may have recalled the author's name incorrectly.

[161] The selling of commissions was abolished in 1871 as part of the Cardwell reforms, so Hardacre must have been speaking metaphorically. Major John Sholto once served in the 34th Bombay Infantry.

[162] This is no longer true. We now understand that the Neolithic hill-forts were primarily constructed during the British Iron Age (c.800 BCE – 100 CE), which ended shortly after the Roman invasion (43-84 CE).

[163] In typical Watsonian fashion, there is no Manor House of Ro-

denhurst on Cranborne Chase. One possible candidate is St. Giles House in Wimborne St. Giles. This manor is closely situation near the many barrows centred on Monkton Up Wimborne and Cashmoor.

[164] The Victoria Terminus, now the Chhatrapati Shivaji Terminus, was begun in 1878 and completed in 1887 by Frederick William Stevens (1847-1900). Kandahar is the Afghan city from which British forces sallied prior to the Battle of Maiwand (27 July 1880).

[165] The hotel at St Pancras Station, designed by George Gilbert Scott and completed in 1873.

[166] Salisbury Cathedral (404 feet) was the tallest building in England after the 1549 collapse of Lincoln Cathedral's spire. It would not be surpassed until 1964, when the General Post Office Tower was completed in London.

[167] The tale of the Viking berserker can be found in the non-Canonical *The Adventure of the Double-Edged Hoard*. The tale of the phantom omnibus has never been fully related, but was referred to in the non-Canonical *The Adventure of the Mad Colonel*. Perhaps Holmes' greatest adventure, *The Hound of the Baskervilles* was published in 1902.

[168] The Sepoy Mutiny, or Indian Rebellion of 1857, was a major event in the consciousness of the subjects of the British Empire and was vividly recounted to Holmes and Watson by both Jonathan Small and Henry Wood.

[169] Kaffiristan covered a small portion of modern Afghanistan on the boundary of the Hindu Kush, and was most famous as the setting for Rudyard Kipling's *The Man Who Would Be King* (1888). The natives of this region practiced a form of ancient Hinduism before their forcible conversion to Islam in 1896 by the forces of the despot Abdur Rahman Khan.

[170] Pushto, or Pashto, is one of the main languages of Afghanistan.

[171] German dentist Peter Baliff designed a hand prosthesis in c.1816-18 where the fingers were activated by elbow and shoulder motion. This was not supplanted until 1916, when German surgeon Ferdinand Sauerbruch, inspired by the tragic injuries of soldiers fighting in World War I, designed a model whose digits were controlled by the transmission of upper arm muscle movements.

[172] Tisane is the more proper term for so-called 'herbal teas' made

from plants other than *Camellia sinensis*.

[173] 'Susurrus' is an archaic term meaning 'whispering, murmuring, or rustling.'

[174] If Miss Victoria Holden carried out her promise after returning to India, she might have made the acquaintance of other notable practitioners of a simple living lifestyle living at that time, including the great Bengali poet Rabindranath Tagore (1861-1941) and Mahatma Ghandi (1869-1948).

[175] The Hindu festival of *Holi*, or *Hoolee* to the fascinated British colonial staff, is the spring celebration of the victory of good over evil. It is famous for the bright colours with which people are liberally doused.

[176] Nostrums, or patent medicines, are commercial drugs, typically containing secret and dubious ingredients. They were extraordinarily popular in the days before medical regulation, but eventually vanished as people began to appreciate that they often killed more people than they helped.

[177] Sadly, as we well know, Holmes was not a whole-souled admirer of womankind.

[178] The term 'Mumbo Jumbo' entered the English language c.1795. It derives from a Mandinka word for the masked dancer of the West African religious ceremonies. Over time, this mutated into a term for confusing or meaningless language.

[179] The careful reader will note many similarities of this tale with a short story entitled *The Story of the Brown Hand*, which was published by Sir Arthur Conan Doyle in *The Strand Magazine* in May 1899. One may speculate that Watson's first literary editor was provided the details of the story, but instructed to erase all details of Holmes' involvement in the case. Fortunately, Watson maintained a copy of the actual particulars, for our current enjoyment.

[180] There was a terrible influenza pandemic from 1889-1890 (popularly the 'Russian flu') which killed about one million people, most famously Prince Albert Victor, eldest grandson of Queen Victoria. However, this cannot be the cause of the Holden's deaths, as Watson was clear that this story took place after Holmes' Great Hiatus. Therefore, Watson is most likely referring to a lesser epidemic that lasted from 1898-1900.

[181] There is no village of Georges Parva on Cranborne Chase, nor a

Mannering Towers. This editor proposes the village of Tarrant Hinton and the country house of Crichel House as possible candidates.

[182] The Earl of Uxbridge was Field Marshall Henry Paget (1768-1854), a distinguished cavalry officer who lost the lower part of his right leg at Waterloo. General Sir James Chatterton (1794-1874) was another officer during the Peninsular War and Waterloo, who received a special gold medal at the 1838 coronation of Queen Victoria and carried the banner at the Duke of Wellington's funeral in 1852. Charles Babbage (1791-1871) was a famous polymath, while Sir Charles Berry (1795-1860) was an architect, best known for rebuilding the Houses of Parliament.

[183] A recourse in law through which a person can reported an unlawful imprisonment to a court and request that the court orders the custodian of the person, usually a prison official, to bring the prisoner to court, to determine whether the detention is lawful.

[184] Named for the royal hunts that took place on its downs, starting with King John, Cranborne Chase was a crown property until 1616.

[185] According to the Game Act of 1831, pheasant season begins on 1 October, so Holmes is a bit early.

[186] In 1871, Theophilus Murcott began manufacturing hammerless shotguns at 68 Haymarket. His most famous gun was known as 'Murcott's Mousetrap' because of the loud sound of its snap action cocking.

[187] The details of this case can be found in the non-Canonical tale *The Adventure of the Wrong Hand*.

[188] The Great Fire of Hindon, a village on Cranborne Chase, occurred on 2 July 1754. Almost one hundred fifty buildings were destroyed.

[189] 'Goose Day' is an archaic term for Michaelmas, the Feast of St. Michael, which was celebrated with the eating of a well-fattened goose to protect against financial need for the following year.

[190] In his work *Airs, Waters, Places* (c. fifth century BCE), Hippocrates mentioned comparative pathology and insisted that diagnoses should be based on experience, observation, and logic. Holmes would have been very familiar with the work 'Is Disease a Reversion?' (c.1884) by Dr James Mortimer. The *Bhagavad Gita* (c. 200 BCE) is a dialogue between Arjuna and Krishna about the ethical duty to uphold the cosmic order through selfless action. Lane Fox

was the professional name of Augustus Henry Lane-Fox Pitt Rivers (1827-1900), an innovator in archeologic methodology who spent most of his career excavating upon Cranborne Chase.

[191] The Seringapatum Medal was awarded to all British and Indian soldiers who participated in the British Victory at the Battle of Seringapatum (5 April – 4 May 1799) during the Fourth Anglo-Mysore War. Troops under General Sir David Baird, including Colonel Arthur Wellesley, stormed the fortress of Tipu Sultan. Over fifty thousand medals were made, most of tin or bronze, with only 113 of gold.

[192] The name of the South Kensington Museum, founded in 1852 as the Museum of Manufactures, was changed in 1899 to the Victoria and Albert Museum. It was intended to hold 'practical' art, with 'high' art contained at the National Gallery and 'scholarly' art at the British Museum.

[193] The Company was an informal term for the East India Company, an English joint-stock company founded in 1660. At the heights of its power, it seized control over large parts of the Indian subcontinent with its private army. After the Indian Mutiny of 1857 brought to light some of its abuses, the British Crown assumed direct control of India's government, effectively dissolving most of the Company, which was completely defunct by 1874.

[194] A gun dog can refer to various breeds of dogs developed to assist in an aspect of hunting, such as pointers, flushers, or retrievers.

[195] Presumably *Vanity Fair* (1847-8), the story of the adventuress Becky Sharpe's social rise and fall.

[196] The Battle of Assaye (22 September 1803) was a major battle of the Second Anglo-Maratha War, where General Arthur Wellesley led less than ten thousand British troops to victory over a force of greater than fifty thousand men.

[197] Watson is referring to events that transpired during *The Adventure of the Norwood Builder,* which took place in August 1895.

[198] It is a matter of debate who precisely should get credit for the use of fingerprints in detection. Here Holmes appears to come out on behalf of Henry Faulds, a Scottish surgeon who published 'On the skin-furrows of the hand' (1890) in the journal *Nature*. Holmes' monograph on the subject has sadly been lost.

[199] Now known simply as the *Salisbury Journal,* this paper was

founded in 1729.

[200] Corrosive sublimate is an archaic term for mercuric chloride, a former topical treatment for syphilis. Alexandre Dumas' collection *Celebrated Crimes* (1839-21), a work with which Holmes was surely familiar, details the case of Desrues, but the case of Bille has been lost to history.

[201] This lost case of Holmes was also noted in the non-Canonical tale *The Gate of Gold*, suggesting that it took place before 1884.

[202] *Il Trovatore* (1853) was Giuseppe Verdi's opera about an Aragonese soldier obsessed with a young noblewoman, who instead loves a mysterious troubadour. Adelina Patti (1843-1919) was one of the most famous sopranos of the 19th century.

[203] As noted in *The Final Problem*, Watson's Italian was limited, but plainly he was conversant enough enjoy Italian opera. The modern reader should recall that surtitles were invented only in the 1980's, such that audiences were previously expected to follow along in the original language.

[204] A slight misquote of 'Three can keep a secret, if two of them are dead' by Benjamin Franklin in his *Poor Richard's Almanack* (1732-58).

[205] The Royal Courts of Justice, commonly called the Law Courts, is a building upon the Strand that houses the High Court of England and Wales.

[206] Reminiscent of the will belonging to Mr. William Shakspeare, the merchant and one-time actor of Stratford-upon-Avon, commonly mistaken for the great playwright who released his works under the pseudonym William Shakespeare.

[207] Instead, Watson plainly gave his write-up of Harry Bertram's case to his literary editor, Sir Arthur Conan Doyle with instructions to remove all trace of Holmes' involvement. This was eventually published in *The Strand Magazine* as *The Story of B24* (1899).

[208] Watson is paraphrasing from Shakespeare's *Hamlet* (Act 1, Scene 2).

[209] *The Adventure of the Lion's Mane* is dated to the end of July 1907. Given Holmes' reticence, Watson clearly related the history behind the events at the Half Moon Inn to his first literary editor, Sir Arthur Conan Doyle. Conan Doyle then re-worked it as a short story, which he entitled *The Pot of Caviare*, publishing it in *The Strand Magazine*

in March 1908. Conan Doyle enjoyed the tale so much that he then adapted it into a play by the same name, with its first performance on 13 November 1908.

[210] The Great War ended in 1918, but the lingering effects were felt for years afterwards. The general strike of 1926 was a nine-day attempt by transport and heavy industry workers to force the government to act on behalf of coal miners. Although unsuccessful at the time, it sparked the rise of the Labour Party under Ramsey MacDonald. Herbert Greenhough Smith edited *The Strand Magazine* from 1891 to 1930, the entire era of the fifty-six Canonical Holmes short stories. Watson appears to have forgotten that *The Adventure of the Lion's Mane* was actually published a month earlier in the United States in the magazine *Liberty*.

[211] Watson presented himself as Dr Hill Barton in *The Adventure of the Illustrious Client*, and impersonated Holmes himself in the non-Canonical case, *The Adventure of the Double-Detectives*, published in the collection *Round the World* (2019).

[212] Watson appears to be referring to the non-Canonical case *A Cold Dish*, published in the collection *The Schoolroom of Sorrow* (2018).

[213] There is no Half Moon Inn in Alfriston, though there is a Star Inn. Many of the subsequent details appear to match those of the Star.

[214] Holmes appears to be referring to the treatise *Poisons, Their Effects and Detection* (1884) by Alexander Wynter Blyth.

[215] A well-known children's story tells of King Alfred the Great of Wessex (848-899), who took refuge in the home of a peasant woman while on the run from Viking invaders. Not recognizing him, she asked the king to watch over her cakes – small loaves of bread – as they baked by the fire. However, distracted by thoughts of his problems, he allowed the cakes to burn, thereby earning him a round scolding by the woman.

[216] The Somerset Levels are a coastal plain and wetlands area near Glastonbury. The Vikings successfully besieged Chippenham in 878, but were decisively beaten by Alfred's forces at the Battle of Ethandun later that year.

[217] Fortnum & Mason was established as a grocery store in 1707 by William Fortnum and Hugh Mason.

[218] The *Transactions of the Entomological Society* was first published

1836. This editor has been unable to locate the issue containing the description of the *Lepidus Mercerensis*.

[219] A light cavalry corps formed in the 1830's. Until 1914, there were only six regiments, so Watson is hiding something.

[220] The Siege of Sevastopol (1854-5) was part of the Crimean War, fought between the French, British, and Ottoman upon one side versus the Russian Empire. The Franco-Prussian War of 1870 was a conflict between the Second French Empire and the Kingdom of Prussia leading the North German Confederation. The 'Mexican Adventure' refers to the Second French Intervention in Mexico (1861-7), which concluded with the execution of Emperor Maximilian I.

[221] The Protectorates in North Africa included both Algeria (1830-1962) and Tunisia (1881-1956), and later Morocco, as part of the colonial French Empire.

[222] The Long Man of Wilmington is a 235 feet tall hill figure cut into the grass. It has long been thought to have been carved in the Neolithic period, though the earliest mention of it dates to 1710, so some now consider it a Tudor-era carving.

[223] The White Horse of Litlington is a chalk figure of a giant horse carved in 1836, one of a dozen or so such representations in the England. Most are only a few centuries old, though the precise reasons for their carvings are unclear.

[224] A reference to C.A. Gifford's *The Life of the Most Noble Arthur, Duke of Wellington* (1817).

[225] A fair assessment of the Battle of Waterloo (18 June 1815), which was a 'near run thing.' Wellington's troops fought a masterful defence, but most historians agree that the Imperial Guard would have overrun his lines if not for the timely assistance of the Prussian army.

[226] The town in Belgium where, on 18-19 June 1815, the Battle of Wavre was fought between the forces of Marshall Emmanuel de Grouchy and General Johann von Thielmann. Although technically a French victory, the heavily outnumbered Prussian III Corps' blocking action kept over 30,000 French soldiers from reinforcing Napoleon at Waterloo, while simultaneously allowing 72,000 other Prussian soldiers to advance upon Napoleon's flank.

[227] Dymchurch in Kent and Eastbourne in Sussex are the sites of

the two Grand Redoubts, or fortifications, on the south coast built in 1804-5 to repel Napoleon's planned invasion. They were never tested.

[228] The twin battles of Jena and Auerstedt (14 October 1806) were decisive French victories over the forces of William III of Prussia, putting it under French control for the next eight years.

[229] Germany would not build such a defence until the construction of the Westwall (known as the Siegfried Line in English) in the 1930's. This was the German response to the French Maginot line, itself built out of desire to avoid the disastrous trench warfare of the First World War.

[230] The events leading to Dr MacDonald's imprisonment in 1887 can be found in the non-Canonical tale *The Adventure of the Dawn Discovery*, collected in *Fortunes Made and Fortunes Lost* (2018).

[231] Benjamin Haughton (1865-1924) was a minor English landscape painter. One of his best-known works is 'Autumn, Weald of Kent' (1904).

[232] More properly 'On the South Coast' (1899) by Algernon Charles Swinburne. It begins with 'Hills and valleys where April rallies his radiant squadron of flowers and birds, / Steep strange beaches and lustrous reaches of fluctuant sea that the land engirds, / Fields and downs that the sunrise crowns with life diviner than lives in words...'

[233] As of the most recent publication prior to September 1907, *The Adventure of the Second Stain* (December 1904), Holmes was still active. His retirement to the South Downs was not made public by Watson until the Preface to the collection *His Last Bow* (1917)

[234] The HMS *Dreadnought*, a Royal Navy battleship launched in 1906, was both the fastest and most heavily armed capital ship of its time. It revolutionized naval power and set off an arms race during the build-up to the First World War.

[235] The third plague pandemic officially began in 1855 in Yunnan, China, but was known in the West due to an outbreak in Hong Kong in 1894. It was there that Alexandre Yersin finally isolated the bacterium that causes the disease.

[236] The Boxer Rebellion was an uprising in China led by the Militia United in Uprising, known in English as the Boxers due to their practice of so-called 'Chinese Boxing' or martial arts. The Boxers were

anti-Imperialist (against the Empress Dowager Cixi of the Quing dynasty, who was ineffective at resisting foreign influence), anti-foreign (as numerous European nations were attempting to colonize China and exploit its resources), and anti-Christian (whose missionaries were abusing their positions and aggressively attempting to supplant traditional Chinese religions). Although there were long-simmering tensions between the Boxers and these groups, a major drought, followed by floods, is thought to have been the major trigger for sparking the fuse of the rebellion. The Boxers have been vilified by Western accounts for their participation in the massacres of many missionaries (and their families). The Boxers were ultimately defeated by an alliance of eight nations (Austria-Hungary, France, Germany, Italy, Japan, Russia, the United Kingdom, and the United States), followed by the victorious troops engaging in general looting and punitive executions.

[237] Limehouse is a district of London upon the northern banks of the Thames. At the time, it was poverty-stricken, with a strong maritime character, and a large Chinese community.

[238] A 'postiche' is a covering of false hair, typically used for either adornment or disguise.

[239] In this regard, Holmes was not infallible. He failed to recognize Jefferson Hope in the form of Mrs. Sawyer (*A Study in Scarlet*, Chapter V) or Neville St. Clair in the form of Hugh Boone (*The Man with the Twisted Lip*).

[240] There was no such ship. There were only two Centurion-class battleships, the *Centurion* and the *Barfleur*, both of which supported operations during the Boxer Rebellion. They were made obsolete by the appearance of the HMS *Dreadnought*.

[241] China Station refers to the former Royal Navy formation (1865-1941), with bases at Singapore, Hong Kong, and Liugong Island.

[242] Jourliac, located at 99 Rue des Petits-Champs, was a seller of coiffures and postiches in the early 1900s.

[243] Technically, a mitigatory defence that one was provoked into the act. If successful, this could drop a charge of murder to that of manslaughter, but would not have absolved Miss Patterson of the crime entirely.

[244] There is no town of Ichau, though some of the particulars seem to match the town of Tianjin, where German officers staffed a

military academy. In June 1900, the Boxers were able to seize control of much of Tianjin. On June 26, European defence forces heading towards Beijing were stopped by Boxers at nearby Langfang and forced to turn back to Tianjin. The foreign concessions were under siege for several weeks. In July 1900, troops of the Eight-Nation Alliance recaptured the town.

[245] Sangars are temporary fortified positions made of stone, sandbags, or similar materials, used to cover troops from enemy fire. They were typically constructed in terrain where digging of ditches was impractical, or where rapid advancements were possible.

[246] '*Potz-tausend*' is generally translated as 'Upon my soul.'

[247] Lachryma Christi is a celebrated Neapolitan wine produced on the slopes of Mount Vesuvius. Archaeologists have determined that it is the nearest equivalent to the wine drunk by the ancient Romans.

[248] Practitioners of traditional martial arts, in popular culture the Boxers were believed to have possessed a semi-mystical sense of their own invulnerability, which led to their massacre at the hands of modern weaponry.

[249] Mauser is a German arms manufacturer founded in 1811 by Andreas Mauser; its M71 rifle was popular with the Qing Dynasty. Maxim is a former British arm manufacturer founded in 1884 by Sir Hiram Stevens Maxim; its recoil machine gun is the weapon most associated with British Imperial conquest.

[250] Unfortunately, this literary editor is unable to locate any records of the Siege of 'Sung-Tong' (or even a place of that name) in 1889.

[251] '*Assez*' is French for 'enough.'

[252] The phrase 'the eleventh hour,' meaning at the very last moment is taken from a passage in the parable of the workers in the vineyard (*The Gospel of Matthew*).

[253] 'Peking' is the name given to China's capital by 17th century French missionaries. The spelling 'Beijing' was adopted in 1958.

[254] The game that was to become modern Polo was introduced to British soldiers in India. The oldest club was founded in Calcutta in 1862 and the sport then spread to England.

[255] Literally, 'he should live high.' The German equivalent of 'for he's a jolly good fellow.'

[256] Pearls of amyl nitrate came into medical use in 1867 to treat heart diseases, such as angina. They can also be used as an antidote for cyanide poisoning by inducing the formation of methemoglobin (which turns blood a bluish colour), which in turns sequesters free cyanide.

[257] The latter moth has apparently been renamed in the last century – perhaps due to its connection to its original discoverer – Mr. Vandeleur, later realized to be a pseudonym of the villain Rodger Baskerville.

[258] 'Tartars' are a general term for the inhabitants of Tartary, a blanket term used by Europeans to describe Central Asia, Manchuria, and Siberia.

[259] The first desertion refers to the period of time when Watson married his first wife and returned to practice. During this time, some evidence suggests that he resided on Cavendish Avenue in St. John's Wood.

[260] The second desertion occurred when Watson wed Mary Morstan in the spring of 1889, approximately six months after the adventure they shared together. During this time, Watson's practice was reportedly located at Crawford Place in Marylebone (approximately May 1889 to May 1890), followed by Earl's Terrace (which backed up to 'Mortimer Street') in Kensington (approximately May 1890 to April 1894).

[261] The dating of *The Adventure of the Second Stain* is one of the most controversial of the entire Canon. Watson himself deliberately attempts to obscure the date: "It was, then, in a year, and even in a decade, that shall be nameless, that upon one Tuesday afternoon in autumn we found two visitors…." Baring-Gould places it on October 12–15, 1886 under the very reasonable hypothesis that it must have occurred during a year when two different men held the offices of Prime Minister and Foreign Secretary.

[262] While the identify of Watson's third wife is unclear, it is apparent that he wed her in late 1902, from which time, he practiced out of rooms at Queen Anne Street until his own eventual retirement to Southsea.

[263] Collected in paperback as *Light in the Darkness;* independently published by The New World Books (2017).

[264] Collected in paperback as *Light in the Darkness;* independently

published by The New World Books (2017).

[265] First published in *The MX Book of New Sherlock Holmes Stories, Part I: 1881 to 1889;* David Marcum, Editor; MX Publishing (2015).

[266] Collected in paperback as *The Treasury of Sherlock Holmes;* independently published by The New World Books (2018).

[267] Collected in paperback as *The Treasury of Sherlock Holmes;* independently published by The New World Books (2018).

[268] First published in *The MX Book of New Sherlock Holmes Stories, Part IV: 2016 Annual;* David Marcum, Editor; MX Publishing (2016).

[269] First published in *Holmes Away from Home: Tales of the Great Hiatus;* David Marcum, Editor; Belanger Books (2016).

[270] First published in *The MX Book of New Sherlock Holmes Stories, Part VI: 2017 Annual;* David Marcum, Editor; MX Publishing (2017).

[271] Collected in paperback as *The Gathering Gloom;* independently published by The New World Books (2019).

[272] First published in *The MX Book of New Sherlock Holmes Stories, Part XI: Some Untold Cases;* David Marcum, Editor; MX Publishing (2018).

[273] First published in *The MX Book of New Sherlock Holmes Stories, Part VIII: Eliminate the Impossible;* David Marcum, Editor; MX Publishing (2017).

[274] Collected in paperback as *The Gathering Gloom;* independently published by The New World Books (2019).

[275] First published in *Sherlock Holmes: Adventures Beyond the Canon, Volume II;* David Marcum, Editor; Belanger Books (2018).

[276] First published in *Tales from the Stranger's Room 3;* David Ruffle, Editor; MX Publishing (2017).

[277] Collected in paperback as *The Travels of Sherlock Holmes;* independently published by The New World Books (2020).

[278] Collected in paperback as *The Travels of Sherlock Holmes;* independently published by The New World Books (2020).

[279] First published in *The MX Book of New Sherlock Holmes Stories, Part XVIII: Whatever Remains... Must Be the Truth;* David Marcum, Editor; MX Publishing (2019).

[280] Collected in paperback as *The Chronicles of Sherlock Holmes;* independently published by The New World Books (2021).

[281] Collected in paperback as *The Chronicles of Sherlock Holmes*; independently published by The New World Books (2021).

[282] First published in *The MX Book of New Sherlock Holmes Stories, Part XXV: 2021 Annual;* David Marcum, Editor; MX Publishing (2021).

[283] First published in *Sherlock Holmes, A Year of Mysteries – 1881;* Richard T. Ryan, Editor; Belanger Books (2021).

[284] First published in *The MX Book of New Sherlock Holmes Stories, Part XXIII: Some More Untold Cases 1888-1894;* David Marcum, Editor; MX Publishing (2020).

[285] First published in *Sherlock Holmes: Stranger than Fiction;* Derrick Belanger, Editor; Belanger Books (2021).

ACKNOWLEDGEMENT

First and foremost, I must give a grateful acknowledgment to Sir Arthur Conan Doyle (1859-1930) for the use of the Sherlock Holmes characters. Without his words, this could not have been written.

For reference, I consider Leslie S. Klinger's 'The New Annotated Sherlock Holmes' (2005 & 2006) to be the definitive edition, which builds upon William S. Baring-Gould's majestic 'The Annotated Sherlock Holmes' (1967). I also frequently consult Jack Tracy's 'The Encyclopedia Sherlockiana, or A Universal Dictionary of the State of Knowledge of Sherlock Holmes and His Biographer John H. Watson, M.D.' (1977), Matthew E. Bunson's 'Encyclopedia Sherlockiana, an A-to-Z Guide to the World of the Great Detective' (1994), and Bruce Wexler's 'The Mysterious World of Sherlock Holmes' (2008).

Finally, many of these stories owe a massive debt to David Marcum, author and editor of several wonderful compilations of Sherlockian tales, whose praise and encouragement prompted me to continue unearthing these lost cases of Mr. Sherlock Holmes, written long ago by his biographer Dr John H. Watson.

ABOUT THE AUTHOR

Craig Janacek

In the year 1998 CRAIG JANACEK took his degree of Doctor of Medicine of Vanderbilt University, and proceeded to Stanford to go through the training prescribed for paediatricians in practice. Having completed his studies there, he was duly attached to the University of California San Francisco as Professor.

The author of over a hundred and fifty medical monographs upon a variety of obscure lesions, his travel-worn and battered tin dispatch-box is crammed with papers, nearly all of which are records of his fictional works. These include several collections of the Further Adventures of Sherlock Holmes ('Light in the Darkness', 'The Gathering Gloom', 'The Treasury of Sherlock Holmes', 'The Travels of Sherlock Holmes', & 'The Assassination of Sherlock Holmes'), two Dr Watson novels ('The Isle of Devils' & 'The Gate of Gold'), the complete and expanded Adventures and Exploits of Brigadier Gerard ('Set Europe Shaking' & 'A Mighty Shadow'), and two non-Holmes novels ('The Oxford Deception' & 'The Anger of Achilles Peterson').

His short stories have been published in several editions of 'The MX Book of New Sherlock Holmes Stories, Part I: 1881-1889' (2015), 'Part IV: 2016 Annual' (2016), 'Part VI: 2017 Annual' (2017), 'Part VIII: Eliminate the Impossible' (2017), 'Part XI: Some Untold Cases' (2018), 'Part XVIII: Whatever Remains Must be the Truth' (2019), 'Part XXIII: Some More Untold Cases' (2020), and 'Part XXV: 2021 Annual' (2021). Other stories have appeared in 'Holmes Away From Holmes: Tales of the Great Hiatus' (2016), 'Tales from the Stranger's Room 3' (2017), 'Sherlock Holmes: Adventures Beyond the Canon' (2018), 'Sherlock Holmes, A Year of Mysteries – 1881' (2021), and 'Sherlock Holmes: Stranger than Fiction' (2021).

He lives near San Francisco, California with his wife and two children, where he is at work on his next story. Craig Janacek is a nom-de-plume.

ABOUT THE AUTHOR

Sir Arthur Conan Doyle

In the year 1885 ARTHUR CONAN DOYLE took his degree of Doctor of Medicine of the University of Edinburgh, and (after diversions in Greenland, West Africa, and Southsea) proceeded to Vienna and Paris to go through the training of an ophthalmologist in practice. Having partially completed his studies there, he was duly attached to a consulting physician at 2 Devonshire Place, London. The patients were few in number and, to bide his time, he turned his attention to the writing of fiction.

The author of twenty-four novels, some two-hundred odd other fictions of all genres, and more than a thousand other works (including plays, poems, essays, pamphlets, articles, letters to the press, and architectural designs). Although he personally preferred some of his other works, he has been forever immortalized as the creator of one of the greatest and most famous characters to ever be set down in print – Mr. Sherlock Holmes.

In 1902, he was made a Knight Bachelor by King Edward VII. He is buried in Minstead, New Forest. The epitaph on his gravestone reads simply: 'Steel true / Blade straight / Arthur Conan Doyle / Knight / Patriot, Physician and Man of Letters / 22 May 1859 – 7 July 1930.'

PRAISE FOR AUTHOR

" 'The Watson style is deceptively difficult to imitate. Good practitioners include....' I'm now adding the stories in Craig Janacek's series, 'The Midwinter Mysteries of Sherlock Holmes' as well."

- DAVID MARCUM, EDITOR OF 'THE MX BOOK OF NEW SHERLOCK HOLMES STORIES', IN 'THE DISTRICT MESSENGER' (JANUARY 2014)

"Craig Janacek combines the puzzle mystery and the paranormal brilliantly in 'The Adventure of the Fair Lad.' "

- 'PUBLISHERS WEEKLY' (DECEMBER 2019)

THE FURTHER ADVENTURES OF SHERLOCK HOLMES

A large cache of manuscripts by the biographer of the world's first consulting detective, Mr. Sherlock Holmes, has been found! Restored, edited, and compiled into thematic collections, these tales augment and expand upon the Victorian world so vibrantly laid forth in the 60 original adventures. Setting forth from their base at 221B Baker Street, herein, Holmes and Watson come upon friends – old and new, and villains – both cunning and tragic. Fully annotated, these editions contain a cornucopia of scholarly insights which compare these newly unearthed tales by Dr John H. Watson to the classic adventures from the Canon of Sherlock Holmes.

Light In The Darkness

Sherlock Holmes returns! He must deal with a series of cases which encompass the broad range of the human experience, from the grim workings of physicians who have violated their oaths, to the magnanimous moods which every man – no matter how cool and emotionless – feels at the time of Christmas. Comprising the collections 'The First of Criminals' and 'The Season of Forgiveness,' all seven recently-unearthed adventures in this volume are narrated by Dr Watson in the in the finest tradition and spirit of such classics as 'The Adventure of the Speckled Band' and 'The Adventure of the Blue Carbuncle.'

THE FIRST OF CRIMINALS: Descend into the horrors that lurk in the minds of doctors who have gone terribly wrong in this quartet of stories featuring the world's first consulting detective, Sherlock Holmes, and his able assistant, Dr John H. Watson. This collection includes the tales 'The Adventure of the Monstrous Blood,' 'The Adventure of the Mad Colonel,' 'The Adventure of the Fateful Malady,' and 'The Adventure of the Barren Grave.'

THE SEASON OF FORGIVENESS: Celebrate the spirit of the season with the world's first consulting detective, Sherlock Holmes, and his able assistant, Dr John H. Watson. This collection includes the tales 'The Adventure of the Spanish Sovereign,' 'The Adventure of the Manufactured Miracle,' and 'The Adventure of the First Star.' It also includes 'The Grand Gift of Sherlock,' a final letter from Holmes to Watson at the very end of World War I, which is sure to delight bibliophiles with its depiction of Watson's bookcase and its moving testament to the enduring power of friendship. Also published as 'The Midwinter Mysteries of Sherlock Holmes.'

The Gathering Gloom

Embark on an exploration of the darker corners of the human experience with the world's first consulting detective, Sherlock Holmes, and his able assistant, Dr John H. Watson. Comprising the collections 'The Schoolroom of Sorrow' and 'An East Wind,' all ten recently-unearthed adventures are narrated by Dr Watson in the in the finest tradition and spirit of such classics as 'The Problem of Thor Bridge' and 'The Adventure of the Bruce-Partington Plans.'

THE SCHOOLROOM OF SORROW: Dive into the deepest abysses of the human soul with Mr. Sherlock Holmes and Dr John H. Watson. From the days before his career as a consulting detective to years of his restful retirement, Sherlock Holmes has all too often encountered terrible events that served to shape his philosophy. To Holmes, every adventure holds the possibility of teaching an earthly lesson regarding the nature of good and evil. This collection includes the tales 'The Father of Evil,' 'The Adventure of the Dishonourable Discharge,' 'The Adventure of the Fatal Fire,' 'The Adventure of the Awakened Spirit,' and 'The Cold Dish.'

AN EAST WIND: In the time of England's greatest need, Sherlock Holmes and Dr Watson stand ready. A great and awful war is brewing in the East, and foreign agents will do everything in their power to see England brought to its knees. Only the swift actions of Sherlock Holmes can prevent the empire's secrets from being sold to its enemies, thereby dooming thousands of brave young men to terrible deaths upon the fields of Flanders and in the frigid waters of the North Sea. This collection includes the tales 'The Adventure of the Third Traitor,' 'The Adventure of the Unfathomable Silence,' 'The High Mountain,' 'The Adventure of the Defenceless Prisoner,' and 'Their Final Flourish.'

The Treasury Of Sherlock Holmes

Embark upon quests for buried treasure with the world's first consulting detective, Sherlock Holmes, and his assistant, Dr John H. Watson. Comprising the collections 'Treasure Trove Indeed!' and 'Fortunes Made and Fortunes Lost,' all eight recently-unearthed adventures are narrated by Dr Watson in the in the finest tradition and spirit of such classics as 'The Musgrave Ritual' and 'The Adventure of the Six Napoleons.'

TREASURE TROVE INDEED!: Things get lost very easily in England. Across the realm, from the remote Peak District to the sea-faring shores of Bristol, from the ancient manors of Devonshire to the warrens of London, Sherlock Holmes is faced with a series of challenging cases. Ranging in time from his days at university until shortly before his retirement, these adventures span the gamut of Holmes and Watson's time together. This collection includes the tales 'The Lost Legion,' 'The Adventure of the Pirate's Code,' 'The Adventure of the Queen's Pendant,' and 'The Adventure of the Silent Drum.'

FORTUNES MADE & FORTUNES LOST: The pursuit of fortune may lead a man to riches or to ruin. From Cambridge to Scotland to London, Sherlock Holmes and Dr Watson must face the darker side of treasure hunting, as they contend with criminals driven mad by their quest of fortune and glory. The full brilliance of Sherlock Holmes is on display as he solves an ancient curse, the singular adventures of the Grice Patersons in the island of Uffa, and a mysterious cipher. Meanwhile, with Holmes thought lost over the Reichenbach Falls, Dr Watson must attempt to employ his methods in the solution of an exotic tragedy. This collection includes the tales 'The Adventure of the Double-Edged Hoard,' 'The Adventure of the Dawn Discovery,' 'The Harrowing Intermission,' and 'The Adventure of the Sunken Indiaman.'

The Travels Of Sherlock Holmes

Embark on a series of journeys with Mr. Sherlock Holmes and Dr John H. Watson. Although Holmes was at his best amongst the ghostly gas lamps and swirling yellow fog of London's streets, he was occasionally willing to venture forth to strange locales whenever a sufficiently-interesting adventure called. Comprising the collections 'A Prompt and Ready Traveller' and 'Round the World,' within are eight recently-unearthed cases which induced Holmes to set forth to the Continent, the Colonies, and even the Americas. All are narrated by Dr Watson in the finest tradition and spirit of such classics as 'The Disappearance of Lady Frances Carfax' and 'The Adventure of the Devil's Foot.'

A PROMPT & READY TRAVELLER: While Sherlock Holmes protested leaving London for too long, for fear of causing an unhealthy excitement among the criminal classes, Dr Watson was always a prompt and ready traveller, who could be counted upon to encourage his friend to take up a peculiar case, no matter where it might lead them. From a spiritual visit to the exotic Kingdom of Hawai'i to the dangerous boulevards of Paris, from to the dark catacombs of Rome to the posh resorts of Bermuda, Holmes and Watson must deal with private revenges and matters of grave international importance. This collection includes the tales 'The Adventure of the Missing Mana,' 'The Adventure of the Boulevard Assassin,' 'The Adventure of the Boulevard Assassin, 'The Adventure of the Secret Tomb,' and 'The Adventure of the Dead Man's Note.'

ROUND THE WORLD: Sherlock Holmes would recommend rejuvenating trips round the world for certain of his clients, but it took a strong force for him to do the same. And yet, occasionally, he would don his travelling cloak and ear-flapped cap and set forth to deal with challenging cases. These adventures include a faerie kidnapping in Ireland – featuring one of the most fantastic deductions of Holmes' career – and a trip to the American South to face the return of a terrible enemy – the K.K.K. Closer to home, the return of a tragic adversary – Dr Leon Sterndale – coincides with the emergence of a new horror. Finally, we learn the true story of whether or not Holmes ever visited the silver fields of California, as previously reported by an American author of some repute. This collection includes the tales 'The Oak-Leaf Sprig,' 'The Adventure of the Double Detectives,' 'The Adventure of the African Horror,' and 'The Adventure of the Fair Lad.'

The Assassination Of Sherlock Holmes

Embark on an epic adventure featuring the world's foremost

consulting detective, Sherlock Holmes, as told by Dr John H. Watson in the finest tradition of the Canonical stories. Comprising three parts, 'The Adventure of the Pharaoh's Curse,' 'The Problem of Threadneedle Street,' and 'The Falling Curtain,' these tales relate one of Holmes' final and most gripping adventures. This special Collected Edition also contains the previously unpublished tale 'The Red Leech.' For the first and only time, rather than a stranger, it is a desperate Dr Watson himself that is sitting in the client chair at 221B Baker Street. Can Holmes help save him from the clutches of the repulsive Red Leech?

THE ADVENTURE OF THE PHARAOH'S CURSE. October 1909. Sherlock Holmes has been retired to the South Downs for six years, resisting all entreaties to return to his career as the world's foremost consulting detective. But the brutal murder of one of his former colleagues from Scotland Yard has finally galvanized him back into action. Dr Watson at his side, Holmes journeys to London's British Museum, where a series of singular disappearances have taken place. With the museum staff convinced that the curse of a four thousand year-old pharaoh is emanating from the Egyptian Gallery, it is up to Holmes to prove that the worst horrors come from the minds of men. But will the echoes of the past prove to be his undoing?

THE PROBLEM OF THREADNEEDLE STREET. November 1909. Sherlock Holmes has been called out of retirement to successfully solve the mystery of the British Museum's Pharaonic curse. But while he longs to return to his villa on the South Downs, a new threat has arisen. A twisted riddle of the sphinx suggests that Holmes and Dr. Watson are wading through deep waters. And when the main vault at the Bank of England is inexplicably plundered, Holmes realizes that his enemies may be trying to bring down the nation itself. Only the piercing acumen of the world's foremost consulting detective could see that this theft was but the first blow, and that the villain is certain to mount another daring robbery. From a baffling series of seemingly unconnected events, Holmes must make the brilliant leaps of deduction required in order to determine where his adversary next plans to strike. Only then can Holmes set his own traps and turn the tables on his foe. But will Holmes be able to anticipate all of the forces that are aligning against him?

THE FALLING CURTAIN. November 1909. Sherlock Holmes has successfully prevented further robberies of England's greatest institutions and captured one of his most dangerous enemies, but something is still rotten in the streets of London. A series of attacks threaten not only his life, but the lives of those few individuals that he calls 'friend.' With Dr. Watson injured, his defenses crumbling, and Scotland Yard deaf to his appeals for succor, Holmes must call upon some irregular help and use every means at his disposal to determine what adversary is stalking him from the mists of the past. From the cells of Wandsworth to the heights of Tower Bridge, Holmes is once more on the hunt. But is he willing to make the sacrifice required to put a final end to this monstrous menace?

Printed in Great Britain
by Amazon